The
Jumping
Off
Place

Also by Garet Rogers

A CORNER ON ANGELS

PRISONER IN PARADISE

LANCET

THE
JUMPING
OFF
PLACE

by
Garet Rogers

THE DIAL PRESS
NEW YORK   1962

Printed in the United States of America

By The Haddon Craftsmen, Inc., Scranton, Pa.

For Snatley

. . . quis custodiet ipsos custodes?

Who's in charge of the keepers?

—Juvenal

The
Jumping
Off
Place

1

Alas, Mickey

"Name me a more peaceful place in which to spend my declining years," Dr. Ouita Rosebend liked to say of Pawksville State Hospital for the Insane. She was the senior staff member in years as well as service, and though her mind was subject to the infirmities of those in their seventies, she performed her duties with ease. She was in charge of wards Eight through Ten, and custom and Dr. Ouita Rosebend both spoke of them as the Old Ladies' Opens, meaning that the wards were unlocked during the day and that the inmates were not in any strict sense of the word patients. They were cast-off grandmas, maiden aunts, an occasional used wife, and in general the refuse of the families of Pawks County, sprinkled here and there with a lady of maniacal antecedents whose psychosis had burned itself out along with the other fires of youth.

Through the incandescent summers of Pawksville, Dr. Ouita rested in her cool office and knitted for her many grandnephews, and—nieces, while on her Open Wards her ladies sat and tatted, and poked Copenhagen snuff into the swollen alveolars of their gums, and fanned themselves with fans from the Pawksville Mortuary, and ignored the tele-

3

vision set. Every so often, tottering around on the highly polished floors, one of the ladies would fall and break a hip, and
Dr. Ouita would have to immobilize her in the airy room
with all the other ladies with broken hips, and hang a weight
from the foot; every once in a while one would die and Dr.
Ouita, clucking cheerfully, would come round to pronounce
her dead.

There was rarely any rush; questions never burned for
Dr. Ouita, at best only flaring up fitfully, and matters did
not press. On this August morning she was idly enjoying the
view from her window, while her fingers knitted on, swift
and unerring. Her rounds were done, though later in the
day she would administer a liver shot to the sister of the
Clinical Director, and some time soon she would have to dispense more placebos to the bored, irritable wife of Dr. Heall.
The female members of the staff families fell to Dr. Ouita's
care when there was nothing seriously wrong with them.
There rarely was.

There were some who said that Dr. Ouita had been sitting on the fence waiting for Pawksville State Hospital to
open. Others insisted that she had obtained her position on
the staff by getting and preserving the goods on someone, then
to settle down secure and forgotten; though her victim's suc-
cessors hadn't the faintest idea what she knew about whom,
and it is doubtful if even the good doctor herself remembered
the exact way of it. Like any state hospital for the insane,
Pawksville had been a sagging and treadworn plank in the
platform of every reform governor—and they were all such
—from the time when memory runneth not to the contrary.
It was again, in fact, for the present reform governor was
sore beset by the aspiring next reform governor, and the incumbent gentleman was due shortly to inspect Pawksville.
The Pawksville grapevine, a hardy growth thick as a dino-
saur's ankle, had it that the incumbent had damn well better
find that all was in order, or heads would roll. Dr. Ouita's
excepting; like Barbara Frietchie's, each gray hair was
charmed, was utterly safe.

The first breath of the day's heat entered Dr. Ouita's window, a portent so telling of the swooning mugginess to come that it seemed to flow into the office on a lassitudinous wave, sluggishly undulating inward and enveloping all that it encountered. Dr. Ouita bestirred herself, thinking to adjust the Venetian blinds, when Nick Bartholomew appeared in the doorway.

"Got a moment to spare, Doctor?" Nick said, and if he noticed the knitting in Ouita's hands his expression did not reveal it. He was an immense man, doubly so in his whites, and his assertive manner had been habitual long before he was appointed Clinical Director. Because he had paid for his medical education by performing whatever manual labor came to hand, Dr. Ouita's admiration and liking for him was just a shade under extravagant. In the clear northern light of her office his tanned skin appeared quite dark, and the macadam-black eyes disconcertingly direct. That is, he was able to disconcert others with a single slashing glance; Dr. Ouita, on the contrary, met his gaze and told herself yet again, "Poor Nick. Since his wife died he's taken to work like drink."

For his part, poor Nick was having difficulties with the chair Dr. Ouita had indicated he take. It was a dainty, most unofficelike object with a fancywork seat, and as Nick was a hairbreadth from burliness he lowered himself gingerly onto its uncertain support. "Just thought I'd better check with you on something," Nick said, still testing the chair's ability to support him by leaning forward. The deceptive mildness of his manner did not escape Dr. Ouita, for Nick, when roused, was a tongue-lasher of the first order.

Dr. Ouita nodded her assent, and counted a stitch or so. "Nice morning, isn't it," she said in the measured cadences of one timing speech to some other activity.

"Not so far, no," Nick contradicted her pleasantly. He took out a great handkerchief and ran it under his collar. Dr. Ouita immediately recognized the handkerchief. Years ago, when the new Hospital building was going up, the con-

tractor had given her some fifty blueprints with the instruction that she wash them. A doubtful Ouita had rinsed out
the blue dye, to find herself in possession of a windfall of
oblong on oblong of finest linen. All one year her ladies had
cut to size and rolled hems and tatted edges onto the squares.
Not a medical staff nose in Pawksville but had been wiped
with these works of art. Ouita was touched to see Nick still
plying his. Dabbing almost up into his wiry hair spotted with
gray, he pocketed the handkerchief and proceeded without
preamble, "Superintendent Keeney had bad dreams last
night, and woke fearing for his job. He called me off a ward
to come hold his hand."

"That's nothing new, Doctor," Dr. Ouita sniffed. "The
only time we see hide or hair of Superintendent Keeney
around here is when he does remember where he works. If
you'd seen the number of superintendents come and go I
have, Doctor, you wouldn't give it a second thought."

"I'm afraid Keeney is giving it second and third
thoughts."

"He'd better watch out," Dr. Ouita cautioned, "or he'll
be using up his thinking quota for the entire week in one
morning." She held out the baby jacket she was knitting
and examined it critically. "Superintendent Keeney's a fuss-
budget. With you running Pawksville for him, he has no
cause for concern at all. Things are smooth as cream around
here. I challenge you, Doctor, you name me a more peaceful
place in which I could spend my declining—"

"Bedlam," Nick Bartholomew suggested in that soft
drawl that betokened his most dangerous mood.

Dr. Ouita was on the verge of taking this as a witticism,
then recalled that if Nick were some thirty years her junior,
he was at the same time her superior on the staff. She took
refuge in briskness. "Oh?"

"The Superintendent is the victim of any number of
floating anxieties this morning, but I managed to nail down
two of them. The first is the impending visit of the Governor."

"Oh that. The Governor isn't due for ages."

"The Jubilee is less than a month away," Nick reminded her.

"Really?" Dr. Ouita said lightly. "That soon."

"And the second floating anxiety troubling Superintendent Keeney is the Special Patient. Since he's under your care, I thought I'd consult with you before talking to him."

Dr. Ouita put her knitting to one side. "Doctor, do you mean you want to do a mental examination on Titus Graham? If so, I'd like to see him first, and prepare him for it. He has his setbacks, you know, and I wouldn't vouch for his not getting disturbed if his routine is upset too abruptly."

The tanned skin grew darker, though Nick's voice was controlled. "Would you be more explicit, please?"

Dr. Ouita longed for a moment to tell the Clinical Director to go stir his tempest in a teapot elsewhere. She had seen Special Patients come and go, she had observed the last of the dust of too many forgotten superintendents to name, and clinical directors bobbed on the seas of her memory like so many reform governors cast adrift. Like the dye in the blueprints, everything came out in the wash. "I mean," she said carefully, "what I say. The slightest break in routine disturbs Mr. Graham. He likes to keep to himself in the Special Patient's Cottage, with just Mr. Hamshot to care for him, and my dropping in every so often on my rounds. He looks on the Cottage as a—retreat——"

"Retreat, hell," Nick said politely. "It's a hideout, Doctor."

Ouita plunged on gamely, "I know we disagree on his diagnosis. Be that as it may, he has shown improvement. Why, ever since I stopped his receiving or sending out mail——"

"Oh, you did?" Nick asked lazily.

"Why—of course, Doctor. All that mail was much too much in the way of hyperactivity and excitation. He was sending letters and great thick folders of I don't know what,

where, and receiving more in return. And all that busy business was simply strengthening the foundations of his delusion."

"I was not aware," Nick said, "that he entertained any
delusions."

"Why. . . . Doctor! He thinks he's world-famous. And
not just because his cousin is the Governor's wife. He be-
lieves himself to be an ambassador also."

"That is not quite an exact statement of his belief,"
Nick corrected her quietly. "If I recall correctly, he told me
he was an ambassador-at-large of the cultural community of
the nation, and therefore a statesman. Not a mere politician
like the Governor, mind you—a statesman."

"There, you see!" Dr. Ouita's voice carried a modest
ring of triumph. "That's why I curtailed his mail privileges.
The only way he feels he can cope with the world is to draw
his delusions about him. As it is, Mr. Graham's shown some
very nice improvement because he doesn't have to cope. And
I've had him under supportive therapy for some time now,
of course. . . ." Her eye strayed toward her knitting and an
instant later, all unawares, she was plying the needles again.
With the calm of a woman who employs her hands at useful
work while talking, Dr. Ouita resumed, "Naturally, I can't
predict for Superintendent Keeney—or even the Governor
for that matter—how long Mr. Graham's full recovery will
take—"

Nick announced, "I can. You'll find him completely
cured the day the local constabulary are no longer interested
in binding him over for trial. He was incarcerated here,
Doctor, in case you've forgotten, for beating a young boy
unmercifully. But he made the sole mistake of doing it in
Governor Leroy Jackson's political back yard. It's one thing
to make an ass of yourself at a statewide political rally by
declaring yourself to be a cultural ambassador-at-large. That
artsy-crafty crowd the Governor's wife runs in probably
thought Titus Graham quite chic. He just should have been a

little less artsy and a lot more crafty when he went after that young boy, Doctor."

"We mustn't lose sight of the fact that the man is insane," Dr. Ouita said, taking advantage of her years to permit a tone of reproof to enter her voice.

Nick ducked his head. When he looked at her again there was no trace of a wry grin on his face, if such had ever been there. "I differ. But you stick to your guns, Doctor. That's all Superintendent Keeney wants to know. That one of us is willing to declare the Special Patient psychotic. Should the need arise, that is."

Dr. Ouita nodded vigorously, confronted with the inner vision of Titus Graham in his therapeutic tepid bath. Time and again on her rounds she had come upon him petulantly slapping pat-a-cake on the lapping waters and shouting at her. He would be progressing so nicely, and then there would be a relapse heralded by unfounded accusations and compulsively reiterated nonsense syllables. Only a day or so ago such a scene had taken place, he had beaten the edge of the tub steadily with his water-shriveled palms, denying that the tub soothed him, bawling at her that he was no *proost* or *prewst,* or whatever the word was, he was a poet. Those had been his exact words: a poet, not a *prewst.* And this had been his totally unresponsive rejoinder to Dr. Ouita's bright inquiry, "And how are you feeling today, Mr. Graham?" Dr. Ouita looked at Nick sternly and said, "Oh, he's not out of the woods yet, Doctor."

"Then I will suggest to Superintendent Keeney that he refer the Governor to you on the matter," Nick said smoothly. "In case the Governor wants Graham kept under wraps for a while longer. Or if—by some chance—some nosy reporter asks after his condition. Because if my opinion were asked, I would have to say that I consider Titus Graham in full possession of his faculties, and that he belongs in prison and not in the Special Patient's Cottage taking up the full attention of an attendant. In short, that he is vicious but

sane, and should be punished for his crime." Nick grinned
suddenly and admitted, "Which noble statement would get
me fired. Whereas if nothing but sweet concord prevails between the Governor and myself, I aim to hit him for more
funds for Pawksville. Every other institution in this state
is knee-deep in the pork barrel, while our patients don't
even get a drop of bacon grease for their dry crusts. Those,
Doctor, are my sentiments."

The matter put in this light, Dr. Ouita lowered her
gray head and pretended to count stitches. She too had a
favor to ask of the Governor. And if Titus Graham was to
be the means of having her petition granted, then she must
prepare a report for the Governor showing Graham's slow
but steady improvement. This, in turn, would demonstrate
to the Governor that on Graham's eventual release the
shocking event—whatever it was, Dr. Ouita was inclined of
late to become hazy on details—would not re-occur. She rolled
up her knitting. "You just leave the Special Patient to me,
Doctor."

"Gladly. And if he gives you trouble," Nick said,
"remind him that the Special Cottage is infinitely preferable
to the state pen."

"If he were sane, I wonder if he would agree with you.
The sane look on Pawksville as being strong punishment."

"Those who are not themselves in need of surgery look
on an operation in the same way," Nick said evenly. "I say,
let the sane take their punishment in the proper institutions,
then. And not add to the overcrowding here."

"Some people," Dr. Ouita said, rather surprising herself with her cryptic remark, "have to take what punishment they can get." Then before Nick could challenge that,
she took a turn for the bland. "How is Miss Bartholomew?"

"My sister's getting along fine. She still needs the cane,
of course."

"Remind her she's due for her liver shot," Dr. Ouita
said, and Nick thanked her and was on his way.

As Dr. Ouita had not gotten around to setting her Venetian blinds aslant, Nick had gazed from time to time past her to the view beyond her windows. What met his eye pleased him, for the landscape was manorial, parklike. There must have been a school of architecture around the close of the last century known as State Hospital Gothic, and its members must have prospered. Imagine, if you will, the House of Usher rising from rolling lawns, with madmen shouting like muezzins from its towers, and with crenelated battlements of stone splendor. This is the Annex. It is annexed to nothing, and stares over the trees at the great dome of the Administration Building. The administration of Pawksville takes place elsewhere, and the Administration Building consists of five brick wings of wards converging on a four-story rotunda topped by the heavy dome. The front of Administration may scarcely be called stark—some nine ornate columns rise to support the protruding upper lip of the third story, lending to the façade a slightly repressed or suspicious expression. Within this upper lip is contained a complete house, private elevator, four bedrooms, living room commanding a view, kitchen, paneled library, and all, wherein dwell the current Superintendent and his family.

At Pawksville too there is a power house, and the Special Patient's Cottage, and an Auditorium, and a Morgue House, and even a Hospital, still uncompleted since it is only seven years old, and the reform governor before the present reform governor. . . . Only Dr. Ouita would have the correct facts on why the contractor walked out before finishing up the job. As most state hospitals take their names from the nearest village, so did this, for it lay in the meadows outside a small southern town called Pawksville, located in a state you wouldn't know from Tennessee unless someone told you otherwise. To the cognoscenti, therefore, Pawksville always meant the State Hospital, just as the Hospital always meant the uncompleted building. Complicated though it might sound, one accustoms oneself to Pawksville traditions with no strain.

Leaving Dr. Ouita's office, Nick moved as if powered by his deep meditation alone. He found himself in the rotunda. The light from the high dome filtered down on his head, or, rather, because of the frosted panes so far up, the light drizzled down; in any event sunlight never was seen in the rotunda. Smack in the center of this great area, and dwarfed by the tiers of galleries, there plip-plopped a gloomy fountain in the perpetual dusk. Toward this fountain Nick was drawn to gaze thoughtfully upon an ugly utilitarian spigot of sorts which supplied the waters of the pool in dismal spurts. Along with the wheeze and thump of the elevator, the fountain was the only sound to be heard in the cathedral immensity and hush of the rotunda. No one was about in mid-morning to be heard; the acoustics of the dome were such that hollering from the tiptop gallery produced a faint ghostly cry, whereas two whisperers anywhere else would inform all within sixty feet of their inmost secrets.

To the staff the fountain was unsettling as a weeping nag. It cheered no visitors, patients to no avail had tried to do away with themselves by submerging on hands and knees, and only Dr. Ouita maintained with the sharp insistence of nostalgia that once the fountain had charm. As an uncertain newcomer to Pawskville, Nick had listened with full attention to Dr. Ouita's story of the stone boy. In place of the spigot had stood a little boy gravely urinating a stream the color of consommé from his rusty tap. Almost fifty years ago the medical staff—the then-young high-spirited Dr. Ouita among them—had taken daily notice of the stone boy's state of health. "Diabetes mellitus," or "Cloudy amber . . . Ought to check him for albumin. . . ." Alas, the stone boy had offended some Superintendent's wife, and he was summarily banished and never seen again. Mickey had purportedly been his name, Nick reminded himself as if this were a fact newly brought to life, Mickey—short for micturation.

Nobody believed Ouita's story, the consensus being that it was some ancient hallucination rooted in thwarted maternal instinct. In any event, Nick dismissed it, for it had taken place—if it had—before he was born.

His thoughts plip-plopped as drearily as the fountain. Were all to go well, were—he was being visionary now—the Governor and his retinue and every reporter in the state able to take up residence in the wards, even, and never find anything amiss; and were the rest of Pawksville able to allay the Governor's fears of a rotten spot in his administration; were the Purchaser able to account for certain time-honored discrepancies in his department; were Superintendent Keeney at his bland and bibulous best; were he, Nick, able to hold his snapping temper on a firm leash; were all in order save what had been carefully swept under the rug, then Nick could and would do what everyone else in Pawksville was dreaming of doing. He would ask the generous Governor for a small favor.

To the Superintendent's modest request for a new sports car (he had already declared Pawksville in sad need of one); and to Dr. Heall's plaintive bleatings for a *genuine* leather couch for his analytical sessions; to the Purchaser's heartrending entreaties for twenty-five cents more per day per patient (the Purchaser, a political appointee, dabbled in the stock market); to these Nick would add his own hopeful demands for more male nurses, a half-dozen more physicians, and the completion of the Hospital. Little enough to ask, considering the funds at the Governor's disposal. Why is it, Nick asked himself heatedly, that when the wants are small the need always has to be so great?

And were Pawksville itself a model of orderly felicity, he thought, there was still the Special Patient. It was not in Nick to look the Governor in the eye and declare Titus Graham insane, not even for the sake of his job. Perhaps, though, for the male nurses, and some psychiatric internes, and a decent drug budget. . . . No, it rested with Ouita. She believed in the man's insanity, and, thank God, the truth was in her.

Heartened, he was about to turn away from the fountain. Then he paused, wondering what special little gift Ouita might want of the Governor. He was wondering even as he bent down to scrutinize the slight unevenness in the stone rim of the fountain. Some ornament or other must once have been fastened there.

2

The Bespoke Schizophrenic

"I really do look like hell, don't I?" the heretofore clean-cut young Marion Pierce said in actual pain.

"Indisputably."

Thus crisply reassured, young Pierce turned from the hotel mirror, and, practicing his shambling walk, went to the hotel window. Below, the bright town square of Pawksville was so like that of his own hamlet of origin that he would not have been too astonished to see his late father entering the courthouse opposite. Marion was conscious, almost angrily so, certainly defensively so, of the opinion his companion held of Pawksville. "Faulknerland," Mr. Ellis had said immediately upon debarking from the train, then reeled from the heat, though he tried to give the impression that it was dismay that was unsteeling him. "Marion, did your father actually have a law practice in a town like this?" Mr. Ellis had next asked, and indulged in his cultivated titter.

Brooding on these remarks, Marion Pierce was not at all diverted by Mr. Ellis' present observations. "Do you know, Marion, this morning I was actually treated to the sight of a woman sitting in a wagon giving suck to her infant. And at that a loutish toddler fully three years old, I give you my word."

Young Pierce held his tongue, longing to snap, "Well, at least she didn't have to pay a New York pediatrician two hundred dollars to introduce her to the fact of breast-feeding." Contenting himself with a mild, "The back-country people are still given over to many of the old ways, sir," Marion turned from the window.

"They seem very *real*," Mr. Ellis granted as though there had been some question about this.

"We're human," Marion said touchily.

"Now, now, Pierce. . . ."

Scratching his unshaven chin, loathing his unwashed self, Marion shambled back to his peeling cane chair.

Having judged this performance with a critical eye, Mr. Ellis said chattily, "Good. Excellent. That psychiatrist schooled you beautifully. And I've every faith in the couple I found. They're perfect for our needs. She's genteel and grasping, and he's a crumbling alcoholic." Mr. Ellis sought his own elegant image in the dresser mirror and gazed in chilly reproof at a tobacco-color stain on the glass which laid a birthmark along one lean chop and silvered temple. Moving an inch or so to the left he delicately touched his handkerchief to the temple as if to remove a faint dew of perspiration, though his skin was absolutely dry, as Mr. Ellis prided himself on aging—as the French had it—*sec*. "I feel we can trust this couple," Mr. Ellis resumed, "simply because they are so—spineless. The weak are always so strong in their failings. Wouldn't you say, Marion?"

"And you think," Marion said with great control, "that this pair resembles my own parents?"

"Not in the least. This heat has us both on edge. It's simply that they look the part, and—to put it bluntly—are willing to perjure themselves. I'm sure—" Mr. Ellis went on gallantly "—your own parents would have turned down such a proposition as mine forthwith. Surely they were hardly the type of people who would commit a strange young man to Pawksville for money."

"Sorry," Marion said. "I'm just a little nervous about all this, that's all."

"*Gadfly* Magazine and I have every faith in you," Mr. Ellis said as stoutly as if he were pounding Marion on the back. "Shall we go across to the courthouse? It can't be more stifling there than in this hotbox of a room."

A last glimpse of himself in the mirror, seedy, unkempt, and loose-grinned, was sufficient to speed Marion on his way. He and Mr. Ellis met no one on the stair, but crossing the blazing square they afforded amusement to two loafers by treating them to the picture of the shaggy Marion supporting the gasping Mr. Ellis under the direct glare of the sun.

". . . every faith in you," Mr. Ellis gasped, breathing as if it were his last, as they gained the black shade of the courthouse corridor. Falling into the nearest chair, and narrowly missing falling asprawl, Mr. Ellis sighed. "Heat . . ." he managed. "Unseasonable?"

"Southern summers are usually like this, sir," Marion assured him. Yet he too had broken out in a chill sweat. "Sir—— the more I think of this scheme, the crazier it seems."

Recovered, Mr. Ellis said gaily, "Precisely. That's why we're having you committed." Again he tittered with that quiet eloquence of his, so that he seemed the last exponent of a dying art.

Marion Pierce pressed on in a low urgent voice, "But it's really like looking for the proverbial needle in a haystack. There are at least a couple of thousand patients at Pawksville. Why, I could be locked up for a year in a padded cell and never so much as——"

"Not," Mr. Ellis cut in incisively, "if you use your head. Do bear in mind that we went to the best psychiatrist in New York to work out your affect and ideation. You ought to find yourself in the next bed to him."

"But what if they don't put me where he is?" Pierce

asked passionately. "There're probably a lot of wards in Pawksville."

"Make them shift you around."

"How?"

"Show improvement."

"And if I still don't meet him?"

"Worsen," Mr. Ellis advised simply.

"That's all very well, provided he's really insane!"

"Hardly a remote possibility," Mr. Ellis said. "Taking into consideration his latest efforts, or should I say *attempts*, at poetry *Gadfly* has received from him. Or would you, with your vast experience in literature, call the 'Canticle for the Holy Dove' a masterpiece?"

The opening lines of the disputed Canticle spoke themselves in Marion's mind:

> Shush now, now shush, now,
> Shush. Now you all shush.
> The Lord's atalking, wants
> A Word with me.

"My theory is," Mr. Ellis said suddenly, "that he's decided to play at madness as an expedient. In which case we'd best leave him undisturbed so he won't have to stand trial. But if he really is insane—and we're all relying on you, Marion, to find this out—then we'll see about having our attorney file a writ of habeas corpus. We can't let his genius be ruined by quacks, or his freedom made a political—"

"Football," Marion said. "But, sir, we can only get a writ out if he's not receiving proper treatment. Isn't that what the attor—"

"Shall we leave the legal work to those so qualified to act?" Mr. Ellis showed open disfavor at Marion's flagging courage. "All I ask of *you* is that you keep your head. And your ideation in mind at all times. And your wits about you. And remember your kinesthetic arabesques."

Marion (who had forgotten about *them*) dutifully

demonstrated a few meaningless stylistic gestures with his hands.

"And don't fail," Mr. Ellis went on, "to find out who's sneaking his work out for him. We're open to nothing short of extortion there, as I doubt a lover of poetry is performing that service for us."

"I'll do my very best, sir," young Pierce said, trying to rally.

"Splendid. I know you will. In the meantime, I'll be thinking about that advancement for you. Achieving the status of editor of the most eminent poetry magazine at the age of twenty-three. . . . Well, time enough later—after you've made your report—to discuss that."

"Yes, but what if they won't let me make a report?"

Mr. Ellis suddenly lost all patience. "Marion, I'm not sending you to prison. I'm sending you to a hospital. On a very serious mission. And should the least trouble arise, or I not hear from you within a reasonable time, I'd simply have my attorney— Instead of borowing trouble I suggest you concentrate on serving the cause of literature."

"Yes, but I can't help feeling a little like Orpheus——"

"Ah . . ." Mr. Ellis interrupted in a voice that rubbed its hands together in satisfaction. "Here come your, ah—" he nodded at the bright doorway "—parents, Pierce." He rose, his distant smile at once summoning and subduing the couple advancing down the corridor.

Marion Pierce remained seated, remarking to himself with a shock that the pair did remind him strongly of his own dead parents. The woman wore the same shabby clothing and shabby dignity, and the man carried himself with the careful usage of his body, the same husbanding of energy that any Southerner with a "heart," a demanding occupation, and an insufficient income must employ to function at all in the heat of a Southern summer. When his own widowed mother had been scrabbling for every penny to send him to Yale, she would have perjured herself for a good cause (and a good price) twice as readily as this woman. Against instructions Marion jumped to his feet at the woman's approach.

"Will you sit down!" Mr. Ellis whispered sharply. "Or is that your idea of how a hebephrenic schizophrenic acts? Bite your hangnails, for heaven's sake!"

Young Pierce slumped down and sat regarding his slovenly attire.

". . . shouldn't take ten minutes for the whole proceeding, I've been given to understand," Mr. Ellis was saying briskly to the accomplices of *Gadfly* and literature. "This is Pierce, here. And he came from this state originally, so it's all perfectly legal. Or legal enough." Discreetly he took an envelope from his inner coat pocket and displayed it, maintaining a tight grasp on it the while. "Then this will be yours, and I'll be able to catch the noon train. We all know what we're to say?"

"You brought our poor sick boy home to us," the spurious Mr. Pierce murmured, shamefaced.

"He's more than sick, he's hopelessly deranged," Mr. Ellis said loudly, as if bearing gladsome news. "Shall we have him committed now?"

The woman looked down at Marion uncertainly.

Marion said softly, "I appreciate your kindness, ma'am. But it's what I want to do." He then shouted something loud and unintelligible, and the courtroom door opened to admit the head of the bailiff.

"Yall the Pierces?" he bawled directly to a startled Mr. Ellis. "If yar, bring um on in then, the Judge ez bout to leaffer lunch."

Mr. Ellis recovered and bent to pull Marion to his feet. Suddenly he sank down next to Marion and touched his forehead. "Could you two drag him in, please," he said to the ersatz Pierces. "I'll wait here for you unless I'm needed. This heat is simply . . . too . . . unbearable."

Marion submitted to the grasps of the strange couple,

yelling nonsense syllables over his shoulder to Mr. Ellis, reassuring that gentleman that, the mission undertaken, he would not fail. Yet in his mind Marion Pierce was saying fearfully: Oh, Lordy? Lordy, what am I . . . as he was dragged forward.

3

The Old Nick

Pawksville had a number of prized sayings, many of them first given coinage by Babs Heall, the pretty wife of Dr. Sonny (né Sidney) Heall. Having come as a bride to Pawksville and noting the misery and degradation which insanity inflicted on its victims, Babs was immediately of the firm opinion that "Any buddy who'd go crazy would have tuh be plum outta their mines." To this assertion, couched in her own inimitable sorghum accent, she held fast, regarding the patients as beneath notice and only a cut or so above contempt.

Driving home from what she persistently called the beauty parlor, though she had promised herself time and time again to say "hairdresser's" instead, Babs was not in the best of moods. The net which had been placed over her curls while she was under the dryer had bitten deeply into her forehead, leaving a red ugly crease that lent to her face an expression of extreme disgruntlement. Just ahead of her on the highway was the Sheriff's station wagon going at a fair clip, and Babs did not pass it, wanting no truck with those gentlemen on the subject of speeding. Instead, she was idly amusing herself by watching the antics of the man in the back seat, secured between two deputies.

He was a young man, so far as she could determine, and an active one. He was full of broad gestures, and seemed to be quite the conversationalist as well, for he turned from one deputy to the other, busy as a gossip just home from a long trip. Another nut, Babs announced to herself, speaking freely in her mind a word never uttered aloud in Pawksville.

Tiring of observing the psychotic young man, as she rapidly tired of any form of entertainment with which she could not identify, Babs bent her gaze to the rotunda, rising ahead, shimmering in the midday heat. She beheld it with distaste. Pawksville bored her; she found its occupants dull in the extreme, with the exception of herself and Nick Bartholomew. In Nick she saw a romantic figure, marred only by the fact that he had three children and was, to Babs' way of thinking, an idolator of his daughter. At least, though, he was a widower of several years standing, and this in itself served to enhance Nick for Babs. Off and on she was prone to grow desirous of him, in particular when he was angry, for then his aspect was formidable. Immaculate in his whites, his virility overpowered them; and Babs could not rid herself of a secret fancy of what he might do when furied, or to what lengths his rage might carry him—were she helpless and within reach.

Dwelling on such pleasant conjectures, Babs followed the station wagon through the gates, then brought her car to a tire-scorching halt. The wagon had gone on ahead, but a work detail of male patients had begun to shuffle across the driveway as aimlessly as sheep. Armed with hoes, bent of shoulder, and with lackluster gazes wandering purposelessly under straw hats, the patients appeared less than human, burdened under the disease which had claimed them. Babs lighted a cigarette and then sat examining the work detail, not blowing out the match until her thumb and forefinger stung. A lone patient, a straggler being shoved along by an attendant, had caught her eye. Hatless, head up, he took the sun without flinching. His face was afire with sunburn, shades darker than his golden-red hair, and because of his emaciation and a certain burning quality about him that had nothing to do with his coloration, he was altogether remarkable. He was a catatonic, which, in the forbidden language in which Babs communicated with herself, meant that he was a "dummy"—a patient who neither spoke nor responded when spoken to, an unreachable refugee from reality.

Will you jus looka that, Babs invited herself. She was filled with the mounting glee of the idle woman scenting conflict among those around her. Jus wait, oh jus you wait til lil ole Doc Jane Carmody claps eyes on that. Her very own lil beau-boy bein treated no bettern anybody else!

Thus highly diverted until the work detail had moved on, the red-headed patient prodded from behind, Babs crushed out her cigarette. An unease had seized her, and for a moment she did not recognize it as a charitable impulse until she reflected, Guess Pawksville's no play-party for Carmody. I sure wooden like to be in her shoes.

The drive free, Babs swung around past Administration and on to Hospital. There the Sheriff's deputies were in the act of delivering their charge to an attendant. Babs stuck her face with the hair-net line like a scar on her forehead out the car window in time to hear a deputy say to the receiving attendant, "Name of Pierce. He's all yours, boys." The babbling young man was induced to get out of the road and onto the Hospital steps, so that Babs might safely pass on. *Ruckus-raiser* was her only mental comment on Pawksville's newest acquisition, name of Pierce.

The Hospital behind her, she turned into the tree-shaded lane that led to the Annex. Her thoughts returned again to the work detail. As if some slight, long rankling, had at last been assuaged, Babs told herself warmly that Nick was a devil, all right. A real devil, putting Maginnis to work and Carmody in her place in one stroke.

Now the Annex came into view, the old brick façade appearing deceptively cool. What a devil, that Nick, Babs was repeating to herself, when a favorite remark of her husband's abruptly presented itself for her further examination.

Sonny Heall, Nick's lieutenant, second in senority to himself, had once summed up Nick: Of course, Nick's super-ego has him by the short hairs, but he's a swell guy aside from that.

Having long pondered this, Babs now suddenly chanced on the right construction of it. Sonny meant that Nick might act uppity, like he wanted to be perfect or something, but his heart was in the right place, you had to grant him that.

4

The Downcast and the Divine

Wrestling with her conscience was a new and demanding sport for Dr. Jane Carmody. In her twenty-nine years she had heretofore managed to do the right thing—if not always the correct thing, which is something else again—without too much effort or sacrifice. She and temptation had had little more than a nodding acquaintance; her girlhood had been placid, if industrious, and being an only child she had been a touch overprotected. As her mind was commodious and disciplined she was demonstrably good material for medical school. Now, on the sunny side of thirty, she was still too pert and given to an occasional gaucherie to be called a "handsome woman" and yet feminine enough for older females to bark in resentful disbelief "*Doctor* Carmody?" upon being introduced to her. One would instantly take Dr. Carmody for a pediatrician. Actually she had planned to specialize in gynecology, until one day she had walked out on a residency in Nashville to come to work at Pawksville.

Dr. Carmody had an office in the Annex which she rarely entered, having taken up the slack in the lab, which had been run in a manner most haphazard until her arrival. The lab was a cool refuge in the basement of the Hospital, and there, amid urine samples and soothed by the hum of the refrigerator, Jane smoked and sat on a stool to run analyses, or drifted to the battered desk to tend to her case histories, or sprinted to the refrigerator to hide a bottle of wine after a shopping trip to the village, and occasionally laid her neat beige curls among the rubber tubing and the slides and the Petrie dishes and wept.

Loathing herself for these lapses into the tearful, yet certain that one would befall her every so often, Jane found privacy of the essence. Her gratitude, therefore, had been little short of boundless when Nick Bartholomew had assigned her the little single apartment in the upper story of the Morgue House for her quarters. Her gratitude had taken a rapid slump when he had, in the next breath, assigned her the back wards for her duties. But her sense of fairness dictated that she attend her charges with all due dedication until such time as Nick rotated the staff assignments.

Over three months later such time had not arrived, and, in fact, no longer seemed very likely to. Nick Bartholomew, she was beginning to learn (if she wasn't learning much else at Pawksville) took resolute prodding; all her hints had failed.

In the heat of the August afternoon she was lingering a moment longer in the lab, before her conscience drove her to her duties. She was making work and she knew it, puttering with some glassware in general, and in particular rinsing out a beaker in which she had warmed a can of soup for her solitary and therefore peaceful lunch. That deliberate tread which caused her to look to the lab doorway announced the coming of Nick Bartholomew an instant before he appeared. Jane found time to assume the exact comradely smile the situation called for as Nick entered.

His manner was easy, and because he was rarely in the lab he rather made a quick inspection while he was at it. Satisfied with what he saw, he took a lab stool. "I missed you for lunch."

"Sorry, I didn't know I was on the menu," Jane said, risking the flippant to sound cordial.

Nick appraised her at his leisure. "I just wondered if something was bothering you."

"No. No. I simply wasn't in the mood for Sonny's psychoanalytic gems of jargon. Not to mention——" She spread out her hands and shrugged. "You know, the usual cattiness that passes for conversation. Is there something on *your* mind, Nick?"

"That's my question. Keeney had me over bright and early this morning to keen about the Governor's visit, so I'm by way of taking a poll. I'm gathering complaints, if such there be, from the staff. See if there's anything I can put to rights."

"You can indeed," Jane said promptly. "I've a large resounding complaint."

"Oh?"

"Yes, *oh*. How's about putting me on the acute wards for a change?"

Nick shook his head. "You couldn't handle acute and back wards both."

"I wasn't suggesting I handle both." Jane made a futile attempt to outstare Nick, to make a contest of it. "I mean," she said in her most conciliatory manner, "if you could perhaps rotate assignments. Not that I'm telling you how to run Pawksville, Nick, but——"

"You relieve me, Jane. For a moment there I thought . . ." Nick let the rest drift and, picking up a piece of filter paper, idly began pleating it. "I was afraid," he said, reverting to his former topic, "that you were—hiding away in the lab here because you were depressed."

"Depressed! Good Lord, Nick, those filthy wards day in and day out would put anyone in one unending glum. That's not what I came here for. I came here to learn psychiatry——"

"So you told me," Nick said, his demeanor suddenly dangerously mild.

Jane turned away from him. "You should take up massage. You could pick up the last few pointers, then, of how to rub it in. If you guessed right away why I wanted to work in Pawksville, why did you hire me?"

"Well, I needed every addition to the staff I could get. I can't afford to look gift motives in the mouth." There was a rustling movement and he added in the same collected tone, "Cigarette?"

"No thank you," Jane said formally. "I must be off on my rounds." When she looked at Nick again she saw he was not smoking either, but finishing off his pleating of the piece of filter paper. He had only to bend it in half to make a toy fan of it.

"You'll never forgive me, will you," Jane said bitterly. "For trying to hoodwink you when I came for a job interview."

The fan completed, Nick dropped it on the lab bench. He said quietly, "There is nothing to forgive, Doctor. Your personal—motivations were not for me to judge. But as for getting over my initial disappointment, that's something else again."

"Hold a grudge, then," Jane said, and in the next moment advised herself aloud, "and I'd better hold my tongue."

When he grinned at her, she recognized that his geniality was genuine. He slid off the stool and gravely slid the fan across the bench toward her as if it were a peace offering. "Here, cool yourself with this."

"Sometimes, you make me so uncontrollably furious—" Jane began, but with a jaunty wave of his great hand Nick was on his way.

Moments later Dr. Jane Carmody emerged from the lab, jingling her keys in her white jacket out of habit to insure their presence. In the sun she paced herself a cadence or so

faster than a stroll; to hurry in such heat invited collapse.
Around the shade trees were collected groups of Dr. Ouita's
old ladies endlessly at their tatting, while along the dusty
walks male work details trudged heavily as if in chains, their
attendants slouching beside them, hot, baleful, and ready
with a furtive blow.

Rounding the refectory, Jane glimpsed first the white
curtains of her bedroom in the Morgue House hanging still
and virginal in the motionless afternoon, and then, rising
like nothing so much as the frozen glass moon of all lunatics'
moons, the rotunda resting clumsily on its irradiating wards.
Within earshot and noseshot of her wards, Jane caught a
flash of the only spirited figure on the breathless landscape.
Caddy Bartholomew's ponytail flipped upon her Tee-shirted
back as she hastened along a walk, her stride announcing a
purposefulness far beyond that of the average self-important
youngster. But then, Caddy's every mannerism spoke to
Pawksville at large of a child hopelessly indulged and endlessly pursuing some mischief or other. In her mind, clinically likening Caddy to the merry maniacs sometimes produced by chronic syphilis, Jane thought, Funny kid, she has
all the carefreedom of a happy paretic.

Within the lee of the ancient back wards with their
screened populous porches, Jane paused to sop at her forehead with her handkerchief and brace herself. Then with
firm step she entered into the dark close corridor and unlocked the first door. The stench was ripe, the uproar routine.
Locking the door behind her, Jane was greeted by the chattering and gesticulating and shouting and macabre chortlings
of her charges. Women stripped and women in strait jackets
roamed aimlessly; lined along the walls the silent ones, with
mouths ajar and eyes uninhabited, lolled in their messes and
(some old hands had it) fancied that they lay in clover
scented with spring rain. There was the usual commotion
sounding in the washroom where some filthy patient was
receiving an unwelcome bath.

Billie Noon came tramping down the ward to gratify Dr. Carmody with news of the day's fractures, gouges, abrasions, concussions, and similar mishaps. "Well, same old milk run today, Doctor." Miss Noon's whistle strung on a cord around her neck bounced from side to side against her weight-lifter's biceps.

"All in order, I see," Jane said dryly. "Has Ethel calmed down on her paraldehyde?"

"Well, she hasn't threw a chair at anyone for over an hour," Miss Noon said, all cheerful optimism. She indicated a nearly bald girl with a jerk of her head. "Cherry's been foolin with her hair-do again. Shall I restrain her?"

"You'd better, unless you want to contend with another infection like the last time."

"Gawd ferbid," Billie Noon prayed. "It's been pick–pluck–pick–pluck all morning. It's really something, I mean. Nineteen years old, and she's already snatched herself bald. But I kinda hate to restrain her, Doctor. You know? She'll just bang her head against the wall then."

"Tape her down."

"Like all last week," Billie Noon said in resignation.

Like some young and vastly influential prelate with a wise workhorse of a lay reader as honor guard, Dr. Carmody and Miss Noon began the rounds. "How are you feeling?" Jane said to the babbling, to the vacant, to the frenzied. In turn she was advised to go to hell, to kill babies, that Peter had a pepper full of pickpockets, and that on occasion the President of the United States took up residence behind the radiator.

"And that," Jane said, referring to a woman who crouched naked on all fours, "is the result of one hundred and ten EST convulsions." Together she and Miss Noon looked down on the swayback, the thin flanks and the head hanging low between elbows with great protuberant knobs on them. The patient looked like nothing so much as some beast of burden abandoned to starve.

"Well," Miss Noon said pleasantly, "I haven't seen any heralds of fidgitation out of her for months now." Miss Noon's terminology was of her own devising; she would have spoken in the same breezily competent manner to Dr. Bartholomew or even Superintendent Keeney without fear or even the thought of correction. "She goes to the toilet when you take her there, and she don't bite the hand that feeds her any more." Perspiring cheerfully, Miss Noon took a step from Jane's side to indicate they should continue on the rounds.

"How are the women taking the heat?" Jane thought to ask conscientiously.

"It don't cool them down none," Miss Noon grunted. "Doctor, for the millionth time, can't somebody do something about my porches? The only way my ladies—" Miss Noon's rather mountainous face forbade Jane to smile at her borrowing the term usually reserved for Dr. Ouita's patients "—my ladies can get a breath of air is go roast in the afternoon sun. You'd be bat—goof—cra——" Tangled in her struggle to avoid the use of expressions frowned upon at Pawksville, Billie Noon gave up the struggle. "You'd be disturbed too, Doctor, shut up in this heat. When the Governor comes, I'm telling you, I'd just like to invite him to set a spell on that porch. Maybe it just might come to him that a little air-conditioning wouldn't hurt Pawksville none."

"I'm not acquainted with Governor Jackson," Jane said, "but I'm afraid he'd still feel that Pawksville has certain more demanding needs."

"Yeah, like a Lincoln convertible for Superintendent Keeney's daughter to jazz around college in," Miss Noon interrupted with the insolence of one who has worked faithfully for over twenty years in a job no one else in his right mind would dream of taking. "Don't give me that, Doctor."

The conversation had run aground. In silence Jane glanced out on the porch. The blaze of sunlight and stench seemed one, like some fiery steam that caused the sweat to pour from the skins of the half-naked women without cooling them.

"And Doctor Heall once tried to tell me those schizies go schizie for the fun of it." Miss Noon sniffed and flexed her biceps. "That's some retreat from reality, I sure wouldn't say. You hadn't come here, had you, when he tried to analyze Carrie Hodget? She poked him one on the button." Miss Noon chuckled in a burst of admiration for Carrie's acumen. Then before Jane could murmur some chastisement or other, Miss Noon took a turn for the anxious. "Oh, Doctor, one thing you can do for me. Have the Holy Dove sent over to the dentist when he comes. I think a tooth's bothering her."

"I'll have a look at her."

"She won't admit to it," Miss Noon said in warning. "The tooth. But one side of her face is kind of swole. She's in cleaning the washroom."

The Holy Dove was indeed in the washroom, engaged in scrubbing the artwork from the walls. She was a magnificent woman, wearing her sixty-odd years as she might royal robes. Her person and faded cotton house dress, despite her present task, were neat; the long (a concession in the case of the Holy Dove) white hair wrung out from the crown and braided and coiled round and round her head in the fashion of those who would be queenly. She was on her knees when Jane entered the noisome, humid washroom and rose with a weighty grace. On her feet, the stance of the Holy Dove was that of some imperishable eminence like a snowpeak. "Good afternoon, Doctor," the Holy Dove intoned in her ecclesiastical contralto, at the same time unobtrusively executing some ritualistic shorthand on the air with a crooked chapped forefinger.

"Good afternoon, Holy Dove," Jane replied with an unconscious note of deference, taking the opportunity to gaze penetratingly at the Holy Dove's jaw. "How are you feeling?" This was said far less casually than to, say, a garrulous patient in a strait jacket.

"I am splendid, Doctor," the Holy Dove observed, some-how giving the impression she was reporting on herself in the third person.

Miss Noon's eyes signaled her concern to Jane: Look at the left side of her face.

"Miss Noon would like you to take the dentist's detail over, when he comes Thursday," Jane said dutifully.

The Holy Dove conceded, "Oh, yes. That must be man-aged."

"And have that tooth of yours looked at, now, Holy Dee," Miss Noon so forgot herself as to blurt.

Trying not to look pained, the Holy Dove continued to address herself to Jane. "That won't be necessary, Doctor. The tooth is not at all burdensome. Moreover—"

"Moreover me no moreovers," Jane said firmly, knowing when the Holy Dove wished to be coaxed. "If that tooth poisons your system and incapacitates you, it will be most burdensome to Miss Noon, I assure you." The humidity of the washroom was causing Jane to feel unreal; this minuet of manners with a petted paranoid (she was thinking, and then collected herself—it was dangerous to slip into alliteration around the Holy Dove); this orderly progression of civil-ities, the greeting deferential, the address correct, the request politic, the command gracious, all protocol and expedient when dealing with the Holy Dove, were remote as some radio star from what Jane had calmly imagined she would be doing and saying as she rounded the third decade of her life. She belonged in a cool tiled clinic, a silent matronly nurse at her side, as she said: On the table, please, Mrs. Smith. Put your feet in the stirrups, that's it. The pain is on the left side, you say? "Isn't there a little tenderness on the left side of your jaw, Holy Dove?"

"A trifle," the Holy Dove admitted. "I'll have the dentist draw the tooth."

"You'll do no such thing, Holy Dee," Bille Noon said

heatedly. "If the dentist wants to fill your tooth, then you let him——"

"Pain," the Holy Dove was explaining to Jane, "is part of my martyrdom, Doctor. I embrace it."

"As a doctor, I must prevent pain," Jane was saying a touch wildly. "Now, I'm going to order you something for that tooth, Holy Dove. And Miss Noon will see to it that you take it. You've got Miss Noon all upset about you, Holy Dove——"

"I have always done anything and all that Miss Noon asks of me," the Holy Dove put in, mountain-lake blue eyes chilly. "Nor will I dash this cup from my lips." Having capitulated and won the day as well—a habit with the Holy Dove—she said no more, gazing upon Jane and Billie Noon alike with a superior kindliness.

Miss Noon bristled with relief. "Well, that's better! I declare, Holy Dee, trying to keep a thing like that from me, when you know good and well a tooth can cause a gen'ral infection in ladies our age . . ."

But the Holy Dove had already turned away to contemplate where next the tiling needed washing down.

It was this very immutable devotion to what she saw as her duty which had led the Holy Dove to her downfall. Or was that the term for it? Jane wondered, leaving the washroom. For the Holy Dove was the glory of Pawksville; most state hospitals have some prized inmate, but few could boast so classic a paranoid. In the opinion of Nick Bartholomew she was seemingly sane in all matters save the sole delusion of her divinity. "I am," she had announced, upon meeting Jane and to the beaming pride of Billie Noon, "the Holy Dove of the Trinity, the Fourth of Three. Believe in me."

Each year, in fact, a group of divinity students came to Pawksville for a day for a quick briefing on what might be termed abnormal pastoral psychology, topped by a lecture from the Holy Dove on some very esoteric points of theology. Nick Bartholomew, bursting his buttons but straightfaced, introduced her, knowing the Holy Dove would give the earnest young men aces and spades before she was done. That was the topnotch paranoid the Holy Dove was.

From the moment she had emerged full-blown into her paranoia, the Holy Dove must have been a psychiatric marvel. She could have been a stunning lecturer or an executive of a corporation. Unfortunately, her delusion had caused her to found a cult—and a good one, as cults go—and her commitment to Pawksville was foreordained. For several years the cult had prospered, her disciples gradually hardening themselves to endure lives of sacrifice and good works, and many who had come to her little temple to scoff remained to join. When the Iscariot made his appearance, he did so by sidling in under the guise of a meek little clerk in a dry-goods store. The Holy Dove knew him beyond all disguise, but kept her counsel. One day the clerk revealed himself by speaking to the Holy Dove in the sacred tongue, the alliteration of *m*s. "Magnificent morning," he had remarked with a greasy smile. "Must make every minute——" The Holy Dove knew what must come to pass. To that end she gave a Last Supper and poisoned the clerk. He didn't die, but he nearly did. The Holy Dove, through inexperience, had shown a certain ineptitude with toadstools. She had thus taken the short step from cult to chaos. And commitment.

At Pawksville the Holy Dove promptly offered herself up as an uncomplaining drudge. Backward through the wards she worked her way down through the years. The attendants fought over her, each declaring herself most in need of that sturdy back and those willing hands. Billie Noon fought fiercest, plaguing the doctors and wheedling her fellow attendants until the Holy Dove was hers. For years now the two had labored in the endless heat of a filthy ward. In winter when the radiators were turned on full to keep the nude patients warm, the Holy Dove went around preventing the catatonics from resting their faces on the searing metal or dragging the raging off the icy porch. She forced kicking, clawing patients into the tubs, warding off blows with one hand and restraining with the other. She broke up fights, and had many a time come sailing into a fray to rescue Billie Noon. Withal the Holy Dove was encased in her paranoid calm, her superior kindliness.

Billie Noon once said the Holy Dove had such a way about her with their poor "ladies" that she was half of a mind to believe the Holy Dove was who she said she was. Having said it, Miss Noon flexed her muscles and would not take it back. It had never been necessary for Billie Noon to tell anyone, including the greenhorn Dr. Carmody, that she treasured the Holy Dove above every other friend.

Having ended her round of Miss Noon's ward, Jane paused before the door for Miss Noon to open it. It was a little courtesy the brusque older woman liked to perform for Jane in return for favors. "Thanks for fixing up the Holy Dove," Miss Noon said gruffly. "Stubborn! Sometimes just to get her to take her little walk every day I have to almost kick her in her sacred behind." Miss Noon swung the door open.

From the door across the dim corridor there sounded the shrill tweetings of an attendant's whistle, accompanied by much shouting and similar freedoms of expression.

"Having themselves a free-for-all on Six, all right," Miss Noon commented merrily.

But Jane was already gone.

Locking the door of Ward Six behind her, Dr. Jane Carmody leaned against it and rested in the gloom. There was a slight bruise on her temple and her jacket pocket was torn. She was not a strong or muscular woman, and wrestling with a combative patient (without ever once resorting to an exchange of blows) came no easier than struggling with her conscience. She wondered for an instant if she actually detested her work, but put the thought from her mind. To paraphrase the Holy Dove, she told herself wryly, My cup runneth over, don't waste any more of your best rare old vintage gall on me.

But her daily stroll through a holocaust was over. She could hide in the lab and have a Coke and a smoke, then run some routine analyses. If it would only rain, she thought, looking out into the burning heart of the afternoon.

Walking bareheaded under the sun, she weaved for a step or so like one stunned. Then, adjusting to the glare, she increased her pace. Nearing the Hospital, she looked to the Morgue House and the drift of white that was her bedroom curtains, inviting as seafoam. Eyes fastened on that beckoning promise of coolness and quiet, she was almost past a group of male patients working among some wilted flower beds. Only one patient, Sean Maginnis, did not wear a straw hat. His dark red hair bleaching to copper under the sun, his thin nose purple from burn, he stood staring off into infinity, eyes almost gentian blue in their catatonic ecstasy. A trowel dangled from one listless hand while the other played an arpeggio on air. Ten feet away from Maginnis his attendant picked his nose in the shade of a magnolia tree.

"Where's that patient's hat?" Jane asked the lounging attendant in a voice so hoarse, so abrupt, that he started. Recognizing her, a slow knowing smile accompanied his shrug. "What, Doctor?" He did not trouble himself to rise or look toward his charges.

"I said where's that man's hat? Can't you see he's in danger of sunstroke? Look at his skin! You take him back to his ward——"

"Sure, Doctor, only Doctor Bartholomew instinctly told me to puttim to work." The smile was broad now, inviting provocation as well as provoking. "I figure maybe I better wait till Doctor Bartholomew—"

"Put his hat on for him!" Jane shouted.

Insolent, indolent, grinning, the attendant rose and shambled out into the sun. Moving among his patients as if they were so many grazing sheep, he reached the red-headed one, lifted a straw hat from the dust and clapped it on his head. The patient remained motionless, the hat dumped ludicrously over his ecstatic gaze. "So O.K.?" the attendant asked in mock servility.

Jane turned away hurriedly. Trotting for the lab, she could not have said whether she was perspiring heavily or crying.

5

Duet in a Dour Key

Life on a receiving ward had proved to be far beyond the inventive limits of young Marion Pierce. *Garish* was the way he summed it up to himself. After a whirlwind physical examination by a Dr. Parry or somebody, he had been thrust into the ward, shown his bed, and not introduced to anyone. This in itself unnerved him, even though his greeting in reply would have been some rehearsed piece of gibberish. It was, he supposed, the shock of his first encounter with a group of people who did or said exactly what they chose and as long as they chose, until cuffed or mauled or restrained. He had seen battles, listened to ravings, and watched in helpless fascination a fellow patient devour with relish a rubber bathtub stopper. As he had been permitted to wander the length and breadth of his ward, he satisfied himself on his first day in Pawksville that the man he sought was not in Receiving. Marion then rather poked about, observing much —adding here and there a gesture or a twitch to his own repertoire—until he found his horror abating and a helpless pity taking its place.

He had been informed by his attendant that on Thursday—Staff Meeting Day—he, Marion, would be required to

trot out his talents for the ladies and gentlemen there assembled. Thus on Thursday morning an edgy Marion took
his place in the breakfast line. Ahead of him an ancient der-
elict, someone's cast-off grandfather, did not want to move
with the line, bleating some recital or other about wanting
his robe. The attendant stepped before Marion and gave the
tottering old creature a shove that spun him. "Don't do
that," Marion heard himself say.

Marion found himself the subject of the attendant's close
regard. He decided it was time he himself moved on, but
found his route again blocked by the elderly one. This time
the attendant clapped a hand seemingly the size of a small
leg of lamb on the fragile shoulders and flung the old man
halfway across the ward hall.

It was then that Marion first acted in a truly insane
manner. He clipped the attendant neatly but ineffectually
on the jaw. Then he himself was snatched from the line and
tossed into a chair. Another attendant was already approaching him with a strange garment made of heavy canvas. Into
the canvas sleeves went Marion's arms; he noted curiously
that his hands did not emerge, but were confined by a draw-
string much as if he were being tucked into an infant's beddy-
bye sleeper. Next the jacket was laced up his back, and lastly
his arms were crossed over his chest and drawn taut by having the drawstrings secured behind.

Long before the August heat claimed the ward, Marion
was casting about in his mind for random thoughts, lest the
pain of his arms drive him clean out of it.

This Thursday too, on or about the time the Holy Dove
would be convoying her two or three complaisant catatonics
to the dentist, Nick Bartholomew would be girding himself
for the ordeal of listening to Dr. Sonny Heall's choice utterances in Staff Meeting. Each week the Holy Dove liked to
take a break in her little jaunt about the grounds and relax
on a shaded bench not five feet from the opened windows of

the Staff Room. In such wise her knowledge of the doings at Pawksville in the summer was second only to Nick Bartholomew's and infinitely superior to that of Superintendent Keeney, who, it was commonly noted, hadn't the faintest idea of what was going on at Pawksville—ever.

Once again, notwithstanding the pain of an extraction, the Holy Dove would lead her charges for a rest to the selfsame bench. Not so much as a muffled whimper would escape from any of the little group, for they (in the tradition of catatonics everywhere) held their peace even unto the dentist's chair.

All that morning, then, the surface of Pawksville appeared to be unruffled. Just before noon, however, a ripple appeared when Nick met Jane Carmody in the clinic. Not replying to his casual greeting, she turned her back.

"Anything doing here?" Nick said in a slightly louder tone, and putting a soupçon of authority into it for good measure. Still he was presented with her rigid back, along with a certain pinkness of the ears.

"Dr. Heall asked me to do a spinal for him," Jane said stiffly.

"I'll bet he did," Nick commented. "He all but has tears in his eyes when he asks me to do one for him." He waited a moment and then said, "Jane?"

Though he had been hoping to avoid it, he was not surprised by her outburst. "Tell me, Doctor, is sunstroke your concept of a new therapy? Is sunstroke your idea of how to liven up things for a patient? Is sunstroke——"

"No, it isn't." He debated calling her Doctor or by her first name again, then avoided the issue entirely. "Your husband has a bit of a sunburn, that's all. I gave the attendant hell for it."

"How gratifying."

He was tempted to touch her; in the back of his mind he was discovering that he would have, but for the fact that he was so deeply tempted to do so. As a compromise with

himself Nick said, "Jane, will you please face me while
you're talking to me? That's an unfair trick, you know,
turning your back on me. You might as well ask me to go
stand in the corner."

"So go stand."

He waited, and in an instant she was turning, her face
flushed becomingly above her whites. "Ought I to be
abashed?" she challenged.

"It would be good form." Again Nick wanted so to touch
her, to place his fingers on her cheek or hand, that he welcomed the approach of an attendant and a patient, at the
same time wishing to throw the two of them bodily out the
clinic door. "Well now," he said, and wondered what on
earth to say next, but was relieved of the choice by the look
on the patient's face. "Headache pretty bad?" he asked the
patient, and (glad of something to do with his hands, at
last) placed one lightly on the patient's arm.

The patient looked about him dolefully. Then with the
resignation of his years at Pawksville, he took off his shirt
and climbed up onto his seat. This was a gangling chair that
was constructed somewhat as if the furniture-maker had had
in mind a cross between a lifeguard's tower and a high chair.
The chair was painted white, as was about everything else
except the instruments in the tiled clinic. The patient, chilly
with fear in spite of the heat, sat with his back curved, his
head hanging down. He was visibly of two minds about the
puncture, knowing that only a draining off of a few cubic
centimeters of spinal fluid would relieve him of the clam-
orous headache from which he had been suffering for almost
a week, and yet in horror of the great needle Jane was preparing to thrust between his vertebrae. His terror was not unfounded, for patients had reared back in uncontrollable
panic upon entrance of the needle and snapped it off, leaving
it buried to the hilt in flesh.

But Nick wore on his face all the makings of a grin
when Jane, with a cool brief glance at him, calmly picked up

the needle. (Sonny Heall, Nick remarked to himself, would honestly rather take a beating than perform a puncture; when one inserted and missed, and jabbed and missed, and became all sweaty fumbles while the patient rapidly and understandably grew impatient, matters could get out of hand in a hell of a hurry.) Behind the patient's back, Jane dipped a pointed, carefully cultivated long fingernail of her left forefinger into some alcohol. In her right hand she held the needle in readiness. "Here we go," she said to the patient quietly, and poked the fingernail deep between the vertebrae. The patient yipped, half-reared, then relaxed. At this moment Jane easily and taking her careful good time inserted the needle into the depression left by her nail and pressed home. All unaware that this was the moment of terror, the patient sighed with relief.

"Nice going," Nick said, not free to comment further upon her ruse. There was the faintest trace of pleasure in her returning smile. She liked to be deft, he knew that of her; it gave her a sense of worth to be able to ease pain without momentarily increasing it. He found himself wishing heavily that he could do the same for her. He said only "I'll see you at Staff Meeting, Doctor" and left to go upstairs to lunch.

Frequently Nick lunched in the staff dining room, as did his children when they were around. But the twin boys were away for the summer at a dude ranch; they were too old to be cared for by a patient any longer and too young to be at the mercies of his daughter Caddy. On Thursdays, however, he always lunched in his apartment, a habit carrying over from the times when his wife Nancy was alive, and he found in her the peace and quiet he needed before Staff Meeting.

Again this summer, his Thursday habit had taken on meaning, for his sister, Al, was visiting him. Incapacitated by a multiple fracture of the left leg, she came to Pawksville to mend. If there was an awkwardness about her visit, it had arisen so far only from her careful avoidance of mentioning how she had come by her injury. Her silence on the subject of auto accidents, well-meaning but clumsy, had a greater impact on Nick than if she had shrieked it out: Nancy got killed in her car.

If Nick had been required to describe his sister, he would have said that in his opinion she wasn't a bad sort. It was that her professional gruff solicitude of the private nurse had long since colored not only her personality but her outlook on life. She was prone to treat adults as if they were children, and children as if they were sparring partners (which they so often were, when it came to getting medication down them or administering hypodermics). Nick could not remember when it was that he and all who knew her had ceased calling her Alberta, and used instead the pointed Al. But Al she was, it suited her—just as her brusque manner did, or the stout Hamilton watch she wore strapped to her wrist at all times, and upon which she placed the same stern reliance a locomotive engineer would have.

Leaving the clinic, Nick passed the treatment rooms and posted himself before the elevator, pressing the button. The self-service elevator remained stationary, ruminating for its customary length of time before deciding to obey Nick's command. Opening its doors to engulf him, it then with much effort (needless effort was the impression it managed to give) jolted him up past the acute and hospital wards, past the surgery, and up to the unfinished top floor. There it opened its doors and contemptuously spat him out before dropping from sight as if crashing, which it had never done. So far.

The only flooring was a wooden walkway laid over steel beams, which trembled under Nick's heavy step as he began the long journey to his apartment. On either side of him stretched the uncompleted story, a windowless area—the contractor had walked out on the job in a huff—lit only by four naked bulbs suspended from the roof. Halfway across the great gloomy expanse a second walkway branching off from the first led Nick to his door. It came to him, as it had before, that this short trip was somewhat like walking along an amusement pier, desolate and dangerous of a still winter's night. Nor was the effect lessened by the heat, even in summer.

None of this gloom, however, penetrated into the sunny rooms of his apartment. There, in a fit of chintz, Nancy had once covered every stick of state-hospital furniture with flowered or striped materials, and had hung more of the same at the windows, until Nick had pronounced the place quite unlivable. Only in the kitchen—with its tan or brown, or maybe it was gray, wallpaper (one couldn't remember the color even when looking at it) did he feel at state-hospital home.

On the sound of the powerhouse's noon whistle, Nick skirted an inlaid table on which a jigsaw puzzle was slowly taking form and stuck his head into the kitchen. The banquette was set for three, but no one was about. Nick eased his great frame into the banquette and called out, "Anybody home? Where is everybody?"

"Within hailing distance, obviously," Al said and appeared in the doorway. Her limp was rather pronounced and he frowned, wondering if the leg bothered her or whether she was merely favoring it unconsciously. She was a hearty woman, older than he (and cheerfully looked it), but in all other respects the Bartholomews were remarkably alike. "Keep your seat, keep your seat," Al said as Nick commenced to rise. "I've got a chilled salad and cold chicken in the refrigerator."

"Where's the patient?"

Al carefully balanced herself on her good leg and slammed the refrigerator door shut with the other. Setting the food on the table she announced flatly, "I sent that idiot back to the ward where she belonged."

"Al, around Pawksville we don't refer to——"

"I was reining myself in, if you must know," Al said,

composed. She slid behind the banquette. "She was busily putting my puzzle away—*away* in its box, mind you—when I caught her at it. Besides, she got on my nerves. She spent half her time at the sink with a sour dishcloth in her hand, muttering to herself. Frankly, Nick, I just can't bring myself to like the insane."

"They're like olives," Nick admitted. "Pour me some tea, will you?"

Al complied, pouring over the ice cubes a brew so black and bitter it gave itself medicinal airs. "I suppose you've had an absolutely nerve-shattering day? Or was it rib-tickling?"

"Bone-chilling," Nick declared. "I had decided a little yard work might do Carmody's husband some good, and the attendant let him burn his little nose in the sun."

"Cut it out," Al remonstrated.

Nick broke the back of a lettuce leaf with his fork. "All right. But I get in an uproar every time I think of Jane's throwing her life away on him. Incidentally, she found out about the sunburn and gave me a couple of very uncomfortable moments this morning."

"Good for Jane."

"Yes, it was good for Jane. Better she lets off a little steam than mooing to herself secretly in the lab." Nick stirred his iced tea, tasted it, plainly showed his disbelief, and dumped in four cubes of sugar. He went on reflectively, "You know, she's got a nice spinal puncture on her, that gal. I'd like to see her out practicing medicine. She'd be good, I think."

"What, pray, is she doing here?"

"Brushing up on her hysterics."

"Nick, you're becoming a curmudgeon."

"Mebbe. But I'll tell you something, Toots. One fine day I'm going to inform Carmody that lover-boy Chopin's piano-playing days are done. I'm even going to break the news to her that he's catatonic. That compared to him a blank wall is vivacious. That he's incurably insane."

"Barring medical advances," Al said.

"And excepting miracles," Nick concurred impatiently.
"For all practical purposes, he's finished. Nuts. Bats. Wiggy,
the works. If she can get that through her head, maybe she'll
pack up those records of his and that hi-fi set and go out in
the world where she belongs. Why she ever married that long
skinny drink of water—"

"Guess," Al said.

"Him?"

"A lot of women find that slim-reed-in-the-wind type
overwhelmingly sexy," Al assured him comfortably. "Don't
ask me why. I go for the manly sand-hogger build myself.
Which is only seemly in a lady of my—ah—years and girth.
I could snap Maginnis like a twig. But then, Carmody's just
a bitsy thing herself, isn't she?" After a pause Al repeated,
"Isn't she?"

"Isn't who what?" Nick asked, suddenly intent on his
chicken.

"Carmody," Al said, the picture of patience. "Bitsy."
She refilled her plate complacently, secure in the knowledge
that her proportions became her. She went on innocently,
"That's what I said about Nancy when you two were first
married."

Nick took a turn for the reserved. "I'd forgotten." As if
counting noses, he looked about the banquette. "Where's
Caddy?"

"At the library. I apprised her of the fact that lunch is
at twelve noon. I suggested that she walk in that door no
later than one second after the whistle blew. You may observe
the results for yourself."

"She could have forgotten it was Staff Meeting day and
gone to the dining room."

"Her absence might admit of that explanation, yes. On
the other hand, I think there's a bit of hidden conflict between myself and Caddy. She's afraid I'll try dominating
her. And she's not cut out for the poor-motherless-little-tyke
routine. I did think of exercising a kind of loose surveillance

over her, but then I decided it would take the militia to do that."

There was a hint of disappointment in Nick's manner. "Oh. I was rather hoping, Al, that this summer you could make Caddy—"

"Thanks to your kind offices, I have a feeling no one has been able to make that girl do anything since she was four. More tea?" Al threatened his glass with the pitcher of black brew.

"My daughter is not exactly wayward."

"No, but she's full of bliss and ginger." As Nick received this with a scowl, Al, enjoying herself, went on chummily, "She's all Bartholomew, that kid."

"She resembles her mother closely."

"Well, yes, that," Al agreed politely. Not wishing to resume the hostilities of a burnt-out war, she examined the wallpaper as if to determine once and for all whether it was really gray or tan. "All I'm saying is that she's a country mile from being disciplined the way we were. Times change. Caddy is almost thirteen, isn't she?"

"Almost. What does she do all day in the library, anyway?"

"Among other things I am given to undertand she's writing an Ode to the Pawks Boys. She fully expects, unless I'm mistaken, to read it to the Governor when he comes here for the Pawks Boys' Day Jubilee."

"Oh my God," Nick groaned, "I thought she's gotten over her poetaster stage."

"Don't let Caddy hear you calling her that. She knows the difference between a poet and a poetaster, even if you don't. Besides, it keeps her out of mischief."

"And it's unhealthy," Nick burst out. Then, borrowing one of Sonny Heall's favorite words to describe the self-centered, he went on, "That kid's getting a little too damned autistic to suit me."

Al snorted and handed him another lemon slice.

"I don't suppose," Nick ventured, "you could just make an overture—"

"I've made so many overtures to my niece I sound like an album of concert favorites. Nick, don't ask me to do, or undo maybe, what should have been done, or undone, or whatever. . . . What I'm trying to say is that she's never been reared, she was fetched up. By patients. All right, I know; it's standard operating procedure in state hospitals. But a patient can be a pretty permissive—"

"Substitute?"

"Did I say 'substitute'?"

"You were making a headlong dash for it. Your implication being that long before Nancy's death, my kids were being neglected."

Al said crisply, "I stand corrected. I have no right to judge your wife. Admittedly, I felt like shooting the two of you when you got married. Getting yourself kicked out of your internship—" Al broke off sharply. "Permit me," she said with no little dignity, "to take all that back. You loved that girl and you married her. There's no law against a nurse and an interne marrying. Just grossly unfair hospital rules. You should kindly excuse the outburst."

"Nothing to excuse," Nick said. The ensuing silence was diplomatic, each Bartholomew granting the other a moment to collect himself, but each, notwithstanding, feeling that he was fully in control of his temper. After a suitable pause Nick remarked, "Still scrapping, aren't we, Al?"

"Yes, but it was more fun before you outgrew me."

"I don't know why, but I seem to spend my Thursday noons building up a mad."

In civil tones Al said, "One has to be mad to deal with Sonny Heall on equal terms." She selected a new topic, "By the bye, has little Babs dimpled at you recently?"

"She has," Nick said largely. "And she's looking better to me every minute."

"Dear me. And I would have said your thoughts were elsewhere."

Nick looked at her directly. Saw, or pretended to, that she was speaking in jest, and let the moment pass. "How'd you like to drop over to Staff Meeting with me?"

On that point Al was positive. "No thanks. I'm not feeling that sprightly. Besides, I run into enough psychotics among my rich old ladies. Frankly, I think you have to be a real gung-ho humanitarian to devote your life to the insane. The acute set my teeth on edge, and the chronic make me feel incapable and helpless. I have the feeling that the harder you fight the disease, the harder the patient fights back. Somehow, incurable insanity is more frustrating to me than death. Or does that make sense?"

"It always has," Nick said and struggled out from behind the banquette. "And don't do those dishes yourself. I'll have a patient sent up."

"You will not. I'm doing them, and then I'm going for a walk. Exercise, I believe, was your instruction."

"If you bump into Caddy," Nick said, "will you give her a sizable piece of hell for me?"

"Certainly not. I like the kid. When it comes to hell, *I'm* hellbent on insinuating myself into her good graces. Alienation of affection, I think it's called. I just may make the delicate observation that she has been neglecting what she calls her 'vile-in practice,' but that's as far as I intend to go."

Nick stood irresolute, then braved what could bring a most forthright reply. "Alienation of affection? From whom? Why?"

"You, in part. The way things stand now, if and when you decide to take to your bosom a new wife, Caddy's going to go sky-high."

Nick bent on his sister that cool appraisal with which he greeted unwelcome levity. "I haven't the faintest idea what you're talking about. Who would I marry?"

"That is a burning question," Al said, laughing at him as he stalked from the room.

Al finished off her tea with relish and wandered out

to the chintz living room for another look at her jigsaw puzzle. Her taste in puzzles ran to those which came in plain numbered boxes that gave no hint whatsoever as to the subject matter. The completed border had raised her hopes that she might have a seascape. But her eye now fell on a piece that strongly suggested part of a sheep's face, and she feared that it would turn out after all to be one of those boringly placid pastoral scenes.

Back out in the unfinished part of the building, Nick moved through the gloom toward the elevator. I'll thank my sister, he thought, I'll thank Al not to, I'll let her know in no uncertain terms that I do not appreciate her taking cracks at Nancy, I'll ask her to kindly take her criticisms elsewhere, I'll not. . . . All right, then, Nancy was no great shakes as a mother. But I wanted her from the minute I laid eyes on her walking down a hospital corridor, carrying a kidney pan.

He had turned and followed that kidney pan as if it were the Holy Grail. Come to think of it, Nancy had been no great shakes as a nurse either. But she proved to be that matchless woman—a practicing romantic. In their lovemaking she released for Nick that tenderness which is locked up in so many powerful men. Where other women had expected—had wanted—him to grapple with them, Nancy caught up his massive hands and kissed his knuckles for him. When they were done she would offer her fragile shoulder as a pillow for his head.

Still, they—he—had been careful. She a nurse and he a lowly interne, they were mindful of all they had to lose. But one night—he was never to know which—he had begot Caddy.

There was only one type of hospital that accepted married internes with pregnant wives. Pawksville gave them sanctuary.

Thirteen years later, even with Nancy gone for almost four of them, Nick would not have exchanged one of his

operatic schizies for all the rich coronaries in the world.
Nancy had given him his love, his three kids, and inadvertently his career, before killing herself in her car.

Stepping into the elevator, he thought, Wonder when I'll
get over feeling lonely. It came to him that here was the source
of his sympathy for Jane Carmody. Alone by herself, night
after night in the Morgue House, listening to her records——

And alone, he told himself, is the way it jolly well better
stay. He thrust his hands into his pockets, those hands which,
of late, were suffering from a strange new need of Jane.

6

Of Cant and Canticles

At just about the time Nick and Alberta Bartholomew were enjoying their exchange of mild rebuffs, young Marion Pierce was being hand-fed like an infant. Thanks to his offer to give an attendant a drubbing, he was still in his jacket. Nonetheless, thanks to the jacket, he had been able to spend the morning reviewing his affect and ideation, and reciting to himself "Canticles for the Holy Dove" I, II, and III, which in themselves brought back to him the full seriousness of his undertaking. Completely satisfied that remaining on the receiving ward would serve no good end, he was looking forward to being presented at Staff Meeting with a certain sense of the adventurous. Thus preoccupied, he forgot to open his mouth for his next spoonful of soup, and received it full in the face instead. "Ya damned schizzy," the attendant informed Marion, over a good hour before Nick Bartholomew or Sonny Heall would have their say.

That Sonny Heall liked to have his say at Staff was groaningly known to all his colleagues. Having bolted an early lunch, Sonny was in his office reading up on his Brill. Like Napoleon snatching the crown, Sonny had been unable to wait for an official appointment, and so, after reading one book and a week after his arrival at Pawksville, had appointed himself the staff psychoanalyst. If Sonny suffered an id–ego conflict, it stemmed, he darkly suspected, from Nick's smile every time Sonny uttered such terms of art as *affect hunger,* or *passive algolagnia,* or *ego organization,* or *polymorphous-perverse sexuality.* Sonny's tincture-green-soap eyes would lose their boyish shine and his fat firm chops would droop; each time, each time, he so hoped for an encomium from Nick, or at least recognition of his accomplishments. He would then read yet another book, and trot out for Nick's edification *oral erotization of the analysis,* and Nick would smile and say, "That's an interesting concept, Doctor." That and rarely more; Nick stubbornly refused to be knocked galley-west by Sonny's conviction that psychoanalysis would empty every state hospital in the country.

It had never been a mystery to Nick why Sonny had come to Pawksville as an interne. What kept Nick awake at nights was wondering how Sonny had ever gotten through medical school, war shortage of doctors or no. But so long as Sonny attended to his assigned duties (he had several receiving and acute wards) Nick gave him his head on analyzing certain patients who caught his fancy.

In some eight years at Pawksville, Sonny's efforts had been commendable, if not triumphs. Opposite his desk was a bookshelf of ledgers, especially constructed for Sonny by a grateful patient who had been released from Pawksville, had gone home to his basement workshop to construct the shelves, and then had systematically run every stick of furniture in the house through the saw. On the bottom shelf were closed cases, a ledger for each analysis with the name of the patient lettered on the spine by Sonny himself. The middle shelf were current, the top were pristine ledgers at which he sometimes gazed, envisioning the names of certain incurable patients writ there. The very first top one was invisibly lettered: *The Holy Dove.* Impossible to effect the cure of

Nick's pet paranoid? Sonny would have given his flabby
if relatively spotless soul to do so. For it would ease from
Sonny's conscience yet another ledger, of which neither he nor
Nick ever spoke. Thoughts of this ledger threatening his
composure, Sonny stifled them through sudden activity.

Jumping from his desk chair, he left his office and with a
rather pronounced, or even athletic stride, made his way
toward Staff Meeting.

The conference room where Staff Meeting took place was
just off the second gallery of the rotunda. The room was
pleasant and light, the combination of the white Venetian
blinds and the distant drip of the fountain presenting the
mind a vision of coolness though the temperature was in the
nineties. The staff sat along a polished table, all but Nick
Bartholomew and the patient to be interviewed comfortable
in captain's chairs. Bartholomew's chair was a swivel desk
affair, and the patient's a leather home-library lounge which
was designed to put him at his ease, but did not in that he felt
dwarfed with his chin inches above the table. Here and there
were glass ashtrays, one conspicuously placed for the use of
the patient, should he care to smoke or throw something.

The staff was assembled upon Nick's entrance, and he
was greeted with all due formality by his second-in-command,
Sonny Heall. As Nick had not lunched with the staff, he
assumed—actually he would have taken an oath on it—that
he and his family and their doings had been the topic of
conversation. In any event, the smirks of two young gentlemen, the doctors Parry and Diljohn, would have assured
Nick that he, or Al, or Caddy, any or all, had received
critical attention over the iced tea and potato salad. With
genuine unconcern Nick nodded at Dr. Parry and Dr. Diljohn; what those two impossible incompetents, those mere
medical handy men, thought of him moved Nick not in the
slightest. For his part, Nick looked on Diljohn half in com-
passion, half in contempt, for the poor creature was fighting

a losing battle with the bottle; he felt deep pity for Dr. Parry, both because that young man was an epileptic and because he thought Sonny Heall to be one of nature's noblemen. Nick was long since resigned to having to work with such promising material as this pair. Were he at one of the more advanced state hospitals, Columbus, for example, or Rockland. . . . But he was clinical director of sturdy old inner-directed Pawksville, and he worked with what material came to hand.

Taking his seat, Nick had a pleasant smile for Dr. Ouita (busily knitting), and a more reserved one for Dr. Jane Carmody, for he was troubled over her. Next to Nick sat Sonny, acting for all the world as if he were brilliant, when no one in his right mind would even call Sonny able. Nick found Sonny's affectations relatively harmless; besides, Sonny was not a particularly happy man. His pretty wife Babs had had so many miscarriages that she preferred to bear Sonny grievances instead.

As Superintendent Keeney was absent—and Nick would have taken alarm had he shown up—all were present and accounted for, and they were ready to commence. "Shall we begin?" Nick said.

Sonny cleared his throat importantly, and opened the file in front of him. "This is—uh—Marion Pierce. Male, white, twenty-three years of age. Hmmm. Oh yes, Yale graduate. Was working in New York and began to show signs of cracking up. He came from around here, evidently, so a friend brought him home. Committed by his parents. No history of psychosis in the immediate family. However, the father—" here Sonny colored slightly out of deference to Dr. Diljohn "—the father showed all the signs of alcoholic addiction. Broken venation of nose and cheeks, that sort of thing. The patient hasn't suffered prior breakdowns, though his mother admitted to his being 'nervous' and 'excitable' as a boy. Only child. I had the impression, talking to Mrs. and Mr. Pierce, that they weren't too well off. So this could easily be one of those cases where the parents make great sacrifices to put a child in an expensive school and then he cracks up under the strain of trying to live up to their expectations. He's only been working one year. In some kind of publishing house or something."

"Did you talk to the friend who brought him home?" Jane Carmody wanted to know.

"Now that's a funny thing," Sonny said. "He just brought Pierce home, or actually to Pawksville, and had the parents come get him. Took the next train out."

"Too bad," Nick commented. "As it stands, we have no case history on the patient at all. Anything else, Doctor?"

"That's all, Doctor," Sonny said formally. "Shall we have him in?"

"Tsk! Dropped a stitch," Dr. Ouita murmured, knitting.

The staff smoked and doodled while Marion Pierce was being ushered in. Marion was wearing for the occasion a clean white shirt, wash pants, and a do-or-die look on his face. He sat where shown, in the deep leather chair, and, in sudden inspiration, rested his chin on the table. A glance into Nick's macadam-black eyes had Marion's gaze scuttling away from that quarter, only to collide with the tincture-green-soap regard of pudgy Sonny. Marion hastily took to squinting down the table at the doctor who looked like he hit the bottle too much.

On his pad Sonny Heall wrote: Suspicional expression.

Jane Carmody noted: Carried self well on entering room.

Dr. Ouita wrote: Remember get No. 6 pink yarn, also pearl buttons.

"Would you care for a cigarette?" the big bruiser of a doctor with the steady dark scrutiny asked Marion carelessly.

Marion declined by staring straight ahead.

The amenities taken care of, the pudgy doc leaned forward with a look on his face which Marion could only identify as being sappily commiserative. "Would you tell us your name?"

Marion Pierce looked at Sonny as incuriously as he was able, and refrained from replying.

"Isn't your name Marion Pierce?"

Marion acknowledged this with a cautious nod of his head, swiveling about on the point of his chin.

"And do you know where you are, Mr. Pierce?"

A rush of saliva filled Marion's mouth. God, did he not know! A morning in a jacket such as he had spent would inform a corpse of its surroundings. His arms and shoulders were still so sore, in fact, that he could no longer maintain what he considered to be his very effective hunched-over position, and he was forced to lift his chin from the table.

During this time the staff had opportunity to note that the patient was disoriented. In short, he hadn't the slightest idea of where he was.

"Is this like a prison?" Marion asked, his voice coming out as dry and insubstantial as cotton candy, and, oddly, once he began to speak his mouth suddenly felt as dry and full of sugar splinters as if he had been devouring the stuff.

"No, you're in a hospital," the pudgy doctor informed him bracingly.

Marion snorted. The effrontery of such an announcement was more than he could countenance. "This—abattoir? A *hospital?*"

The fountain pens raced.

They're falling for it, Marion congratulated himself glumly. Out of the corner of his eye he could see the rather pretty lady doctor noting that he, Marion, appeared to be hostile.

"Do you know the date?" the pudgy doctor pressed on.

There was a silence; then "A bellwether," Marion said suddenly, confidently.

"Perhaps you would like to tell us about the bellwether?" the plump doctor said smoothly.

"So how's your sex life?" Marion asked Dr. Ouita conversationally, and knew he was flushing to the roots of his hair when that lady smiled at him in motherly forbearance. It was not, Marion discovered with a sense of disappointment in his lack of confidence, as easy as Mr. Ellis and the New

York psychiatrist had assured him it would be. For example, the big doctor at the head of the table, the big shot, Marion had not doubt, was writing down nothing, observing all, and keeping his mouth shut. That one, Marion counseled himself, is the one to work on.

"Does the subject of sex bother you?" Sonny was pushing on determinedly.

"You talk too much," Marion complained in a whine. "My father had my tail docked like a puppy." This revelation concerning a carefully worked-out castration complex had the fat doctor beaming on a bewildered Marion. "And he said if I wasn't good he'd cut off another inch or two," Marion improvised wildly. "So I got this job cleaning the guano out of mares' nests." To get away from the beaming of his inquisitor, Marion looked appealingly at the good-looking young woman doctor. "I had a girl friend, a really lovely girl, but she decided not to have anything more to do with me. She said I was crazy." Marion laughed comfortably. "I guess you can't blame her. If a girl thinks *you're* crazy, *she's* crazy to keep going with you." He blinked, wondering that this pleasant innocuous observation should bring bright anger— or something else?—to the cheeks of the young woman doctor. What the hell did I say, he asked himself. I'm only here to prove I'm insane, not insult nice women. But to show insanity, one has to bring a few incivilities to bear—the psychiatrist impressed that on me enough.

"You feel you are mentally ill?" the fatty doctor asked silkily.

"I think I'll button your big fat lip for you," Marion assured him. He paused so that all who wished might make further notes. Again he fell under the scrutiny of the big shot at the end of the table. "Go chase yourself, quack," he advised that black gaze. "What're you, anyway, a pig-gelder? I'm a practicing warlock myself, I've got more notions for potions than you ever heard of." Marion was beginning to sweat copiously, begging of himself, Oh God, are my aberra-

tions all in order? Am I talking the way any sensible psy-
chopath would? "You're no doctor," he said again to the big
man down the table from him. "Man," he added anxiously,
"I got you pegged."

"Do the voices tell you he's not a doctor?" the plump one
resumed with great interest.

The big shot at the end of the table made some soft
sound of annoyance. In a burst of gratitude (Marion had all
but forgotten about the voices aspect of his psychosis) Marion
was nodding eagerly. "Voices?" He cocked his head. "You
attuned, man?"

"Are they the voices of men or women?" the plump doctor asked rather unsteadily under the cold stare of the big one.

"Oh, cut the waltzing around, Doc. The committee
couldn't break me because I've got a drip-dry brain. You
can't brainwash a synthetic." Marion again cocked his head
in a listening position, then looked gleefully over at the
alcoholic gentleman. "He did? You'd never guess it to look
at him, would you?" As this sally was received without comment or question, Marion remembered to giggle foolishly,
while trying at the same time to decipher what was being
written down about him.

"Tell me, Mr. Pierce," the big shot asked suddenly,
"what is five times five?"

"Twenty-six," Marion said with confidence.

This appeared to satisfy the big man, for he took to gazing idly at the smoke issuing from his cigarette.

The young woman doctor asked quietly, "Would you
tell us more about the voices, Mr. Pierce? Do they say nice
things? Or threaten you?"

"The last thing in the world I'd eat would be a dove,"
Marion said. He grew solemn, "Doves are holy things, you
know." He was quite happy to have gotten this in, for if
Titus Graham was daft on doves (and his latest efforts all
pointed in that direction), why then, it wouldn't hurt for
him, Marion, to exhibit the same tendencies. This was a

touch of his own, the psychiatrist in New York not having thought of it.

There was a silence, the old lady doc knitting along placidly.

"Any other questions, Doctors?" the big shot asked.

"Yes," the old lady said. "Mr. Pierce, are you comfortable here? We want you to trust us, because, you see, we're going to get you well."

Marion Pierce hated like sin to have to tell the sweet old duck to go jump in the lake.

"That will be all, then," the pudgy doctor said, pleased as punch. Over what, Marion could not for the sanity of his mind divine.

Marion Pierce had departed. Nick Bartholomew lit another cigarette. Without glancing at the few notes he had taken, he opened, "Schizophrenic. Hebephrenic."

Thus informed that hebephrenic schizophrenic or better was required to get in the pot, Sonny Heall said, "Paranoid."

Dr. Parry raised him, "Paranoid schizophrenic with catatonic side effects."

"Catatonic?" Dr. Jane Carmody questioned. She would see it. "Paranoid schizophrenic with paranoid affect."

"Did you notice the most operative and redoubtable super-ego?" Sonny murmured insinuatingly out of turn.

Nick Bartholomew bent his gaze on Dr. Ouita. "Oh, dementia praecox," that lady said, taking a firm stand for the use of the good old terms.

"I thought I detected a certain manic-depressive—" Dr. Diljohn ventured, but as suddenly decided against it and dropped out.

"Any delusions?" Nick prodded Sonny.

Peering at his notes dutifully, Sonny decided not. Then with a glow he recalled one, "Just a minute, Doctor, how about the docking of his tail like a puppy's? I thought that had a tremendous Oedipal punch. It will be interesting to

learn who the voices of the auditory hallucinations are. I'd
lay even money on one of them being either God or Pierce's
father."

Nick called it. "Agreed, then? Paranoid schizophrenic
with hebephrenic affects."

All nodded. Dr. Ouita looked up from counting stitches.
"Then it's dementia praecox? I thought so."

"Well, Doctor?" Nick said to Sonny.

Sonny was happy. "Since the patient is in excellent physical condition, and this is his first mental break, I think we've
got a very, very good chance here. I'd like to see him started
on a course of Metrazol right away. That would break up the
ice pack and make him accessible to analysis. Actually, a lot
of it seems quite close to the surface. All those allusions to
various animals. Yes, I'd like to get going on him right away.
Ten shots of Metrazol could do the trick. Why, even five could
render him accessible to analysis!" Sonny cried optimistically.

"Very well, Doctor," Nick said. "Unless anyone else has
further suggestions, we'll give it a try. Who's next on the
docket?"

But the next patient, sunk in the twilit gloom of catatonia, failed to hold Nick's attention. He mused on Marion
Pierce's eastern-seaboard locution. Still, Pierce had gone
north to college, and then on to New York, and would have
dropped his mush-mouth Pawks County accent long ago.
No, something was amiss. Young Pierce had been too pert,
alternating with spurts of fright at his own outrageous behavior. He's too impeccably silly—not quite the true Tom-
Fool ring of the hebephrenic, Nick thought. As if—paranoid
notion that it was—someone had coached him. And he had
recalled the voices. He *recalled* them, Nick told himself. But
not until Sonny shot off his mouth by bringing up the subject first. And when he found himself in murky waters with
Carmody as to the sanity of a woman who clings to an insane
lover, he beat a hasty retreat. Pierce's sense of decency, an
inborn delicacy had stilled his tongue. Carmody had been

beet-red, and everybody in the room—Pierce included—knew she was taking it personally. As for telling me that five times five are twenty-six, that was at once too responsive and too calculatedly silly. He did better when he kept his head and reluctantly told old Ouita to go jump in the lake. Thought that too was, in its way, responsive. His entire show of hostility, of course, was sham.

Nick smoked and reflected, a faint grin on his face. He himself had undergone each and every type of therapy offered to the patients. The fiery convulsions under Meterazol had left him shaken for days, and he bore those of EST—electroshock therapy—little better. And though Nancy had raged and demanded to know if he thought himself Jesus Christ, he had proceeded on to the sweating coma of insulin. Come to think of it, he hadn't cared for insulin either. He had spared himself only massive sleep, an extensive and artificially induced coma of many days' duration; and that because massive sleep was a therapy of questionable value, and still in such an experimental stage that he had used it on only three or four manics who had been whooping it up to the point of complete physical collapse.

Thus, what Marion Pierce was destined to undergo Nick had undergone. Nor would he be the first sham patient to come to Pawksville. There had been an occasional reporter come to work up a nice little by-line exposé for his paper. The gentlemen of the press never hung around very long somehow. They went over the nonexistent fence at the first opportunity.

Reporter or no, Pierce's commitment would want looking into. There was just the possibility—and this thought caused Nick to sit bolt upright—the fellow was a spy from Governor Leroy's rival camp. Nick brightened. Why, all the better. Let a howl arise and Governor Leroy would have to loosen the purse strings. Three new psychiatric internes, Nick daydreamed: not the dregs of the graduating class, but young men genuinely interested in psychiatry. And a raft of

RNs, male and female. And a drug budget so lavish he could dispense tranquilizers by the handful, careless of cost; and some decent lighting for the surgery; and—hell, why not— get the top floor of the Hospital finished, they could use the room; and. . . .

And if he is a spy (Nick daydreamed luxuriously, knowing full well it probably wouldn't be easy to get at the bottom of the matter), *if* he is, I hope to hell he finds out about that goddam Great Poet the Governor rammed down my throat. I hope to hell, oh, to hell and back, he finds out about that, and opens the whole scandal up again, because that would bend Leroy right over the barrel, and he'd need my considered opinion that the Great Poet is cracked as the Liberty Bell, and in all truth and honesty I could say that he is as aberrant as a cowpath, and Sonny and Ouita would more than back me up, but oh the bill I'd present to Leroy when it was all over!

On the other hand, Nick warned himself, I may be imagining things. We'll see how he comes along on treatment, before I go leaping at every inviting conclusion that comes along. This could just be one of my more paranoid days. . . .

Sonny Heall, too, was meditative. Marion Pierce and his painful burden of childhood guilts had wrung Sonny's vitals. Long ago another patient had touched Sonny deeply, and he had sought to help her. And in the doing—— Glancing at the thoughtful Nick, Sonny asked God (in whom he wasn't certain he believed) right humbly that Nick was not remembering too.

Sonny had been at Pawksville about six months when the then reform governor allocated funds for a Pawksville swimming pool. The heat of summer was a joy that year, those patients who were able sporting in the pool to their untold physical benefit. When the day attendants came off the wards at five-thirty, Sonny could hear their happy splashing from his office window. But he himself never took a dip until after his afternoon's analytical session was over. He was struggling with a case tailored to his talents—an involutional melancholiac, a woman whose husband and children had great need of her at home. Her name was Neely. ("How are you feeling today, Mrs. Neely?" Sonny still said to her brightly in his nightmares.) Mrs. Neely was convinced that she had committed the Unpardonable Sin. The elements of this sin she would not name. With her gaze full on Sonny, she wept and would not corrupt such a fine young doctor with the Evil Knowledge. But of every spiteful or selfish or wicked thing she had done as a child she spoke freely. Events long suppressed, old aches, old guilts were brought out into the open. Sonny was confident they were doing famously; his pen raced across the pages of her ledger.

He told Mrs. Neely's attendant that a dip in the pool every day with the other patients might spark her appetite. On an August morning Mrs. Neely walked into the crowded pool at the shallow end, and kept walking. She was still lodged at the bottom of the deep-end ladder when they found her.

After that, the pool was drained. Naturally, the next year when Superintendent Keeney's daughter had houseguests the pool was put into operation—until Nadine and her guests went off to Virginia Beach for the rest of the summer. As she grew older Nadine was never around Pawksville for the summer, so Superintendent Keeney saw no need to fill the pool. Anyway, the reform governor—the new one—allocated funds for a Greek reflecting pond. Let one of those nuts drown themselves in that! Reporters! Never saw the like!

Sonny, of course, had a bit of explaining to do to Nick. He covered the auspicious progress of the analysis carefully. Each hour more conflictual debris had been sorted over by the two of them, Sonny and Mrs. Neely. They hadn't gotten to the Unpardonable Sin, to be sure, for Mrs. Neely—Sonny was certain—had been saving this as a gift to him. A parting gift, the verbalization of——

"Doctor," Nick interrupted softly, "don't you know what the Unpardonable Sin is?"

Sonny Heall grew pink; his green-soap eyes avoided Nick's. "I've told you, Doctor, we hadn't—the analysand hadn't—"

"Biblically speaking, Doctor, it is to blaspheme against the Holy Ghost. You can find it somewhere in Mark. As we are not ministers, but psychiatrists, we must label the Unpardonable Sin a delusion. In your career, Doctor, melancholiac after melancholiac will tell you he or she has committed the Unforgivable or Unpardonable Sin. And when they do, I advise you not to exacerbate or strengthen the delusion by mucking around in their childhood misdemeanors and magnifying them all out of proportion. Hereafter, make the castration complex your stomping ground. You'll keep out of trouble that way."

"Yes, Doctor," a woeful and contrite Sonny said.

"Well," Nick said briskly, "that about covers it. Just remember, Doctor, to each his own Unpardonable Sin. The delusion, to be stuffy about it, is called *hadephobia*."

Sonny had greeted this new addition to his vocabulary with the solemnity it deserved; but when he attempted to bring Nick up to date on some term, Nick always smiled and turned to other topics.

Struggling also with words in the midday heat was Caddy Bartholomew, belaboring her Muse. Nearby Caddy slumbered the librarian, Miss Wurde, at her desk, undisturbed by the noisy fly bathing in the quarter-inch of iced tea left in the bottom of her glass. The library fan whirred softly (it had rubber blades, for patients often took it into their heads to stick their fingers into the oddest places), turning in a lazy arc, ruffling at each completed journey a loose strand of roan hair on Caddy's forehead. Each time the strand vibrated, Caddy stuck out her under lip and blew upward, causing the strand to float lightly to the crown of her head. Her eyes, the color of two fingers of Scotch, never

moved from the pages of *Gadfly*, the small magazine she was
studying. Her ponytail, protected from the fan, hung limp.
At the moment there were no flies on Caddy. Under her
elbow, secured from the fan's breath, lay a number of back
copies of the same publication. Though all were addressed
to Titus Graham, it would appear by the very proprietary
manner in which Caddy rested her elbow on them that Mr.
Graham had never exercised even temporary title to them.

To one side of Caddy's current study lay a scarred copy
of the *Oxford Book of English Verse*, a *Golden Treasury*
with both a fractured spine and a broken back, and on top
of both a clipboard to which was secured an unfinished
"Ode To the Pawks Boys," on which Caddy occasionally and
desultorily worked because she had told her aunt she was
so doing, and it was too easy, if a bore, not to make a liar
of herself. Caddy had been at her occupation most of the
morning, even unto holding down the fort when Miss Wurde
roused from her slumbers at eleven to amble out to lunch.
Undisturbed by the browsing of patients with ground privileges, and merely pointing silently at a copy of the television
log from the Louisville Sunday paper when asked by one of
Dr. Ouita's ladies, Caddy's concentration had so far proved
fruitless. Only when the Holy Dove had hustled in to see
if the new shipment of pocketbooks from the Friends of
Pawksville contained anything lively for Miss Noon had
Caddy raised her gaze from her endeavors. It would have
been unthinkable to refuse Pawksville's finest one's fullest
attention. Having selected those books which appeared to
Caddy's practiced eye the most vulgar and therefore suited
to Miss Noon's taste, and impressing on the Holy Dove that
she, Caddy, had first dibs on them after Miss Noon, Caddy
had slumped to her library table seat again with a forlorn
sigh.

"Troubles?" the Holy Dove asked, as if she knew the
answer beforehand, but it was only polite to ask.

"My Muse," Caddy admitted, "is just plain catatonic today."

"We all have our days, Caddy," the Holy Dove said in a voice that firmly excluded herself. She shifted her load of lurid books more comfortably, the illustration of a disheveled B-girl leering out just under her sacred chin, and announced busily, "Well, I've got to run along, dear. Miss Noon will be needing me, if I'm to take a little flock to the dentist later on. And do give Miss Bartholomew my regards. Tell her her recovery is going to be very rapid. Very rapid," the Holy Dove repeated impressively.

"Oh, I will," Caddy said. Born and bred to Pawksville ways, it did not occur to Caddy to question the extent of the Holy Dove's knowledge of her aunt, or her aunt's leg for that matter. By way of being a minor local oracle herself, Caddy could only stand in awe of the Holy Dove's store of Pawksville lore, past, present, and—it had happened—future. "I certainly will tell my aunt you said so," a pleased Caddy said. A rapid recovery, she repeated to herself, watching the Holy Dove's magisterial departure. A hope not quite formulated lay in the back of Caddy's mind. Were Aunt Al to enjoy a rapid recovery and return to her private nursing before the twins came home from camp—why then, she, Caddy, could have Nick all to herself for Jubilee. And after reading her Ode to the Governor, he would doubtless invite Nick and herself to join him at the watermelon feast, and what thrilling eventualities might come to pass after that not even Caddy could imagine. Although it would seem only reasonable that the Governor would wish the Ode to be placed among his official papers. All this, Caddy felt, would come about readily, but for one thing; if Aunt Al were still around she might put a spoke in Caddy's wheel. Though not a hoarder of recriminations, Caddy could well remember her mother saying of Al that she was "far and away too bossy." Caddy could only hope, therefore, that the Holy Dove knew whereof she spoke.

Returning to her work, Caddy thought, I'm going to show her some of the Canticles when I think the time is propitious. Sure as hell the old Dove will be pleased. But the time of warm self-congratulation passed, and knowing that dwelling on past triumphs only encouraged that sullen bag, her Muse, to loaf, Caddy left off lollygagging and picked up her pencil. At the sounding of the noon whistle she had swept up from her mind one more dusty line for the dispirited Ode, but her inspiration lay not in that direction. Too, the whistle had distracted her, but forgetting that it was Staff Meeting day, she resolved to struggle a quarter-hour more before going out to the rotunda to see if Nick were about. Putting aside the copies of *Gadfly,* she let her gaze wander to the window.

Beyond the pillars of the Greek reflecting pool could be glimpsed a green dense grotto, the center of which seemed incongruously, crazily busy. Here dwelt a troop of acrimonious spider monkeys, detested by all of Pawksville, not excluding the mournful Mr. Hamshot—whose task it was, among others, to feed the spiteful creatures. Some Special Patient or other long ago had brought the tribe with him to while away the hours of irksome if expedient confinement, and had abandoned them to Mr. Hamshot when the heat was off and he could leave. Not infrequently Caddy had business in the grotto, entering its shade which was damp and hot and airless like a dungeon, from the far side, safe from the prying eyes of a Sonny Heall, or that roving black orb which Nick cast on all within his purview.

Rendered uncomfortable, even itchy with guilt at the very sight of the grotto, Caddy took to dreaming out at the shallow surface of the reflecting pool, which mirrored only its own simpering columns and the cloudless bilous sky. At that moment her Muse stirred. I want, Caddy thought, something . . . limpid. Something absolutely ageless, like Herrick. Just a few simple lines and they knock your eye out. About

love. She turned over the "Ode to the Pawks Boys" and wrote
on the fresh page

O love

She had seen worse opening lines. In all fairness, she had
seen much worse. The fan swung her way, purring in rubbery
content, and she absently blew the strand of hair to the top
of her crown. She was caught up, lifted up, wafted. She
scribbled joyously, the words pouring out of her:

> Love, had I told thee nix,
> Would I now need 6o6?

Then with a snort of exasperation she drove the point
of her pencil into the library table. It wasn't ageless, it was
old hat. Nick never gave 6o6 any more except to a few
diehard paretics. Everything was penicillin now; romance
was dead. Those summer Saturdays when Nick had gotten
the 6o6 shots on the road at eight in the morning—one
patient after the other, slamming the needle home and telling the protesting, "You've heard of Sal Hepatica for the
smile of beauty? Well, this is Salvarsan for the smile of
health. Next!"—so that, clinic over, he and Caddy could
roam the meadows about Pawksville. They were past, over,
done with.

She rallied. Not all the good things were gone, the tried
and true cast aside. Perhaps. . . .

> Serenity, with me abide,
> Given an ounce of paraldehyde.

No. Not limpid enough.

Besides, if Nick could talk the Governor out of a decent
drug budget, he'd start using those lousy new tranquilizers
anyway. And whatever else Caddy wanted her poetry to have,
permanence was foremost. It came to her that this was pos-
sibly what *Gadfly* had in mind when it stated that the artist
needed but two things—privacy and stability.

Neither of which were to be granted her further, for
Caddy suddenly beheld her Aunt Al standing by her side.
Caddy clutched her clipboard to her breast. "Aunt Al! I
didn't hear you——"

"Caddy, I can hardly be said to have crept up on you.
Not stumbling around the way I do." Al rested her bulk
against the library table. "We missed you at lunch, so I
thought I'd just mosey over and see what you were up to."

"Don't tell me this is Staff Meeting day!" Caddy said
this several times, showing a fine range in deplorations.
"Don't tell me——"

"I won't. But it is."

"Is Nick mad at me?"

"Let us say that you've incurred your share of his wrath
today."

Remembering her manners, Caddy mumbled, "And you
walked all the way over here on your bad leg, just to warn
me."

"Well, no. I was on the good one at least half the time,"
Aunt Al said in her literal way.

Caddy worked up a croak intended for merriment over
her aunt's sally. Then when it had died away, she found
herself mired down in one of those pauses of Aunt Al's which
could disconcert even the most assured. Gathering up her
books, Caddy regarded glumly the prospects of the jigsaw
puzzle which awaited her. Such an innocent pastime was for
those cut from another bolt than Caddy's; her restlessness
drove her to roam Pawksville bent on her various enterprises.
Her possessions hugged to her person, Caddy rose.

Casually Aunt Al said, "Your father would like you to
practice your vile-in this afternoon. I'm relaying the message."

"Thank you," Caddy said, matching her aunt careful
nuance for careful nuance. "To tell you the truth I'd forgotten all about practicing." She followed her aunt out the
door.

In the rotunda where the fountain plip-plopped drearily,

Caddy restrained her brisk stride to accommodate Al's measured pace. Footsteps sounded from a corridor, and the galleries took up the noise and echoed it. Searching for the source, Caddy spied her father just a few feet from Staff Meeting room, talking to Dr. Carmody. His head was to one side as he bent to hear her, though his macadam gaze was full on her. Dr. Carmody grinned and said something, and then Nick's laugh rolled down the corridor and reverberated clear to the dome. At this, the pair turned as of one accord and walked away, disappearing around a corner.

Some aspect of the scene created an unease in Caddy; it was as if she had witnessed an intimacy. Almost in defense of Nick, though he was not under attack from any quarter, Caddy said, "Dr. Carmody's husband is a *patient*, you know, Aunt Al."

"Yes, I do know. But since everybody on the fourth gallery probably knows it too, let's get out of here, where we can talk in normal voices."

And with the stately tread of one favoring a leg, Aunt Al made her way with Caddy out onto the lawn and the walks shimmering and appearing to undulate in the heat. Far to the left Caddy could glimpse the grotto, but resolutely directed her gaze elsewhere lest she draw her aunt's attention to that forbidden spot. Caddy ventured, "I think I'd better do my practicing under a tree somewhere, Aunt Al. The racket I make, nobody can *think* even. So if you want to work on your puzzle——"

"Good idea. You're indoors too much."

Caddy chose not to contradict. "I guess I have been spending hours on my poetry and all." Caddy waved her clipboard, "A poet has to be alone a lot, you know."

Since this threatened to lead to certain awkwardnesses, Aunt Al said, "Caddy, I think I'm going to sit on that bench over there and rest." Indicating a shady spot, she let her invitation to Caddy to join her speak for itself.

All consideration, though with her customary reserve

with her aunt, Caddy obediently turned off the walk and joined Aunt Al on the bench. Sitting on the very edge, as if poised to take flight, she directed Aunt Al's attention to the rotunda massed against a cloudless sky. "I think that's the best sight we've got in all Pawksville," Caddy said. "Oh, I like the Greek reflecting pool, and the Morgue House is just darling, but somehow the rotunda—"

Aunt Al interrupted quietly, "Don't chatter at me, Caddy. *Talk* to me. And while you're at it, why don't you simply call me Al. *Aunt* Al always makes me feel as if I should be wearing a lace cap and carrying a bunch of bluebells in one hand."

The vision summoned up caused Caddy to lose her dignity and snicker.

"Especially," Al went on, "since you call Nick by his first name. And you called Nancy by hers, as I remember."

With a let's-see-where-this-is-leading-to caution, Caddy admitted, "Yes, I did. Al . . ." Still perched on the edge of the bench, she crossed one leg over the other, and stared straight ahead.

Al suddenly asked gently, "Caddy, why the icy reserve with me? Are you looking upon me as an interloper?"

Caddy evaded, "Mebbe I'd better look up that word first." She examined her clipboard as if it might be, by some chance, defined thereon.

"I'll save you the trouble. An interloper is someone who moves in where he wasn't wanted."

Unwittingly or no, Al had touched a sore spot. "Like me?" Caddy cried passionately. "Someone who wasn't wanted, like me?" her ponytail flew straight out behind her as she flung her head around.

A startled Al said, "What?"

"Getting myself born," Caddy said. "You felt that way about me. Because Nick had to give up his internship and marry my mother. Nancy knew just how you felt, Aunt Al, I mean, Al, about her. And you felt the same way—"

"Caddy, what differences your mother and I might have

had were resolved before you got your first tooth. I know you are protective of your mother's memory, you should be. But Nancy and I—"

"And you still think it's a crying shame Nick's here at Pawksville." Gathering momentum, Caddy went on wildly, "All because of me. I know all about me, you bet I do. Don't you think I know I was a six-and-a-half-months baby, with all my fingernails on! Why, I never even *saw* the inside of an incubator. I weighed seven pounds and I had all my fingernails. Some premature baby I was!"

"Very well, Caduceus," Al said with the determination of one breasting a fierce current. "If you're adult enough to level charges, then you're adult enough to listen to a few home truths. I'll admit I didn't greet the news of Nick's marriage with yelps of joy. All I could think of was the years of hard work he'd undergone to pay his way through med. Only to toss——only to direct his efforts elsewhere. It was none of my business but—" Al grinned disarmingly "but did that ever stop anybody? So my brother and I were—strangers—for a while. You see, when we were kids struggling for our educations we were very close. We each went without things to loan the other the money for tuition or what-not. We were ambitious and self-centered—you have a touch of both too, Caddy, it's the Bartholomew in you—and we were both quite sure that the medical world would fall into decay unless we came along and rescued it. By the time Nick reached med school, I was nursing, so I could help out a bit more. You see?"

Caddy demanded furiously, "You mean you—what I mean is—you're telling me you put Nick through med school?"

Al came dangerously close to falling into one of her pauses; her silence would have constituted a damning accusation. "Oh, of course not," she said smoothly, amused. "Caddy, that would smack of ridiculous self-sacrifice. I simply helped Nick out, as he had helped me."

"And then Nancy came along and ruined everything!"

"She didn't ruin anything, she changed—matters. That's the whole story. I adjusted, and Nick and Nancy and I mended our fences. I'm sorry my nursing kept me from seeing more of you—all of you. Maybe you wouldn't resent my being here now, if we'd seen more of each other in the past. I would have come after your mother died, but I was nursing a little girl who was very sick and very dependent on me. Any change in her routine. . . . Well, let's just say it wouldn't have done that little kid any good. I don't know whether you remember it or not, but when you were about two and a half, I did come here for a weekend. Nancy and I got along like a house afire. She was such an extremely pretty woman," Al wandered off randomly. Then forcing herself on the path again, she said, "But I just didn't want to take on even the appearance of interfering."

A smoldering Caddy countered, "Whyn't you think of that when I was born? Instead of writing Nick what he *had* to name me."

"Caddy, I didn't issue a royal edict, I merely suggested—"

"And Nancy didn't want to call me Caduceus, she told me that. She wanted to name me Nicole after Nick. But no, you had to come up with an ugly . . ."

"I lightly *suggested* that since your mother was a nurse, and your father a doctor, that the symbol of medicine would make a very pretty and most unusual—"

"Any girl who gets named after a stick wrapped with a couple of snakes has a pretty unusual name, all right, all right!"

"And a pretty venomous tongue in her head, when she wants to use it," Al commented mildly.

"Excuse me," Caddy said, stiffening. "I try to show you great respect, *Aunt* Al."

Al sighed. "We're not getting anywhere very fast, are we, Caddy?"

"That's because I'm on Nancy's side," Caddy said tightly. She bore Al's scrutiny rigidly, long a familiar of the thought-

ful, unwavering, unreadable Bartholomew gaze. "And nobody is ever going to take her place. Not while I'm around."

"Caddy, I'm not here to take your mother's place. I'm
Nick's sister, your aunt. And there was never a feud worthy
of the name to take place between your mother and me. We
may have had our misunderstandings. Or rather, you may
have misunderstood something Nancy said about me. Or
maybe you exaggerated some chance remark; kids are apt to
do that, but. . . . Well, maybe I should have come around
more when Nancy was alive. But I was busy, and one thing
led to anoth—"

"We always enjoyed your Christmas cards, Aunt Al,"
Caddy said, politesse itself.

Al Bartholomew leaned back against the bench. "Caddy,
I'm just a middle-aged lady sitting in the shade on a breath-
lessly hot day. I have a game leg, and I'm just not in fighting
trim. Will you please go pick on someone your size?"

"I'd better go practice my vile-in now," Caddy decided.
She rose, hesitated, and then asked, "May I bring you some
iced tea or a Coke or something?"

"Caddy——" Al began on a confounded note, then said
only, "No thank you. But it was thoughtful of you to ask."

A released Caddy trotting away thought, if Nancy hadn't
told me how Aunt Al really was, I'd think she was swell. She
just makes these *suggestions,* and the next thing you know,
she's got you chained to your oar, like Ben-Hur or somebody.
The thing of it is, we've just got to keep being pleasant to
one another in the evenings—which we have been—with Nick
around. What with the Governor coming and all, he shouldn't
have anybody else on his mind.

The Special Patient's Cottage—once dubbed the Sans
Souci for Society-page Sociopaths by Nick Bartholomew—lay
on the far side of the grotto, hidden from the gaze of the windows of Pawksville. Once the Cottage had housed the Superintendent and his family, but this was before the sumptuous

house within a building had been fashioned in the innards of the rotunda. Only the elder wise folk of Pawksville, people such as the Holy Dove and Billie Noon and Dr. Ouita, remembered the days before the Cottage had lent sanctuary to a succession of embezzlers, rapists, rich old ladies intent on squandering the family fortune to the noisy anguish of their heirs presumptive, drunks, and drug addicts. Currently an equally illustrious personage dwelt there; a poet, to be exact, of sound reputation among those few if vocal intellectuals who knew of his work. Upon admission this gentlemen was learned to have severely beaten a young boy; though his crime was susceptible of several explanations, Nick Bartholomew, in the press of work, had laid it to homosexuality and let it go at that. Sonny Heall, armed with a new ledger, had galloped to the Cottage for an audience, to be roundly turned out; and so the current Special Patient was left to his own devices and to the morose ministrations of Mr. Hamshot, the Cottage attendant. The assignment of this Special Patient fell to Dr. Ouita; that good lady read a poem or so of his in *Gadfly*, promptly banned all poetry and banished *Gadfly* to the library, and then ordered a course of soothing baths and fresh air to get the patient's mind on healthier things.

Still, the word got around in old Pawksville tradition, and Caddy was quickly in joyous receipt of the intelligence that a Titus Graham, a Great Poet, was in residence in the Cottage. Her discovery of *Gadfly* as a new addition to the library's periodicals soon followed.

So, on the blistering August morning whiled away so pleasantly by Caddy poring over *Gadfly*, the Great Poet was also attending to matters concerning that publication. Chewing on his rather unkempt curry mustache, he defied Dr. Ouita by applying himself to a rickety typewriter left behind by some former tenant. When angered or determined, Titus Graham's eyes were a tigerish gold, and were so small that they appeared no larger than the gem-stone in a man's ring. The eyes were suspicious of one another, glued closely to each side of his nose as if keeping a watch on each other. There was always a quality of spite in them, but never more so than when trying—so far futilely—to establish contact with the outside world. He was in the midst now of a heated letter addressed to Mr. Eliott Ellis, publisher of *Gadfly,* in New York.

. . . don't know whether this missive will reach you either. Or is it that you gladly accept my work, and then refuse to have other dealings with me? I had, for a time, been using a patient to play mailman for me, but as no word seemed to be getting through, I've taken on someone else in my employ.

I don't know what, if anything, you may have read in the papers about my getting sent here. I can well imagine the imprecations poured on my head by the local tabloids. God knows, I didn't want to come South in the first place, but you talked me into attending that one-horse Writers' Conference in Nashville. *You,* Eliott, you *insisted.* Otherwise, I'd never had had occasion to drop in on Leroy's rally. But my cousin can be most importunate when it comes to showing me off before her phony artistic pals. It gives the Governor's Mansion "class," she avers. Nauseating.

You could have done what I did, Eliott. You could have found yourself in a crummy hotel room, drunk and out of your element, and disgusted with yourself for having performed like a bear for a pack of red-necked politicians, you could have done it. You. A single gesture toward a bellboy, misinterpreted, and then the slimy little creature setting himself up then and there for a shake-down. If I had him here now, I'd do more than break his jaw for him. I'd snap his teeth out one by one and pack them up his nostrils. He was worse than a tart who threatens to yell and tear her clothes off if you don't pay her double her quoted price.

What must I do, or say to you, before you will lift a hand to aid me? Or is it that you do not know how? Eliott, I urge you to get in touch with Governor Leroy Jackson *in person,* at once. Surely if I have endured the durance vile of this unspeakable humidity and heat for months on end, you can withstand it long enough to talk sense to Leroy. Remind him that

it was my cousin, his wife, who was responsible for my appearing at the rally, and ultimately being sent here in lieu of the
pen—by a pack of howling bigots. The whole thing has long
since blown over, so it's time someone nudged Leroy.

Unless you act soon, I actually fear for my sanity. I have for
companionship one lugubrious attendant, whose sole joy it is
to feed peanut-butter sandwiches to a treeful of vicious monkeys, and a senile old bat of an attending physician who desires
me to sit in a tub all day, like Proust, and calm myself.

Outside of you, I've one slim chance left in the world to me
to extricate myself from this intolerable situation before I go
mad. There is talk of Leroy's appearing here for a backwoods
heathen ritual called the Pawks Boys' Jubilee, or some such.
All will be in readiness for him, including cake booths run by
the local citizenry, lotto games, and a pack of loonies on their
best behavior trotted out to listen to Leroy make a speech
and have a watermelon feast with him. I very much doubt that,
gaining his ear, he would listen, under the circumstances.

Eliott! I beg of you. Think of my work, if not of me. I am
perishing! I am

The Great Poet let his slim white hands slip from the
keys. He examined them as he would curiously fashioned
weapons. They had propensities all of their own, and the
strength to be lethal. If they—not he—so wished. There was
a child once in Capri, an urchin who had died near a cool
dark water cave, held under by those hands. No one had
missed him.

The Great Poet stirred, the vision of those water caves
had stolen into his mind unasked, triggered by Mr. Hamshot's running the water for his bath. Oh God, I'm not forty
yet, he thought. The exilian years stretched ahead. Parched
summer after parched summer. And then the chill sullen
rains of autumn. Sometimes, Mr. Hamshot said, the rains
were so persistent that almost the whole of Pawksville was a
marsh. Yet rain or shine, the inexorable Dr. Ouita, blandly
assuming he was psychotic—and he soon would be, oh, he
soon would be—would enter, babbling cheerfully of her no-

tions of supportive therapy: the tub. *Supportive!* She was
insupportable. As insupportable as that burly bastard, Nick
Bartholomew, blandly assuming he was sane. Which he still
was.

Or had he ever been?

Beneath his watering eyes, the Great Poet's fingers struck
from the keys: Let me out of here, I am as insane as you are.
I am not a refugee from swift justice, no; I have been, instead, removed beyond the reaches of sweet retribution.

Gazing at this message to himself, the small gem-bright
eyes squeezed shut in derision. Again he contemplated making his escape from Pawksville. Walking off the grounds with
only the few coins in his pocket doled out to him by Mr.
Hamshot, for tobacco and (had Mr. Hamshot but known it)
postage. He could make his way to New York, and have Eliott
Ellis ship him to Tahiti——

There to live on what? Eliott's doubtful bounty? Not by
half would Eliott consent to that. And the Great Poet's own
tidy little fortune had been placed in the trust of some fool
ex-judge or other, a political pal of Leroy's.

And were he to make his escape good, why, in the meanwhile, back at the funny farm, the officious Dr. Bartholomew
would yell cops, and Leroy would call out the troops; and
back he would come, until Leroy saw fit to set him free.

All because some little male slut of a bellboy. . . . Hollering blackmail at one moment, screeching for the gen-
darmerie the next. Over what? The drunken prank of an
artist toying with a mildly outré sensation. (Not at all like the
boy in Capri, where he had really been beside himself, and
as helpless as the boy. As who does not lose his temper on
occasion, and suffer guilt thereafter? He, the Great Poet, knew
well the burning night-sweats of remorse.) But this time there
were police, followed by Leroy dragged in from dazzling his
constituents, eyes bulging with heterosexual outrage, his
mouth so full of you-alls he could barely eke the expletives
out.

There was no telling Leroy of the artist's low threshold of aggravation; Leroy thought only in terms of the nearest closet into which to shove a family skeleton. And it would be like trying to establish communication with a Martian to attempt to explain to the loutish Dr. Bartholomew that the gifted are only too frequently caged up within their own skins with an uncontrollable demon and must not be held accountable at all times.

Maniacs among the magnolias. Along with senile old bats and dictatorial brutes calling themselves doctors. And himself struck dumb through self-pity and self-loathing entwined, unable to defend himself against his keepers. Ah yes, *Sed quis custodiet ipsos custodes?* Juvenal knew the question to ask all right: But who keeps an eye on the bastards running this outfit?

7

I Murdered for Mitzi

On the shaded porch of Ward Seventeen, a patient sat scribbling away in a ring-bound notebook. Had one of Seventeen's busy attendants taken the time or interest to read this curious document, the entries would have gone roughly as follows:

29 May
I feel that one writing a journal should speak his truth, or turn to fiction entirely. One is almost obliged to begin: The witness deposeth and sayeth the following. . . .

And having undertaken a journal (though defacing the walls with whatever comes to hand is more *comme il faut* around here, incidentally, than committing oneself to paper), I propose to say what I think, recognizing no need for the maintenance of a façade between myself and me.

I awakened refreshed this morning, so much so that I believe last night's sleep was the most restful of a decade. I would have said I was in my twenties rather than my thirties but for the fact that not even the most ardent seeker after experience could have found and traveled down the strange by-ways that I have at twenty-five. I felt somehow flooded with memories this morning, many of them pleasant, and not a few uproarious.

83

During breakfast, old Judge C. Luther Plathe tottered into my mind. He was retired; an elderly sunny-natured pixie whose passion it was to work on a cookbook entitled *Murder Made Easy*. His object being to discover those herbs, spices, condiments and what not, which would mask the taste of various poisons, or, in some instances, enhance them. A simple recipe would be:

> Vanilla ice cream
> Cynanide of potassium
> Crème de Noyaux

> Mix cyanide thoroughly through ice cream. Rechill. To serve, pour Crème de Noyaux generously over each helping.

I can picture so clearly the old boy puttering around in his kitchen with his Sauce Béarnaise and arsenic, or his Garni Deadly Nightshade (the *Gourmet Cookbook* and a treatise on toxicology chummily paired off on top of the refrigerator) and sipping from a glass of a sweet wine called—don't ask me why—*Est! Est!! Est!!!*. To be invited to dinner at the Judge's exhilarated some and shattered others. I recall a lady gazing nervously at a fried grasshopper and inquiring, "Have —uh—— I take it these things have been—drawn?"

But aside from serving delicacies which could not rightly be called commonplace, the Judge had more and rarer entertainment up his sleeve. It was his pleasure to announce at the end of a princely meal, "Ladies and gentlemen, I have just poisoned one of you." Which, you must admit, is one way of starting the conversational ball rolling. He had not, of course, but it got the game started; each of the guests trying to guess which course might have been the poisoned one, what poison was used, and what exotic preparation of that dish had concealed the dire act. If I recall correctly, it was the Four Thieves' Vinegar in which my artichoke had been pickled which did me in. Or would have, had the poison been present. It was sweet old Judge Plathe's contention that all of us are murderers at heart, and we had best find for ourselves some harmless way of simulating homicide. With all due respect (I being a humble lawyer) I disagreed.

That was before I became a murderer myself. It was before I was even aware of Mitzi's existence, so I could scarcely have imagined myself committing a *crime passionel* over her. When my time came I should have taken a leaf from the Judge's book—cookbook, that is to say—and polished off my man in a civilized way. But by the time I had caught up with him and Mitzi, it was the old story of forcing my way into their squalid love nest, and finding Mitzi shabby and abject, and he surlily amused at my having followed them clear across the country to this benighted State. "Well, if it isn't the legal beagle from L.A.," was his drawled greeting. There was a Western in progress on the television. A considerable amount of shooting was going on. I joined in with the spirit of the thing.

I did a neat job too, for an amateur. One of my colleagues in Los Angeles, apropos, never drank anything but Scotch, and that neat. One neat Scotch after another, while he remained coherent and upright and staggered the rest of us. One can only conclude that one man's neat is another's poison.

7 June

I've been reminding myself to put down how easily I came by this handy notebook. The beautiful part of being incarcerated in an insane asylum is that everyone takes it for granted that you are mad, and conveniently (conveniently for me), forgets that one may be methodical nonetheless. I had only to ask the attendant for pencil and paper, with the asinine explanation that I wished to map out my strategy for obtaining my release, to receive same. The attendant smiled knowingly, quite as if I had announced my intention to talk to the President of the United States over my secret short-wave set. A perfectly valid assertion around here, by the bye.

Yon patient pacing the porch admits to being in the paid
employ of the Serbian FBI. But had I said, *par example,* I
wish to write my memoirs—— Naturally I didn't. I may have
been certified as psychotic, but I'm far from crazy.

I used to go around saying that were I of independent
means I would like to be a writer. As it was I had to earn my
living at the law. I must have said it once too often; Fate
overheard me and provided me with the necessary leisure. If
I were to give this a title, what should I call it? *Memoirs From
A Madhouse?* Or would the very nineteenth-centuryish ring
of that lend to these hentracks a dignity they cannot claim?
The people who publish those paperback books might like
I Murdered for Mitzi. Especially as that is precisely what I
did. How horrible, and yet thrilling, that simple declarative
sentence appears when in one's own handwriting. But I hasten
to add that I am essentially a good person. To be a great sin-
ner is to be an even better opportunist. My law practice
taught me that. Sin is not easily come by, only a scant few
happen on it—the till carelessly, invitingly left open; the teen-
age virgin crossing the vacant lot at midnight; or your closest
enemy bleeding to death in the wreckage of his car, while you,
accidentally having blinded him with your headlights, speed
merrily on—no, crime is a hard way to make a living, and
they say the pay is execrable. I am not an artisan murderer,
only a fool would hire my likes. Nor is this to say I've lived
my life as if every day were January 1. That stern day of setting up exercises, cutting down on smoking, firm rejection of
the third martini, the laborious start on Vol. I of the collected
works of just about anybody—no, I am only an ordinary human being who happened to commit a murder for that brace
of reasons dearest to a juror's heart. I killed for jealousy and
love. I killed Mitzi's knavish lover before her very eyes, dis-
patching him with one bullet, if you will pardon an amateur's
prideful declaration of marksmanship. I loathed him, but I
did not claim his life for revenge. I suspected that he was
tiring of Mitzi, would soon abandon her, and had never, in

fact, had the slightest intention of marrying her. He had taken her from me for a lark, but however cruelly he might have used her, no entreaty on my part would have brought her back to me. I could only shoot him before he could hurt my fragile Mitzi further; she now thinks he loved her dearly and that I was crazed with jealousy. I heard her swear to exactly that, and the jury wasn't napping either. As I could not offer into evidence the beastliness of my victim, the jury gave me the nod on guilty, and then—these days I believe more fervently than ever before in the mercy of capital punishment—then they agreed I should rot for my shot. My lawyer was fantastically pleased; he had been determined all along to save my hide at the expense of my sanity. Perhaps I should have handled my own defense, but the old saw came between me and common sense: The lawyer who takes his own case has a fool for a client, and the client a numbskull for a lawyer. The court graciously appointed a Public Defender for me, a gallus-snapping remnant from the Darrow era. I was his Last Stand, his one and only *cause célèbre*. You would have thought him in fear of being drummed out of the American Bar Association had I been invited to set and visit a spell in the hot seat. (It comes to me that I am addressing this to someone. My gentle reader? I have none. Myself? I think not. And I most definitely prefer that this journal, if that is what it is, not fall into the hands of the attendant. My fellow patients couldn't care less. Psychosis is so demanding that it takes up all their time. Then to what sympathetic eye is this directed? Maybe it will dawn on me.)

Damn. Dinner time. I sit on this thing when not scribbling, and I sleep with it under my pillow. I am like the rest in that. So many of us have something from which we will not be parted. Some harmless object to which we cling, symbol of the wide range of possessions of the lowliest of poor whites outside. A woman walks past the porch clutching a worn shoe box. Another toys everlastingly with a short length of

string. I have this, my journal. I will go to the dining room
and sit on it.

21 June

There is talk already of some sort of bazaar, held an-
nually during the first week of September. A clambake of
sorts, I am given to understand. I find myself rather looking
forward to it, I am becoming a Pawksvillian. My surroundings are not uninteresting, and when the attendants have the
opportunity they like to gossip. I was interested to learn that
there are no Napoleons at Pawksville, though there are two
Adolf Hitlers and one Holy Dove. The latter, a woman of im-
pressive composure, has ground privileges and visits, it is
said, different benches on different days, ostensibly to rest.
Every Thursday she interrupts her constitutional by relaxing
on a bench under the Staff Meeting windows. At the end of
other hot afternoons, she is to be found briefly catching her
breath on a bench under Dr. Heall's office. Oh, and my attendant informed me that one of the Adolf Hitlers is convinced he has committed the Unpardonable Sin. I replied,
"Who hasn't?"

This innocent venture into wit earned me the exact stare
my attorney wore as we prepared my defense. No case has
ever been discussed with such utmost delicacy. A stranger to
the proceeding would not have had the faintest notion of the
crime with which I was charged. "The event," he kept murmuring, or "the act in question," whenever he wished to refer
to my passionately straightforward perpetration of lying-in-
wait murder in the first degree.

But there, no special pleadings to you, dear reader.
(Come out, come out, whoever you are.) Why rehash the
niceties?

What luxury this is, rambling along. I who have been
trained to particularize, to be concise, am drunk on gener-
alizations. I am mad with the freedom of my pencil. A double
meaning there, for, in state hospital parlance, I have been en-

trusted with a potential weapon. I could stab out an eye in a twinkling. I could penetrate to the jugular with one try. But I am mad in no other way, Dr. Heall. (There it is! Be damned! Flushed you out, *Herr Doktor*.) Whereas you, Dr. Heall, are mad to psychoanalyze me. Was it you who gave me the permission to have notebook and pencil? Did you hope, in that way, to steal past my reserve? Do you plan to take these jottings from me without a single pang of compunction? Sonny Boy, I will eat them page by page before I would let a word fall into your infantile pudgy hands.

Why did I detest you on sight? Your office was pleasant, you offered me a cigarette, you asked if the light was just right. Your green piggy eyes were bright; it was time, you said, we had a little chat. Somehow, I just wasn't in a talkative mood.

Dr. Heall, my honest opinion of you would read like unconscionable character assassination. And all unfounded, I am sure. My canons of conduct demand that I own up to this. Surely your marked tendency to nosiness should not alone call down my vilifications on your balding head. Yet for all your little attentions, you made me feel from the first moment as ill at ease as a delegate at a union convention in a prison-labor suit. And when, yesterday, on your rounds, you stopped to ask me, "Well, how do you feel this morning?" I was helpless but to snap, "Through the employment of my tactile sense as always, Doctor."

Belatedly I perceive I may have lost the round yesterday. Your smile shone on steadily; you tendered me benevolence for my malevolence. This is not turning the cheek in a war of wits; it is parry and thrust. Surrounded by those whose wits have gone aroving, I shall have to keep a closer guard on mine hereafter. Not to mention exercising maximum security on this journal, waking or sleeping.

My thoughts turn to Mitzi. I am unable to summon up her face, and recall only a "studio portrait" she had made of herself. I never really cared for the photograph—the camera

had caught that almost imperceptible aura of vanity that sur-
rounds the very pretty girl. She had "autographed" the thing
for me. Yes, her pitiful pretensions were an essential part of
what went into the make-up of Mitzi. In her cultivated chic
backhand she had promised: *Always faithful—Mitzi.*

But I, not caring for the pose, had blurted, "Why didn't
you write *Simper fidelis—Mitzi?*"

Someone else must have told her what I meant, for she
pouted for days.

8

Babs, the Fetching

All that spring Babs Heall had been reading a book by O'Hara. It was a lengthy work, and what with bossing her own private maid around, a patient, and giving herself pedicures, and dreaming in a most disrespectful manner of Nick Bartholomew, she kept busy. She and Sonny occupied a number of cool high-ceilinged rooms in the Annex, furnished most tastefully—had Babs but known it—with heavy hand-carved furniture, a bed whose headboard almost reached the ceiling, and marble-top tables. It was in this very bed that Babs had once malingered so daintily, whimpering to Sonny, "Shugar, Ei jus feel delicate, thass all." And delicate she appeared too, in the massive bed with the nylon ruffles on her bed-jacket inviting the eyes toward rather than concealing what lay beneath them. To Sonny's anxious questions Babs could only say that she felt "Tarred out," and "Wore clean down." Certain it was that she didn't feel chippah, but there was no need for Shug to take on about it, if she weren't so tarred she'd sit up and la-euph, the look on poe Shug's face was that drow-ell.

Ably translating all this, but more perplexed than ever, Sonny sent for Nick. And to Nick Babs repeated her recital in her soft little dra-ull, peeking past his shoulder to her tousle-haired and quite fetching reflection in the monstrous dresser mirror. Nick was all suave bedside manner, hoping to allay Sonny's groundless fears, but poor Babs herself finally struck upon the right diagnosis. "Ei jus seem to heve all these asserted aches and pains," Babs concluded.

If there was one thing in this world Sonny was certain of, it was his recognition of a Freudian slip when he heard one. Babs could assert until the cows came home that she was feelin porely, but Sonny was already thanking Nick and ushering him out of the room. Whatever assorted excuses Babs might think up in the future in order to favor Nick with a glimpse of her in her sheer bed-jacket, this little drama of the wan if rounded beauty and the virile physician was played out. Sonny had no placebos to hand, so he truculently handed Babs an aspirin and stalked out.

Babs continued with her reading of the O'Hara book.

After all her miscarriages, that lethal coyness which had once drawn Sonny to Babs and kept him enchanted for several years drained out of Babs. It was not remarkable then, that shortly after the Nick episode, Sonny was both amazed and ravished to find he was in great demand with his wife. True, her lovemaking had taken a strange new turn. Eschewing every last vestige of coyness, Babs would lie in bed issuing commands in joyless barks. "Hurry up! Can't you see I'm dying for you? Well, what're you waiting for?"

Puzzled but obedient, Sonny was having himself quite a summer. It is necessary to state that Sonny hadn't read a novel by John O'Hara, or anyone else for that matter, in years.

9

Dementia Praecox, Or Whatever They Call It Nowadays

In the late afternoon Nick was in his office in the rotunda, having an animated phone discussion with Dr. Parry. "Well, where *is* the bathtub stopper lodged? Then if he chewed it up first, I should have thought he'd have passed it yesterday. Oh . . . another stopper. He's *what?*"

Dr. Parry talked on jubilantly.

Nick interrupted, "The chain is in the upper intestine? Oh, that's where the ten-penny nail is. The chain is next to the razor blade, I take it. Doctor, will you kindly tell me how the hell that patient got hold of a razor blade in the first place? I don't give a damn if it *was* before your time. With a collection like that in him, he's all but been ripping up the floorboards and chomping them down in front of you, to get all that down him. . . . Well, if there're no perforations, he can probably survive another twenty-four hours as a walking hardware store. I'll be over to look at the X rays. Yes, Doctor, if I do perform surgery, you can assist me. Yes, Doctor. . . . All right, Doctor—— Come right in, Doctor. No, not you; Doctor Carmody just came in." He hung up a moment or so later, and said,

"Sit down, Jane." When she did, her mouth stern, he went on, "What's this to be? A confrontation?"

93

"I've come to apologize," Jane said stiffly. "For rowing with you about Sean's sunburn. I know it's not your fault that half the attendants around here are such—scum that Pawksville is the only place they can get a job. But I do question, Doctor, your wisdom in sending Sean out to grub around in the dirt like a . . . like. . . ."

"Your apology is accepted, Doctor," Nick said with just a touch of tartness in his voice. He offered her a cigarette which she accepted with hauteur. Nick looked away to conceal his sudden dismay. When had discussions with Jane over her husband ceased merely to pain him and become instead acutely painful? He forced himself to say unemotionally, "Jane, as soon as you're done with the unbending act, you will let me know what's on your mind, won't you?"

Her grin was sheepish. "Sorry." Then she too averted her face, and he noticed a tiny pockmark on her temple. Chicken pox, he thought, thinking also, like a lover discovering a new attribute of his beloved, that the pock lent to her pleasant open face the subtlest touch of the exotic, such as a cleverly placed beauty-patch might. "Nick," she was saying, "I want you to put Sean on massive sleep."

"No."

She looked at him, beseeching him.

"No!" Nick repeated. "Are you out of your mind? Asking me to put a catatonic into a three-week coma? What's the matter with you?"

"Grasping at straws," Jane said faintly. "And since he does seem to be improving on insulin, I thought maybe a radical change of therapy——"

"You thought no such thing," Nick said shortly. "What you are doing is tactfully suggesting that I spend ninety per cent of my time on one patient. Namely your husband. It's understandable enough. No, it isn't actually. What you forget is that he's been under treatment for something less than five months. If you were a layman, or if you were still taking your residency in GYN, then I wouldn't necessarily expect you to understand. But you've been around Pawksville long enough to begin to suspect, at least, the tenacity of insanity. Sure, if this had been his first break, we might have made some spectacular strides by now. But—"

"But," Jane echoed in a flat voice. "But. It's his fourth. The fourth, and he's twenty-eight years old. He's an old hand at schizophrenia, is that what you're telling me, Nick?"

"He knows the way in," Nick conceded, then added judicially, "and he knows the way out. Three times he managed to do it all by himself in those concentration camps they call private sanitaria. This time he's being stubborn."

"You can't mean that. You sound like Sonny Heall," Jane said, snatching up a cigarette. "You sound like you just read a popular tract on psychoanalysis. You sound——"

"You sound, Jane, like a woman. Let's discuss this like doctors. All right?" This proposal was made in a temperate tone, though something in Nick's manner, perhaps only that he was too close to a purr, should have warned Jane to modify her attitude.

Recklessly she accused him, "You're demanding that I discuss this in a professional manner, whereas you are entitled to react in a personal way. Is that it? You accuse Sean of being stubborn. What you're really saying is that he hasn't the backbone to straighten out. You don't like my husband as a human being. Admit it, Nick! Yes, I've been around Pawksville long enough to observe that favoritism obtains here, as everywhere else. I saw Sonny Heall grow positively beamish over that Marion Pierce, just as I see you all deferential smirks with that pompous Holy Dove. They're trick people, aren't they? Their little ways appeal to you. Or if some patient comes in here climbing the walls, and you can send him back to his plow after six months of EST, why we're all expected to squeal with delight. But the—"

Nick put in mildly, "Yes, I do somewhat rejoice when I can send a patient back to a useful life. That patient you're referring to had a wife and I don't know how many kids, and when he suddenly snapped out of it—"

"Sean, of course, isn't useful. He may have a wife, yes.

but he doesn't know a plowshare from a speculum. Is that the criterion around here for preferential treatment?"

Nick made a pretense of deep thought. "Let's see, your husband is a piano-player, is that right, Doctor?"

"He's a musician, and you know it. A musician."

"Well, I've never heard him play, so I could hardly be basing whatever attitude I have toward him on that basis, could I, Doctor? And my attitude toward him, since you seem to be making accusations there, is that of a physician watching a patient deteriorate in spite of his best efforts to prevent it."

"Deteriorating! Dammit, give him a chance!"

"Then let us say," Nick countered, "that Sean Maginnis is rapidly not improving. And I am trying, Doctor, to give him every chance. He's had EST. He's on insulin now. Metrazol next. Or EST again. He has gotten the works, and he'll get them again. What else can I do?"

"Turn him over to me," Jane said.

"Oh." Nick took the cigarette from Jane's fingers, and put it out for her. "Is it your suggestion that I have him continue on with his shock therapy in the mornings, and then deliver him to your care for the afternoon? You'd prefer, I suppose, I have him sent over to the Morgue House. You two could listen to his records all afternoon. Or you could take him for long healthful walks when the weather turns cool. Dr. Ouita, I presume, could take over your wards. You will try, won't you, to find time to perform your gynecological examinations—at least on the incoming patients? Will I see you in insulin clinic any more? At least while your husband is receiving that therapy? I'll see if Doctor Diljohn can spare a few afternoons for the lab. On second thought, why don't you just have his parents take him home, Doctor? They committed him only at your request, they are most anxious to take him out of Pawksville. You could care for him there. Is there anything else you wanted to talk about, Doctor?"

After a moment Jane said wearily, "I asked for it. I got

it. You're his last best hope, and I know it. But I must resign myself to the fact that there are two hundred others like Sean with equal demands on your time. I hope you can bring yourself to forgive me for accusing you of neglecting him. You've never neglected a patient in your entire——"

"Yeah," Nick said comfortably. "People are always rushing up to kiss the hem of my garment, I'm that dedicated. Look, it's my job. When I send 'em home cured, that's my bonus."

"My position is somewhat different," Jane said with difficulty. "I do not consider myself my brother's keeper. I'm an only child."

"If I thought you lived up to that, I'd kick you out on your ear."

Jane managed a passable laugh. "Well, Doctor, I just can't tell you when I've had such a comfy little visit. But— back to Billie Noon, the Holy Dove, and assorted hollering assaultive filthy sisters-under-the-skin. Come to think of it, there is one more thing."

"Yes?" Nick said lazily.

"You remember that youngster, Cherry Fielding? The patient who gave us so much trouble with a scalp infection last spring?"

"Sure. Chronic schizzy. First year she was here, I threw everything at her but Diljohn's Southern Comfort. Nothing worked."

"She's getting disturbed again. Could we—you—try massive sleep on her?"

"Now you're talking, Jane. Send her over to Twenty-One and *you* try it. Be a feather in your cap if you could snap her out of it."

"It's a deal," Jane said, rallying. "You tend to your head-dress, and I'll look to mine. Thanks for the sympathetic ear, Nick. Not to mention," she added wryly, "the tongue-lashing."

He chose to receive this for what it was worth. "Any

time, Doctor. The latchstring is always out." He rose as Jane did and went to open the door for her. "Do me a favor," he said, looking down on her. "Start your vacation next week. Get away from it for a while."

"With the Governor coming and all? Land sakes, Nick, I thought you wanted all hands to battle stations."

"He won't go within a hundred yards of your back wards. Parry can handle them. Or I'll give Sonny something to do besides brushing up on his Breuer, or pestering patients about their toidy-seat reminiscences."

"Thanks, but no dice," Jane said positively. "I'd rather stick around for a while and see how Sean progresses on insulin. See you around, Boss."

Closing the door after her, Jane thought, Nick is kindness itself . . . at times. But at others. . . . Take his inability to understand my concern over Sean. Sometimes Nick displays a dismaying poverty of affect.

Nick sat at his desk and smoked several cigarettes, musing. Jane distressed him mightily; she could not bring herself to accept as fact his slender expectations for her husband's recovery. Daily he grew more troubled over her; his fondness not blinding him to her increasing neurasthenia.

10

A Shocking Event

A trembling Marion Pierce was being led down the busy hall of Ward Thirteen, Male Receiving. As he had done little but shiver in the intense heat since his admission less than a week ago, shivering through his physical examinations, trembling as he sought to eke out a few drops into a clammy lab-sample bottle, fidgeting anxiously as his blood was drawn—destined for that same lab—he had lost weight and appeared a victim of the ague. Or would have so looked, he knew, to the average person; but, owing to his accelerated education in the office of a New York psychiatrist, he acknowledged that he was exhibiting as well extreme motor unrest. His every movement appeared to his own eyes a kinesthetic arabesque, and in trying to control himself he but exaggerated the effect. He had no doubt but that anyone could tell at fifty paces that his self had been overwhelmed by his id and his ego was either fragmented or destroyed, but inoperative in any event. He took no comfort from his performance, for of Titus Graham's whereabouts he had learned nothing, and he could have conducted his psychosis so poorly that everyone automatically would have taken him for a suicidal melancholiac, for all it had gotten him.

Wearing hospital pajamas and a threadbare robe, he was shown into a room containing two vacant beds and, from his authoritarian appearance, a male nurse. Having been told to remain in his sleeping garments and refused his breakfast (which acrid coffee and pitted-cement oatmeal he would not have eaten anyway), Marion's suspicions were aroused. He had been hard at allaying them, assuring himself that he was probably due to be removed from Receiving and, thanks to his sound performance and cool nerve, would likely find himself in quiet consultation with that other boldfaced fraud, Titus Graham. If fraud he were, though the New York psychiatrist was not of that opinion.

Ordered by the attendant to get on the first bed, "Wh-what——" Marion very much wished to know.

"Get on the bed," the toplofty stranger ordered curtly.

"Yes, but—"

"Relax, Buster," the attendant advised.

Marion found himself unable to meet with this request. His eyes swiveled from the taciturn attendant to the other gentleman present. That creature, wearing his knee-length smock with military splendor, bent a teardrop face over Marion and returned Marion's timorous glance with righteous implacable self-esteem. "Has he," the righteous one asked of the attendant, "been disturbed?"

"Mr. Dick, he was combative from the minute he got here."

"That's not—" Marion began, only to lift his head at the sound of rubber-soled footsteps.

Dr. Heall danced in, looking fit and sassy, as if he had just spent the most excellent of nights, starting off with Southern Comfort on the rocks and the company of a pretty woman, and continuing on from there. "Good morning, Mr. Pierce," Dr. Heall sang. "How do you feel?"

Suppressing what could have been his finest kinesthetic arabesque, Marion rose to the occasion. "Oh, just—— Dandy. I guess the FBI has had a little chat with you by now." He

winked at the radiant Dr. Heall, the wink a triumph of
conspiratorial silliness. "You'll be sending me on to another
cell-block, won't you?" he ended, with rather too much sup-
plication.

"We don't have cell-blocks in a hospital," Dr. Heall said,
busying himself at a treatment stand that Mr. Dick, with sly
importance, had rolled forward. "Well, now," Dr. Heall
said, "we're going to have you feeling a lot better soon. A few
treatments, and then we'll see about sending you to another
ward."

"Treatments?" Marion quavered. He attempted to rise
but was held firmly by the attendant. "You're not going to
give me that electrical shock business! Listen, Doctor, you're
not going to use that medievalism on me!" Observing Dr.
Heall's practiced serenity, Marion began to shout, "You don't
have permission to do that! Don't you have to get permission?
Who gave you permission? Just tell me——"

"Have you had to restrain him much?" Dr. Heall murmured to the attendant, who replied, laconic, "I can handle
'em a lot more disturbed than him, Doctor."

Acutely disturbed, Marion was yelling, "What about
those new tranquilizers? Why don't you give me one of
them? My God, don't you even read the *Reader's Digest*?
Look, Doctor, electric shock is a thing of the past. Catch up
with the times, this is nineteen-fifty——"

"Do you see an EST machine anywhere in the room?"
Dr. Heall interrupted in his sunny manner.

Marion went limp. His roving gaze encountered only the
treatment stand and the other bed. Not too familiar with
electrodes, he yet saw nothing that approached his concep-
tion of one. Nor was there anything remotely resembling a
machine. "Oh," he mumbled lamely, faint with relief.

Dr. Heall picked up a syringe and needle. "This will
calm you down a bit. Just relax, Mr. Pierce."

"Why didn't you say so," Marion muttered tearfully,

submitting to the alcohol swabbing. But of course his hysterical panic had been entirely of his own making. He had only to use his head to realize that he was still in his sleeping garments because Dr. Heall intended to tranquilize or sedate him or something.

"Make a fist," Dr. Heall said.

Marion complied, grinning sheepishly when he winced, intending to remark on his childish fear of the needle, when Mr. Dick suddenly thrust one of those wooden tongue depressors, wrapped in many thicknesses of cloth, into Marion's mouth. Marion frowned up at Mr. Dick, his fear of the needle was hardly all that devastating. . . .

The explosion in his skull was that of blinding blue flame, followed, like a string of cherry bombs, by erratic sharp bursts crackling here and there in the dark. For an instant the circuitry of his brain went dead, but slowly, humming wires glowed and swayed, the blackbirds riding the incandescent cables in a high night wind. Connections fused, and a thin electric melody sang among the fiery cells. Bright memories flashed and were gone, a voice long since forgotten spoke solemnly, and detoured unused bridges of association were lit up in the night and the heavy colorful traffic darted over them. . . .

Simultaneously with the blue explosion in Marion Pierce's brain, the attendant had thrown himself across Marion's legs, while Mr. Dick lay in lofty expectation across his chest. Sonny Heall cast the needle aside and secured Marion's head, his left hand pressing strongly on the tongue depressor. The Metrazol slammed Marion's spine into an arch, raising Mr. Dick into the air. Bridged on head and heels momentarily, Marion attempted to swallow his tongue, was prevented from this by the depressor. The spinal bridge collapsed and Marion Pierce's legs initiated a wild dance, which was at once taken up by the rest of his body, so that the attendant and Mr. Dick rose and fell and were jerked this way and that, riding their frisky charge.

"Go, man, go," the attendant panted.

"He's having a beauty," Sonny agreed. "Watch his leg, there."

A last lick of the Metrazol like heat lightning, and a fitful spasm now and again, and Marion Pierce's first convulsion was over. He shuddered and was still. Mr. Dick, with a questioning look to Sonny, relaxed his hold; the attendant was still distrustful of a knee.

"Quite a reaction," Mr. Dick said perfunctorily.

Sonny said with somewhat more respect, "Very satisfactory." And when Marion opened dazed eyes, Sonny asked cheerfully, "How do you feel, Mr. Pierce?"

Marion's mouth tasted of blood, his teeth ached sullenly, and his entire spinal column felt like box-cars slammed together and just come to rest. Certain strings and joints and obscure muscles complained unceasingly. "B–before God," Marion whispered unsteadily, "what was that, Dr. Heall?"

Dr. Heall bent down, smiling. "Do you know where you are, Mr. Pierce?"

"What was that . . . fiendish . . . drug?" Marion quavered.

"Now, now, it wasn't as bad as all that," Dr. Heall said playfully. "You know where you are, Mr. Pierce?"

"Pawksville State Hos—hospital," Marion managed.

"Good. Now you just take a little nap, and then you can have your breakfast." Dr. Heall murmured to Mr. Dick with satisfaction, "Lucid . . ."

Marion sat up and clutched at Dr. Heall's jacket. "Doctor Heall, I must talk to you immediately. It's urgent! If you could just spare me a few moments or so. It is absolutely essential, of utmost importance, that I tell you some—"

Dr. Heall took a turn for the disapproving, his green eyes turning chilly. "You mustn't go getting yourself disturbed all over again."

"Doctor, any rational person would be disturbed by
. . . this problem! I tell you, I absolutely must——"
"Problem?" Dr. Heall echoed helpfully.

Within Sonny's mind, with another patient outside the
door humbly awaiting his morning convulsion, a weighty
decision had to be made. Sonny struggled to reach a fair
balance. So precious little time was allotted him for his
psychoanalytical therapy that he must distribute his largesse
stingily. He could benefit one patient only at the expense
of another. Though he knew he had already made his choice,
his thoughts continued to dwell longingly on a certain Leslie
Erskine. It was only just—here was young Pierce, accessible,
eager; and Erskine had proved unapproachable. Mute. Thus
cogitating, with many a *moue* of importance, and wearing
the remote expression of the sought-after, Sonny's manner
toward Marion Pierce unbent. "Mr. Dick, could you have
Mr. Pierce in my office this afternoon at four-thirty?"
Mr. Dick could.

Marion Pierce attempted to collapse in relief, but was
unceremoniously hustled off the bed, bumping clumsily
into the humble patient at the door. Creeping into his own
bed on aching legs, Marion asked of himself: But what was
that hellish stuff? What did it do to me? I swear to God,
I'm going to expose these quacks and their inhuman methods
when I get out of here! Is this what they did to Titus Graham! No wonder he went off his rocker. No won— I'm going
to find him, and then I'm going to shout to a shocked and
unbelieving world—— I'm going to write a five-foot-shelf
exposé, an encyclopedic indictment, I'm going to . . . . A
thought had come to him of such staggering horror that he
thrust it aside. I'm going to get the hell out of here! Let
Ellis come down and submit to torture, if he wants to.
Let . . . .
Don't let, oh God, don't let anyone ever give me that

apocalyptic drug again. They wouldn't dare subject anyone to it more than . . . than . . . ?

He could not panic. Shivering in the growing heat of the morning, Marion Pierce took hold of himself. He began to marshal his thoughts, to prepare himself for the ordeal of revealing his part in a hoax to Dr. Heall.

11

Pippa Passes

Since she could first remember, or very nearly, summer had been Caddy's season. She could not truthfully say she disliked the Pawksville Grammar School, furnished as it was with girls who lent admiring ears to her poetry and boys who shuffled from foot to foot and looked at her with hesitant expectancy, but she could point out by way of illustration that the firecrackers of Christmas sounded almost soggy in comparison with those of the Fourth, and especially those of Pawks Boys Day; and therein, in a pinch of powder so to speak, lay the difference between school winters and her summers.

This summer, though, had all the earmarks of becoming glorious due to the absence of the twins. The menace of Aunt Al's establishing herself as boss of the Bartholomews was ever-present, of course, but Caddy believed that her strict loyalty to Nancy had so far helped her in avoiding this threat. No, this summer would prove to be the glorious one. She was free of the twins, able to live to the hilt without them tagging after her, yowling of her doings to the whole of Pawksville. She could writhe through the Pawks Boys Day watermelon patch on her belly, and encounter a snake (he and she both recoiling, her nerves—and she supposed his—turning brittle as pencil lead at the supposition that he was a rattler and she a snake-killer, though neither was either) without having the twins scare the snake into a heart attack by screeching their heads off. She could lurk for hours in the library; and best of all, she could join Nick in the clinic when she was of a mind, and have him all to herself while he wrote up a few reports and she cleaned needles for him by pressing the dried blood or medication from them with a thin wire before dropping them into the sterilizer.

Sensing that she was living in her Golden Age, Caddy liked to waken of a morning even before Nick did, and long before Aunt Al, who fooled with her puzzle or read until all hours and then had to take a Seconal. A little after six Caddy's eyes would open fully like windows thrown up. Needing not a moment for orientation, she recognized rapturously and at once that she was herself.

This morning was like all others. The grounds were fresh with dew and the watermelon patch off in the distance was blue with wraiths of summer mist drifting across it. Toadstools lay everywhere, a blistering of them far below her window. Opposite, the dome of the rotunda appeared as coolly opaque as a moon of dry ice, half risen.

Her bronze ponytail confined in its rubber band, and dressed in Tee shirt and shorts, Caddy tiptoed down the hall past Aunt Al's room. Nick's door was ajar, permitting her a glimpse of him awake, one arm under his head, smoking thoughtfully. Sticking her head in, she blew him a kiss and was rewarded with a drowsy grin.

She was about to skirt the inlaid table in the living room with the puzzle on it when a certain piece gave her pause. Into what appeared to be the beginnings of a lazy shepherd and his flock, Caddy fitted her own contribution. The sleeping shepherd turned out to be a soldier, and he was very much dead. Thus enlightened, she went into the kitchen.

She ate a handful or so of dry cereal, gulped down a glass

of milk, and then fed the crumbs of the cereal to the cockroaches in the sink. Straining her ears, she could barely detect
the sounds of music drifting from the Morgue House. Honestly, Caddy thought idly and without rancor, you'd think
all that music of Dr. Carmody's would wake the dead. With
a faintly wicked grin, Caddy then wondered what Dr. Carmody would say were she to learn that the back door to the
Morgue House was unlocked—night and day; and who
should know this better than Caddy, who had herself sneaked
the key from Nick's chain while he was showering and replaced it a day later. Dr. Carmody wouldn't think much of
anything about it, Caddy decided; she's been around Pawksville long enough to know you couldn't be safer. The patients
are all shut up at night, and burglars are scared to death of
the place.

Reasoning in this practical manner, Caddy left the apartment at her leisure. She had time and to spare before catching the first library mail. Long before Miss Wurde arrived
on duty, Caddy would have sorted out the periodicals she
wished for her own use and stacked the rest neatly where
they belonged.

Crossing the grounds, her sneakers stained with dew,
Caddy experienced the familiar enchantment that seemed the
very air she breathed that summer. The back wards of the
Administration Building were taking on life now; a patient
had already manned her shrieking post on the porch and at
a window above another called hoarsely over and over for
help. The monkeys were chittering in the distance for their
breakfasts, and along the walk were snail trails, delicate filaments from a lacquered brush. Glorious, glorious, Caddy
thought, head lifted, while the woman at the window intoned
in the steady clangor of a deep bell, "Help me, help me, oh,
somebody help me——"

Caddy's mind could not but quote Browning: "God's
in his heaven—All's right with the world!"

From the Holy Dove's lofty outlook, it was a troubled world, and Pawksville was in a sorry state. Like Caddy, she had awakened early that morning, but unlike Caddy to a dull headache that rather wandered about, in and out the Holy Temple (the left, that is), then drifted, now to the crown, now the brow, at last taking up lodgement in the socket from which the sacred molar had been drawn. Conquering the pain or, actually, cornering it and then overcoming it, the Holy Dove lay with her eyes closed and contemplated the world. Human existence, that much desired amalgam of mystery and flesh which constituted the paradox and martyrdom of the Holy Dove, the Fourth of Three, had been the first stage of the Holy Dove's trials. The second and greater, and therefore the more welcome, was her ignominious incarceration in Pawksville. If, on rare occasions, she cried out silently at her abasement, it was the flesh alone protesting drudgery—specifically the region of the lower back, after wrestling with the patients in the tubs all day. Her sacrum notwithstanding, her soul was subject to no state but perfection. A state which the dedicated if brusque Dr. Bartholomew described as being perfect paranoia. A smile touched the holy lips; dear kind-hearted quick-tempered Dr. Bartholomew. . . . His courtesy to the Dove was touching, and never more so than when the divinity students came to Pawksville to hear her discourse on her true identity. The Holy Dove did not mind in the least these annual theological palavers, the polite questions, the smiles hidden behind discreet hands, even Dr. Bartholomew's black glower should a muffled giggle seep out—all were part and parcel of her martyrdom. Someone had to heap scorn on her, sooner or later the whole world would have to commit the Unpardonable Sin—blasphemy of the Fourth Member of the Trinity— before humanity could partake fully of salvation.

Minor matters now occupied the Holy Dove. Though she held Dr. Bartholomew most dear, she regarded Dr. Heall only with pontifical reserve. For poor little Dr. Carmody she bore a great pity; her husband was hopeless. Soon Miss Noon's key would sound in the lock, and the Holy Dove contemplated the inner vision of that stout soul, flexing her biceps, with all the warmth of an abiding friendship. Hmmm, the Holy Dove mused, recalling what she had overheard of Marion Pierce's presentation at Staff Meeting. That young man was no more insane than she was. Her years at Pawksville had taught her to recognize fakery when she heard it. Young Pierce would bear watching. Just as little motherless Caddy Bartholomew always bore watching.

Of a sudden the Dove was stricken by the heartache that abounded in the world. Dear Dr. Bartholomew a widower, and poor Dr. Carmody in straits more severe than widowhood. She saw them clearly, each so immaculate in whites, Dr. Bartholomew looking quite—nifty—even, as he bent over Dr. Carmody, his hand jingling the keys in his pocket. Why, he's very nearly in love with her, the Holy Dove divined. Oh my, something drastic will have to be done about that. . . .

Also indulging sad thoughts was Nick Bartholomew. His initial disappointment over Jane Carmody had never quite left him. He had received her application for a position at Pawksville with all the keen gratification of an unsung Schweitzer receiving a truckload of drugs and blankets for his tuberculous Indians in darkest Arizona. His first glimpse of her pale face and shadowed eyes, under which a few childish freckles stood out, had him asking of himself *Who?* He had known other doctors secretly to follow relatives or mates into institutions, and this young woman with her enforced enthusiasm for psychiatry he suddenly suspected of being such a one. Yet—which of some three thousand patients had drawn her to Pawksville? He had narrowed it down almost overnight to five or six recently committed males. He wondered if it was not his revenge for his disappointment that had caused him to give her all the women's back wards. Not that Jane wasn't a worker; at times she slaved. But her heart wasn't in it, and to Nick she therefore wasn't practicing medicine. He would be working with her that morning in the insulin room, her husband on Nick's side of the low screen which separated the male from the female patients. He dreaded it, he doubted if ever he could restore to Jane more than a burnt-out mind in what had always been, at best, a second-rate piano-player.

Mebbe, Nick thought, I could get Father Muldroon to talk to Jane. He fancies himself as one of those subtle princedom-upsetting Renaissance priests, but he does have a way about him. Yep, for once someone might make use of Father Muldroon for something other than his own ends.

On her way to the watermelon patch, her head in the clouds, dazzled by the utterly meaningless poetry she had just read in the new *Gadfly*, Caddy left the cement walk for a small, still dewy footpath and accidentally crushed a lizard under her weight. Were it not for Nick, the temptation to pass on, to crash on through the grass like some uncaring giant, leaving the maimed and dead in her wake, would have been overwhelming. She could not do it, bound by Nick's code she must stop and give aid, or if she had hurt a small creature beyond repair, then she must assume the solemn and horrible duty of finishing it off. She stooped and saw that what Nick would have called the hindquarters, the twig legs and prehistoric tail of the lizard, were smashed. It tried to zip away from her and managed only a zigzag frenzy that took it to all four corners of the globe without moving from the walled pit of her footprint. The ruined tail swatted once, then was still, the miniature crocodile mouth weaving. Caddy huddled over her victim. Were she to take it up gently and put it among the grasses, would it survive? Or would it begin to drag itself toward some green tunnel where death awaited it? She shouted silently to the lizard's Creator, Can't You look where I'm going! He's Your lizard not mine, You could at least take better care of him!

There was no avoiding her duty by accusations or recriminations. The lizard was twitching, and as she bent very close one eye rolled round to inspect her. The gaze of that single eye, fearless, judicious, unblinking, knowing, commanded her. There was a stone to hand, or something between a rock and a pebble, and Caddy picked it up. She brought the stone down hard, grinding with one hand and burying the lizard in mud with the other. She murdered on and on, until she was done. Then, patting the rest of the mud in place, she smoothed over the area. Only a shining pool of brown earth marked the plain where the scion of dinosaurs had been destroyed. She heard herself sobbing in a dry cackle; now it was flawed, what had started out to be the single perfect Golden Day of her life. No imperfection in the entire world had met her eye until one carefree misstep had revealed to her that ugliness was everywhere.

She rose and began running toward the watermelon patch, flinging tears as she went. She had never even suspected that a merciful killing could entail such a sense of guilt and attendant sorrow.

Looking out of his office window, Sonny Heall said to himself, Now what's that Bartholomew brat up to? He sharpened his scrutiny, observing the fierce demise of the lizard. She seems to be killing something, Sonny told himself clinically. It's Nick's business if he chooses to overlook the fact that his ewe lamb is suffering from schizothymia, but overt sadism is something else again. The way he lets her run around, doing anything she likes, getting into God knows what mischief, you'd think he was secretly hankering for disaster. Mark my words, Nick's got a case of *lapsus calami,* if ever I saw it. . . . A desire for disaster.

By the time Caddy had reached the watermelon patch and was going about her harvesting, rapping on each melon, listening intently with tearstained cheek resting on the dark-green rind, attuned for that deep *thunk* denoting ripeness,

Jane Carmody was also engaged in listening for certain sounds coming from the abdomen of a patient.

She and a slovenly female RN and Nick Bartholomew were in the basement of the Administration Building, subterranean floors under the rotunda. The room was long and arched and had once contained wooden cages for the repose of the acutely and destructively disturbed. In a far corner, for display purposes only, a single cage remained, resembling a large coffin on legs with rungs along the sides and across the top. There were two broken hasps on the runged lid. Thrown carelessly over this was Jane's jacket, and on it, Nick's. In this airless dungeon Jane was working with sleeves rolled up, moving from one comatose woman patient to the next. The patients lay on cots, foam-rubber pillows under their heads. Deep in insulin coma for over an hour, they had sweated until their sheets and pillows and gowns were as wet as if they had just been lifted, dripping, from a washtub. Those still in deep coma moved murmurously, the copious sweat running in glistening streams. On Jane's side of the screen a patient or two was recovering. On Nick's, there were somewhat greater signs of activity. Carts containing slabs of bread thickly smeared with syrup and cups of tea sweetened to the consistency of fine silt were being rolled among the beds by working patients.

Jane permitted herself a glimpse of Nick's side of the room. Sean Maginnis was still semi-comatose, the tea a patient was holding to his mouth dribbling down his chin. His eyes, so fiercely blue, were as devoid of purpose as ever. Jane turned away; she was learning to live with heartsickness as others indulge their ulcers. One of her own patients required her attention. Accepting the greased tube from the sour-smelling nurse, she slid it expertly up the patient's nostril and down into the throat. The tube down, Jane stuck the other end in her mouth, and at that point laid her ear on the patient's abdomen. She blew into the tube and was rewarded by a burbling of the contents of the stomach beneath her ear. Satisfied that she had not introduced the tube into the lung, Jane motioned for the nurse to pour the thick tepid tea down the tube. Moments later Jane's efforts showed results. The patient, enjoying lucidity brought on by the coma, looked up at Jane. "Are you a nurse?"

"No, I'm Doctor Carmody. How are you feeling?"

"I'm not sure," the lucid one said weakly. "Is this a hospital?"

"Yes. Do you know who you are?"

"Of course." The patient said in wonderment, "Why, I'm Helen Daniels."

"How old are you, Mrs. Daniels?"

"That would depend," Mrs. Daniels said ruefully, "on how long I've been crazy. The last I remember I was twenty-four."

"You still are," Jane said. "You're going to come along rapidly from now on. A few more months and we'll see about your going home for a trial week end. Won't it be nice to see your baby again?"

"That substitute thing? That thing of rubber and straw they tried to tell me was my baby? That thing they put in my arms after I'd killed my own baby? That thing? That thing they gave me when I went crazy and killed my own baby? That thing? Thing?"

"Mrs. Daniels," Jane snapped, "you have a fine healthy boy at home, and you did not kill him. You've never so much as harmed a hair on that child's—"

"Thing?" Mrs. Daniels was asking. "Thing?"

Dammit, Jane thought. For an instant she entertained the deep desire to slap Helen Daniels repeatedly. Beat the psychosis out of her, pummel her into sanity.

"Doctor Heall said I didn't want my baby. Doctor Heall said I resented him because he ruined my figure. That's why I killed him, and then they gave me that thing thing thing——"

Some day, Jane promised herself, I'm going to pick up

The Complete Works of Sigmund Freud and swat Sonny senseless with it.

After a time the patients were able to sit on the edges of the cots, swaying with weakness. Attendants were arriving to convoy them back to the wards, and Jane watched the witless Sean Maginnis being led out. The cavernous sunburned cheeks were peeling in what looked like strips of ancient Cellophane. His thin hands hung lifeless at his sides. He shuffled past within a foot or two of Jane, and she said to herself quite as if she were repeating syllables after someone else in an unknown tongue, That's my husband. I'm Mrs. Maginnis. I know the touch of those waxy hands and that slack mouth. I love that sweaty, smelly animal slouching past me. He goes by me without a sign of recognition, and I am his wife.

"Doctor Carmody!" Nick said sharply. "Could you give me a hand here?"

She stared at him without comprehension until his expression steadied her. She moved toward him as if he had extended her a hand. When she reached his side, he said, "Roll with the punches, Toots. We're not licked yet."

"He breaks my heart," Jane said simply.

"Yeah. The trouble is, so do you." Nick looked at the last of the attendants going out the door. "Well, alone at last." He pushed a cart toward her, grinning. "What say to a dish of tea?"

"You'd have to be crazy to drink that goo," Jane said in a voice that meant it. She sat down on a revolving stool and stared at the cots and the sodden sheets. "Nick, what's insulin shock like?"

"Not too bad."

"And EST?"

"Rugged."

"And Metrazol?"

"Most terrifying thing I can think of. Next to insanity." As casually as if he had not ventured onto ice as thin as membrane, Nick went on, "Incidentally, I'm taking your husband off insulin. I tapered him forty units today."

"Nick, give him time. He's had just fifty-two—"

"Sorry. Listen, when you were looking at him, did you really look? Or just moon? He's emaciated, and they've been having to force-feed him. He can't take a beating like this every day. I'm going to give him a rest for about a week, and then start him on Metrazol."

"No," Jane said flatly. "Too much danger of fractures. I won't have him snapping his arms."

"In medical school I learned how to reduce a fracture," Nick said mildly. "There's no particular knack to it. I've done it innumerable times."

"A funny man like you ought to charge admission," Jane began. "We're on a screamingly funny topic, I know, but—"

"It must be. You're screaming."

She wilted. "If you must put him on convulsive shock therapy, make it EST."

"Again . . . sorry. I don't seem to get the results with it I can with Metrazol. I want him to convulse to a fare-thee-well. He's got to get the works, Jane."

"Don't sound so satisfied about it! You think I don't know what's going on in your mind? Hell, I experienced the same thing myself this morning. When that Helen Daniels came out of it, and then two minutes later was merrily off on her pet delusion again, I wanted— I wanted to pleat her nose in for her. But we don't rough a patient up, do we, we just order some disciplinary course of treatment. I can put Helen Daniels on Metrazol, and then I can watch with many a fat chuckle while she puts hairpin crimps in her spine, and twists her arms out of their sockets. That's grand fun——"

"So you've reached that stage," Nick said with an easy smile. "You'll weather it. I mean thinking that the patient and the psychosis are in league against you, and that your sole weapon is the severity of the therapy. Later on, only the psychosis will engage your—anger, say—and you'll hit it with everything you've got, within the patient's physical limitations. Let me put it this way, to be squeamish is to be sentimental, and at the patient's expense. Does it matter whether I say, 'Administer electro-shock therapy to the patient for the subsequent ameliorative calmative effect,' or simply, 'Give 'im a hefty jolt to take the fight out of 'im'?" Listen to what I say, not how I word it. And while I'm on the subject of what the ancients used to call 'heroic measures' when they meant adopting a kill-or-cure method, they knew whereof they spoke. Over the ages experience has taught us that unnatural physical states directly affect the mind. From boring a hole in the head all the way up to modern times when they infected them with malaria to induce high fevers." He knew himself to be covering over what had threatened to become an ugly exchange by lecturing. But of late his responses to Jane were so heightened that he had to control himself lest he mate her mood to mood. "Look, Jane, all we're trying to effect, in a manner of speaking, is the reverse of *tortura insomniae*. Ever hear of *tortura insomniae*, Doctor? A medieval form of brainwashing—simple, to the point, and in all instances effective. Keeping some neurotic female awake day in and night out until she came to believe, and readily confessed to, being a witch. And I mean *believe*. Embrace the delusion. Now, take massive sleep—shouldn't it be able to dissolve a delusion? The French psychiatrists think so. Doesn't always work, though. Then, in excessive sleep, there's always the danger of oxygen starvation of the brain tissue."

"You digress," Jane said sullenly.

"I'm giving you time to collect your thoughts. Just the same, our medieval psychiatrists were right on the track when it came to treating those who were genuinely psychotic. Beat the bejasus out of them. With chains. Do you know how successful their therapy was? On a percentage basis, no less than ours. That's why—even though I'm going to get down on my knees to the Governor for some tranquilizers—I've no intention of giving up the more rugged forms of therapy. From what I have seen of these new wonder drugs, too frequently their use is tantamount to neglect. Sugar-teat therapy smoothing the surface over the inner turmoil. Yet get what the boys who write articles like to call a 'transient reduction.' That means that a whole bloc of patients can walk out one door, tranquilized to the eyeballs and sane to all appearances, and a year later they're brought back in the other, combative and acute. Even Sonny Heall has brought his towering intellect to bear on the subject and reached the same conclusion. Under the loving influence of Serpasil a patient will spill his guts to Sonny, but the revelations have no emotional sock behind them. Sonny's gone back to shock, because after a violent opening up of the clogged passages, Sonny and the patient can really get down in there and root around in the mud. My methods are different because I believe I'm dealing with a disease, or a chemical imbalance of the brain, if you like, as opposed to cutting through the scar tissue formed by a thousand traumatizing experiences. That's why, in some instances when a patient proves to be chronic and inexpressibly wretched, when the process appears to be irreversible, then I will consider lobotomy as being not only indicated but merciful."

"You sound like Superintendent Keeney," Jane accused.

"I do not. If he had his way, every patient in Pawksville would be lobotomized, so Keeney could feed them on gruel and dispense with a medical staff. He would amputate a leg because of a troublesome boil; I would resort to it only in case of gangrene. Just as I will resort to whatever treatment, however harsh, promises maximum results. Is that clear, Doctor? Impugn my motives all you like, just admit that my means work. Admit that, and I'll make it so hot around here for Sean Maginnis that even snapping out of it and going back to a neurotic nag of a wife like you will seem like paradise. Agreed, Jane?" He looked at her steadfastly

thinking, She looks tired; dammit, this dame is really beginning to get to me. He asked, without knowing he was going
to, "Jane, do you love him?"

She braced herself visibly, "What he was, yes. Now he
needs me, of course."

"You mean you need him to need you."

"Don't go Sonny Heall on me, Nick," she said sharply,
so that he knew the matter must end there.

Looking away, his attention was suddenly taken. He
spied his daughter passing along above. He could see only
her lower trunk, the rolled legs of her shorts extending an
inch or so below her shirt. He was struck by the fact that she
looked extraordinarily pregnant, even to her hands clasped
protectively across the abdomen. Only her walk differed from
that of the pregnant, for she was executing a furtive scamper.
Close on wondering what she was up to, he decided that whatever it was he didn't like it. He wished she would hang
around Al more, or practice her violin or something. There
was a thought—tie Sean Maginnis to a chair and force him
to listen to Caddy at her scales. It would restore the man
to his senses in a trice—or send him off the deep end once
and for all. Smiling slightly at this conceit, he looked down
from the high windows to find Jane staring at him intently.
More than intently, she was bending on him the suspicional
regard of the incipient paranoid. "Don't think that," she
said tightly.

"Think what, dammit!"

"Whatever it was you were thinking about Sean."

"I was merely observing my daughter going by," Nick
said calmly.

Before his eyes Jane managed subtly to rearrange her
features. The pinched Modigliani stare of the persecution
maniac gave way to her usual wide-eyed look. The mouth
filled out, the red rushing in to erase the white fold of taut
lips. "Sorry," she said in a placatory tone. She laughed shak-

ily. "It must be catching around here. I'll be hearing voices next. Maybe I need a little therapy."

"The day you do, I'll hit you so hard and fast you won't know what happened to you. I'll be merciless. I happen to like you for a sidekick. You start cracking up, and I won't bother with Metrazol. I'll just haul out the chains."

"As a professional courtesy," Jane said in all seriousness.

"Right. Well. . . . Are you going to permit me to extend the same courtesy to your husband?"

Her voice was faint. "The works."

"I was afraid for a minute there," Nick admitted, "that we were in for a heated exchange." He rose, extended a hand as if to touch her (Are you at *that* again? he asked himself heatedly), then awkwardly redirected the hand to fiddle with the teacart. "Jane—— When your husband is able to go home with you, what are you going to do? About children, I mean. You should keep in mind that you're running a certain hereditary risk. Instability, if not actual insanity, has a habit of cropping up—" He broke off, then said, impatient with himself, "I forgot. He is Catholic, isn't he?"

"Very much so." She was listless. "His family made a concession in that direction where I was concerned. When they were wife-shopping, they were more interested in my profession than my Protestantism. They're a lovely crew, all right. As for kids—Sean and I played Vatican Roulette. But that was only to be until I'd completed my residency. After that, I was hoping to . . . but he cracked up—again—so soon after we were married. You know, don't you, Nick, that he has an aunt in a sanitarium. And a grandmother died here in Pawksville."

"Yes, I know."

"Nick, why can't I buy Sonny's psychogenic theory? Why must I believe that insanity is hereditary? Sonny says that you're full of . . ."

"Full of what?" Nick prodded her.

"Somatogenic superstition," Jane said miserably. Her

hand went forth to rest an inch away from his on the cart.

"Yes, that does sound like our Sonny. Jane, can't you find it in yourself to walk out on your husband? Leave Pawksville, go on about your life? I'd still go on doing my utmost for him. But outside you might meet someone—I'm saying this stupidly, I know—but you owe it to yourself——"

"I can't. It isn't as if he were dead."

"I'm afraid it is, though."

". . . or happy. If he were like the Holy Dove, glorying in a spectacular delusion, then, yes, perhaps I could abandon him."

"I've toyed with the notion of firing you, you know that?"

She looked at him abjectly. "Don't. You might think you were doing me a favor, but you wouldn't be."

"Oh, Christ," Nick said and went over to the ancient cage for their white jackets. Slipping hers on for her, he said in an altered tone, "My daughter went by a few minutes ago looking as if she were in imminent danger of giving birth to twins. I must look into it."

"That would be wise."

"I'll have lunch upstairs, I guess. See what my sister and brat are up to."

"Caddy's a good kid," Jane said with a hairbreadth more politeness than conviction.

Nick shrugged on his own jacket. "I'll tell her you said so. Even Caddy feels the need of a kind word now and again. Shall we lock up?"

"Are we circling one another for advantage?" Jane asked lightly.

It was only then that Nick discovered he had an arm around her. He held her closely, rested his cheek against her temple, and looked past her to the vacated cots. He was alone with her, safely alone and in a room full of beds. "And you," he said against her hair, "you have to have a husband who was comatose on one of them not an hour ago." Then turning abruptly away from her, and leaving her to lock up, he fled.

Caddy would have said it was in the nature of a private tradition for her to swipe watermelons intended for the Pawks Boys Jubilee. When she was younger she would let them drop to the ground so that the twins might gobble from the fragments; it was one way of shutting them up for a while. Free of the pair, she nevertheless continued her raids on the patch. Interested less in the melons than the exciting mechanics and techniques of theft, Caddy had elaborated on her tradition to the extent of chilling them in the Morgue House icebox. Hence the unlocked back door which, facing the meadows, was hidden from the view of Pawksville, and which door, as well, she had unlocked at a time when Dr. Carmody was upstairs with her husband's piano records going full blast on her hi-fi.

She had made only a modest raid on the patch, a sortie of two small melons. In the interests of daring alone, she transported her booty somewhat in the manner of one playing Missionary and Cannibals, moving first one to a hiding place under a tree or vacant bench, and then returning for the other, to sprint like a football player with it, fifty yards to the cache of the first. In this way, both melons had come to rest within minutes of each other under the staircase of the Morgue House. Above, Dr. Carmody's radio sang to itself unattended, as it was a clock radio set to wake itself each morning with a burst of classical music, and Dr. Carmody, for some private reason, rarely bothered to turn the thing off, except to interrupt its tinny outpourings with her hi-fi.

The noon whistle had sounded; Caddy was behind schedule. She crouched under the stair, hidden behind the instrument cabinet, listening. Dr. Carmody, Caddy deduced then, had gone directly on to the staff dining room from insulin clinic. Emerging from her place of secrecy Caddy went to the built-in refrigerator and opened the first door that came to hand. A tug on the tray revealed that it was occupied. The second was equally taken up, and lifting the sheet idly Caddy looked down on the face of the cadaver. Under a snow-white state-hospital bowl haircut there was the face of an old woman, the wrinkles chill and firm in the way the rays of a molded aspic are firm. She put a fingertip to the nose; the cartilage felt as brittle as an egg shell. The draw-string mouth was bunched tight, surrounded by the faint white beard of old women, each bristle a tiny icicle, like frost needles. Lingering, looking long on death, Caddy sought to comprehend it.

When Nancy was killed, Caddy and the twins had been taken over to the mortuary in the village by Dr. Ouita, who spoke during the short drive in terms of slumber, rest, naps, and the like, so that the twins were convinced they would see their mother dozing. Instead, they were ushered into a hushed room with a closed coffin and Nick seated by it. Nor had he looked like Nick particularly, for he was wearing a dark business suit which made him appear pale and strange and impassive. After a moment or so, Dr. Ouita led the children back out into the sunlight, and then remembered that she wanted to pick up some more Pawksville Mortuary fans for her ladies, and went back in alone for them.

Once again Caddy sought to believe in death; her mind refuted it. It was only a catatonic catalepsy, or, in line with Dr. Ouita's explanation, an extended extended massive sleep. Until Nick lets me watch a post, Caddy thought, naturally employing the abbreviation for post-mortem, I just won't catch on to what being dead really is. So that you're not a person any more, you're just another corpse.

She could have mulled such thoughts for an hour, examining the evidence, but for the imminent return of Dr. Carmody after lunch. Slamming home the tray, she moved in the cool gloom of the Morgue House to yet another tray. The old folks of Pawksville died like flies during the dog days of August, and silently reviling the lazy attendants who used up all the lower trays first, Caddy came to the end of the row. The entire lower tier was tenanted. It was necessary for Caddy to climb on one of the precariously high stools meant to accommodate those performing autopsies on the slab in the middle of the room and, balancing, open a door, peek in, and, in finding it occupied, climb down, move the stool, clamber up and have at the next door. The callous disregard of the attendants in hogging the lower tier for their own purposes had Caddy muttering and growing careless in her haste. Dr. Carmody sometimes picked at her food at table, then abruptly rose and hurried from the dining room; Caddy had seen her do just this on more than one occasion. It was always a mystery to Caddy, for she could recall no incident which might have provoked Dr. Carmody's strange behavior. It was everlastingly the same old chatter in the staff dining room about who (not being present at the time) was getting more paranoid every day, or whatever; for her part, Caddy more often than not was in accord with the diagnosis. Insofar as it might relate to Dr. Carmody's husband being an inmate, such sensitivity was beyond Caddy's ken. One medical problem was to Caddy as factual, colorless, and commonplace as the next.

Dr. Carmody's compulsive states aside, or the reasons therefor, Cady recognized that she must take into consideration that the Doctor could easily come bursting into the Morgue House at any moment, her only warning being the swift twist of her key in the front-door lock. Ignorant of whether Dr. Carmody were a tattle or not, it was not a revelation Caddy cared to risk. Were Carmody to catch her and then snitch to Nick, then Nick—as Dr. Heall would probably say—would get very Oedipal about the whole thing and raise a ruckus.

Greeted again on the second tier by the cold carven face of death, Caddy grumbled, "Oh, fiddlesticks," and tried for another door. Success rewarded her second effort, but as she was endeavoring to keep her balance on the stool and hoist the watermelon onto the tray, she dropped it. Caddy climbed down and contemplated the mess. Inaction seized her, a state Nick had warned her people fell into when thoroughly disgusted with themselves. Still, the loss of her own self-esteem would be as nothing compared to Nick's reaction were he to learn of the back-door key, and Caddy set about to bustle. The big chunks of melon went straight into the autopsy bucket, followed by toweling dripping with juice and seeds. Time, she feared, was flying, with the second melon yet hidden under the dark stair and behind the instrument cabinet. The bucket would have to be emptied lest someone came in that evening to do a post. And there was a syrupy stain on the floor, but that, Caddy sensibly told herself, would hardly cause comment, lying to one side of the slab as it did. No, her first concern was the bucket——

Dr. Carmody's key clinked against the front door. Caddy shoved her stool next the slab and retreated to the depth of darkness under the stair, heart thumping against the cool surface of her remaining melon. She peeped past the instrument cabinet.

Locking the door behind her automatically, Dr. Carmody mounted the stair slowly, heavily for such a graceful little woman; mounted it with all the eager tread of one climbing up to a scaffold.

Then, pausing just above Caddy, with only a foot of gloom, an inch or so of wood, and some threadbare carpeting separating them, Dr. Carmody sank down.

Dr. Carmody began to sob.

Caddy turned her face upward like one after a long Pawksville dry season welcoming the first drops of rain. Appalled, she was crying out soundlessly. Now, now, Doctor, there, there. . . . Oh, honestly, there, there!

Well that's over with, thank God, Caddy told herself with relief, when, with a self-conscious honk of her nose and a muttered "whining, lacrymose female," Dr. Carmody got hold of herself and continued on up the stair.

Not long after, Dr. Carmody's step, light and pert now after her good cry, tapped over Caddy's head softly. There was the sound of the front door opening, and from her hiding place Caddy beheld a startling thing. A shaft of sunlight slashed across the druidical gloom of the morgue, straight to the slab where it drew silver fire from the center drain. Some savage forebear of Caddy's cried out inwardly, pierced by the silver brilliance. Enraptured, she made her vow. Nick's edict that she could not watch a post until she had entered high school diminished her resolution not in the least. The next post Nick performed, she would be hiding exactly where she was now, making her due acquaintance with death.

The door cut off the sun; and her second melon safely tucked away, Caddy emerged presently to empty the bucket.

In their pleasant island of light set in the ocean of perpetual night that was the top floor of the Hospital, the Bartholomews were seated at the banquette. Nick was hot and tired, his mood shading on the grumpy, and Al, though rested, was edgy from the heat as well.

"Well, it's your business," Al was saying. "But I do wonder at your letting the kid roam all over Pawksville at will. After all, Nick, there are patients, males, at large on the grounds."

"No one knows that better than Caddy. My daughter is not a fool. Moreover, for the last four summers—"

"She had the twins to ride herd on," Al reminded him. "Safety in numbers. Admit it, you haven't the faintest idea what's with her from dawn to dark."

"I saw her late this morning, going past the insulin clinic windows. Al, you just don't understand state-hospital brats. They're different from ordinary kids; they have to be. They're more self-reliant, more knowing. Listen, the things I've told Caddy, the things I've had to warn her about, would curl the hair of the average thirteen-year-old."

"If I were you, I'd worry less about curling some other kid's hair, and more about putting a crimp in Caddy. Okay, okay," Al said on a rising note, precluding a rebuff.

The door to the apartment slammed and Caddy bounded in. "Lordy, I lost all track of the time! Nick, I didn't know you'd be having lunch with us or I'd've——"

"But you were aware that Al was expecting you?" Nick said sternly.

A downcast Caddy said, "Yes, sir." With that impregnable politeness she extended verbally to Al, she added, "I'm very sorry, Aunt Al."

"Humph," Al said, not unpleasantly. One of her silences came over her; during it she noted Nick's inability to maintain his disciplinary scowl and Caddy's sudden resumption of her perkiness.

"I see you are safely delivered, Madame," Nick said, with a pointed glance at Caddy's middle.

"Oh, Nick, you must have seen me," Caddy giggled. "I was walking around with this pillow. I don't know why I'm so juvenile sometimes."

"I just might come up with a reasonable explanation," Al offered. "And I would like to know why you were late, Caddy. Care to tell us?"

Caddy was all contrition. "I dunno. I meant to be prompt, but one thing somehow led to another. Somehow . . ." she ended, dawdling on the "somehow" as long as she had breath, forestalling further questions from Al.

"What things?" Al asked in genuine curiosity.

"Yes, do particularize," Nick twitted.

"Oh, Nick," Caddy tittered in outrageous flirtation, "you're pulling my leg!"

"I sit and listen to this," Al remarked to the tan (or was it gray?) wallpaper, "but I don't really credit my senses. The two of you sound as drafty in the attic as the rest of them around here." Glancing up, she discovered both Nick and Caddy looking down their noses at her.

"We don't use expressions like that around Pawksville, Al," Nick said.

"I distinctly recall you, Nick Bartholomew, saying *bats* and *wiggy* the other day. To mention just two."

"That was different," Nick defended himself. "I was making a point."

Caddy nodded quite as if she had been present at the time.

"I stand corrected," Al said. "You just don't catch on to Pawksville decorum overnight, I guess. What's on your agenda this afternoon, Caddy?"

"She's going to practice her violin," Nick announced. "Right?"

"Yes, Nick," Caddy said, alert and winning.

"And the luncheon dishes for Al?"

"I'll be glad to."

"Well, now that you girls are getting along so well, I have to be off," Nick said. He pulled Caddy's ponytail. "Do what Al tells you to, hear me?"

"Yes, sir," Caddy said demurely. And followed Nick with sparkling eyes as he left the apartment.

Alone, the two Bartholomew females measured one another without any outward show that they were doing so. Al remarked with calm deliberation, "Nick works very hard, Caddy. What with running Pawksville and the various clinics and his acute wards and the sick wards, he's got his hands full."

"Yes, I know, Aunt Al."

"You're pretty much the bright spot in his life."

Caddy's eyes became less guarded and began to glow. "Well, the twins, too," she said modestly. "But I guess because I'm older, he can—you know, kid around me more. We have a whale of a time just sitting around and——"

"Somehow I haven't seen much evidence of that during my visit here. You've rather isolated yourself in your room evenings, reading or working on your Ode."

"But you and Nick get to talk about old times, then," Caddy pointed out artfully. "It isn't as if Doctor and Mrs. Heall or Doctor Carmody or somebody were up here saying the same old thing over and over."

"What you're saying then, is that I'm a welcome, if temporary, break in Nick's routine. But when I'm not here, doesn't Nick still need adult—"

"He gets that all day," Caddy said positively. She began to gather up the plates. "I purely believe he'd scream if he had to listen to Doctor Carmody all evening too. Like this winter Nick's going to teach me to play chess with him. The twins can have the television, and Nick and I'll set up the board right at the table here . . ." An unfathomable expression on her aunt's face caused Caddy to falter. Rallying, Caddy went on, "Or maybe we'll use the table you have your jigsaw on."

"Funny thing about that jigsaw," Al said pensively. "I could have sworn it was going to be a pastoral scene. And instead, it's turning out to be some obscure battleground. It looks like such an unlikely place for a war."

"Well, from what I've learned in history class," Caddy said, "one place seems to be as good as another." She turned on the water in the sink, bringing the conversation to a close.

In the shade of the old Monkey Tree, the Great Poet, Titus Graham, awaited his trysting mate impatiently. With the exception of the mournful Mr. Hamshot (armed with his peanut-butter sandwiches, to be sure) one was ill advised to sit on the circular wood plank bench at the base of the tree unless he were furiously smoking a noisome pipe. The rapist, or murderer of parts—The Great Poet could never remember which—who had originally brought the spider monkeys to Pawksville was no exception; it was Mr. Hamshot's one venture into the thick underbrush of humor to describe that gentleman smoking passionately as he chained his pets to their leafy prison. Somehow when he departed Pawksville, the rapist (or murderer) had left his creatures behind, putting them in his past along with the full syndrome of his psychosis. The Great Poet, doubtful inheritor of the Monkey Tree, early in his stay at Pawksville had disdained all of Mr. Hamshot's most sorrowful warnings and betaken his then-athletic self to sit under the tree and invite his soul. The monkeys had crashed the party, rattling their chains in a frenzy of affection as they leapt upon the Great Poet's head and neck and shoulders, there to wrap their prehensile tails about him and cuddle. Amused—flattered, actually, as many are when strange animals fall in love with them— the Great Poet had spent a most enjoyable quarter-hour diddling the monkeys. He then wished to put them away. It took Mr. Hamshot, along with numerous hastily smeared peanut-butter sandwiches and two pipes fired up with Prince Albert, to rescue the Great Poet. Bitten and embittered, dubious of all animal affection now, as he was always of that of human beings, the Great Poet had made his escape. If the Monkey Tree were still his refuge, he came prepared, and the spiders kept their distance, clanking their chains, complaining pitifully, and fighting among themselves. One of them had gone so far as to withdraw completely from his fellows, sitting high in the bower above all others, his chain stretched to its limit, as he picked at his mangy fur and sorrowed in silence.

There was a story that once a wretch, a fearful guilt-ridden involutional melancholiac, had strayed too deeply into the grotto and been captured by the monkeys. Each attempted rejection of them had earned him ugly bites and lacerations about the chest and face. They say he sat thus, long into the night, thinking of many things, but in the main of his commission of the Unpardonable Sin, and certain that his punishment, the eternal caresses of the demons cradled on his person, had finally befallen him. The searchers found him, of course, but he was unable to recover from the experience. He managed to do away with himself shortly after by ripping up his bedsheets and packing his throat and nostrils with the shreds.

A pretty tale, the Great Poet reflected, and—as are so many pretty tales—true. As the able Pawksvillian for whom he waited was late, the Great Poet amused himself by taunting the monkeys, blowing streams of smoke upwards, agitating them. Only the lonesome one was above all this, figuratively as well as literally. Of him the Poet could see only the tail with its worn leathery underside, looping down in a coil that managed to speak volumes on despair.

If, like a coin, the Great Poet had had an obverse side, that side would have been Nick Bartholomew. Contemptuous of most of his fellows on sight, Titus Graham had had to invent a special detestation for Nick, had had to tailor it to Nick's specifications. For Titus, Nick embodied all that was burly and bungling and fatuously dedicated. Titus took only satisfaction from the realization that Nick looked on his own Greek athleticism as being tainted, effete; just as Nick always took great care to view Titus's fine curry-colored mustache as if he were looking at a laboratory animal that had died on Friday night and wasn't discovered until Monday. Nick was of the opinion that if Titus had a reputation of note in the world outside it was due to his peccadillos, not his Alexandrines. This also served Titus as a source of amusement. And Titus had been roundly entertained when, at the conclusion of his first interview with Nick (he was not to be subjected to Staff Meeting, under strict orders from Superintendent Keeney, under strict orders from Governor Leroy Jackson), Titus had requested to see what Nick had written, and was promptly accorded that courtesy:

"Claims," Nick wrote in a fury of resentment at being saddled with yet another Special Patient, "to have a reputation of international standing. It does appear that he has published some verse in obscure magazine. Attaches an importance all out of keeping with reality to these infrequent appearances in print. Is opinionated, authoritative, has de-

lusions of grandeur—thinks he is related to political bigwig—
and that the literary world is aghast at his confinement. Is
abusive to me, *e.g.,* 'You sweaty Phillistine,' etc. His attendant
reports he has not been assaultive as yet. Grumbles a lot
about food, airless rooms in Special Cottage, etc. Speaks of
his brutal molestation of male adolescent lightly, dismisses
victim as being of 'no consequence.' Flat affect. Marked
blunting. Considers self above law or morals. No prior history
of hospitalization. Paranoid schizophrenic with manic-depressive side effects. Therapeutic measures yet to be decided
upon."

"Excellent, Doctor," Titus said. "Now will you please go
to the board and write Philistine one hundred times? One *l,*
if you please."

A man with a curry mustache and ginger eyes was bound
to be considered a spicy personality, and the Great Poet had
long since gone to work on living up to the impression.
Being forced to languish under the Monkey Tree, therefore,
he was growing peppery, one exquisitely veined hand
clenched about his pipe, the other resting on his manila
envelope. His pleasure in giving Nick Bartholomew tit for
tat, by taking Caddy into his employ in return for Nick's
having turned Titus over to the merciless motherliness of
Dr. Ouita, was lessening each moment the brat was later.

So when Caddy did, at last, burst into the grotto, the
Great Poet snarled over his second pipeful of Prince Albert,
"Where in hell have you been?"

"Had to practice my vile-in," Caddy retorted, curt as
he. "Got anything for me?"

"Most certainly I have! Do you think I seek out your
company for the pleasure of it?"

"Nope," Caddy said with state-hospital sagacity. "You're
not supposed to like girls."

The Great Poet puffed on his pipe, raising enough
smoke to protect him while he spoke. "I've some work here
for you, but I'm afraid I'm going to have to ask you to carry
me on credit this—"

"Not on your tintype," Caddy said without hesitation. "I'm not running a business, you know. You keep asking me to carry you on credit because you think that way I'll keep coming back. Well, it won't wash. I read that in a book. Every penny of your money goes for your stamps. I don't like you as a person, but we poets have to stick together. Cough up the dough. We're running low on stamps, and since I'm supposed to go to the village this week and see this girl friend, I can buy them then. That is, if you want your stuff mailed out any more."

Grunting with dislike, Graham laid his manila envelope on the bench and plunged his hand into his pocket. Again he availed himself of the opportunity to puff on his pipe and received in reply an angry chiming of chains. Caddy, meanwhile, took a cursory look upward, noting that the solitary monkey roosted like a sleeping bird, with its head sunk to his motheaten chest.

The Great Poet spun a fifty-cent piece in the air and Caddy caught it expertly. "Thanks."

A nickel then followed the first coin. It fell to the dust. "What's that for?" Caddy asked.

"I thought you might like to buy yourself an ice-cream cone," the Great Poet said, barely concealing his dislike for her under his magnanimity.

"The last of the big-time spenders," Caddy scoffed. "Besides, I don't eat ice-cream cones. Doctor Heall says that people who do are reverting to the pap. He means nursing, you understand."

"That man has the vilest mind I've ever encountered."

"Oh, do you think so?" Caddy cried, warming to the poet for an instant. Her happy tone was echoed by a monkey chittering down at them, his cheepings filtering through the leaves like the thin hot strands of the afternoon sunshine. Some play of light on the Great Poet's face instantly dampened her spurt of girlishness. Gathering her dignity about her, she said in her chilliest voice, "I'm having a spot of trouble with my Ode. What rhymes with flag?"

"Rag," the Great Poet said as if glad of the opportunity to speak nastily.

Caddy sniffed. "Very funny. I must say, that's a new high in something or other. You'll be having a *flight of ideas* next, if you don't watch yourself. That's when you get to rattling off a lot of stuff that doesn't have any meaning. Kids do it a lot, but my father never let us even get started on it." Having stated the latter in the manner of one being most kindly and helpful, Caddy veered back to business. "*Pawks* and *hawks* rhyme; that won't give me any trouble. I'll just say something about 'The hawks of the dawn.' " She made a sound of disgust. "I'm getting bored with the whole thing, frankly. Having to make it standard Tennyson, you know. Or Sidney Lanier, or sombody. He's what I ought to shoot for."

"Time somebody shot at him."

Caddy had fallen into a study. "You know. . . . There's something to your 'flag and rag.' You know? It's—bitter. It would sure make 'em sit up and take notice." Her face fell. "Naw. . . . It'd be kind of chancy to recite something that off-beat for the Governor. Nick—that's Doctor Bartholomew, of course—" Caddy corrected herself, not wishing to extend the courtesy of a first-name basis between her father and a mere patient "—wants everything nice and proper for Jubilee. And, besides, if my Ode is to go among the Governor's private papers——" Certain uncouth sputterings on the part of the Great Poet caused her to glare suspiciously. He appeared to be choking on his pipe, and, mollified, Caddy resumed, "No, I'll have to write the Ode in the same old way. A way I'm afraid I've just outgrown."

"Why write it at all?" the poet snapped, as if she irked him unbearably. "The whole Jubilee is rubbish, and you know it."

A practical Caddy said, "Well, they'll publish it in the Pawksville paper, for one thing."

"Is publication all you think of?"

"Just about," Caddy said cautiously.

"And you value the opinion of the few who will even so much as glance at your dubious manifestations of talent?"

"Sure I value it!"

"And what do they know about poetry? Answer me!"

"Come to think of it, not much, I'm afraid," Caddy said truthfully.

"Or they wouldn't print your garbage."

Reining herself in, Caddy cast about for a new topic. "Wouldn't it be interesting to know what Doctor Heall thought of *your* work? He's a psychoanalyst, you see."

"From what I've heard of that fathead, you're making a pretty broad assumption that he can read at all."

"He can," Caddy assured him with surprising heat. "He read an ode of mine. I was just a kid then, and I wrote it and sent it in to the Pawksville *Courier,* and they printed it. And Mrs. Heall saw it and . . . um . . . brought it to Doctor Heall's attention. As they say. I was going to spring it on Nick—that's Doctor Bartholomew—for a surprise. But Doctor Heall quoted it first in the staff dining room."

"Indeed?" Puff, puff. "And how did your ode go?"

Now that she was called upon to do what she had obliquely hinted for, Caddy hung back. *Vis-à-vis* with her first peer critic, she cleared her throat with a troubled snarl. "Oh, it wasn't much. Just something that the power-house smokestack inspired."

"Let's have it," the Great Poet commanded cruelly.

"I see. . . ." she declaimed in a fluttering voice, then fell mute.

After a time the Great Poet observed. "It does have a certain compactness. But I think it's a little early in your career for such stark obscurity. You need a bit of imagery to green it out."

"I see," Caddy blared desperately, "a smokestack rising/ Against a rose-tipped sky/And to me it is a symbol/Of a hope that cannot die. . . . That's the first verse."

"I'm inclined to agree with Doctor Heall," the Great Poet gasped, convulsed.

"How do you know what he said?"

"One doesn't have to be that baroque Holy Dove, running around sticking her nose into everything, to guess," the poet said in gusts. Confronted by Caddy's outrage, he sought to control himself sufficiently to ask for the next verse, but his efforts were unavailing.

More than aware of his mockery, yet only vaguely sensing that his unspoken contumely embraced more than the poem, more than the poem and Caddy put together, for that matter, Caddy drew herself up. Pocketing the fifty-cent piece in her shorts, she said, "I'll be going now," and took up his manila envelope.

Leaving the grotto, head held high, she did not look back. The sound of striking matches and the squalling of the monkeys told her that the Great Poet was firing up, preparatory to taking his own leave.

Making her way from magnolia tree to magnolia tree, slipping in and out of their secret shade as she made her way toward the back wards, Caddy's soul twitched in unrest. Surely not all the intrepid poets of *Gadfly* were despicable as well? Were she to continue on with her art, instead of or even in spite of choosing medicine as her profession, would she end as the Great Poet had? Torn between wishing to fulfill Nick's dearest dream—coming down the aisle to show him her M.D. degree—and embracing poetry and the world well lost, she learned suddenly what it meant to be rent by conflicting desires. To feel as Nick said the poor schizzies felt. Rounding a corner of a back ward she nearly bumped into the Holy Dove, and cried out in glad greeting to that stately figure and fond smile, "Oh, hi, Holy Dove! Isn't this a perfectly *rotten* hot afternoon?"

"Yes, it's very bad on my ward, Caddy," the Holy Dove agreed tranquilly. "Miss Noon was nice enough to insist I go for a little walk under the trees." The Holy Dove narrowed her glacier-lake eyes to focus on Sonny Heall ambling towards his office in the rotunda. "I must go, Caddy. Miss Noon will be needing me back soon."

"You take it easy in this heat, now, Holy Dove!" Caddy admonished.

"Bless you, Caddy," the Holy Dove replied in a manner so heartfelt that Caddy half-believed she probably was.

The Holy Dove out of sight now, Caddy ducked into a dark doorway to make her familiar trip in the semi-black down a flight of stairs. Deep under the rotunda, passing along unused arched corridors, she came to her secret hideaway —the old, abandoned lab. Here was a Bunsen burner on a scarred table, a sink, and an old roll-top desk, the key to which Caddy had discovered in a pigeon-hole drawer. She produced the key from its pin on the inner waistband of her shorts and opened the desk. Inside lay Caddy's counting house. There were paper, the cigar box of stamps, and an ancient office typewriter. Next she lit the Bunsen burner; placing a chipped beaker of water on a ringstand over it to boil, she searched on the lab bench equipment closet door for a wad of gum affixed to it, and protected by a piece of yellowed filter paper. While the water came to a boil, Caddy washed the filter paper from the chewing gum at the sink, firming up the gum in the process, and, lastly, popped the wad into her mouth. Chewing with great swinging motions of her jaw, she waited for the steam to rise from the beaker. When it did, she carefully, calmly steamed open the Great Poet's manila envelope.

Seated at the desk, she then rolled a fresh sheet of paper into the typewriter. Punching the keys with her forefingers only, and with many a frown of bafflement, she began copying the latest segments of the Great Poet's major work: *Ex Povertium.* Her scrupulosity in putting down each (to her) misplaced mark of punctuation could, under other circumstances, easily have earned the Great Poet's approbation. To tamper with the work of another would have struck

Caddy as being first-degree Unpardonable Sin. Her copying done, her knotted-brow attempts to understand the Poet's latest efforts caused her own Muse to rouse and squirm. In the shadows of the desolate room, dwarfed by the high arches down which streams of collected moisture ran, Caddy experienced again a twinge of schizophrenia. She felt alone; worse, she felt bereft of herself. All the events of the day, presenting themselves suddenly, alarmingly, in vivid color, passed through her mind. The rotunda in the dawn, the doomed lizard, Dr. Carmody sobbing miserably yet somehow crankily on the Morgue House stair, Aunt Al's disjointed observations about Nick, the downright orneriness of the Great Poet, the sun, fur, and dust filtering down through the foliage of the Monkey Tree, all and up to that glimpse of Dr. Heall strolling to his office, his round balding head compartmented into thousands of musty nooks and corners wherein he stored the mildewed secrets of Pawksville, all— and this last too—lifted Caddy until she was soaring free on a poetic flight of ideas. Brushing aside "Canticle for the Holy Dove," VII, she rammed a fresh piece of paper into the typewriter, and began:

HEBEPHRENIA

Hereafter
Keep your lizards out
From underfoot.
You know damn well people
Don't look where they're
Going.

Never neck with a monkey.
He gets assaultive when
You want to
Quit.

And while I'm on the subject,
Stay away from the Monkey Tree

It's a back ward if ever I
Saw one.
And I've seen plenty in my
Time.

The whole world is going to the dogs.
Down curs! Down and
Heall.

At once replete and drained, Caddy sank back against the rickety office chair. After a time of emotional replenishment, she lifted "Hebephrenia" from the typewriter and read it over. Give it a whirl, she thought, and included it with the retyped pages of the Great Poet, along with, to be sure, "Canticle for the Holy Dove," VII. Placing all in the manila envelope, she resealed the flap with a tongue coated with rich chewing-gum-induced salivation, and then pounded it secure with her fist. She affixed some stamps from the box.

Her rituals before the altar of art almost done for the week, she put her feet on the desk and relaxed with the latest copy of *Gadfly,* chomping and cracking her gum loudly. The mail truck would be along in a half-hour.

Caddy would be there to meet it.

The masthead of *Gadfly* asserted, far better than it knew: *Ars una, specie mille.*

12

The Walrus Hour

It would be safe to say that Marion Pierce, like any correct young boulevardier, had entertained the hope of coming to grips with himself one day by "enjoying a salutary experience with his analyst." The phrase was not Marion's originally, though he had made it his, along with others of a similar "conceptualization" gleaned from conversations with a friend of his who was "enjoying an adequate medical encounter"—or was, to make short shrift of it, undergoing psychoanalysis. The friend had been graduated from his Alma Mater straight to the office of his God-the-Father figure as naturally as a chemistry major sets out to obtain his Master's next. Marion, not having the wherewithal for his analysis and being of the conviction that group therapy was *déclassé* (not to mention the unsavory types one might become embroiled with in such a circle—after all, one was *supposed* to regard them almost as siblings), Marion, then, had to content himself with saving his money and looking to the future. Certain it is that his darkest horse of a nightmare never presented him with the fact that his analyst would be on the staff of a backward back-wards backwoods booby hatch, that same analyst assuring him with a single smile that he, Marion, was severely deranged.

Close on the heels of his shocking experience, Marion took pains to express himself most rationally whenever he was addressed by his attendant or anyone else. His unprecedented recovery, his virtual leap into lucidity, seemed to him to go maliciously unremarked. He chafed through an endless day until the lordly Mr. Dick came to escort him to Dr. Heall's office for his first session. During the short walk there, Mr. Dick replied in curt monosyllables to Marion's most ardent conversational advances. It was all Marion could do to keep his eyes dry and his voice steady. In the late afternoon sun the grounds of Pawksville were peaceful, patients sat about becalmed as sheep in a nineteenth-century pastoral scene, and the trees guarded secret places of hot black shade, the undersides of their dusty leaves a lustrous amber. The menace that Marion sensed lay in the studied tranquility of the state-hospitalscape. "But it's like Kafka!" he burst out, in spite of all his intentions not to babble.

"Where?" Mr. Dick said. "That another state hospital you been in?"

"Oh no!" Marion cried with wild good cheer. "No, I've never been committed before. No, Kafka, Mr. Dick, is. No. Well. Let it go."

Dr. Dick grunted with his customary disdain, his gaze momentarily held by the fiery rotunda, setting behind the back wards like some horrendous sun as viewed from a planet that had strayed too close. "Pretty, huh," Mr. Dick commented in the same tone he would have employed to remark that Armageddon was a fair-to-middlin' scrap. Convoying Marion through a door, he led him under the rotunda, skirting the dreary fountain. Inside, the galleries were deserted and everything, even the motionless air, appeared to be tinted a dirty orange.

His apprehension deepening, Marion whispered (one simply did in the rotunda, it was that kind of a place), "That was a nice fountain."

Mr. Dick looked at him as if he had made some mention of his teddy bear.

Leaving the rotunda, a brief walk brought the pair to the office of Dr. Heall. A single glimpse of the room was enough to proclaim Dr. Heall's theory of psychoanalytical decor. The analyst's office should be pleasing, soothing, but not furnished with such distinction as to be distracting to the analysand. To this end the Venetian blinds were slanted against the hot glare of the August afternoon, and on the beige walls were a pair of oils of the Pawksville landscape, painted during a rainy spell in occupational therapy by a manic-depressive, since departed.

Dr. Heall's desk was properly imposing, placed in front of some bookcases, so that he sat with his balding head and glossy cheeks framed by the works from everyone from Mesmer to Reik (whose name Sonny did not know how to pronounce, and was called one day *Rike, Reek* on the next). The Couch had been reupholstered in some synthetic—one hoped it was synthetic, otherwise it was inexplicably but compellingly reminiscent of tanned human skin—and was set on such short legs that the analysand could not but feel he was operating on a very low level indeed. To Marion's right, as he entered, was a bookcase containing a number of ledgers, their spines neatly lettered. Dr. Heall looked up in greeting, his fleshy face wreathed in a reassuring smile.

There is absolutely nothing surrealistic about all this, Marion told himself sharply; he had to refuse to notice that the word ERSKINE on the spine of one of the ledgers had run and, furthermore, that Mr. Dick was receding with great hauteur, rather than departing, through the door. So rapidly had Marion become accustomed to being locked in that he waited for the sound of Mr. Dick's key. When no such sound was forthcoming, he felt weirdly insecure.

"Well, how are you feeling?" Dr. Heall asked.

"Doctor—Doctor Heall, I'm in a perfect state of health. And a perfect frame of mind. I mean state of mind! I mean, my mind is exactly as it should be. What I'm trying to say is that my mental outlook, no, not my outlook, my general outlook, my——"

"Wouldn't you like to sit down?" Dr. Heall asked— meaning "Wouldn't you like to calm down?"

A compact young man, Marion had never before felt so ungainly. "Why, that's very nice of you, Doctor." He was within a foot of the desk before he saw that no chair was provided for him. There were two chairs in the corner, but unless he and Doctor Heall were to shout at one another. . . . With a thrill of premonition, Marion awkwardly sat himself on the couch. "It's awfully kind of you, Doctor Heall, to give me this—uh—interview," Marion announced.

"Hmmm?" Dr. Heall murmured in a way that fell un- pleasantly on the ear, its avuncular, even folksy tone not- withstanding.

Marion grinned winningly. "I guess I might as well spit it out. What I came to say. If you haven't caught on. . . . Well, even if there is still some doubt in your mind, I don't think I could keep up the masquerade much longer. You doctors are too hep to be taken in for long."

"Hmmm?"

"Yes. I'm not going to make a Walrus Hour out of this interview, Doctor. You know, the time has come, the Wal—" Dr. Heall's eyes were fastened on Marion's hands, of which, the fist of one was pounding into the palm of the other. Horrified at the aggressiveness of this new kinesthetic arabesque, Marion was hard put not to sit on the offending paws. Slowly Dr. Heall raised his twinkly green eyes, "Hmmm?"

Marion crossed his arms over his chest. After a deep breath he proclaimed to a volume of Horney in the library to the left of Dr. Heall's ear. "It was really foolish of Mr. Ellis and myself to think we could hoodwink practicing psychiatrists. And cheeky on my part. I really mean that, Doctor. You realize, of course, that I'm not in the least in- sane. In view of the fact that my conduct at Staff Meeting, as opposed to what it is now, you understand. I'm trying to say this too fast; I'm getting ahead of myself," Marion said, braking what threatened to become headlong gabblement. "The truth of the matter is that I don't belong at Pawksville, and should never have come. Whatever my private reasons were. And at the time I thought they were perfectly valid. You see, I had myself committed deliberately. For a particular purpose. I guess that's what they all say when——" He broke off to laugh in croaking horror at what his tongue was doing to him. "I'll just get down to business," he took up, rattled. "You don't want me to lie *down* on this couch, do you?" he put in parenthetically, as if he were two people, each vying for Dr. Heall's attention.

"Hmmm," Dr. Heall breathed, a touch chilly.

As compromise, Marion leaned over and rested on an elbow. He encountered at once Dr. Heall's smiling scrutiny. "Doctor, you can verify everything I'm going to tell you. Just write to Mr. Elliott Ellis of *Gadfly* Magazine, New York; the address is. . . ."

Dr. Heall sat immobile, his hands folded on the desk before him.

"My God, Doctor, this is the truth! I came here only to get in contact with another patient. I had myself put here for that reason alone. You see, the intellectual world is in a froth about this other patient. It's vital that *Gadfly* determine whether he's actually insane, or only here for—uh —asylum. You see? Until such time as a certain ill-advised— ah—occurrence has been forgotten. I'm sure you know who I mean," Marion pressed meaningfully.

"Hmmm?" Dr. Heall wanted to know noncommittally.

"Well, of cour—— Don't tell me Pawksville has more than one patient of world-wide renown! I just don't want to have to call a spade a spade unless I have to. This is a very delicate matter, and it's bad enough as it is. The last thing Mr. Ellis would have me do would be to call down a scandal on our heads. *All* our heads." Marion drew himself up short. He was not cleaving unto the point—namely that he get

himself out of Pawksville before Dr. Heall turned up the
ward again to give him, Marion, that Treatment. "Doctor,
I was *coached* to be a hebephrenic in New York. I know I
sound paranoid, but this is the gospel truth. Look at it this
way. If I was hebephrenic in Staff Meeting, how come I'm
suddenly paranoid now? Surely I don't have to tell you,
Doctor Heall, that the truly insane don't jump from category to category like that, do they? I mean, *do* they?"

"Hmmm," Dr. Heall disagreed not very helpfully.

Marion hung his head, then chanced another look into
the tincture-green-soap gaze. Dr. Heall's eyes were so small,
set deep in his wealth of cheek, that he appeared ever to be
peeking out at one.

"I guess I'll have to take your word on that, won't I?"
Marion either laughed or sobbed, he could not have said
which. Intending to resume soberly, he heard himself en-
treating, "Doctor, if you won't take down Mr. Ellis' address,
how about contacting the people who brought me here? The
ones we paid to pretend they were my parents. I'm sure if
they were to be confronted with the truth, I mean, that the
jig's up, and promised them, of course, that they wouldn't
be prosecuted if they admitted their part in the—— Doctor,
if I were to tell them right in front of *you* that I *wanted*
them to admit the *truth*—" Another glance at Dr. Heall's
prudently blank expression and Marion fell supine with a
groan. "So they double-crossed me," he whispered. "Cooked
up a story for just this contingency. Set it up so that even if
I told the truth about their not being my parents, it would
sound like a delusion. That's what the insane do all the time,
isn't it, deny their wives, or their relatives?" Marion wailed
and flopped about. "That's exactly what they did, told you
not to be surprised if I said they were complete strangers
to me. But they are! I swear to you, that until last week—"

Dr. Heall delivered himself of a sympathetic "Hmmm."

"Doctor Heall, I'm not crazy!" Marion screamed, shooting up.

Dr. Heall rose and came round the desk. Passing the

fist-into-palm-pounding Marion with a comforting smile, he went to the far bookcase, selected a new ledger, passed Marion again with the selfsame smile, and reseated himself.

Marion's face temporarily sought the refuge of his hands. "All right," dribbled from between his fingers, "let's suppose for the sake of argument, that my story about Mr. Ellis and those people is a fabrication. A delusion, if you will. I agree. It was a delusion, and I held it firmly until that Treatment this morning. But I don't have it any more. I'm all free of it now. I mean, you've been so patient, so empathic, that just being able to talk to you, like this, I mean, has done me more good than a hundred of those Treatments. . . ." Marion peered, heart in his mouth, at Dr. Heall.

"Hmmm," said Dr. Heall, considering this offer like a shrewd old horse-trader. He stood the ledger on its edge, spine uppermost. Then, with great care, he uncapped his pen and began lettering the spine.

Forgetful of his solemn duty to *Gadfly,* Marion strove to consolidate his gain. "I know you're fearfully busy, Doctor Heall, but if you could just spare me a few more minutes——" He lifted his head and saw then that Dr. Heall was done with the capital *P* and was at work on the *I.* The *I* done, he pursed his mouth, judging how large the *E* should be.

Now, slowly, inexorably, Marion's eyes went to the far bookcase. The fresh unnamed ledgers, the used ones, and those worn from months, years of handling, their names fading, almost illegible. . . .

"I came to Pawksville to meet Titus Graham," Marion bleated. "He's that poet you have locked up here. I can prove this! Titus Graham! Doesn't that bear out part of what I've been saying?"

Dr. Heall looked over in open disapproval. "Hmmm." He held the pen poised over the spine of the ledger.

It came to Marion then that one of them in the room must surely be a madman. The very position of that pen,

arrested in the act of inscribing his name, spoke to him of
many more Treatments before he might find himself in this
office again. Without a sound Marion laid his length full on
the couch. He was dealing with a slippery egomaniac who,
with a single murmured "Hmmm" could cast such doubt on
solid fact that it took on all the aspects of fantasy. With a
chill, Marion recalled that there was a patient on his ward
who had set forth in great detail that he was an agent of
the FBI gathering information on Communist infiltration
in state hospitals. In its essentials that deluded creature's
story was no sillier than Marion's, for Communism existed
no less surely than did Titus Graham. On hearing his fellow
patient's glib tale, Marion had brought to bear all his
popular-magazine psychoanalytical-article knowledge and had
come up with the handy explanation that his fellow ward-
mate was insane, did know he was incarcerated in a mental
institution, and had concocted his FBI "scheme" to stifle
the opposition of the reluctant id, this at the instance of
the dutiful super-ego. Accordingly, Dr. Heall was probably
of a similar opinion about Marion. That he, being of the
literary world, had seized upon Titus Graham as his ego-
saving device, assuring himself that he was not insane even
as he was benefiting from hospitalization. Viewing his plight
in this light, Marion was suddenly convinced he knew exactly
what Dr. Heall was thinking.

Dr. Heall's pen scratched busily as a furtive tear slid across
Marion's cheek into his ear, where it burned like a single
drop of henbane. No matter what I say about Titus Graham
or Mr. Ellis, Marion told himself in despair, that—that
paranoid playing with his ledgers will take it as corroborative
data to support his particular theoretical framework, whatever *that* happens to be. There was no question here of
elimination *versus* illumination; he, Marion, had damn well
better pretend to give up his delusion about Titus Graham,
and damn quick or—

"Hmmm?" Dr. Heall prompted cozily.

"I dreamed," Marion began, resigned, "that I was poor old Haydn. It was kind of a confused dream. . . ."

Dr. Heall interposed helpfully, "Hmmm?" He smiled down on the name *Pierce* on the spine, then laid the ledger flat. He first opened the front cover and pressed it to the desk top, then repeated the operation with the back. Next he opened the pages to the middle and pressed them, proceeded to the last quarter of the pages, and finally the first, thus softening the spine and preventing it from cracking during extended use. This time his "Hmmm'" was sharply prodding.

"Well, you see, Doctor Heall, after Haydn died, a bunch of crazy phrenologists stole his head. I mean it. Swiped his skull. And for years those poor bones, that violated skeleton languished. . . ."

"Hmmm!" Dr. Heall said as warning that Marion was going too fast, and that Dr. Heall wanted to get all this written down.

"And for all I know, Haydn hasn't got his head back yet," Marion maundered on. "I just happened to dream about it, that's all." Think of something else, he begged himself. Offer up anything in propitiation. Gift-wrap it. Be an annalist of your life and times for this unspeakable analyst. Just keep feeding his ravening curiosity, and keep his mind off that Treatment. Time enough later to start planning for my escape. Speak up! Of ships and shoes and sealing— "And then . . . there was this—walrus. He . . . uh . . . was eating oysters. . . ."

Dr. Heall's fountain pen raced. "Hmmm?" said that twinkling tyrant, Dr. Heall.

When Marion's first hour was over, Sonny stood at his office window, smoking and pondering deeply. This had been his first attempt to exercise his own version of client-centered therapy, in which the therapist lent only nonverbal encouragement, while the patient did all the talking, spilling his—— Sonny collected himself. Unbridled, his thoughts were apt to be couched in loose terms or slang; thus he now speedily lapsed into his favorite mental-labor-saving device —jargon. It was with only a tremendous amount of will, he thought, that he had restrained himself from what usually amounted to the psychic enema of the first analytical session. Young Pierce had freed himself of his delusion beautifully, once he had gone beyond the optimal frustration level. And there, Sonny thought, lies the secret! I'm done with this Menninger pampering of the analysand. Shooting the patient a little libido every time he bogs down. That's where I failed with Leslie Erskine. (Except that I didn't fail, of course. Freud himself wouldn't have been able to cope with a patient suffering from hysterical mutism.) Not that Pierce doesn't have a long way to go. Still, with such a splendid beginning, it would be interesting to see how far we could advance without further physical therapy. I think I'll take him off of Metrazol completely and forget to mention it to Nick. I can just see his face some day when he's lecturing at the top of his voice about chemotherapy being the coming thing in psychiatry, and I trot out Pierce for him in Staff Meeting. Show him a schizzy cured through psychoanalysis alone! Nick once told me to make the castration complex my stomping ground. Very well, he asked for it. This Marion Pierce is made to order. The Oedipal situation that caused his break is already half-conceptualized. Anamnestic experiences must have been excessively traumatic, no wonder strong castration complex. . . .

Sonny smoked, his whole career beginning to re-form around Marion Pierce. Lying there, Sonny thought, and telling me he dreamed someone had stolen his head. Well, that's a castration complex for you. His father took his genitality *and* his sanity from him. Classic. By God, I can, I *will* do it! I'll snap him out of it in no more than three years, and then I'll ram him straight down Nick Bartholomew's all-knowing throat! Fired with ambition, Sonny tossed his cigarette out the window.

The Holy Dove, resting during her daily walk, sat on a bench with her hands palms up in her lap. Suddenly a lighted cigarette fell from heaven into her left hand. The pain was exquisite, the Holy Dove biting her lips to keep from crying out at this new humiliation of the flesh, until at last the fire burned itself out. The Holy Dove rose, the way before her long and hard.

13

Father Muldroon's Tale

In earlier times Father Aloysius Muldroon might have changed the course of history; upsetting thrones would have been second nature to him. Nick Bartholomew's senior by a few years, the two were well matched, notwithstanding the fact that Nick frequently proposed and Father Muldroon promptly disposed. As the priest's own parish was small and he found ample time on his hands, it was only natural that long since he had become a unique figure on the Pawksville scene. True, he had patients to visit, and he celebrated Mass in an unusually charming little chapel room in the Annex (when Father took a fancy to a certain crucifix or expensive candlesticks, some member of Father's flock somehow found himself shelling out the money); and should the question arise of terminating the pregnancy of a Catholic patient, Father was on the spot, implacable in his wrath and driving Nick Bartholomew half out of his mind. Barring such emergencies, Father conducted himself like nothing so much as the nuncio to some obscure little duchy.

He had a flair, then, all his own, best typified by the manner in which he arrived for one of his innumerable visits. Screeching his tires past the main gates, he would speed hell for leather straight up the rotunda drive until, almost past the parking site he had chosen for himself, he burned rubber for twenty feet, announcing to all within earshot that he was come, shot backward for ten feet and permitted his shaken Ford to collect itself while he, all urbanity, prepared to mix deeper into the murky doings of Pawksville. From the rotunda he screeched to the Annex and thence streaked to the Hospital. Because of such treatment, he had had a succession of Fords, each one more neurotic than its predecessor, and Pawksville permitted itself its one exception to the rule of *verboten* words indicating psychosis by remarking, to a man, "That Father Muldroon drives like a maniac."

On one such afternoon, Jane Carmody was in conference with an excited Billie Noon when Father came hotrodding it toward the rotunda parking circle. Jane consulted her watch, wishing to be in the Hospital lab by the time Father was done in the Annex. Still, there was an important matter to hand. Namely, the burned hand of the Holy Dove.

"I don't know how she did it," Billie Noon, said for the fifth time, almost tearfully. "The Holy Dee never smokes. And I can't get a thing out of her."

"Well, if she doesn't keep that hand out of filthy water, it's going to be a quagmire of just about any infection you want to name," Jane said. "I'm relying on you, Miss Noon, to watch her like a hawk. See to it she keeps that splint on for several days, and give the penicillin ointment a chance to work. I'll talk to the night attendant about it, as well as writing an order—"

"I can't," Miss Noon fretted, "for the life of me figure out what happened. Coming back here, calm as you please, and I just *happened* to see—"

"Miss Noon, the Holy Dove is insane. You simply have to expect bizarre behavior out of her occasionally."

Miss Noon flexed her biceps sadly, "Yeah . . . I kinda forget that."

Jane was bemused with Miss Noon's forgetfulness

throughout her walk back to the lab. Noble as Shakespearian love, Miss Noon's friendship did not choose to alter where it alteration found. Passing the Morgue House to her right, Jane would have sought the coolness of her little apartment —it was her afternoon off—but for the imminent arrival of Father Muldroon, who would have visited Sean in the meantime. Once in the lab, Jane began a desultory running of some urinanalyses, thinking: Ah, but I don't go along with Shakespeare, I would alter Sean, and if I'd had two brain cells to rub together I would have noticed the heralds of his coming break. Did he really have to stack all his music in the Steinway and set it afire before I caught on? She turned on the radio next the microtome—she was always turning on radios wherever she was—and then ignored it as it squawked to itself of Schubert.

She was smoking, idly remarking the important progress of a cockroach on its way down the sink drain, when Father Muldroon, armed with an umbrella, suddenly stood in the doorway announcing his presence loudly. "Hot enough for you, Doctor?"

"Come in, come in. Unless—" Jane warned "—you come here to make things hotter, Father."

As he was well on his way to his customary lab stool, he merely nodded imperturbably, seated himself, determined the degree of gloom into which she seemed plunged this day, nodded again (this time in confirmation of some prior expectancy, and, another expectancy presenting itself to his mind, looked pointedly at the lab refrigerator. "Why is it," he asked pleasantly, "that when I show up, everybody immediately presumes I'm here to raise hell? I work to beat hell, admittedly, but that's something else again . . ." He permitted himself to dwindle off, and, master of the bag of tricks that he was, looked at Jane pointedly, the very picture of red-faced thirst.

Jane twisted on her stool. "Would you like a glass of iced tea, Father?"

"I would not."

Jane laid her cigarette in a Petrie dish, lifted a test tube from the rack and swished the contents in the flame of the Bunsen burner, then put the tube back. "A Coke, Father?"

"Are you toying with me?" Father Muldroon demanded heatedly.

A rare lightheartedness wafted over Jane, like a fresh breeze promising rain. She knew herself to be grinning; the expression felt almost therapeutic for a mouth usually held in restraint. "I wonder, then, if I might tempt you with some Chablis? I just happen to have—"

"Sure'n and I'd laid me life down you did," Father said, the bogus Irish accent laid on with his light touch.

Jane went to the refrigerator, removed a flask labeled *Acetic Acid,* then took down two clean 500-cc. beakers from the shelf, set them in front of Father on the lab table, re-seated herself and, unstoppering the flask, murmured, "Say when, Father."

Father Muldroon sat examining carefully the rack of tubes, the cluttered desk, glanced briefly to a rainbow cast by the sprinkler on the lawn outside, and finally at Jane's brave smile. When his beaker was full he spoke politely. "When." He waited for Jane to serve herself.

She poured four fingers of wine into her own beaker.

"I'm a fist man myself," Father informed her, and demonstrated by wrapping his great hand around the beaker so that only the rim and lip showed. "Your health, Doctor."

"And yours, Father."

They drank and then Jane got out a clean Petrie dish for Father in case he should want to light a cigar. Performing these little tasks of the hostess, Jane reflected that there were times when she and Father had a way with each other—the way being that of two canny diplomats met to discuss a *casus belli* over a bottle and a bird. His very demeanor today, that of the harmless thirsty Irishman, not to mention what he must have conceived of as being a master stroke—his toting about under the blistering sun the black umbrella of a bumbling parson—suddenly lessened her lightheartedness, putting her on guard. Indicating the umbrella, she inquired innocently, "Do you think it will rain?"

"Has to. I washed and polished my Ford this morning. I'm expecting a cloudburst. The drought is at an end. Hence the bumbershoot." His tone was easy. He held his wine to the light. "The essence of a chill spring dawn, wouldn't you say?"

When Father Muldroon took meandering turns in his conversation, Jane knew mischief was afoot. "I would say so," she agreed levelly.

"High in the Urals. Wouldn't you say high in the Ural Mountains, Doctor?"

"I'll turn polished phrases like cartwheels for you, Father, if it will help you come to the point."

"Ah. I fear I was free-associating a trifle. Bear with me." He took out his cigar case and made a selection, a prissy habit of cigar-smokers which confounded Jane as one cigar of a brand was to her mind exactly like the next. He took the Bunsen burner and rolled his smoke carefully, lighting it evenly all round. He released a gust of smoke from his mouth and studied the tip. "Oh, I've just come from Sean."

"Yes," Jane said. She looked at Father so openly that he was forced to return her steady regard. "How did you find him?" There was no levity in her voice, for the probing gaze of Father Muldroon could conceivably discover what even Nick Bartholomew had overlooked.

Father Muldroon said thoughtfully, "I did not find him exactly—tempestuous, Doctor."

"Catatonics rarely are. Unless, of course, they are in an excitement."

"That's so," Father said, nodding. "Also, he pretended not to know me."

"Nonsense," Jane said sharply. "He *doesn't* know you. He walked past me the other day—closer than you and I are

now—and there was not a sign of recognition. That's hardly
pretense, Father!"

Father shrugged. "He looked directly at me. In his eyes
I read recognition. Grudging recognition."

Jane seized the moment. "What were you saying to him?
Talking about me?"

"No." Father smoked at his leisure. "I was giving him
hail Columbia for turning his back on life."

"You were!"

"I don't hold with all this Freudian claptrap, need I say.
This 'recognize that we are all beasts' and then conduct ourselves in as beastly a manner as possible. That's Sean's
trouble. Some psychologist or other filled his head with such
swill. And then when he acted on it—"

"How acted on it? Father, whatever Sean might have
done in his sickness, which I suppose, could include marrying
me, a Protestant—"

Father Muldroon had himself some more wine. "I am
Sean's confessor, not his doctor. But if you will control your-
self, Doctor, I will tell you that the sins I'm referring to
have nothing to do with your marriage. Sean knows his sins.
But he must be convinced that catatonia is not sanctuary.
Sooner or later he will be held accountable for them. I
merely suggested that he straighten up and face them now.
He heard me, too."

"Father, I don't—I can't—believe in a word you are
saying. I'm not disputing your jurisdiction over Sean's soul,
but you take too much upon yourself when you—you—tor-
ment a sick man——"

"The worthy Doctor Bartholomew tells me he wishes to
put Sean on Metrazol," Father said smoothly. "A treatment
calculated to hurtle him into reality with terrifying force.
Yet you have the courage to accept that for him."

"He is deteriorating," Jane said, embattled, and turned
her head away. The radio was chuckling a snatch of Schumann now, and she tightened her fingers about her beaker.
"He's not responding to insulin."

"He appears to be no worse than a week or so ago,"
Father argued.

"Lack of improvement in and of itself is a sign of deter-
ior—" Jane rubbed her forehead. "Father. Father, you've
heard Sean play. Did you ever hear him do that Schumann
Sonata . . . in G Minor, I think it is?"

"I may have," Father admitted cautiously.

"In that Sonata—— Well, Schumann was rather a wag. A
nut in his own right, I suppose. So in the Sonata he indicated
the tempo to be *prestissimo possibile*—as fast as possible. But
later on Schumann is after the pianist to play even faster. And
he winds up demanding 'Faster than that.' I've one of Sean's
private records playing the Sonata lickety-split. It's headlong
. . . pell-mell. . . . It's the way Sean goes at anything. Including schizophrenia. *Prestissimo possible*. And faster than that.
So. . . . Let's not talk about his grudging recognition of you,
Father, or his appearing to be no worse than he did a couple
of weeks ago." She lit a cigarette fiercely, almost singeing
her eyelashes in the flame of the burner. "More wine?"

Father Muldroon thought that that would be nice. "I
saw," he said suavely, "his parents last week."

Jane set the flask down hard. "And?"

"They want to take Sean out of Pawksville."

"Is everyone in that family insane? Take Sean— No, absolutely no. He's got one last chance and that's taking his
lumps from Nick Bartholomew!"

"They signed the commitment papers," Father reminded her softly. "They have the say as to what treatment
he gets, and where he gets it. And if, as you say, he's not
getting better here, maybe you should go home with him.
They're perfectly willing to hire a male nurse to help you."

"I ought to do it," Jane said grimly. "I ought to take
him home, and then invite his mother up for a front seat
when I give him Metrazol. His father could ride-a-fat-horse-
to-Banbury-Cross on Sean's legs while he convulses. Maybe
then, those—" She jabbed out her cigarette in the Petrie
dish. "Listen, Father Muldroon, you take them this little

message from me. They had their turn. I've never raised anything like the hell I should have when I learned of the
scummy trick they played on me. Sean was entering his
fourth break—he was actually in a violent state—before
Mummy so much as hinted to me of 'nervous breakdowns.'
Before then, any moodiness or withdrawal was simply 'artistic
temperament,' and wouldn't I kindly recognize it and respect
it. Not one word of the fact that Sean was chronically schizophrenic did they ever breathe to me. And after all that,
I made a deal with them. They put Sean here and I'd give
up my residency and follow. I'm not pointing myself out as a
marvel of wifely devotion, Father; I married him because I
loved him, and because I was dazzled by his charm and his
talent and his money. I didn't stop once to wonder why they
welcomed Plain Jane into the family with open arms. That
was my fault, not theirs. But now we're doing it my way.
They try taking Sean out of here and I'm going to court!
And Nick will back me up to the hilt. They sanctioned our
marriage only because I'm a doctor. Okay, now I've got some
mighty bitter pills for them. They make one move in Sean's
direction, and they'll never set eyes on him again. I'm his
wife, and I have the legal right to say where and how he
should be treated. Not they! You got that Father? Then
have some more wine." Jane swept out a hand as if to table
any and all suggestions, comments, counterproposals, or com-
promises Father might venture.

"Ahem," Father said with deliberate mildness. "That
does seem to cover it, Doctor. Remind me to brush up on
my pastoral psychology. I seem to have slipped up somewhere." Again he raised his beaker to the light. As if they had
done nothing but gossip, cozy as two cronies, he murmured,
"This raising a glass of wine has almost become an 'activity
mannerism' on my part, wouldn't you say, Doctor?"

Jane summoned a hospitable smile. "Tut, Father, jargon-
izing. Have you been talking to Sonny Heall?"

"No. Doing a bit of reading. I read where a psychiatrist

set himself to talking a catatonic out of a stupor. Did it too.
Took him something like twelve hours, as a I remember.
He was hoarse at the end. But before he quit the patient an-
swered him. Lucidly."

"Drivel," Jane blurted. "Sorry, Father, for some reason
I'm touchy today." She cast about for some graceful topic
on which they might end what had threatened to become
a pitched battle. "Will your parish be having a booth at the
Jubilee?"

"Certainly." He dusted the ash of his cigar delicately
along the rim of the Petrie dish. "The good ladies and I have
decided to sell cricket watches to the credulous relatives and
members of the Governor's entourage. Of all people, I will
be there. I promulgated the Jubilee, didn't you know that?
My, yes. . . . Years ago. When I was by way of being the
Pawksville antiquarian. You see, my parish once wanted
to hold a bazaar and raffle off a few items. Furniture, watches,
the like. But the rest of the local citizenry yelled 'gambling.'
Naturally—" Father went on lazily "—I had to skin my cat
some other way. The Pawks Boys Jubilee on the lawns of the
hospital served nicely. Would you care to hear the nerve-
tingling, shattering, heartbreaking story of those two brave
lads, the Pawks brothers?"

"Father, whenever you start playing the genial old
windbag, I know you're up to devilment. Let's have it; I'm
avid."

"Legend has it," began Father, savoring his delicious
anecdotal tone, "a legend fostered, to be explicit, by the
Pawks family and tributaries and other brackish branches of
same, that the Pawks brothers, twins, had set out together
from Belle Isle, the family plantation, to fight under the
Stars and Bars. They kissed Sister Lululu on the forehead,
Mater on the cheek, and wrung the Gov'nor's hand in farewell.

"Having then won First Manassas, among other battles
too numerous to mention, single-handed, they received fur-

loughs. Nearing the beloved acres of dear Belle Isle, they were warned of a platoon of drunken Union soldiers camped nearby. (This is confusing, but then, it was a confused war.) So, in the dark of night, stained with walnut juice to look like darkies, or Nigras, if you will, the Pawks boys—I did mention they were twins? I thought I had—embarked on what sounds surprisingly like a Commando raid against the hapless Union lads. With knife and garrote they killed the sentries, wounded two more soldiers, and killed the rest. Then, dressed in the uniforms of the fallen Yankees, the Pawks boys bethought themselves to take similar groups by surprise and finish them off. (At eighteen they were enterprising, you must grant them that. Their combined IQs, however, probably wouldn't total— Well, that's neither here nor there.) First off, though, they had to return the horses to the plantation. Someone, it seems, had stolen them. Namely, the Union soldiers had, come to think of it.

"They approached beloved old Belle Isle in the dawning. Nut-juice-stained and mounted on spirited Beau and Orion, the mighty hunter—"

"Orion? Somehow I doubt that," Jane muttered.

"—the mighty hunter, Orion, they neared the colonnaded front po'ch. Unfortunately, Sister Lululu (pronounced Lew-looloo) chose at that moment to stick her golden curls out the upper window to view the dawn. What she sighted instead was a pair of *black* Union soldiers, riding up on Beau and Nimrod, the mighty——"

"That's better. I was beginning to think it was nothing but a preposterous lie," Jane said, triumphant.

"Orion had gone lame," Father snapped. "So they saddled up Nimrod next. They had more than one hunter at Belle Isle, let me tell you.

"Seeing the invading soldiers, Lululu got a gun, drew a bead, and shot her brothers dead. The story is not ended. Close on the heels of the brothers, now slain, their precious blood enriching forever the earth (now the rotunda parking circle), came a trio of real Union soldiers. Seeing what they took for their own kind dead, they rode their horses straight up the colonnaded po'ch and into the great Hall, Lululu having run out of ammunition in the meanwhile. But Faithful Sam, huge, black, and himself born in a cabin not a hundred yawds from the Big House, had heard the shots and come belatedly to the rescue. He stopped in the dawning to weep on the bodies of the Pawks brothers; he, a year older, had always loved them as if they were his own brothers—the which, come to think of it, they were—and had gone to the University of Virginia with them as their valet and could as a consequence converse fluently in Greek—and still weeping, Faithful Sam gained the po'ch just in time to receive a screaming Lululu, who he promptly put behind his back in time to accept into his own breast the shot meant to end her life. Inside, under the crystal chandelier, Massa and Missy lay dead. Then the soldiers fired Belle Isle, and left it a smoldering ruin. Only Lululu escaped to tell the tale of woe before dying.

"Being the father of the Pawks Boys Jubilee," Father interrupted himself in a modest aside, "I must stand ready to substantiate these facts which I have just related, and to which my research led me."

"You don't grace a pulpit for nothing, do you?" Jane submitted.

"There once stood a plantation house on the very site of the rotunda. That it was called Belle Isle stands to reason. Every so often, Doctor, after a particularly wet autumn, the water is no longer carried off, and Pawksville is something of a marsh. Except, of course, the ground on which the rotunda is situated, which is, you may have noticed, on a slight rise. Can't you just see Belle Isle with its columns rising through the mists and the marsh like a dream?"

"Not to mention the mists and rather swampy family history it had to rise above too," Jane said. "Tell me about the real Pawks family, now, Father."

"Why," Father said blandly, "as far as I can ascertain a man named Pawks entered this county around eighteen sixty-six, coming from parts unknown. He presented to what passed for the courts then a deed for all the land hereabouts and demanded a declaratory judgment of quitclaim against all and sundry with claims to the contrary. He said he had inherited the property from some dead cousins. He then unpacked his carpetbag and settled down. Naturally, since the land proved to be a disappointment, his heirs sold it to some reform administration or other."

"And you told that outrageous fable to the present Pawks family so they'd help you throw your church bazaar on the grounds here?"

"I may have hinted at it," Father conceded. "Purely in jest, may I add."

"Yes, but—" Jane poured the last of the wine into Father's beaker "—how did you dispose of Lululu? You didn't say what happened to her."

"Heart failure."

"Heart——?"

"I hadn't the heart to go on with it," Father explained, gazing into the pale gold depth of his wine. He drank it off, looked expectantly at the refrigerator door, then returned to Jane. "I must be off," he said with finality when it appeared the wine supply was exhausted. "Would you care to reconsider the offer to take Sean home?"

"I would not. No and no and no. I could go on from there, but out of respect for your cloth I'll save the intemperate outburst. Tell them this, though: one more bright idea like that, and I'll see to it that Nick cuts off their visiting privileges. Incidentally—and this is not for Maginnis ears, Father—I should have gotten a whiff of what was in the woodpile the other day. Nick and I almost came to blows over putting Sean on Metrazol. He set me straight just the way I did you this afternoon."

"Well," Father said. "That's it." He caught up his um-

brella, looked past her to the window framing the cloudless
sky, said, "I'd better hurry along if I don't want to get
drenched," and rose, sober and suddenly sober of mien, with
a thousand cubic centimeters of wine in him. "You both have
my prayers . . . Jane." He saluted her. "See you at the Jubilee,
Doctor."

Father Muldroon was gone; outside in the still afternoon
the Ford roared at his urging and sped along the curving
driveways of Pawksville, tires wailing. Then all was still.
Jane turned off the Bunsen burner, rinsed the Petrie dishes
of ashes, forgot as usual to turn off the little radio, and entertained thoughts of a long tepid soak in her tub.

Locking the lab behind her, she went along the corridor,
past the clinic, past the room where she did her weekly GYN
examinations and performed such treatments as those examinations might show were required, and came to the outside door. However she braced herself, the blast of the afternoon sun always struck her anew. Off in the distance she saw
patients in the watermelon patch, tenderly at their horticul-
ture for the coming feast, while scant yards to her left an
attendant and more patients were fussing with a recalcitrant
sprinkler. Standing quietly under a shade tree where the
attendant had left him, and with that perfect submissive-
ness of the catatonic, was Sean Maginnis. Unnoticed, Jane
joined him. "Come with me, Sean," she said quietly, putting
her hand over his. "I want to talk to you."

She led him, lifeless and shuffling, around the treetrunk
and out of sight. When they came to the Morgue House, she
unlocked the front door and pushed him inside. Again he
stood with the infinite patience of the catatonic until she
locked the door behind them and pushed him ahead of her
up the stair.

In her cool living room with his records everywhere
and the hi-fi, Jane brought them to a pause just inside the
door. She inspected him sadly. The last of the sunburn was

peeling and his lips were cracked. His eyes were riveted straight ahead, the expanded pupils giving them a soft, lost, velvety appearance. Inches away from his face Jane scanned his thin features. With a fingertip she touched the lips, murmuring, "I'll put a soothing lotion on them for you, darling." She ran the fingertip down the jaw and neck to the pulse-point. Then, overwhelmed by pity for the two of them, she took him into her arms and pressed his head down on her shoulders. Kissing his temple and running her hand along the back of his neck, she held him and promised, "Sean, I'm going to get through to you. I'm going to get through and then I'm going to lead you out. Maybe not all at once, poor baby, but I'll do it. . . ."

She held him, patting and petting him for many moments.

14

The Sockdological Mantrap

The patient who had been granted the privilege of note-book and pencil (the pencil being taken away every night, of course, and returned in the morning with only a regulation state-hospital sneer), had not been idle. There was much of interest for any astute observer in Pawksville; and when the doings of others palled, introspection drove the pencil across line after line. Some of the entries could conceivably have won from Sonny Heall that same passionate attention which Babs was devoting to the collected works of O'Hara.

6 July

The fireworks are over, such as they were. In other state hospitals, I am given to understand, the Fourth is the day when everyone except the bedridden and the combative are led outside and fed box lunches and watermelon. This is the annual pandemonium day, with the fireworks contributing no end. We at Pawksville have our Jubilee later on. I've already learned that Southerners consider dates of Confederate importance (to speak loosely of our Jubilee) rightly take precedence over the Fourth, Christmas, and V-Day all rolled into one.

The local wiseacres say that if this dry spell doesn't end soon we are in for a "drout." I always pronounced it as it is spelled—*drought*. In California the word is uncommon, we take it for granted that there won't be so much as a drop of rain for over six straight months of the year. Sometimes I think of California the way some little minion of hell who got caught up in the mighty clash of political bigwigs must recall heaven.

Yet what could I say of my childhood that would command the interest of the most exacting of sociologists? My parents were average, he an attorney, she ineffectual but well-meaning. I was an only child. I fell in and out of puppy love as the young will, but nothing came of it. I had followed my father into the law, and had to take over his rather chaotic practice when he fell dead. Law school and my father's scrambled affairs sufficed to keep me out of the lists of love.

Until Mitzi. She came to me for a divorce, her jaw set, her eyes uncertain. (Shifty, I thought at the time, but I didn't love her yet.) She's dark and has a liquid melancholy about her when her face is in repose. Her eyes are plum-colored, I swear. Long, long before her divorce was final I was in love with her and joyfully believed she reciprocated. I spent my weekends in her apartment, where she brought me the Sunday papers on my breakfast tray, and fussed about tucking me in as if I were an invalid. But come, chèr Herr Doktor Heall, enough of the minutiae of my love life with Mitzi.

Suddenly she was gone. Gone off to this benighted state (sometimes I could *swear* it was Tennessee) with one of those braw lip-licking tourists who turn up in California to "case the broads" and scoff at innocuously middle-class Hollywood. He left, taking Mitzi with him as casually as a bumpkin toting home a Kewpie Doll from the County Fair. She wrote me a pitiable letter (her spelling was pitiable) asking me to forgive and forget, along with all the other platitudes so at home in my poor Mitzi's mind.

I boarded the first plane in pursuit of her. Once in the glorious community of Briggsburg where I found them, I spied on them. I sat in my rented car and looked up at the windows of the crummy apartment where they were staying. And one night, when I didn't have anything better to do, I went up and knocked on their door, and walked in, and shot him.

From the instant he expired, Mitzi was in her element. There were solicitous policemen, awkward as bears, soothing her hysterics. And there were reporters and sob-sisters camping on her doorstep day and night.

In my cell I sat surrounded by newspapers, all with front page photographs of a prettily weeping Mitzi. Her anguish became her. But that was always part of her charm, that though she was wayward she was never a merry Magdalen.

17 July

I shall never forget our first encounter, Dr. Heall, though you would prefer, I am sure, it be called an interview. I am convinced that when you have one foot in the grave, the other will be firmly planted in your mouth. To give you your due, you did ask me how I felt, and invited me to be seated. You were unable to conceal your chagrin when I *did* seat myself, stalking past The Couch to plump myself in one of the chairs lining the wall. After a moment's agonizing hesitancy on your part, which I enjoyed thoroughly, you conceded the point and brought my chair over to your desk. You offered me a cigarette and I accepted with alacrity. Silently.

"Well," you ventured in a small voice that begged me on its knees not to take offense, "you certainly don't look the type."

A graceful opening, Doctor: mannerly, cultivated, designed to put me at my ease. How rude of me that I sat there stonily smoking, silent for the full thirty or so minutes you blabbered at me, hoping so appealingly to win me over.

Oh, the bonhomie of that sweet half-hour. While you delivered yourself of little quips, and then applauded them with your neurotic nicker, an unspoken flow of epithets passed between us. I had not known the extent of my command of billingsgate, dear Doctor, and your own talent in that direction I am bound to recommend.

Your eyes, I should like to note, are as bright and fixed and glassy as those in your mother's old fur piece.

Allow me to continue, you are staying with this effusion, are you not?

During our second interview (or skirmish) you asked me, like a child wheedling for a sweet, of what I had dreamed the night before. I was not unprepared for this poser; you were unprepared for my answer—or any reply at all. "Unicorns," I said, being laconic and at the same time, for me, garrulously responsive.

"Unicorns?" you echoed, and the falling notes of your voice sprinkled the two of us with an iridescent fountain of insight and delight.

"Unicorns," I assured you solemnly, and smoked. I had spoken.

You were not aware of this. "Tell me, what were the— ah—" you fairly slavered over the question "—unicorns *doing?*"

I repeat, I had spoken. And after a most unrewarding barrage of questions—what were they doing, were they doing it to each other, was I a unicorn, were there any other people in the dream, was it a happy dream, have I ever dreamt of them before, what does a unicorn represent to me, *und so weiter,* you, as I had long minutes before, fell silent.

I wonder how long it was before you, Doctor, looked up unicorns? Did you learn that the lovely mythical beast appears only to virgins? It submits only to the caress of the *virga intacta.* A charming conceit.

Incidentally, though it is infra dig around Pawksville

to employ such expressions, may I pass along to posterity that you are goofy, Doctor Heall?

I weary of this thing. I weary of Pawksville. My sanity is a burden too great for me to bear.

Finis

1 August

Shucks, *malgré moi,* Doc, I am at it again. I have logorrhea. I should write a novel. *Love and Logorrhea.* You know exactly what most people would think that was about. Because that's what *you* think it's about. Look up the word, chum; be outcountenanced.

I had a dream for you. I was prepared to bargain for ground privileges with it. But you graciously ordered them for me without asking anything in return. Well, have I not conducted myself decorously in my stay here? But it is nice to be able to walk under the trees, and to sit in some shady spot and scribble away. Also I am now in a position to observe the cunning staff at their pranks. Is it true sweet old Dr. Ouita has the visual hallucination of seeing (or once having seen) a little boy relieving himself into the rotunda fountain? And who, pray, is that mincing creature with the sulfur mustachios who frequents the Monkey Tree? And why does little Caddy Bartholomew have assignations with him there? I do declare, I seem to be taking an interest in my surroundings.

It is like being let out of solitary to be permitted to sit on this bench and

Approaches now the Holy Dove. Hurrying by with a thrify smile. Never misses a trick, that one. And Dr. Bartholomew and Dr. Carmody leaving clinic, chatting and parting. She's a trim little thing, and he watches her until she disappears.

And you, Dr. Heall, emerging

You stopped to ask me how I felt. I replied with extreme courtesy, not forgetting to thank you for my ground privileges. (Sitting on this journal, you can be damn sure.) You went on your way.

That's a cherubic rear view you have there, Doc.

                                                    7 August
I must remark unkindly on the hospital library. Doesn't anyone check that stuff before putting it on the shelves? Anyone besides Caddy Bartholomew, that is? She reads everything she can lay her hands on, when she isn't scribbling on that clipboard of hers. The gossip is that she resents her aunt, the redoubtable Miss Bartholomew, because the aunt and her mother were never exactly bosom friends. On the other hand, I wonder if Caddy isn't a mite too possessive in her love for her father. Betcha you could unburden yourself of a few million Freudian maxims on that subject, Doc.

Yes you, Sonny. You're cute as a button; I came to that conclusion while strolling through the rotunda on my way back from the library. I had stopped to gaze into the mournful depths of the fountain. Then I heard you, twice-blessed Dr. Heall, 'way up in the top gallery, a little lower than the angels, deep in a whispered discussion with Dr. Parry. I sense you have a disciple there, Sonny. But such talk I never heard! You went from professional patois into pure prattle.

And then, because you had come in from the blazing sun, and the rotunda is damp the year around, you began to sneeze. In the midst of some *clang association* or other (I got that one out of an old text on psychiatry in the library), you threw back your head and went *Id? Id! Id!! Chew!!!*

                                                    15 August
I feel sorry for the poor little Carmody. The grapevine has it her husband is a shoo-in candidate for a back ward.

She and the burly Bartholomew are more and more to be seen together—going about their duties, you may be sure. He feels a *tendresse* for her, I suspect.

I glimpsed the husband standing still as a stork in a flower bed, while the garden detail weeded past him. Hard to believe, but gossip has it that he was climbing the walls when committed. What a creep. Yet dimly I perceive why she married him. I have noticed in my time that many professional women are extraordinarily naïve. They have to spend so much time, in school and later, proving themselves in what are traditionally men's fields that their social lives are about as busy as that of Typhoid Mary. So I can see Carmody going head over teakettle when she bumps into her first exotic artist. Or was he a musician? I must check on that.

Wonder how much psychiatry Bartholomew expects her to learn on the back wards? Or is he subtly letting her see for herself, day in and day out, what her husband might become? So much, so much to ponder. . . .

17 August

Ground privileges or no ground privileges, I am *not* going to while away an hour, any hour, on The Couch, chèr Sigmund Heall. If my silence rattles you so—and it must, as witness the smeared mess you created as you attempted to letter my name on one of your ledgers—why have me sent to your office?

Moreover, I don't dream. Now that's the sum and substance of it. For a while after I was first sent here I must have been slumbrous with shock, for I slept until I had dreamed myself out. I remember being removed from Receiving to Hospital, for I wasn't eating. I could not for the life of me see the purpose of eating, which was what the wily Bartholomew suspected. It was exactly that—eat for the life of me.

18 August

Superintendent Keeney descended from his ivory tower today to prowl the wards. His mission an evil one. He is seeking candidates for psychosurgery, or lobotomies, I believe they are called. At any rate, some part of the brain which has to do with the emotions, as opposed to the intellect, is destroyed. Thus a wildly disturbed patient is rendered tractable and complacent. He can even go home and engage in some form of work that isn't very demanding. This is the bait Keeney holds out to the relatives to get them to sign their consent for the surgery. Once that consent is signed, the die is cast. A visiting surgeon does the dirty work, and Bartholomew (who runs this joint in every other respect) has no say in the matter.

Yet when I think of what I have seen walking past the back wards' porches, of the stench and the horror and the agony, I wonder if Keeney isn't right—even if for the wrong reasons. He isn't interested in relieving a patient of the tortures of insanity, he just wants him out of Pawksville and off the budget.

And I was astounded to learn (I don't know why) that the officious Father Muldroon approves of psychosurgery in certain instances. I guess it is a medical form of rendering unto Caesar. But, oh God, oh God, unless Pawksville unseats my mind to the extent that *I* end up on a back ward, please don't let Superintendent Keeney render *me*.

28 August

Famous last words are not included in my field of interest, or not those attributed to the dying. Those in which I do take an interest are the words which fall on the ear of the expiring.

These morbid reflections are the result of a patient's dying in the night, in the bed three over from mine. I heard —I had never really taken credence in it before—the death rattle.

It happened soon after the lights were out, and the night attendant was just settling down for a long comfy night's sleep in an easy chair dragged from the common room for that purpose. So, early in the night I was awakened by a dry rustle as of leaves disturbed in some bleak autumnal forest. I sat up, alerted, and again came that disturbance; this time it sounded as if something dying threshed about in those leaves and then lay still. I popped out of bed and was on my way down the hall, when the attendant roused and ordered me back to bed forthwith. I protested, and was angrily promised two ounces of paraldehyde, a jacket, and the firm request that Dr. Heall administer EST to me in the morning, if I didn't stop the goddam racket. I am quoting, not paraphrasing.

"Aren't you going to do anything?" I demanded, while the attendant played a flashlight over the face of the corpse.

"Be just as dead in the morning," the compassionate attendant assured me. "No use waking Dr. Heall to come over now."

I was left to the darkness, the dead, and my thoughts. Three beds over, a human being had died to my racket, my alarums, and my indignation. I bethought me of poor Lincoln, attending a performance of *Our American Cousin,* laughing at the line, "You sockdological old mantrap!" just as the bullet entered his head. Yes, the insane dies ignobly, whether he be an involutional melancholiac and President of the United States, or a burnt-out paretic who had caught the venereal disease years ago, in the gaslight era. In a hansom cab, perhaps.

Will I die with some attendant hollering, "Aw shut up! Or are you hankerin' for a big fat jolt in the morning?"

Very likely.

Ah, Mitzi, Mitzi . . . I shot a man to death and shot my life to hell for you, you sockdological mantrap.

I would have ended this day's entry on the above operatic level, but for life's thrusting itself on me from all sides as I sit and scribble in the shade. One would think me buried alive here in Pawksville, but on the contrary I am *in*

medias res. In the very thickest of things. I offer in evidence
this: Unless my eyes deceived me, I just spied the little
Carmody sneaking her husband into the Morgue House with
her. What has the faintly freckled one got up her starched
white jacket sleeve?

I shall sit on here in the shade, unnoticed but watchful.

15

An Isle of Rapture

Jane Carmody's little bedroom–sitting room–hot-plate closet –and–bath apartment was not without its charm. There were white Priscilla curtains at every window, suggesting breezes when there were none, and Jane was of the conviction that the great refrigerator downstairs was what kept the Morgue House cool and livable all summer. In her sitting room, along with all the records and the hi-fi, was a studio couch covered in blue denim and two superb white wicker chairs (provided your taste runs to wicker chairs, picnic hampers, Gibson girls, and the like.) Her coffee table was a hand-carved inlaid work of art some twenty years old. These tables were everywhere in Pawksville, having been fashioned over the years in Occupational Therapy by an epileptic—who always went into a day-long furore after a seizure and then returned to his art refreshed and full of new ideas. (Sonny Heall used one of his inlaid tables as a footrest while he watched television; and Babs' served perfectly as a handrest while applying nail polish, with the result that the intricate design was almost obscured by globs of red lacquer. Caddy Bartholomew had composed the much-maligned *"Ode to a Smokestack"* on one of theirs. And Superintendent Keeney had a collector's item with chairs to match in his library, over which he and visiting politicos smoked cigars, sipped brandy, and played poker.) On her table Jane kept cigarettes, ashtrays, flowers in season, and a portrait of Sean which she brought out each evening after the cleaning-patients had gone.

It would have been hard to say which of the two—the portrait or the subject sitting on the denim couch in front of it—was the more lifeless. Jane had placed him there when she hastened to change out of her whites. She wanted no uniforms or similar signs of the institutional world to obtrude and strengthen Sean's withdrawal. One of his records was playing softly, a practice record the Maginnis family had cut before they got the tape machine.

She glanced out the bathroom window and saw the work detail still undisturbed, its attendant in deep study of what appeared to be a comic book. Some yards away from the Morgue House another patient sat under a tree, bent over a notebook or letter pad, writing busily. No one, then, had noticed her impulsive abduction of Sean.

Coming out of the bath, clad in a fluffy flowered robe from her trousseau, Jane stood in the doorway watching Sean, hoping for some sign of recognition, if not of her, then of himself as his music, his very essence, spilled through the speaker. She had not been able to rid herself of Father Muldroon's contention that Sean could, by great effort, or by an intimate reminder of strong ties, be reached.

He sat exactly as she had placed him, as he would sit until posed somewhere else. This was catatonia, and sometimes prankish attendants had been known to "pose" a patient with one foot in the air, thumbing his nose, and returned, hours later, to find the patient still as stone in the same position. Now, hearing nothing, seeing nothing, Sean stared straight ahead, the insulin-induced impairment of pupillary reflex lending to his usually brilliant gaze an air of melting ardor. Jane came to his side, turning his face to hers, and holding his hands. If Father Muldroon had gotten through to Sean, then she would—with all the patience and means at her disposal. She began to talk to him softly, speaking of her love and her loneliness, tightening her hands over his and raising them to her lips. She invited him in a soft voice to revisit that wet night she had first heard him play. It was his Master's Recital, and she, weary of the cynicism of internes and the tryanny of head nurses and all the routine backstabbing of a great university hospital, was plodding across the campus to the local movie when she passed a door opened for ventilation and, hearing music, looked in, backstage, and saw Sean's red head lifted as he played in his private ecstasy. "And I went in," Jane said. "Don't you remember, Sean? There was only a handful of people there, and I broke your mood when I plopped-plopped in, all the way down to the first row, and you looked down and glowered at me. And I was so—entranced by you that I tossed my wet raincoat on the seat next to me, and—" Jane grinned, tightening her grip on his hands "and your mother—I didn't know who she was then, of course—gave me a look full of murder, and very slowly pulled her wet mashed mink out from under my raincoat. And I didn't even give her a nod of apology! I just kept gawping up at you. When it came time to applaud, I made a spectacle of myself, remember? You smiled down at me, but I made you a bit nervous too. I pounded my hands until they stung. And when it was over I hung around shamelessly, playing the stage-door Jane, until I got to talk to you. Sean, it's all there in your memory, try to think back! Did strangers come in out of the rain every recital and fall in love with you right in front of everybody? I know you and your family thought I was stark staring out of my . . . mind . . ." Jane whispered, and laid her cheek on their clasped hands. "You were so—precisely—beautiful," she said to his knuckles. "I'd never met a painter, or a musician, or anyone like that before. I thought people like you were just the figments of some spinster's imagination. So you were pretty heady stuff for a hen-medic like me. Then when your family invited me to come along to the party at the house—they had to, to all appearances I was preparing to tag along anyway . . ." Jane laughed shakily. "And by popular acclaim, mine, you played just once more for us, and I was so bewitched that tears came to my eyes, and the crystal chandelier overhead seemed to be made entirely of prisms. You played *L'Isle Joyeuse* for me. I'd never heard it before, and I fell in love with it just the way I fell in love with everything else in sound or sight. Dazzled, I suppose I was; or the warm welcome extended to a brazen intruder would have set me to wondering. Umm, Sean?"

The soft ardent eyes looked at her fixedly.

Gently she laid his hands in his lap and went to the record player. Sean's *L'Isle Joyeuse* lay at the bottom of the stack, for she could bear to play it only when not to had become unbearable. She put the record on the turntable and the opening trill filled the room, gossamer as seaspray. Returning to Sean she kissed his burned nose and wet his cracked lips with her tongue. She stroked and caressed him with tenderness and devotion, lulling his sleeping flesh to awaken to pleasure and to awaken the mind with it. As if bringing him gently out of a too-deep sleep she murmured over him, letting her hands rouse only as much as they soothed. In her own mind's eye she saw the ripples and gradual swell of his music begin to wash over them. She placed his hand at her breast, cupping it, so that the firmness, the compactness of her small frame might be recalled to his fingers. The music was carrying them both toward that moment when the golden blinding Isle itself rose triumphant over the crashing breakers.

Sean stirred and uttered a faint sound.

Heartened, Jane whispered to him, pleading, "Sean, come back to me. . . . I'll help you, I'm here. It's Jane. Don't be frightened. . . ." And then to his locked mind she begged, "Sean, let me in. It's Jane, let me in!"

He was looking directly at her. Malevolently. The cracked lips slowly spread in a vindictive smile. At the instant when the golden Isle rose, and the chords surged forth from his hands, ever mounting—at that instant he raised his hand and struck her across the mouth. That done, he smiled again, head cocked to the record player.

"Sean!" Jane cried out as if in sharp warning that he was in peril.

He sat up, throwing her away from him in such a fury of rejection that her head struck the wall. Then he was on his feet, headed toward the record player, and when she tried to grasp his arm, again crying out his name, he flung her off with all the old strength that hours and hours of practice had lent his hands and arms. His recording of *L'Isle Joyeuse* was the first he destroyed. Then, rampaging, he broke record after record, clawing the albums to shreds. Jane was at him, like the young veteran of the back wards' battles that she was, fighting to protect all that was really left of Sean Maginnis, but he struck her again, casually, contemptuously, so that she fell away from him. Unhampered now, he continued with his destruction. The record player was brushed to the floor, the speaker kicked in; as Jane snatched up the phone, he caught up his portrait from the inlaid table and beat it against the corner of the speaker, puncturing his image through. He tossed the portrait aside with bleeding hands and seized the amplifier, holding it high above his head while the blood dropped on his up-lifted face.

"Get me Doctor Bartholomew, hurry!" Jane screamed into the phone. "Find him!"

The amplifier crashed to the floor.

Jane cried into the phone, "Nick, help me! I've got Sean with me in the Morgue House. Listen to me! He's here

with me, and he's in a catatonic excitement. Yes, he——"
But Nick Bartholomew was on his way.

When Nick had gained the second floor of the Morgue
House, an attendant behind him, he heard the familiar
babbling of a full-blown catatonic excitement. He came a
few steps into the room and looked first at Sean Maginnis,
his destruction of all that was himself complete, his whole
life and talent in shards at his feet, while he talked furiously,
disjointedly, a catatonic outpouring, gesticulating constantly
with his bleeding hands. Huddled on a corner of the blue-
denim couch, Jane looked up, hurt past all weeping, despairing past all means of expression. The attendant hovered uncertainly in the doorway at the sight of Jane's ripped peignoir,
and Nick said to her, "Go in the other room, please, Doctor."

Mute, she obeyed. Hurrying into her clothing, she heard
Nick approach Sean. "Well now," Nick said loudly though
in an unruffled tone, "how are you feeling, Mr. Maginnis?
Wouldn't you like to go back to your ward now?"

There was a scuffle, Sean bellowed once before resuming
his babbling, and then there were the sounds of his departure
down the stair.

In her bedroom, Jane finished dressing; turning to the
closet door, she leaned her forehead against it.

"I'm waiting, Doctor," Nick called out.

She came in and looked at him in entreaty, but Nick
was surveying the wreckage of her treasures. "Nice going,
Doctor," he commented.

"Nick, I thought—— Father Muldroon mentioned—"

"Mentioned you might goad or frighten a catatonic into
an excitement? As a therapeutic measure?"

"I thought——"

"Doctor, that is the most presumptive statement I've
ever heard in my life. You *thought!*" Nick waved a hand at
her. "Sit down, please. This will take a while."

Jane slumped down in a white wicker chair abjectly.

Huge in his whites, massive in his disgust, his face dark
with anger, Nick stood over her. *"Yeess sir!* Nice going. What
were you trying to do? Undo what little I've been able to
accomplish? If you wanted to see him in restraint on a back
ward that bad, why didn't you come ask me? If you really
enjoy your work at Pawksville so much that you want to
stay on and on, you could have chosen some other means
than setting your husband back five years."

"Nick, I thought if I could just get through to him with
love—"

"You stupid, you criminally stupid woman. Prancing
around in that rag like a Hollywood houri——"

"W–hat?"

"Houri! Listen to me. I don't have to resort to obscenities to explain my feelings. Crawling all over him like
a houri, yammering into his ear about luhuve. . . . And playing his records for him for background music, isn't that
what you did? Rubbing his nose in what you undoubtedly
chose to look on as being reality. Making sexual demands
of an emaciated body just emerged from a course of insulin
shock. Shaping up the libido of a maniac for him. What
would you have done if he were dying from cancer? Gotten
all dolled up in that rag and then withheld his morphine
from him until he came across? Oh, you are a physician
among physicians, Doctor. Here, all along, I've been disappointed in you because all the rest of your patients wrapped
up into one didn't mean as much to you as your husband. But
I told myself it was only natural for you to single him out
from the herd. Well, now I can thank God you did. If you
had the same concern for the rest of your patients as you do
him, you'd have ruined the chances of recovery for more
patients than I care to think of."

Jane whispered, "Nick, stop berating me. I can't take
much more."

"You're going to be surprised how much you can take.
That, or get out." He shoved a shard of record aside with

his white shoe. "Looks like you're going to need a new record library, Doctor. Though I'd advise a television set. Instead of the late Beethoven quartets, you could indulge in the late, late movie. This is just a tip, you understand. Look to your own mental health, Doctor. Along with that of your patients, of course. One of whom will not be, and never was—Sean Maginnis. Hereafter, if you want to know how he is, come ask me on visiting days. As his wife. Needless to say, you won't be seeing him on visiting days, or any others. I'll have to take him off the garden detail—which I had hoped would stimulate his appetite, if nothing else— because the very sight of you coming down the walk will send him off into another excitement. Only a word or two more, Doctor. I'll have to be leaving you to see to Maginnis. If he's hard at climbing the walls, as I suspect he is, I want to give him a dose of EST to calm him down. A catatonic excitement can bring on physical collapse in no time when the patient's as debilitated as he is. I've seen them younger and healthier literally burst their hearts with activity. But I don't want to bore you with a recital of what you already know, Doctor. I must remind you, though, that Maginnis is *my* patient. You do keep forgetting that little point. And my patient he remains, receiving my treatment, as long as he stays in Pawksville. Since I have never found it necessary, Doctor, to consult you before tending to my other patients, I see no reason to do so in Maginnis' case. I repeat, if you wish to question me about him, do so during visiting hours. Naturally, you won't expect me to go into medical detail. Wives are better off not knowing such matters. I'll just tell you whether he's improving or deteriorating. And I have a hunch which it's going to be for some time to come. Well, you must excuse me, Doctor. I hate to bring this little visit to an end, and I certainly do admire the way you've got your apartment all fixed up. Very artistic, what with all the broken records and glass underfoot. And tasteful touches of blood everywhere."

"Nick, have a heart," Jane said so softly she could hardly be heard.

"This was your afternoon off, wasn't it, Doctor?" Nick said, ignoring her plea.

"Yes."

"Next time go to a movie." Nick turned on his heel and stamped out, crunching what was left of *L'Isle Joyeuse* to powder under his feet.

16

A Fortnit Late

Some years before buxom little Babs had consented to go on a blind date with a medical student named Heall—Babs always made it a firm rule never to go on blind dates, except with Washington and Lee boys, of course—she had attended a pajama party at Merridale Middleton's house. Well, it had been just a riot all night long. One of the girls, Babs could never remember who, but it isn't important, had been reading this book about how to do it and all, all the ways and all that, and this girl, Babs simply *couldn't* bring her name to mind, but it didn't matter, but she was the funniest girl Babs had ever known in her life, she always could put on this English accent that was a livin' howl, anyway, this girl said that it, the book, that is, reminded her of that googy poem they had to read in school, the one that starts off: *How do I love thee, let me count the ways,* and, you can just bet, they all screamed with laughter, thinking of this book, you see, because it described about ten at least different ways, and they were all sitting on Merridale's bed counting them off, and then this girl, her name would come to Babs in a minute or two, though it wasn't all that long ago, for heaven's sake, anyway she said you could never really tell the

184

you-know *interesting* books just from their titles, like—well
Babs couldn't think of one right off—but anyway you overlooked some pretty good stuff that way, and they all got to
suggesting titles for a book that any girl in the world would
want to read the minute she laid eyes on it, and Babs, for no
reason she could think of, suddenly came up with *Two
Weeks Late,* and they all howled because you know what
that means when some girl says it, and then this girl, whose
name slipped Babs' mind at the moment, the one with the
English accent, said *A Fortnit Late* and they all just laughed
until they cried, really, just simply fell apart and——

"Why, honey," Sonny said, dismayed, entering their
bedroom and finding Babs lying on their bed in tears.
"What's the matter?"

Babs buried her face in the pillow. "Lot more than a
fortnit late . . . ," Sonny thought she might have said.

"Honey, you mean you're—"

". . . wone go through with all thayut again. . . . Jus a
lotta pain and no babies to sheou fa it."

Sonny lay beside her and rubbed her back between the
shoulder blades. "Honey, we'll keep this one. You just slip
right under the sheet and make yourself comfy, and I'll
go get—"

"Don you dare bring Nick Bartholomew in heah!"

"I'm going to get Jane Carmody," Sonny said grandly.
"Why, she was even taking a residency in GYN before she
came here. All you have to do is just relax."

"But Eiii doan paeticulary *liike* her!" Babs howled.

"Well, nobody does," Sonny said, adding with brisk
practicality, "but it isn't as if we're inviting her over here
for bridge, is it?"

"If yew say sew, shugah," Babs consented, and raised her
tearstained face for his humbly grateful kiss.

17

The Revelations of the Holy Dove

How merrily boils the pot of Pawksville! Having watched
the little Carmody sneak her husband into the Morgue
House, I continued my secret vigil, and was soon rewarded
—first with something of Debussy's drifting past Carmody's
curtains, followed shortly by what would have served ex-
cellently as a sound track for a movie train wreck. Soon
there hastened out of Hospital the mighty Old Nick, in full
battle fury, an interested attendant trotting at his heels.
Moments later the attendant emerged from the Morgue
House with a talkative—to say the least—Sean Maginnis in
tow. Much later the Old Nick himself stomped out. Today
rumor hath it that Maginnis is flinging himself a catatonic
excitement like none has even been flang—EST and precious
tranquilizers notwithstanding. And poor little Carmody
creeps past my bench, unseeing, pale and plenty shook up.
Someone ought to shoot that guy for her; but then, my
thoughts naturally run along such lines.

Ho hum, I'll probably go to the "pitchur show" tonight.
Now there's a paradox for you. An auditorium of psychotics
gazing up dully at a flickering substitute for the reality they

have fled. In the first rows we have a conglumeration (that's what I said, Sonny) of catatonics. Then a patness of paranoids, and seated behind them a seethe of schizophrenics. These nouns of assembly are mine, but they are useful in setting the *mise en scène*. Then, all settled down, the attendants keeping a wary eye on the more self-expressive of their charges, a musical stumblebum at the Steinway on the stage desecrates the National Anthem, and we all rise (the catatonics are excused) and bellow whatever comes to mind—and that is rarely the lyrics. A fist fight or two ensue, are brought under control, and, lo and behold the screen lights up and there is Toby Wing! Or Spencer Tracy, no older than your kid brother.

At this juncture, the pianist usually becomes disturbed about something, and begins banging with her fists on the keys, and has to be forcibly ejected. Sometimes it takes two attendants to do it.

Odd thing about that piano. It's a Steinway C-D, I've learned. This is an instrument leased only to concert artists, schools, institutions, and the like. The company prefers that they do not go to private owners, even if they can afford them, as only so many of these magnificent instruments are constructed, and their music belongs rightfully to the public ear. This fact did not give pause to some Superintendent or other, who blandly requisitioned one for his own quarters, for his daughter to practice scales on. Then when she decided she wanted to be a drum majorette after all, the enormous piano was shipped over to the auditorium. Right triumphs in the end, but who cares to live that. . . .

I am altogether intrigued, perplexed, and avid. I was writing the above when that sacred fowl, the Holy Dove, hove into view. The old bird was trotting along on her drumsticks, her beak red from the sun, and one wing immobilized in a sling. An inglorious description of an imperiously handsome woman, I must confess. Always curious about her, I smiled broadly at her and invited her to roost a spell. I offered her a smoke, which she refused quietly enough, though there was a peculiar flare-up in her glacial eye at the same time. Sensing a touchy subject, I hastily put my cigarettes away and introduced myself. We chatted. As you must know, snoopy Sonny, she is a treasure house of secrets. Taking her little airings, the Holy Dove has managed to poke her nose into a great deal more than one would give her credit for. Little Caddy Bartholomew, she informs me, has been systematically raiding the watermelon patch and caching her loot in the Morgue House. Also, the lass has been seen by the Holy Dove coming out from the Monkey Tree grotto bearing something in her hand. Then the kid lurks down in the basement of the rotunda, tap-tap-tapping away on a venerable typewriter, awaiting the arrival of the afternoon mail truck.

Some of this I knew, but not all, and as *quid pro quo* related what I know of *l'affaire Carmody*. We both clucked then in delicious dismay, in the way of gossips the world over. And in this way too, I suppose, we inmates of Pawksville "piece" at life, the way chubby Babs Heall pieces between meals from the refrigerator. (Well, I'm very sorry, Doctor, but she *is* chubby.)

To continue with this recordation, the Holy Dove casually spoke of her martyrdom and divinity, while I issued forth a series of snorts or starts of admiration, and similar noises of rapt belief. This past, it was my turn. I began carefully, "I must make mention that I'm a murderer."

Her reaction was nothing short of beamish. Clutching my notebook tightly, I wondered why murder so charmed the old bat. All right, she's not an old bat, but the Holy Dove is no spring chicken, either. As uneasy as if I were standing full in a searchlight, I sought about for something else to say. "I've been doing a little writing, you know," I heard myself babble inanely.

"About what?" the Holy Dove breathed.

I parried, "Oh. . . . I guess you might call it *Memoirs
from a Madhouse.*" Again she turned the full glare of her
approval on me. Then it came to me. Inadvertently I had
been oddly alliterative. I must make mention that I'm a
murderer . . . memoirs from a madhouse . . . "I murdered,"
I said experimentally, "for a maid named Mitzi."

The Holy Dove nodded with satisfaction. I was in, I was
one of the cognoscenti.

"Mr. Ellis," the Holy Dove said slowly, "is dead."

I expressed my deepest regret that this should be. "Was
he a friend of yours, Holy Dove?"

"Oh, no, no." The Holy Dove, it came out, knew of
the gentleman's demise by virtue of having read of it in
the newspapers. Those newspapers from New York, to be
exact, in which a shipment of bedpans had been wrapped.
Yes, the gentleman had been on a visit to the South, heat too
much . . . ailing on train . . . dropped dead as train pulled
into Grand Central Station. "What do you think of that?"
the Holy Dove inquired, tapping me most significantly on
the knee.

I mumbled something in keeping along the *tsk-tsk* line.

The Holy Dove seemed disappointed in my response. She
sat tapping my knee, her eyes never leaving my face. I wondered wildly if she were hypnotizing me. I could not look
away from those—pellucid eyes of hers. "Now what," she
propounded next, "is going to happen to that poor young
man? The one Doctor Heall is psychoanalyzing?"

Really, I had no idea. What kind of a garbled hypothetic
question was that? The Holy Dove was assuming a few
hundred facts not in evidence, to say the least.

"Immured," the Holy Dove said for me. "Immured
without mercy." She was homing in on some obscure objec-
tive, but I could not follow her. "Perhaps," she continued
on slowly, "Caddy might. . . . But she's only a child, what
can she do?" Something was definitely troubling the Holy
Dove; I prayed only that she wouldn't turn disturbed on me.

"And I," she said, "am only a patient. Doctor Bartholomew would not listen to me. And Miss Noon would only get upset if I tried to tell her of the situation." Here the Holy Dove permitted herself a sad little chuckle. "Miss Noon gets disturbed when I tell her something she can't understand."

I felt rather a kinship with the unknown Miss Noon at that point. Not knowing whether to mumble, gush, or fall back on good old tsk-tsk, I discarded all three.

"You understand, don't you?" the Holy Dove said. (I told myself stoutly, Don't be silly, she's *not* being menacing.)

I ventured, "I'm afraid I'm not clear in all the details." It was as if the Holy Dove were reading from some text, and I had only her marginalia to go on.

"This is a nice bench," she observed. Erratically, I thought. "The bench under Doctor Heall's office window is nice too. After four-thirty in the afternoon. I wonder what will happen to a certain gadfly, now that Mr. Ellis is dead?"

"Do without him," I said with a lot more confidence than I felt.

"Some will and some won't. That man under the Monkey Tree—he's safe. His kind always are." She sounded bitter, and I was growing more nervous by the minute.

"You mean that poet—what's-his-name—" I stammered.

But the Holy Dove was preparing to leave. "A mean man," she said meaningfully.

"Mendacious," I replied, feeling my way; anything to serve for a placatory noise. I had rapidly lost all interest in cozily settling down into a *folie-à-deux* relationship with the Holy Dove. She just might deal me the role of sworn enemy as ally.

"And Marion," the Holy Dove said softly, bringing our chat to a close. She rose, and dusting off her sanctified behind, bade me farewell. I watched her stately figure disappear past some trees. She could have ruled an empire. As it was, she had only riddles and alliteration for her domain.

Posit: the alliterative are positively paranoid.

Yet, she had set me to brooding. The "mean man" she spoke of had to be Titus Graham. For I understand that someone of that name occupies the Special Patient's Cottage and lingers 'neath the Monkey Tree. While the wisenheimers around here laugh their heads off at his claims to being a poet. Well, a horse on you-all, Dr. Heall. Mitzi once had a slim volume of his effusions around, but I don't think she so much as ever read the first—

No, it wasn't a slim volume. It was a magazine, the entire issue devoted to

Doctor Heall. Oh, Doctor Heall! Calling Doctor Heallll!

The name of that magazine was *Gadfly*.

Sorry to disturb your sang-Freud like this, Sonny. But if the Holy Dove won't speak up, maybe I'll do a little nosing around. Just what young man are you psychoanalyzing? Marion? And what has he to do with Titus Graham, and the defunct Mr. Ellis?

It is close on four-thirty. I shall hie me to a shadier and more exclusive bench.

18

Of Mischief Abroad in the Night

From where Nick sat in his chintzy living room, he could watch the last of the glow fade from the rotunda dome as he enjoyed his gin and tonic. Al was at her puzzle, her imperturbable calm all in order so that she appeared cool and comfortable, even though the temperature was in the nineties. Off in the kitchen Caddy was cheerfully at the dinner dishes, happy that her jumping up to do them had pleased Nick. It had come to her that should she begin to display a competency, if not actual talent, in light house-keeping, she could restore to Nick some of the comforts Nancy had once afforded him.

Faintly annoyed by Caddy's dishpan racket, Nick said loudly, "I know she's doing the dishes. But does she have to make such a production of it?"

"Let well-enough alone," Al murmured.

"I can't hear myself think. I must get that patient back we had up here last winter. For one night, at least."

"One night only?"

"Yes. I mean, one night last winter. Not a clatter or a bang or a sound out of her. She simply threw the dinner plates out the window." As Nick finished this brief recital, the rotunda lost the last of its fire and the lights came on all over the grounds of Pawksville. In the building just to the left of the Hospital, the doors of the auditorium were flung wide and light streamed out. "I've got to figure out how to make my peace with Jane," Nick confessed suddenly.

"Try apologizing for that dressing down you gave her," Al suggested.

"Can't. Even if her motives for doing what she did were of the purest."

"Then ask her to do something for you."

Nick watched her fix a piece neatly into its place. "You're no fool, Al."

She owed up to that, adding, "After you've humiliated someone the way you did Carmody—all right, all right, let's not go into your justifications for it—after you've done that to someone, the best thing to do is make some humble request of them. Restores their self-respect."

"And what humble request should I ask?"

"Search me," Al said. "Listen, do you recall any battlefield that had sheep all over the place? Some sort of Massacre of Innocents?"

Not listening, Nick pondered his own problem for a time, then lifted the phone just as Caddy bounded into the room. "Get me Doctor Carmody," Nick said into the phone. "Try her apartment in the Morgue House." He waited, frowning at Caddy who had thrown herself into an easy chair as gracefully as if she were heaving coal.

"Yes?" Jane came on briskly.

Nick's smile was broad and boyish. "Hi. Want to do a post with me this evening?"

"If you wish, Doctor Bartholomew."

"Oh, let's not put it on that basis. I just thought you'd be interested. An old paretic who's been kicking around here since the Spanish-American War. Might be interesting to see in what organs and how far the degeneration has gone. You won't get to see many more posts like this. Penicillin will preclude them." He was gratified to notice that Caddy was no longer slumping in her chair, but sitting up properly as befitted a young lady.

"To be sure, Doctor," Jane was saying. "A patient of yours?"

"No, she was Sonny's. And I can just feature Sonny keeping me company on a hot night like this in the morgue."

"I can't," Jane said, unbending slightly.

"I mean, I just thought you'd be interested." Nick found he was gesturing broadly—to Al's amusement.

"I'm not in the least interested, Doctor," Jane said. "But unless I go to the movie, you'll be prancing upstairs every five minutes for a glass of water, or you'll have run out of cigarettes, or you'll be hoping I just happen to have some tonic—"

"And a dollop of gin to go with it."

"Doctor Bartholomew, you can jolly well bring your own likker!" Jane said and hung up.

Al raised a brow.

"She's in top form tonight," Nick said sheepishly. He leaned back in his chair. "She knows this thing is a spur-of-the-moment inspiration. I'm not that dedicated a pathologist."

Caddy was on her feet. "Well, see you folks later."

"And where are you going?" Nick said, attempting a sternness that was rarely in him toward her.

Caddy was elaborately casual. "Why— I just thought I'd go to the picture show. If that's all right with you?"

"Why don't you ask Al if she wouldn't like to go with you?"

"Oh, would you Aunt Al?" Caddy cried, all sparkling animation.

But Al, silently applauding Caddy's determination to keep things pleasant while Nick was around, rewarded her by refusing. "I think I'll beg off this time, Caddy. I've already seen Tom Mix."

"Caddy," Nick said, "I want you back the minute the picture's over. Walk back with Miss Saunders and her group. If a male patient slipped out of line, he might not be missed for a while. You understand."

"Yes, Nick, I know," Caddy said, at her most demure. She smiled on Al in a friendly fashion, then on Nick in a blaze of adoration, and with a twitch of her ponytail was gone.

Nick finished off his drink. "My brat seems pretty docile tonight. She feeling okey?"

Waiting until the rumble of the elevator subsided, Al surmised, "She's just beginning to catch on that one can attract more flies with honey than with vinegar. And she's drunk on the possibilities."

"What do you mean by that?"

"Nothing extravagant. Just that she's not a child any more, and that sweet are the uses of puberty. Have you ever considered sending her away to school?"

"Hell no."

"Do."

"Do what? Send her away?"

"No. Think."

Nick shrugged it off, there were more important matters to hand. "Well, now I'd better be off to soothe Carmody's ruffled tailfeathers."

"Bosh. You know you like the woman."

"Enormously," Nick admitted artlessly.

He had reached the door when he thought he heard Al say, "Have fun," but since he took it to be another instance of her cryptic joshing, he did not bother to turn or reply.

The front door of the Morgue House was unlocked when Nick arrived, and switching on the lights, he yelled up the stairs, "Hey, Jane! It's me."

"Coming right at you," she called down, and appeared dressed in slacks and an old silk shirt. She's a diminutive thing, Nick thought, noticing the fragile wrist and the thin hand on the bannister. Helpless femininity should have been her forte, but tonight she was all bright lipstick and sleek well-brushed hair and purposeful stride. "Let's have at her," she said gaily, and unlocked the instrument cabinet that stood somewhat under the protection of the staircase. Whipping about, she brought out two rubber aprons and tossed one to Nick. Hers reached far below her knees, flapping heavily as she walked. She did not quite look at Nick, her eyes darting about in what was only a fair-to-middlin' simulation of breezy unconcern. He wanted very much to shake her until she cried, giving him the excuse to hold her and pat her and murmur, Now, now, Jane, take it easy, kid. Instead he suppressed a sigh and went to the refrigerator and began opening doors and examining the contents of the trays. At the sight of the fourth tray he boggled, looked to Jane— who was lighting a cigarette and whose glance caught thus unawares was that of melancholy brooding—and then down at the tray again. "For the luvva—— Doctor Carmody, is this where you keep your midnight snacks?"

Jane went "Ummm?" and then boggled also at the sight of the watermelon on the tray, its skin faintly sweating. "I never saw that watermelon in my life before," she protested.

The ridiculousness of her heated defense eased the air between them. He slammed the tray home, and then the door. "I know some of the attendants have retarded mentalities, but this is going too far. We'll just do our post, and then have a feast."

"I don't eat contraband fruit, Doctor."

"Here's our subject," Nick said, having opened the next door. He took up the sheeted bundle in his arms and placed it on the slab. When fully revealed the corpse proved to be as meaty as a coathanger. One glazed eye stared scornfully at the ceiling, the other lowered in a lewd wink.

"Old lady like that should have been on Ouita's ward," Jane commented. "What was she doing on Sonny's?"

"Evidently she could be a heller when she got going."

"Do you think," Jane said slowly, "she could already have been at Pawksville when I was born?"

"Long before. She came here in her twenties, if I remember her case history correctly. Ouita gave her a couple of walloping doses of malaria back in the 'thirties. It was too late, nothing could burn her spirochetes out. For some of them insanity is just a way of life, I guess. Oh—sorry," Nick said belatedly.

Jane avoided him, stepping on her cigarette with great care. "You can't stop mentioning chronic psychosis around me entirely, Nick. You'd only be tactless if you tried." She flung up her head vivaciously. "It would be like trying not to speak of alcoholism in Parry's hearing. Or bungling stupidity in mine. I was about to say Sonny. But Sonny's bungles are amateurish compared to my—"

"Shut up," Nick said.

"Sure," Jane replied affably. She laughed and looked down at the cadaver. "Are you going to do a post on this subject or not? I'll go open the back door for more ventilation." She was all activity before he could stop her, flinging open the back door and catching up some instruments from the cabinet on the way back. When she saw that Nick had drawn the sheet over the corpse again, she looked at him so searchingly that he experienced actual physical contact. "Well, aren't we the flighty ones tonight," she said merrily. She opened the refrigerator door with a flourish, and bowed as Nick replaced the old woman on her tray. "What is this —musical stiffs?" Jane jeered.

"Knock it off," Nick said. But Jane was laughing with the brittle, inconsolable hilarity of the hysterical. He closed the refrigerator and with one motion took Jane into his arms. Their heavy aprons made it seem as though they were embracing over a fence. She buried her face under his chin, and he could feel her efforts to stifle her giggles. A gasp more like the last shudder of an inner upheaval than a sigh escaped her; she was sobered. He put his mouth to her hair. "There ought to be more than this. You need it."

He could barely hear her muffled, "Do I ever." She pulled away from him and exhibited a smile like one testing a new denture. "As therapy. Only I was never one to ascribe to the theory of sex as salvation."

"No, but it can go a lone ways toward preserving one's sanity."

Her hands came up over their mutual fence to touch him. "You said *lone,* Nick."

"I know. That is, I just caught my own meaning." He took the instruments from her hand and laid them on the cabinet. "Too bad Sonny isn't here to enjoy my Freudian slip. The hell with Sonny. It is a lone way unless the partners feel at least an affection for one another."

"Yes, that's always quite nice."

"We are very fond of one another, aren't we, Jane?" he asked, choosing his words as carefully as if he were under some compulsion to hold himself in check.

"I suspect as much," she said gravely. "But I don't want you to go messing yourself up over me. This will be just a stopgap measure. No passing notes behind teacher's back, no longuers under Sonny's piercing gaze." She stopped and looked up at him sadly, "I was afraid this would happen— that you would get around to me in time, I mean. Only I was more afraid you wouldn't."

"Go lock the front door, and I'll take care of the back."

When they faced each other again, each bearing a jangling ring of keys, Jane took off her apron and laid it on the slab, and Nick covered hers with his. It struck him with the clarity of a revelation how many times they had done just this, with jackets and lab coats, even stained surgical gowns. The implication frightened him and he heard himself fretting inanely, "Jane, that back door wasn't locked when you went to open it, was it? You've got to be more on the *qui vive*," he rattled along. "You know how careless the attendants are——"

"Come along, Nick," Jane said and, putting her hand in his, started for the stair. On the first step she switched off the lights and turned to him behind her. Raised nearer to his height now, he found her mouth in the dark. After a time they climbed the stairs.

At the last moment, in her great Victorian state-hospital bed, he felt her ardor dim, much like the lights of Pawksville when the engineer at the powerhouse changed over from one dynamo to the other. Then he was lying beside her, his body curled around her slight one protectively. He felt such love and pity for her that he thought, If she sheds a single tear, I'll break down and bawl all over her. He kissed her temple where the single tiny blue pockmark dented her skin. "How do you feel, Doctor Carmody?"

She turned to him with a soft troubled laugh. "I'm afraid I wasn't as abandoned as I might have been."

"You pulled your punches a little. Understandable. But you were hardly perfunctory either." He stretched up to get a cigarette from her inlaid night table, lit it, and gave it to her so that he might read her expression in its glow.

Her grin was game. "I must say, Doctor, you came at me with all the aplomb of a boarding party from a Nazi sub."

"That authoritative?" He was pleased.

She drew on the cigarette and gave it to him. "Oh Nick, I wish . . . . Never mind."

"You wish I could stay all night."

"Yes. Under an entirely different set of circumstances, that is."

"But these are all we've got." A breeze came past her Priscilla curtains and they both stirred, luxuriating. "If I could find my persona, I'd go home." His voice sank, "Oh, dammit, Jane, dammit. You know?"

She looked at him sadly, "I know. Yes indeedy, I do." She pulled his head down and kissed him quickly and fervently. "Now. Scram."

He sat up and looked at the window, "Don't I even get

any watermelon?" Then went on without any change in intonation, "Here's food for thought, Jane: I'll take whatever and whenever you offer it. I'll be content with that."

"If that's food for thought, then it's hard tack and water. You know I can't abandon Sean, and we can't scandalize the community either."

He turned his head to look down at her. She lay utterly still for his inspection. He closed his great hand around her ankle, and suddenly bent to kiss her arch. "Thank God we are both out of practice. It's the only thing that could have saved us." He stood up and began to dress. "You realize by now, of course, that I was as badly in need of a little therapy as you."

She sat up and touched his thigh. She whispered experimentally, like a woman trying on furs she knows are far beyond her means, "Nick—My . . . dearest . . . Nick." Then she swung her feet to the floor and reached for her chenille robe.

At the top of the stair they kissed a final time, each a fraction withdrawn; it was over. They walked down the stairs, not touching each other, saying nothing. At the front door, Jane produced her key and unlocked it. "Good night, Nick," she said with such rigidly enforced composure that for a startled moment he thought she was going to offer him a comradely handshake.

Matching his tone to hers, he began, "We mustn't do this again sometime, Doctor. All in all it's been——"

Then he beheld Caddy, her face white as Jane's chenille robe, approaching them.

"You had to lock the goddam back door," Caddy said in the steady voice of implacable jealousy. "And you had to lock the goddam front door. And I couldn't even saw my way through the window bars with a bone saw, without making so much goddam racket I'da waked the dead." Her voice rose and she shrieked, "Some post-mortem! That was sure some post——"

Nick brought her commentary to an end by cracking her across the mouth. "Now get out of here!"

Caddy rushed past them, looking up once in ghostly murderous hatred at Jane, who stood aside, opening the door wider, to let Caddy pass. Caddy's sandals rang on the walk like gunfire.

"You get after her, Nick!" Jane said.

He was already on his way. At the bend of the walk he caught up with her. All sound ceased until there came a thin shrill noise, some incoherent utterance of rejection or repugnance from Caddy, cut off once again by a sharp slap. Another silence and then their footsteps resumed, heavy, measured, forever alienated as the march of executioner and condemned.

At the entrance to the Hospital Nick noticed that the auditorium was still lighted. "Go on over until the end of the movie," Nick said. "There's no need for Al to know anything about this."

Caddy looked at him in such a way that he wanted to weep for her, for Jane, for himself, and perhaps even for Sean Maginnis. "Yes, let's keep Aunt Al out of it," Caddy said. "Maybe she didn't think much of my mother, but that's no reason for letting her know that I'm a liar and you're a skunk." She waited for him to hit her again, and when he did not, she turned away from him and went slowly toward the auditorium.

19

Chums

Sharp on the noon whistle Al looked up from her puzzle to see Caddy decorously entering the apartment. Her ponytail was neat, her shirt tucked precisely into her shorts, and her manner—for her—subdued. She was wearing a smile of vulpine affability, such as Al had noticed on Babs Heall when Babs had found herself in conversation with Superintendent Keeney's mother-in-law at the staff Independence Day cocktail party. "Am I," Caddy inquired earnestly, "on time?"

"For what?" Al said.

Caddy declined to be rushed into garbed declarations. "I was afraid," she said, taking great care with each word, "I was late for lunch. After you'd gone to all the trouble to fix it, and all. I mean."

"No trouble," Al said, and went into the dinette, Caddy hard at her heels. The banquette table was laid, the iced-tea pitcher crowded with cubes, diluting Al's formidable brew. There were only two plates. Caddy did not remark on the fact.

"Did you by any chance think this was Staff Meeting day?" Al could not resist asking.

Caddy assumed a pretty confusion. "Why, no. No! After

all, why should you think I thought it would be? Why should I? Would I, I mean, think it's Staff—"

"In any event," Al cut through Caddy's syntactical flounderings, "you're welcome, kid. Incidentally, Nick's lunching in the staff dining room with Superintendent Keeney."

Caddy received this intelligence with no show of disappointment. "That's right. Doctor Kox is here today. I saw his car." She waited politely until her aunt had seated herself before sliding into the banquette opposite her. "Looks divine," Caddy commented on the same old potato salad. "You've just got to teach me how to fix it, Aunt Al."

Before Al could tell Caddy that the salad had been sent up from the Hospital kitchen along with the rest of the meal, Caddy was chatting ahead brightly, "I've been reading a book."

"No!" Al said and poured the tea, her only contribution to lunch.

"This *Sun Also Rises,*" Caddy enlarged engagingly. "This book, you know."

"I recall reading it," Al admitted, attuned for trouble. Caddy's manner betokened an inner turmoil.

"Did you!" Caddy cried in delight. "Because I've been dying to talk to someone about it." She stirred her tea busily. "You know, Aunt Al, that Lady Brett was kind of long in the tooth to be horsing around like she did, you know?"

"I don't remember her conduct as striking me in that respect," Al said cautiously.

"Really?" Caddy marvelled. "Why, she was even older than—Doctor Carmody!" she shouted gaily. "And when you consider all the trouble Doctor Carmody has seen. She *is* married, you know. And to a patient at that."

"Caddy, don't you think it a touch impudent on your part to discuss Doctor Carmody at all? Let's talk about something else."

Nothing abashed, Caddy took another tack. "This is," she declared with great emphasis, "the best potato salad I've ever had in my entire mouth. But she is, just the same. Married to a patient, I mean."

"How's the poetry coming?" Al asked pointedly.

"The—— Oh, my poetry! Oh. Well, I'm composing this Ode for the Pawks boys, did I tell you? Oh, I did. Well, I just thought of the coincidence, you know? The Pawks boys were twins, and Nick and Rick, my brothers, are tw—"

"I'd already figured it out that they were, but thanks anyway for telling me."

"Oh, Aunt Al!" Caddy howled. "I don't know what we ever did without you. You're just one shriek after another!" She went into gales of preposterously artificial laughter. Al waited quietly through any number of paroxysms until Caddy had succeeded in her recovery.

"Would you like some more tea after your protracted merriment?" Al asked courteously.

"Oh, please! You know, Al—— You don't mind if I call you Al, do you? You're one of the family now, and we've always just called each other by first names."

"Yes, I rather like the custom too," Al said. "Our parents were always very strict with Nick and me. Around our house it was, 'Yes, Papa,' and 'No, Mamma,' all stiff and formal. I guess that's why Nick and I were so close. It was our way of ganging up on our elders. Well, times—" The expression on Caddy's face brought Al to an abrupt halt. Caddy's eyes were so full of woe that they resembled, not two fingers of Scotch, but black rum. "Why, Caddy! What . . . ."

"At least," Caddy said bitterly, "*your* father didn't forget *your* mother practically overnight."

Al said, a mite unwisely, "Well, there were times he probably wanted to."

Caddy greeted this riposte with a morose snicker.

"Come now, Caddy," Al said sharply, "you made an absurd accusation, so I countered with an absurd reply."

Caddy sneered, on the verge of tears. "Well, I think it's just plain sinful the way some people can't seem to remember somebody from one day to the———"

The tartar in Al, grown indomitable from years of quelling intractable patients, stood forth: "*Caduceus!*"

Caddy twitched, her face contorted, then quieted at once, hanging her head.

"You were cutting up like a hellion," Al informed her comfortably. "Now then, let's see if we can work this out in its proper sequence. Caddy, are you still harking back to a minor difference of opinion Nancy and I once had?"

Caddy squirmed. "I guess that's it," she mumbled. "Although I know better."

"I should hope so, kid. And you surely couldn't think that I'm trying to take your mother's place. That's ridiculous on the very face of it. I'm just—"

"I don't see why not!" Caddy cried, rallying.

"Why not what?"

"What you said. Not take Nancy's place maybe, but just—stick around. Nick purely loves to talk to somebody at night. About Pawksville and Doctor Heall and such. And this winter I'll have my homework to do, and so will the twins, so if you were here. . . . Then he'd have you," Caddy ended triumphantly. "I mean, who else would he need?"

Unconsciously Al fell into one of her silences, and thus unwittingly permitted Caddy to supply her own answer.

"Well, who?" Caddy demanded as if in hot denial.

Oh Lord, now what didn't I say? Al asked herself anxiously. "I'll tell you what, Caddy. We'll talk this over again, and if you still—"

Caddy popped out of the banquette. "Then it's all settled. And, Al, it's going to be just dandy. You wait and see." She caught up Al's plate. "If I'm going to get these dishes done—"

A confused Al said, "No, you go practice your violin, kid. Nick wants you to."

Al sat on, over a third glass of tea. Caddy's door banged, then Caddy appeared, violin case and folded stand under one arm. The other clutched her clipboard and some music held together by yellowed surgical tape. "In this heat," Caddy announced, "it's almost impossible to practice. The E string gets so slickery."

"You've got three other strings," Al said; "work on them." She was about to add some idle admonishment about staying out of mischief, when she was startled speechless by Caddy's suddenly kissing her quickly, clumsily, and somehow furiously on the cheek. She heard Caddy growl, "Al, you're the greatest. I don't know what we'd do without you."

Al was still recovering from shock when the sound of the elevator rumbled through the walls, and Caddy was gone.

Al stirred her tepid tea and brooded. Several days ago something must have happened between Caddy and Nick. Some spat or other of which neither seemed inclined to speak. Al felt herself to be the buffer state between two warring nations.

Or rather, Al realized suddenly, Caddy was like an Indian pony. If she could be said to be domesticated, it was as if the feat had been accomplished by savages. Her demonstrativeness of moments ago had been more fierce than affectionate, more demanding than——

Al rose and went to sit before her puzzle, not looking at it. The sweep second hand on her big Hamilton watch was the only thing in motion about her admirably sturdy frame. I'm not a buffer state, she thought. I'm a hostage, captured by Caddy. She suspects too that Nick is in love with that bitsy Carmody—that long-in-the-tooth Doctor Carmody, as Caddy called her—and Caddy will settle for nothing less than unconditional surrender. Well, somebody's got to give, but I'll be damned if I can see either my brother or my niece doing it. . . .

With dogged resolution, Caddy stood under a tree hard at her Etudes, while her mind seethed. At least with Al

around, Nick wouldn't be free to go charging over to the
Morgue House every lousy night; there were just so many
posts any one or two people could perform. And Al had the
freedom of the mild protests and reminders of Carmody's
husband that were denied to Caddy. There was the off chance
that Dr. Carmody would prove to be only a passing fancy
of Nick's, but Caddy could not rely on that hope. If two
people as elderly as Nick and Carmody were set on making
fools of themselves, there was no telling to what limits they
would go.

Actually, Caddy told herself candidly, it's none of my
business. She began to fume, sawing mercilessly on the violin,
growing jealous all over again in Nancy's behalf, not daring
to suffer on her own. Nor was an open alliance with Al
feasible; Al, Caddy was morally certain, would tell her,
Caddy, to take her nose right back out of Nick's affairs.
Moreover, deep down, the Bartholomew in Caddy approved
of this stance. Nick never interfered with her poetry, for
example——

My work. Caddy thought importantly. Yes, my poetry
just might help me pull through the bad days ahead. Then,
in conjunction with this meditation, Caddy looked across
the grounds for signs of activity at the Monkey Tree. She
did have an appointment there later.

20

The Iceman Cometh

Clearly aware that the dog days had his little pack snapping at one another like curs, Nick Bartholomew tried to tread softly. Also there was the incident of himself and Jane; a thing done, and fairly well done, by the easeful look of her, but still a thing done. On the other hand it had been an emotional stopgap measure, an alleviation of the symptoms of loneliness, while the basic causes—her attraction for him and her unending servitude to the Maginnis family —went unchecked.

Caddy's part in the matter had frankly unsteeled him. He was of the firm belief that he would rather have had Babs and Sonny in the same room with them, drinking Southern Comfort cocktails, than Caddy below in the dark, behind the instrument cabinet. Ever since that night Caddy had made herself scarce, picking, he supposed, the petals from her full-blown Electra complex: *He loves me, he loves me not. . . .*

Coupled with all this was the prospect of an afternoon Nick knew he would remember, and might regret, for the rest of his life. He was standing in the dark rotunda, debonair in a fresh pair of iron-stiff whites, awaiting the arrivals of

Sonny, Superintendent Keeney, and the visiting dignitary
in the person of Dr. Roderick Kox. As always the humid
rotunda spoke of coolness through the fountain, which the
body heatedly denied. Nick longed to be placing his feet
under his own banquette for lunch, notwithstanding Caddy's
accusative glower and his own resultant crossness. Failing
that, he wished with all his heart that Dr. Kox were, say,
the visiting proctologist, or any of the other circuit-riding
specialists who practice their arts at regular intervals on
state-hospital patients saved up for them. The proctologist
was a fat, cheery person who babbled cozily at lunch about
piles and the like, brightening the whole scene with his
quips and indefatigable name-dropping. There were few
celebrities whose fundaments were not familiar to the Rear
Admiral—for such he answered to, with a roar of appreciation every time—and he lent to the provincial air of Pawksville the heady atmosphere of gossip-column worldliness.

Dr. Kox was of another stripe. Babs Heall was so re-
pelled by him that she was moved to the *mot* of her life,
"He's got the broad shoulders of a snake, that slinky ole
Doctor Kox." Indeed, Dr. Kox made everyone think in terms
of cool dry scales and fangs. Yet on the surface he was affable
and smiling. He was a surgeon, and it was his wont to arrive
with his own instruments, which were then taken over
by Mr. Dick while the good surgeon lunched with Superintendent Keeney and whoever else was elected to sit above
the salt with him; next to stroll the grounds or, if the weather
were inclement, have a cigar with Superintendent Keeney
in his library; and finally to walk or (were the weather inclement) to drive over to the Hospital where Mr. Dick and
sundry patients awaited him in Surgery. There Dr. Kox
glanced without looking at a number of documents attesting
to the need of his services and the consent thereto, tossed
them aside, and scrubbed. He asked no questions, his attitude that of complete unconcern. He performed psycho-

surgery; he made no claims whatsoever to being a psychiatrist.

Unless requested otherwise, Dr. Kox performed that lobotomy known as transorbital, wherein the surgeon destroys the fibers between the frontal lobe and the thalamus by pushing an instrument resembling an icepick through the roofs of the eye sockets. Effective anesthesia was achieved with electro-shock, a good jolt for each eye. The patients never knew what hit them; and when they did learn, they didn't care. Superintendent Keeney spoke of lobotomies lovingly, to staff and relatives alike. Nick Bartholomew, keeping an open mind, considered them expedient for those patients who were menaces to themselves and everyone else by virtue of their resistant psychoses and violent activities. Too, there were some patients who, by every outward manifestation, were in such mental anguish that the surgery was a simple act of mercy. Sonny Heall came out and openly denounced psychosurgery as a "medical crime." Nick was forever pointing out to Sonny that some patients benefited enormously, to which Sonny replied, yes, and scads of them emerge as insensate as stones. *"Scads,* Doctor," Nick then would say coldly, "is hardly a statistically significant number." All in all, Nick worried and gnawed at himself about psychosurgery; yet the decision rested entirely with Superintendent Keeney, the relatives, and not infrequently with Father Muldroon or some other spiritual advisor.

This day, glooming into the rotunda fountain—and where better a place to do it in all Pawksville?—Nick was frightened. He was about to permit, he feared, an enormity. Yet an attempt at interference could only prove abortive and cost him his job—his lifework at Pawksville—as well.

Thus it did not help to have Sonny come along and state aloud Nick's doubts for him. Also dressed afresh for the luncheon, Sonny was sweating copiously, his green eyes contrasting nicely with his pink cheeks. Sonny inquired waspishly, "Has the Iceman arrived?"

THE JUMPING OFF PLACE

"Think so," Nick mumbled.

"I must say," Sonny remarked, "you're looking hale and heartless, Doctor."

"What do you mean by that?" Nick flared.

"You know damn well what I mean, Doctor," Sonny said manfully.

"Look Doctor, do we have to go through with this every time? You don't approve of psychosurgery. But since your wards are Receiving and several of the Acute, your patients are never selected, and you can be as rectitudinous as all hell without jeopardizing your job. Dr. Kox, in turn, probably looks on your psychoanalysis as so much ganglionic guessing. Which may be as good a way as any other of describing intuitive arrivals at the truth. But between your psychoanalytic fulminations and Keeney's calloused indifference, I'm trying to steer a sensible course of what might be best for the patient involved. I neither sought nor obtained those consents, Doctor. I have in my time, and you know it, gone down on my knees to Keeney to save a particular patient. And I succeeded only when that patient was young, having his first mental break, and the relatives were themselves wavering." Nick took a breath. "And I would also appreciate it, Doctor, if you would refer to Kox's leucotome as being such, and not an icepick, should the subject arise at table. If you're so concerned about the welfare of the patients around here, then look to yours. I thought we agreed that that Marion Pierce should have a course of Metrazol, and yesterday I learn that he's had one convulsion, and one only. I thought we agreed that his history and extreme youth warranted taking a little trouble to help him. I place reliance in you, Doctor. I can't do your rounds, and the various clinics, and my Hospital wards, all in twenty-four hours. And now I find——"

"You found," Sonny interrupted, as rectitudinous as Nick had accused him of being, "that I did take him off Metrazol. I am analyzing him, and most successfully. When you consider how psychotic he is. But at least I haven't stood by while he got scheduled for a transorbital lobotomy. Anyway, we're not talking about Marion Pierce, Doctor, and you know it. If you want my pure and simple opinion, Doctor Bartholomew, if you don't prevent this, then you're the biggest bastard I've ever met."

"Then you step in and intercede in his behalf," Nick said in a low dangerous voice, looking around and above them at the dim galleries, aware of the acoustics of the rotunda. "Tell Keeney that in your expert opinion a deteriorating catatonic, and one going down for the fourth time at that, and with his family history, should be shunted off to a back ward where he'll be safe and happy. He can climb the walls in his excitement every day, until you come along and soothe him with a few snappy psychoanalytic slogans. . . . I'm afraid, Doctor, I just don't follow your line of reasoning."

"You're following me. If I had a crush on a woman, I'd go to bed with her. But I wouldn't stand aside and let Keeney and Kox turn her husband into a vegetable."

"Will you lower your voice!" Nick whispered furiously.

But Sonny was in the mood to continue on. "And I don't care how many signed consents Keeney sticks under the Iceman's nose. So long as *she* hasn't consented, then I'm just telling you again, Doctor, you are the lowest and the biggest and the dirtiest and the choicest example of a—"

"Doctor Heall, are you sure you're feeling yourself today?"

"Completely," Sonny said with more dignity than many would have credited him for. "As you so obviously are, Doctor. You're not lifting a hand, or even trying to, because you think you know what's better for her then she does. You're feeling just like God, as usual." Sonny turned away, "Paranoid as ever," he remarked to the rotunda at large.

"You and your schizzy posturings," Nick muttered after him furiously.

At the luncheon table, directly under the ceiling fan, a natty Dr. Kox conversed urbanely at jovial Superintendent Keeney. Dr. Kox had dressed his skinny length in Palm Beach cloth to point up his tan. He was around Nick's age, but in every other way his opposite. Where Nick was just emerging from burliness, Dr. Kox was entering elegant dessication. Nick's close-cut wire curls were spotted with gray; Dr. Kox was delicately and correctly silvered at the temples. And where Nick would thunder at his opposition, Dr. Kox would puncture it with the same bloodless precision he employed in driving his leucotome—icepick into a human brain.

If Dr. Kox wondered at the granitic silence of Dr. Heall and the black scowl of Dr. Bartholomew, he was too polite to reveal it. He spoke of golf and deep-sea fishing and vacation spots, and Superintendent Keeney joined in enthusiastically and knowingly because he spent three-quarters of the year enjoying the former at the latter. No word of the coming activities of the afternoon passed Dr. Kox's lips, and a flicker of interest showed in his eyes only once, when he saw the brisk entrance of Dr. Jane Carmody into the dining room. Her cheeks were flushed from the heat, and her sun-streaked hair became her greatly.

At this point Superintendent Keeney was asking, "More iced tea, Doctor Kox?" And Dr. Kox murmured, "Wh—? Oh. Yes," and glanced at Sonny, who was staring over his glass at Nick like a cautious horse peeking out of his feedbag. The patient-waitress poured the tea.

At this point, as well, Nick was in receipt of a bright smile from Jane, who inclined her head to hear something Dr. Ouita was chattering at her. Her smile, bridging the distance between the tables, was one Caddy might have sent Nick upon sticking her head in his office and finding him occupied with a patient. An iced-tea spoon rattled loudly against a glass, and Nick discovered with a flush of agitation that it was his own.

". . . Governor will find everything shipshape here at

Pawksville," Superintendent Keeney was crowing. "That right, Doctor Bartholomew?"

Nick dabbed absently at the back of his neck with his napkin. "Well, we are overcrowded, of course. And understaffed. And, uh. . . ." He forgot what he was saying.

"Oh, that," Superintendent Keeney said.

Inwardly Nick was in such a tumult that the simple act of eating and swallowing approached actual pain. Whatever he did might be ruinously wrong; action or inaction smacked equally of betrayal. Once the Maginnis family had their boy back, and boy he would be, a sunny-natured piano-playing thirtyish lad, they'd kick Jane out without a grain of compunction. On the other hand, he, Nick, could suddenly pronounce Maginnis physically unfit for surgery, and the loftily indifferent Dr. Kox would listen unmoved while Nick and Keeney had it out, thus alerting Jane. It would serve my purposes handsomely, Nick thought miserably, if Jane were to threaten Keeney with such a scandal that it would raise the rotunda right up over the Governor's head. And he wouldn't dare fire her. She'd stay on and on while Maginnis was shunted from one ward to the next, ending up in a stuporous state in a filthy ward. Meanwhile Jane and I have mebbe three or four jolly years of hanky-panky in the Morgue House—on her birthday I'd treat her to a motel—until between us, Pawksville and me, we would have wrung her out. By then she'd be well on her way to becoming one of those screechy neurotic hen-medics to whom love would be merely a word with a murky meaning, fit only for Sonny's psychoanalytic vocabulary. But Sonny's evaluation of the situation was incorrect. I don't just have a crush on her, I love her, Nick thought, accepting this realization with no more astonishment than he would have greeted the endless heat outside. Precision is of the essence, Sonny—and, to be precise, I love her. I'm as certain of that as I am that Sean Maginnis is possessed of the inalienable right to be released from his unbearable mental agony.

Keeney's decision stands. Jane will never forgive me, but no matter, because she'll be gone before the month is out. She can pick up her life and find herself a husband this time. And if Sonny thinks I'm playing God, then he doesn't think much of the Deity, for if ever a couple could hit it off in a good marriage, Jane and I are that pair. Instead, I'm going to betray her so she can resume her life and find herself a husband and have kids; and in doing so, I'm making it absolutely certain that what future happiness she may find will not stem from me.

". . . care to join me on my gallery for a cigar, Doctor Kox?" Superintendent Keeney was saying. "You can always catch a breeze there this time of day."

Dr. Kox cared to.

Now alone, Sonny looked across the table at Nick. "I don't want any part of this, Doctor," he said quietly. "I was told to sit at this table, but I'm not in on it. Officially, I don't know one thing about it. He's not my patient. But if I were you I'd try to prevent it. Stall for time. Turn him over to me for analysis. It might work."

"Are you cra— He's in restraint, hollering his head off in a cata—— Sonny, why don't you just stand up and issue a news bulletin? Then everyone would know about it."

"For the last half-hour I've been sorely tempted to," Sonny said.

Both of them conscious of Jane's profile not ten feet away; they were whispering fiercely.

"Don't tell me you haven't heard of his violent reaction to her company the other day," Nick reminded Sonny.

"And that's your excuse?" Sonny sneered. "Doctor, you'd better get your reality-principle in working order fast. Your libidinal desire for her is in the driver's seat."

"The Clinical Director of Pawksville is in the driver's seat, Doctor. And I concur with Keeney's decision that psychosurgery is indicated in this case."

Sonny looked at Nick a moment longer, then started to

rise. A cockroach scuttled across the table between them, bound for Dr. Kox's plate. Sonny watched it, then brushed it off the table just short of its goal. "One thing no reform governor will ever be able to do," Sonny remarked pleasantly, "and that's rid Pawksville of its vermin. Seems like they're really beginning to overrun the place." He rose.

Nick sat on an instant longer, then looking neither to right nor left, he hastened from the room.

21

Descent from Parnassus

While Caddy was depositing her violin in the entrance hall of the Hospital for safekeeping, Titus Graham sat smoking his pipe under the Monkey Tree. The shade of the foliage tinted his face a delicate mint green, and his pendant mustache was the color of vertigris gathered on copper. He was in a pet at the world, and the fauna of Pawksville—from monkeys to Caduceus Bartholomew—were particularly deserving, he felt, of the several forms of harm he ached to deal them. From his boyhood on he had loathed children, and they him. A sensitive child, he had but to make his appearance at a new school to call down upon his head cries of "Sissy!" and become instanter the butt of bullies. Tears were of no avail, though he sobbed his heart out to flint-hearted teacher after teacher. His recitals of slights and downright physical injuries earned punishments for him, not the malefactors. It was not until he grew up that he realized that jealousy, on the part of both fellow pupils and teachers, had been at the bottom of it. To this day he detested self-sufficient youngsters; he longed to punch their happy little faces in, to see how they liked shedding a bitter tear or two. If they whined and begged, he had mercy on them, mercy which had not been

granted him. But if they fought, it was as if they communicated their panic to him, and he in turn drew on that store
of childish savagery that had lain unused in him until he was
fully grown. Fully grown, and with a man's strength—— But
he never intended those excesses. In the weeks after he had
killed the unknown urchin on Capri, he lay awake at night
and wept. He had not wanted the boy's death, his demon had.
. . . My demon, the Great Poet thought. My demon is a
child. He was shaken by the notion; he grew chilled in the
heat dwelling on that relentless, savage little monster he har-
bored in his head. Suddenly he wanted to weep for the dead
boy, and himself, and most of all for his schoolboy demon,
his murderous evil side, his own indwelling version of Peter
Pan.

Then, as suddenly as sorrow had overtaken him he
abandoned his maudlin mood. He experienced a bracing
sense of pervading detestation. He was an artist, and as such
it did not matter that he personally held himself in contempt.
His work was himself, not he. Thinking of his work reminded him again of the Bartholomew brat.

For Caduceus Bartholomew he reserved a special hatred,
a deep retroactive resentment. The girl had no sense of being
in his employ, which to his mind she was; she had even less
recognition of her infinite inferiority, both by virtue of her
years and her intellectual capacities, and sat next him blather-
ing along at him as if she were undeniably his equal. When
she did defer to him on the matter of her poetic efforts, her
manner was still that of the assured primitive pumping the
academician on technique out of sheer curiosity alone. Only
glorying inwardly in the pleasure, vindictive and sensual, he
would derive from striking her served to keep him smiling
and puffing on his pipe.

This smile he now assumed when he saw her approaching the Monkey Tree, the clipboard with the odious "Ode
to the Pawks Boys" on it clutched to her bosom. Without
preamble she plunked herself down on the bench and began
disposing of her betters right and left.

"I've been reading the most confusing novel," she said smugly. "Why can't people who write books say what they mean?"

"How should I know?" he said, barely concealing his exasperation. "I don't read novels. A pastime for idle women and pimply adolescents. The products of hacks with a poverty of imagination." The Great Poet snorted in disgust. "They should be signing paupers' oaths, not publishing contracts." Pleased with this, he looked, in spite of himself, for her visible appreciation, and saw instead that she had received it calmly and was bent over her clipboard.

"I've decided," Caddy said—fatuously, to his mind— "to take out the word *flag* and use *Stars and Bars* instead. That way, *Mars* rhymes. The God of War, you know."

"You are an ignoramus, aren't you, to say a thing like that to me." He puffed on his pipe, welcoming her glower.

Caddy merely shrugged, setting her ponytail to swinging. "I want you to listen to this part, please. It's giving me trouble."

"Spare me your millipedal verse."

Caddy looked up warily. "What kind?"

"Multipedal," he amended, taking satisfaction from her hurt expression. "Too many feet."

"Why," Caddy inquired in the first chilly breeze he'd felt in days, "do you always criticize before you've heard something?"

"Because any attempt at poetry on your part is a stale and profitless undertaking; is now and will forever be. You don't seem to understand, little girl, that I don't come here to listen to your garbage."

"Gar——"

"I come here on a business transaction. You presumably mail my work out for me, your recompense being not my tutoring of you, but your grubby little forages into embezzlement of a part of the money I give you. Time and again I've given you enough to cover my postage twice over. I expect you to make inroads. Naturally. But listening to your—"

"That is a lie," Caddy imparted to him, voice shaking with insult. "I have every last penny written down in a notebook, how much you give me, and how much postage I have on hand. I have exactly three dollars in cash right now, and sixty-three cents in stamps, and I'll buy more stamps and a half-dozen more manila folders for you the next time I go to the village, which will be as soon as you need the stuff and as soon as I can think up another excuse for riding my bicycle three miles in this sun, and then so I won't be a liar I have to stop off and horse around with some boy-crazy girl or somebody for a while, because that's the only reason I can give for riding my bicycle three miles in this—"

He removed his pipe long enough to ask nastily, "And you've not taken one cent for yourself? Hah!"

"I have not."

"Am I to understand that you mail out my work for the simple pleasure of playing the sneak?"

Caddy countered with great dignity, "My reasons are my own, thank you."

"And do those reasons have anything to do with your own disgusting attempts at poetry?"

"Disgusting?" Caddy quibbled nervously. The conversation was taking a dangerous turn.

"I believe the word applies." The Great Poet spoke around the stem of his pipe, breathing smoke at her.

She said nothing, making obvious efforts to efface a curious expression of guilt from her gaze. He examined her carefully, "Well?"

Caddy fidgeted.

"If it isn't money, and it isn't your love of intrigue, and it isn't poetry that motivates you, what does? Are you endangering yourself coming into my foul presence merely to defy your father? Is that it? Do you fondly imagine you're dealing with a homicidal maniac and getting away with it?"

"Of course not," Caddy said sensibly. "I know about

people like you. Not that you can help it," she added chari-
tably. "My father tells me things about the different patients
so I'll be on my guard. The last Special Cottage patient was
a rapist." Caddy paused to recollect. "A Republican, because
the reform governor was. Republican, I mean. This one's a
Democrat. Naturally, I wouldn't let my little brothers come
within a hundred yards of you."

This time the pipe came out of his mouth. The Great
Poet laughed so ominously that the monkeys rattled their
chains in agitation above them. Sunlight flicked at his sulfur
mustache as he swung his head about.

Caddy regarded him calmly until he was quiet.

He puffed a great stream of smoke upward to ward off
the monkeys before asking, "So that's why you're not afraid
of me. To your way of thinking, of course, I'd have to find
some member of the lovely Bartholomew family toothsome,
but you think one of your little brothers would be more to
my taste. Dear little girl, I've seen those puling brats, and
I find them about as captivating as the contents of a pathologist's jar. You can put your fears to rest on that score. I'd
no more touch those mucoid whining—"

"Now just a moment!" Caddy snapped. "The twins
happen to be my father's sons. And I'll thank you not to
criticize his children."

"Excuse me," Titus Graham said, teeth clenched on the
pipe as he bowed slightly. "I forgot about your sick little
obsession for that self-important father of yours. Look at you,
the very mention of him and you begin quivering. Too bad
your mother didn't take those boys with her in that wreck.
Then you could have had your bully of a father all to your—"

Caddy swung the clipboard at him, knocking the pipe
to the bench. Backing off, she tried to escape his grasp by
batting at his hands with the board. He came at her, head
low, gaze a steady conflagration, as he reached round and
caught her by the ponytail. He held her, despite her wild
swing of the clipboard, in profile to him, so that her rolling

eyes could just detect his doubled fist in preparation. A giggle of excitement and glee escaped him. Caddy started to yell and he clapped his other hand over her mouth. "Oh no you don't, little Miss Bartholomew. By the time I'm finished with you, the only sound coming out of that flapping jaw of yours will be a low moan." Again he tittered.

Caddy gnawed and struggled, her rolling eyes bulging from their sockets as he mashed his hand cruelly against her lips for trying to bite. Freeing her ponytail he doubled his fist when she jerked her mouth away and shrieked, her cry bringing the first monkey down on him. There was suddenly a fury of fur and needle-toothed affection around them. As he let go of Caddy she began to defend herself with the clipboard rhapsodic with rage. All chain and chatterings, as if led by Caddy's attack and fighting under her flag, the monkeys enwrapped Titus Graham, biting him in passion, fighting each other for his nose and ripping chunks of mustache for keepsakes. The very leaves of the tree danced in a green-and-silver seizure as bits of hair and flesh and fur and "Ode to the Pawks Boys" and oaths filled the air; the lone monkey above solemnly moving down a limb to observe his brothers. The Poet's attention elsewhere, Caddy jumped from the bench to fall sprawling. A monkey landed on her back and she beat it off with the board, rapidly scooting backward along her bottom, propelling herself by the heels. From a lowly squat of safety she paused to behold the Great Poet, hung now with monkeys as if he were a carnival barker, his eyes round, attentive to his horror of them.

With the merciless impatience of the free with the captive, Caddy yelled, "Are you nuts or something? What you need is a big—fat—dose—of Serpasil!"

Gaining her feet, she clutched the tattered Ode to her breast. The Great Poet sat cautiously immobile while one monkey searched his head for lice. "Hand me my pipe," he said softly, pathetically.

Caddy boldly marched back into danger and picked up

the pipe. She thrust it between his chewed lips and he drew on the smoldering dottle fiercely.

"Hereafter," Caddy said loudly enough to be heard over the anxious chatterings of the monkeys, "mail your own doggerel."

Hugging her "Ode to the Pawks Boys," she departed.

Mulling Nick's strange agitation while lunching with the suave Dr. Kox, Jane Carmody was on her way to the Hospital when she saw Caddy bursting from the grotto, clutching something to herself. Dr. Carmody thought automatically Now what?, then anxiously recalled that the Special Patient frequently sought the coolness and privacy of the Monkey Tree. Jane called out to Caddy but the girl, pretending not to hear—Jane was certain that it was pretense on Caddy's part—swerved from the walk and directed her steps toward the Greek reflecting pool, away from Jane. Determined but not yet alarmed—there were a number of excellent reasons for Caddy's avoidance of her—Jane set out at a fast trot to follow. She moved soundlessly across the greensward and, circling the pool, emerged from a break in the hedge not five feet from Caddy. Caddy, seated at the pool's edge with her sneakers off, looked at Jane stonily, then returned to her contemplation of her bare feet soaking in the water. At her side lay a clipboard, somewhat the worse for wear, with a few tatters still clinging to it. Caddy's ponytail was a snarl and there was a bruise to one side of her mouth.

Observing that bruise, Jane thought, Good Lord, she wasn't letting that man—

"Caddy?" Jane asked softly, seeking not that Caddy admit to the identification but that she quell any number of fears Jane was harboring for her.

"Please leave me alone," Caddy mumbled.

"Caddy, are you all right?"

"I'm very well, thank you, Doctor. You're the same, I hope?"

Jane accepted the smartiness without rebuke. "I question that you are all right, Caddy. You were in the grotto with that Titus Graham, weren't you?"

Caddy said nothing, seeking to exhibit further insolence through silence.

Jane held her ground, appraising Caddy. Then with precision she remarked, "I suppose you hate me, I suppose you have a right to. That's neither here nor there right now. Did that man try to—Did he tamper with you?"

Caddy made a snorting sound, less indicative of derision than shock. A great cloudy tear rolled down her cheek and dropped with a plop into the reflection pool. That lone tear was to be all; Caddy firmly repressed its fellows.

"Did he just try or did he succeed?" Jane pressed.

"Doctor Carmody, do you give a damn?"

Jane walked over to Caddy and jerked her unceremoniously to her feet. A greater plop was heard and both looked in silence as the clipboard sank to the shallow bottom of the pool, strips of "Ode to the Pawks Boys" attracting a fat gold-and-black goldfish.

"I'm sorry," Jane said helplessly.

Caddy's shrug was listless. "It doesn't matter in the least," she said, and took to examining the hedge.

"What does matter," Jane resumed, touching the bruise on Caddy's face, "is what took place at the Monkey Tree. Are you going to tell me?"

"Business transaction," Caddy said sullenly after a long pause.

"What, I mean *what* in God's name do you mean? What business?"

"Monkey business," Caddy said snippily.

Jane seized her by the selfsame handle the Great Poet had found so convenient. A tug of the ponytail and Caddy was forced to look up into the flushed and determined face of Dr. Carmody. "I just may wallop you one," Jane remarked reflectively. "Have you taken leave of your senses? You know what the Special Patients are liable to be. Sane criminals. Hasn't your father warned you not to go within a mile of a Special Patient unless someone has a machine gun trained on him? You snap to it, girl, and tell me just what you were up to with that man."

"Reely," Caddy managed, "I don't see what business of yours it—"

Jane calmly slapped her on the chop, and greeted Caddy's outraged stare with a thoughtful one of her own. Still calm, Jane said, "I am bigger and stronger than you. If I can subdue a violent schizophrenic, believe me, Caddy Bartholomew, I can handle you with ease. Shall we go another round?"

Caddy glowered, rosy as a little Franklin stove on a snowy night.

"If you don't answer my questions," Jane said with quiet menace, "you'll be on an examining table within five minutes. And then we'll see what's what, all right. Don't think your father won't be the first to insist on it. I'm not in the least impressed by your outraged sass. You stop playing the fool, or I'll be forced to treat you like one."

"I mailed out his poems for him," Caddy volunteered sulkily. "Doctor Ouita won't let him send out his stuff to this magazine. So I did."

Jane could not refrain from remarking, "Since you seem to know so much better than Doctor Ouita what is and what isn't good for a patient, I'm surprised Nick didn't assign him to you."

"I didn't mail any letters for him," Caddy hedged. "Just the other. I mean, I was—uh—you know, acting in the interests of poetry."

"Commendable, I'm sure," Jane said dryly, dubious. But she did release her hold on the ponytail. "And? What happened today?"

"He said something about my mother and the twins. And Nick. I . . . hit him."

"My God! And he?"

"He tried to crack me one. I mean actually, with his fist.
Not that—" here Caddy laughed hoarsely "—everybody
around here doesn't feel perfectly free to poke me in the
nose any time they feel like it. In the last week," she went on,
gaining in indignation, "I've been slapped around so many
times, I'm just getting used—"

"What happened when you hit him?" Jane said, cutting
off Caddy's bill of particulars.

"Why, he dropped his pipe and the monkeys came
down," Caddy said, as if Jane were a fool not to have thought
of it.

On a release of breath Jane murmured, "Good Lord, the
simians to the rescue!" She laughed briefly in wonderment.
"If Nick—Doctor Bartholomew—when Doctor Bartholomew
hears of this, Caddy, I honestly don't know what he'll do to
you. If you think all Pawksville has been slugging it out
with you recently, wait until your father gets wind of this."

"*You're* going to tell Nick?"

A serious Jane said, "I really ought to, shouldn't I?"

"Why don't you just say you ought to tattle," Caddy
ranted, "that's what you mean. *Tattle.*" Prompted by her
jealousy, she stormed, "You don't have anything to do with
me and Nick. I don't need you to tell Nick on me, thank
you. I can do it myself. And he doesn't need you either! I
heard what he said before he went to the Morgue House that
night. He said it was just because you were mad at him, and
he wanted to—"

"Stop that hysterical babbling at once!" When Caddy
fell silent, Jane said, "Caddy, you were dangerously close
to indulging in a little tattling yourself. Now you just com-
pose yourself and listen to me. I've decided I'll not speak
to Nick about this. That is, I'll not, if you give me your
solemn word that you've told me all that happened between
you and Titus Graham. And also give me your solemn promise that you'll never go near him again."

"Will you promise never to go near Nick again?"

Jane sighed. "Caddy, you're in waters over your head. Sit down and let me try to explain something to you."

Making a show of reluctance, thought patently eager to delve into fascinating adult peccadillos, Caddy sank to the edge of the pool. Disdaining for the moment a conciliatory tone, Jane said bluntly, "Surely you know of my husband?"

"Yes, Doctor." Caddy had decided to be helpful. "Isn't he that red-headed catatonic who—"

"I am acquainted with both his coloration and diagnosis," Jane snapped without meaning to.

"Excuse me, Doctor."

Jane put aside her sharpness. "Yes, he is catatonic, Caddy. He's very seriously ill, and I'm terribly worried about him. It's an awful thing, Caddy, to wake up to—well—desperation every morning. And still have to go about one's duties. It builds up in one, the tension, the increasing sense of impending disaster. Such anxiety divides one. Or, let me put it this way. If I don't feel that I have a completely split personality, I do have a perforated one. Just tear along the dotted line. . . ."

Caddy looked with open pity at the woman seated on the marble edge beside her. "I guess I hadn't thought of it like that."

"No. So your father—Working with him as much as I do, he began to worry about me, and he. . . . Caddy, are you comprehending this?"

"Nope," Caddy said frankly. "I see what you're driving at, but I really don't take it in. My viewpoint," she explained, coloring, "is a little different." Suddenly confiding, she added, "I wasn't there to snoop on you that night. I was just caught there. I've been in and out of the Morgue House all summer. I swiped Nick's key for a while and unlocked the back door. Say, did you ever eat that watermelon?"

"Water—Did I ever——"

"Watermelon," Caddy said patiently. "I—borrow one every once in a while from the Jubilee patch—and I keep them in the refrigerator. Only I wasn't after my melon that night. I was hiding behind the instrument cabinet because I heard Nick say he was going to do a post."

"You mean a post-mortem?"

Caddy said regretfully, "That's right. Nick said I couldn't watch one until I was in high school. He just doesn't seem to realize sometimes that I'm almost thirteen, and things that would have the twins fainting all over the joint wouldn't even faze me." Caddy snapped her fingers airily.

"Apparently you are fazed more easily than you like to think," Jane suggested with much meaning.

"Uhhh, yes," Caddy admitted sheepishly.

"Well," Jane said briskly, "have we arrived at an understanding?"

They measured one another with sidelong glances.

"About what, Doctor?"

"Is that a piece of deliberate cussedness on your part?" Jane said, poking a forefinger into the water. "Pretending not to understand me? I want two things from you. First that you understand that what happened between your father and myself was a single instance and will not be repeated. And secondly, I want your promise that you won't, repeat *won't,* go near that Special Patient again."

"Oh, I haven't the faintest intention of going near him again," Caddy said carelessly.

Jane looked at her searchingly, and Caddy noted that Dr. Carmody had freckles, of all places, under her eyes. The eyes themselves were clear and reflective like the Greek pool. "I wonder about you," Jane mused. "You're really too devious, too intent on your own pursuits, for me to follow your thought processes very far into the undergrowth. My common sense tells me there is no striking a bargain with a. . . ." Jane cleared her throat and fell silent.

"Say it," Caddy challenged. "A psychopathic personality! Last year Doctor Heall went around telling everybody I had an Electra complex, and the year before that I was an oral—"

"Caddy!" Jane yelped in disbelief. "You mustn't take such gossip—"

"And if anything," Caddy concluded in a burst of indignation, "I've been as manic as all getout all summer. You'd think a bunch of psychiatrists would be able to see what's under their noses!"

"Wouldn't you indeed," Jane agreed, baffled. She dusted off her lap as though they had been picnicking and there were crumbs there. There was a rather disoriented look on her face. Caddy sought and finally cornered the darting bewildered gaze.

Caddy said, "Then it is settled? You won't tell Nick what I've been up to?"

"My dear Caddy, it comes to me that I haven't the vaguest notion of what you've been up to."

Caddy sniggered self-consciously. She felt herself warming to Dr. Carmody, something in her reaching out timidly for companionship with the trace of girlishness still left in Jane. "For one thing," Caddy said confidingly, "I've been getting a lot of poetry out of my system." She looked down at the rapidly disintegrating shreds of the "Ode to the Pawks Boys," a ribbon of which was slowly drifting out toward the center of the pool. "Have you ever read any of the Great Poet's poems?"

"Ohhh, I may have," Jane said uncertainly.

"He's real obscure, I'll say that for him," Caddy conceded. "But so's everybody. I was just wondering if he's really as good as they say."

"Caddy, I'm not sufficiently attuned to poetry to judge. He wasn't brought before Staff Meeting, so I know very little about him."

"I have the strangest feeling," Caddy remarked with rich and mysterious satisfaction, "that his best work is behind him."

Jane was polite. "That so? Look, Caddy, I'd better run along." She put her hand lightly on Caddy's. "We are friends now, aren't we?"

"If we both behave ourselves, we are," Caddy said boldly, yet blushing when Dr. Carmody received her impudence with an appreciative grin.

After Dr. Carmody was gone Caddy sat on, gazing down on the clipboard. A pair of fish were playing tug of war with the final fragment of the Ode.

Well, Caddy thought philosophically, I guess my reputation will have to stand or fall on my Canticles and Hebephrenia. Deep within her, though, was the sublime content of knowing that, psuedonomiously, she had immortalized the Holy Dove.

Someday, she promised herself, I'm going to tell Nick and Dr. Carmody the whole story, all of it. They'll die laughing.

The immortalized Holy Dove came in out of the sun and, going to her ward door, banged on it imperiously. On her walk she had noticed, from a distance, the phenomenon of the Monkey Tree in furious motion, followed by the disorganized departure of Caddy Bartholomew from the grotto. A vision had come to the Dove, vivid and terrible, of what must have taken place (or only nearly did, God willing), and what terrors had either befallen or were sure to overtake little Caddy in the near future. Under the Monkey Tree, that is.

Billie Noon unlocked the door. "Fer pity sakes, Holy Dee, I thought it was the Governor hisself making all that racket. You have a nice walk, Holy—"

"You must call Doctor Bartholomew at once, Miss Noon."

Billie Noon urged the Holy Dove into a chair by the desk. "Now you just sit down here and rest. If you're feeling bad, I'll have the Doc over here so fast——you look funny; are you running a fever?"

"It's Caddy," the Holy Dove said urgently. "She's in danger. Call Doctor Bartholomew at once, Miss Noon!" She drummed her bandaged hand on the desk for emphasis.

"Holy Dee! If you don't care about your hand, I do."
Miss Noon was rapidly moving up the scale as she spoke.
"You take it easy, I can tell you've been walking way too fast
out under that hot sun. And I don't even want to *think*
about you getting disturbed." Muscles rippling, Miss Noon
patted the Holy Dove awkwardly.

"It is vital he knows about Caddy. Now. It may be a
matter of life," the Holy Dove went on with no indication
that she recognized herself to be intoning platitudes, "or
death."

Miss Noon laid her hand on the phone. The Holy Dove's
face was stern, but her pupils were normal and her breathing regular. There were none of what Miss Noon called
fidgitation signals, heralds of an impending disturbed state.
"Whose life or death?" Miss Noon faltered.

"Caddy's. That Special Patient, the one sent here for
molesting a child, tried to harm her."

"My Gawd!" Miss Noon gasped. "And he's got complete
ground privileges." She leaned forward and tapped the Holy
Dove on her sacred knee. "Holy Dee, spill. You tell me exactly what you saw."

"I think we had best get hold of Doctor Bartholomew."

Miss Noon picked up the phone. There were some
around Pawksville who took the Dove for a joke, who said
that what dirt she couldn't ferret out for herself she manu-
factured. Miss Noon did not share that opinion. "Ring Doctor Bartholomew's office," she said into the phone. She held
her hand over the mouthpiece. "Did you see him, you know,
achully. . . ."

The Holy Dove toyed with an untruth. Lest her vision
be dismissed as an hallucination and as haste, not hairsplit-
ting, was in order, she said, "Yes."

Nick located his daughter the first place he tried, the
library. Eyes on his small desk clock, he was exhibiting
enough fidgitation signals to have sent Miss Noon for the
paraldehyde without an instant's hesitation. Dr. Kox would

have finished his leisurely cigar and chat with Superintendent Keeney by now, and be ambling on over to surgery. He was scheduled to scrub at three, and protocol demanded that Nick be there. Protocol or no, Nick sat at his desk, so frightened that when he picked up the portrait of a simpering seven-year-old Caddy, the leather of the frame grew slippery with sweat. At Caddy's shave-and-a-haircut knock on his door, he bellowed, "Come in here, Caddy!"

She entered, poised and expectant, as if she were certain that he had summoned her in private in order to beg her pardon for what had happened at the Morgue House. Then her first cursory glance put her on her guard. "Yes, Nick?"

He came round the desk and grabbing her shirt front slammed her into a chair. "Let's have it. What were you and the Special Patient up to in the grotto?" But before she could reply, he saw the bruise next to her mouth and was too shaken to speak for a moment.

"The grotto?" Caddy stared hard at her portrait on his desk. "Someone's been telling you cock-and-bull stories, Nick."

"Caddy—— Caddy, so help me, I've only struck you twice in my life, and that was the worst mistake I ever made. I should have beaten you senseless while I was at it. Well, I'm going to make up for it now, if you don't tell me the truth about you and that—pervert."

"He's hebephrenic, if you want to know, and getting more so every day," Caddy so far forgot herself as to say icily.

"Is he! And just how do you know all this?"

"I read his poetry in that goofy magazine in the library."

Nick waited, and when Caddy did not go on, he said. "And that is all you have to tell me?"

Caddy's silence would have done credit to her Aunt Al.

Nick said, "Girl, you use your head. This isn't just

a matter of your hiding something from me as a form of
revenge. This. . . . Listen, kid, you could be in a mess. You'd
better level with me fast, or I'll have to take some mighty
drastic actions. Caddy, level with me. Please!"

"I don't level with people. Not any more. I leveled with
Doctor Carmody, and look what happened," Caddy said
bitterly.

Nick leaned over her, placing a hand on each arm of
her chair. "Dammit, let's not dwell on that now. You saw
us together. I'm sorry. You'll never know how sorry, but
this is something else. You have me scared. Baby, do I have
to get on my knees to you?"

Caddy gulped at the endearment, then she hardened
herself against him. Whatever Dr. Carmody had told him
(It must have been a lulu! the voice of betrayal cried out
in her mind), he believed in it religiously. And here not
a half-hour ago, stupe that she was, Caddy had been contemplating welcoming Carmody to the charmed circle of
Nick and herself. She was actually looking forward to making
a clean breast of it to them both, relying on them to accept
her contrition as well as perceive that their own fears had
been groundless. She had had such faith in them, thinking
of them by the Greek reflecting pool, that they might have
been Nick and Nancy all over again. But the moment her
back was turned Carmody hotfooted it straight to Nick to
tattle. "Name your informant," Caddy burst out. "Go ahead,
just name her!"

"Name—" Nick straightened, hit himself on the forehead, and fell into his desk chair. "What in hell has that got
to do with it? All right, the Holy Dove, if you must know."

Caddy looked at him as she had not even when he
struck her. She looked at him as if he had denied his pater-
nity. "You're lying to me," she said as she were uttering
the incredible. "You're lying to me, to cover up for somebody
else. I've lied to you, and I admit it. But I never thought
you'd do it to me. Even when you said you were going

to do a post at the Morgue House, you weren't lying. You did get the stiff out. Only Doctor Carmody got to carrying on like a—"

"But you can't—— Caddy, I'm just a human being. Allow me a fault or two, will you? Stop worshiping me! Even if I were lying to you, and I'm not, wipe that look off your face. The Holy Dove told me she saw you and that patient together. That there was some sort of a scuffle going on." Nick flung the sweat from his forehead with the back of his hand. "Caddy, you've got to set me straight. What happened?"

Caddy sat. He had his version, he was only asking her for hers to corroborate it, his very attitude from the minute she walked into his office proved that.

The silence grew lengthy. Nick pleaded, "Would you tell Al? Or maybe you'd rather tell another doctor about it. Doctor Carmody would understand——"

"The only thing she understands," Caddy said tightly, "is how to be two-faced. And if I do tell Aunt Al, I'll make her promise never never never to speak a word of it to you!"

Nick said slowly, "Caddy, you know enough about medicine to know that there are drugs to make people talk. If it's punishment you're worried about, I swear to you I won't punish you. Or I will punish you, whichever you want."

"Oh, why bother," Caddy sneered wretchedly. *"She's* told you. You wouldn't believe me, no matter what I say. The Holy Dove told you. That's a hot one!"

"Very well then, who? Who do you want me to say? Does it matter?"

"It sure seems to, us cutting up this way," Caddy said at her most withering, but could not maintain the pose and abruptly sniveled.

Hoping to take advantage of this indication of weakening, Nick suggested quietly, "Then let's cut out the cutting up. Come on, Caddy, have the guts. Out with it. You're not—— You don't have some kind of a crush on the guy?"

"*Pttt,*" Caddy snorted as an alternative to snobbing.

"The truth, then."

"W–who told you?"

"All right," Nick said wearily, "I'll have to break this impasse the best way I can, though in a way you might not like. I'll have Doctor Carmody meet us at the clinic in case she is needed, and then it's pentothal sodium for you, kid. That stuff will have your tongue wagging at both ends, and you know it."

"I'll kill myself before I'll let that vile woman touch me," Caddy said tonelessly. "If you're so crazy about finding out the truth, give her pentothal. Or give the Great Poet pentothal. Or the Holy Dove. You'll take anybody's word before mine!" Caddy was exhausted, perspiring profusely from shame at what Nick was obviously afraid had happened to her. Bitter recriminations spoke in her ears, almost as real as auditory hallucinations. *We're friends, aren't we,* said that gay forked-tongue treacher, Dr. Carmody.

Nick lifted the phone. Caddy's glance encountered his and scurried for safety to the simpering photograph of herself at seven. Torpor settled on her as she listened to Nick locating Dr. Carmody. "Jane," Nick said, "I might need your help at the clinic. It's about Caddy and the Special Patient. What do you know about it?"

He ground the phone to his ear, listening, staring at Caddy. "Nothing!" he shouted. "What do you mean, it's *nothing? What's* all over? Dammit, can't anybody make sense around here? My daughter walks in with her mouth mauled, and you tell me——"

"Why don't you all quit pretending?" Caddy burst out scornfully.

"What? Just a moment . . ."

"Everybody pretending to everybody else and having conniption fits over nothing," Caddy went on. "Not that Doctor Carmody isn't good at pretending. When we were talking by the reflecting pool, I began to think she was one swell person. I was even thinking she reminded me a little bit of Nancy. I'm sure no great shakes when it comes to judging character, am I? Well, now that this ruckus is all over, I'll just be running along, Nick. You and Doctor Carmody would rather talk in private, I'm sure. You and Doctor Carmody must have all kinds of little things to talk over." Caddy stood up.

"You stay put, Caduceus! Now, dammit, Jane, I'm going to get to the bottom of. . . . Because I should be joining the Iceman in surgery, that's why! Look, will you just . . . Promised who? That degenerate? Dammit, you sit right back down. No, not you, Jane—Caddy! No, *don't* come up to surgery!" A fleeting expression of anguish came and went with shutter-click rapidity on Nick's face. "I said meet me in the clinic. Well, Kox can wait ten minutes, can't he? *Caddy, you*—"

"Excuse me," Caddy said at the door, and with a catatonic immobility of feature stalked out.

She had in mind to cower and brood in the sanctuary of the old lab. She slipped out a side door and ran lightly under the overhang of a porch. Above her, male voices remarked pithily of the persecution of the federal government through the agency of the television set, or voiced obscenities with the meaningless regularity of a dripping faucet. Never one to attend to the utterances of acute patients, Caddy noted only that her passing made no impression on them, and her whereabouts would remain to them, forever, a mystery. She made a dash through the open for a hedge, and there in its shade she lay full length to reconnoiter.

Dr. Kox appeared, sauntering along in the direction of the Hospital, slipping in and out of the shade so that the dappled patterns on his face blocked out his features as effectively as if he were covered with camouflage paint. Hard on the footsteps of Dr. Kox came Dr. Bartholomew, his dark skin crimson above his whites, his black eyes searching everywhere. Overtaking Dr. Kox, Dr. Bartholomew had a hurried word or so with the Iceman, then charged on. As the Iceman

idled up the front steps of the Hospital, Dr. Bartholomew
had reached the side entrance to the clinic in a sprint.

Caddy was prepared to bolt the instant Nick closed the
clinic door behind him. But as the door did pull to, a patient
came up to a bench not three feet from Caddy and sat down.
While Caddy sweated and fumed, the patient opened a notebook and began scribbling, scribbling, scribbling.

Suddenly the Great Poet appeared, tottering from the
heat, and went straight to the clinic, trying the door. It
opened through the agency of a hand emerging from a white
sleeve, and the Great Poet entered.

The patient on the bench scribbled on.

After a time, Dr. Carmody strode up to the clinic door
and, unlocking it with her key, entered.

The patient on the bench lit a cigarette and then resumed scribbling.

Caddy itched and sweated and bit her ponytail in rage.
After what she judged to be an eternity, she rose up in her
wrath, scratching at her insect bites, and screeching at the
startled patient, "Is this the *only* lousy bench in Pawksville,
dammit?"

Then, having come to the decision to confront them all
—Nick, Dr. Carmody, the Great Poet, and whomever else
Nick had decided to invite or involve, for Pete's sake, he gets
just too Oedipal for words sometimes, or whatever Dr. Heall
would call it—Caddy herself stomped off in the direction of
the clinic to shoo the bats out of everybody's belfries once
and for all.

When Titus Graham tried the door to the clinic, Nick
was at the desk scrawling out a note for Jane. In his annoyance he thought, Can't Jane get it through her skull
about the doors around here? First she's so careless she doesn't
even try the back Morgue House door for weeks on end,
and then comes over here without bothering to bring her
clinic key with her. "I'm coming, I'm coming!" Nick snarled.

Finding himself fact to face with Titus Graham, Nick did not recognize that battered visage for an instant. Moreover, the mustache no longer ornamented the face, and such its absence now proved it to be, for the Great Poet's spicy aspect was gone. The mouth, upper lip black and swollen on one side, appeared on his face like a surgical site shaved and cleansed for the knife. The ginger eyes had taken luster from the full mustache; now they appeared browned and dry like the spines of old leather-bound volumes. The whites had the tigerish tinge of faded gilt lettering. Very circumspectly Titus Graham asked, "May I have a moment of your time, Doctor?"

Nick had to look away from the bald face. Baldfaced, Nick was thinking, tampers with my daughter and presents himself to me baldfaced. "Well, well, you're just the fellow I wanted to see," Nick said dangerously, and yanked the Great Poet through the door, locking it behind them.

"I've got some bad bites on my mouth," Titus Graham said rather unnecessarily. In a more aggrieved tone he enlarged, "The monkeys attacked me." Seemingly unaware, or pretending to be so, of Nick's stalking him down the hallway, Titus, with a brief backward questioning glance, entered the first treatment room.

"Sit down in the treatment chair," Nick said. His voice had taken on the bland tone that almost stroked its victim when fury possessed Nick completely.

Relaxing a notch, Titus Graham seated himself in a swivel treatment chair. Against a white wall and white cabinets and a white examining table, and above his own whites, Nick's head hung over Titus like some blood-black moon. Titus found the effect not unpleasing. He said easily, "I was afraid I could get . . . something . . . any number of things, I suppose, from monkey bites. Mr. Hamshot suggested I have you look me over."

Nick was doing exactly that.

"Mr. Hamshot said I just might catch you in the clinic at this hour."

"Oh, we'd have caught up with one another sooner or later," Nick assured him pleasantly.

"Oh." Titus Graham decided to return to the subject of his injuries. "Just what might I get from these bites?"

"Not rabies, if that's what's troubling you. Our monkeys aren't rabid. The first time anyone was bitten we sacrificed one, but it proved negative. We found no Negri bodies in the brain."

"You don't say!" Titus Graham marveled. "My!"

"Don't sneer at your own good fortune. Immunization treatment is extremely painful. And bitten around the face and mouth as you are, you'd get two shots a day for the first week."

"Oh, isn't medical science just *wonderful!*" Titus Graham caroled. "And you, Pawksville's beloved and dedicated Doctor Bartholomew, are just wonderful too. The consecrated Man of Medicine. Oh, you just don't fool us one bit, Doctor. We all know of your soft interior so insufficiently concealed by your brusquerie. Not that you aren't a man of decision when the necessity arises. Yes, we humble patients just think you perfect in every way. We . . . Oooow, that stings!"

"Sorry," Nick said mildly, wielding a pad soaked in antiseptic. "Don't think you'll need any stitches." He lifted an applicator from the jar, dipped it, and then worked it around a bite on the lower lip. "I'll want to do more on this, but I'm due in surgery in a few moments."

"Oh, yes. Lobotomy day," Titus Graham snickered. "Our beloved and dedicated Superintendent Keeney is quite ardent about lobotomies. Castration of the mind. Isn't that correct?"

"No. Shut your mouth."

"Tut, Doctor!"

"I said shut your mouth. I'm trying to treat it."

The Poet had long since begun to enjoy himself. "My dear Doctor, I mistook you shamefully. I should have known at once what you meant—— That *does* sting!"

"Not as much, I'd venture," Nick said, "as a broken jaw might." He snapped the applicator in half and trod heavily on the bucket pedal. The lid flew up like a hungry bivalve for the tidbit.

"Temper, temper," Titus Graham murmured waggishly. "Are you considering breaking my jaw?"

"I was referring to the fact that you broke the jaw of a young boy."

"That. At the time I was merely being kittenish," Titus said complacently. "I hadn't set out to do it at all. He simply—" the ginger eyes met Nick's boldly "—simply wouldn't hold still."

"For you to beat him to a pulp."

"Rubbish. I was merely trying to experience a certain esoteric sensation. And I was polluted at the time. No need for you to talk as if my moral fiber is threadbare because of one prank."

"If that boy had died," Nick said evenly, "I'd have tossed my job in the Governor's teeth before I'd have let you get safely committed to Pawksville."

"Would you have." Titus laughed as best he was able, uproar claiming the unimpaired half of his mouth. "You mustn't be so provincial, Doctor. Such experiences are sanctioned, not condemned, in over half the world. Children, you know, are viewed in their correct light—at worst as pests, at best as commodities. But you're so naïve around here. If it had been a colored lad with me that night, the police would probably have poked me in the ribs and asked how it was. You're all a pack of pious bigots. Your very indigation smacks of lynch-mob leanings. Speaking of lynch mobs, it's time steps were taken to secure my release. I weary of this place. And that whole inconsequential mess that landed me here is long over and done with. I paid off the parents gen-

erously. Twice what he was worth." Titus Graham waved a
hand in the air in a balletic gesture. "In any civilized country
children can be had for a song."

"Sing," Nick said.

"Did I hear you correctly?" the Poet asked, taking a
turn for the innocent, the artless, and the crafty in equal proportions.

"Sing me a tune for having tampered with my daughter," Nick said almost casually.

Titus Graham took fright and tried to rise, but Nick
slammed him down. "Doctor," Graham began to babble, "I
don't know what you're talking about. I've not so much as
touched the girl. If you'll stop playing the devoted father and
and listen to me——" The Poet was bracing himself for
bodily harm, the mocking light in his eyes dying. "Doctor,
I'd advise you to recall who I am before——"

"Did you tamper with her?" Nick said softly.

"You place very little trust in your own child, Bartholomew. Why don't you ask her? I'm a depraved beast, hardly
competent to give testimony. Of course you have asked
Caddy, and she's denied all. So you think she gave you
the lie. Well, here's the simple truth. She's been slipping out
my work for me. Your daughter, unlike the incorruptible
Mr. Hamshot, saw fit to mail out my poetry for me. She's
quite a little poet herself," Graham went on placatingly.
"She— Look, do you really think I'd come strolling in here,
if I had . . ."

"You are never to speak to, to look at another person
under twenty-one, so long as you remain in Pawksville. Is
that understood? Because if you do——"

"Not so fast, if you please," Titus said, rallying. "No
empty threats, Doctor. Really, this situation does seem to call
for the most outmoded of melodramatics. Come now, Doctor,
I used your daughter as a mail-carrier. If you want the truth,
I find her as unappealing as a baby pit-viper. Now may I

go? And thank you for your attention to my lip. I was afraid
I might get lockjaw or some—"

"You might at that," Nick said. "It's usually fatal, you
know."

Titus Graham settled back, a fleeting spasm of pain
crossing his face. "If I died, you would consider the world
to have suffered no loss at all, wouldn't you? You, of all
people," he said in a strange questioning voice, "a psychiatrist, should be more tolerant of people like myself. And
our little slips from grace. Try looking at that matter this
way: the boy was the offspring of scum, and scum himself.
No sensible person subscribes to egalitarianism where scum
are concerned. In a word, I am the better of just about
anyone I meet. You glower? Glower then. But you think
exactly the same of yourself. The way you stomp around
Pawksville, you are as clumsily arrogant as Hannibal's own
elephant clumping up the Alps. No more than I do, do you
believe that every breathing piece of human trash is entitled
to a certain measure of importance. But I carry it to its
logical conclusion. If they are without worth, why should I
be tender of them? And if one of them affords me an hour's
pleasure at his expense, should I suffer pangs of conscience
afterward? Must I lie awake at night and weep?"

"Have you ever done that?" Nick said gently.

"One does, you know," Graham admitted erratically.
"But it's not genuine remorse—there is no such thing. Is
there? It's sentimentality. Don't give me a priggish scowl,
Doctor; you know I am speaking the unvarnished truth. Or
am I crediting you with a superior understanding you don't
possess? You're just a masterly phony, aren't you? You've
even got yourself deceived. You don't really perceive, or
think, or comprehend; you merely react to a stimulus with a
reflexive jerk." Titus Graham laughed a shade wildly.
"You're just one more reflexive jerk, Doctor. It may be said
of you only that you are not dead. Conversely, I—I am alive!
In sum, *sum*." Again he managed a laugh in salute to his

little pun. "Am I keeping you from your work, Doctor?"

One hand resting on the examining table, standing quietly, Nick said, "You are my work, Mr. Graham."

Titus looked at him attentively. "You can't imagine how starved I am for conversation. Hamshot, you see, considers *'duhhh'* brilliant repartee. Your daughter I found the world's foremost bleeding bore. You've no idea how safe she was with me. Only she took offense to a criticism of mine and swung at me with the "Ode to the Pawks Boys." Then those little beasts came down out of the tree on us. A case of monkey see, monkey do, ummm?" Titus began to twirl himself in thirty-degree turns on the treatment chair. "No matter, I won't be needing little Miss Bartholomew's services any longer. I intend to demand of Leroy that he have me released, when I see him at the Jubilee. His wits aren't exactly nimble, but he must realize he can't keep me imprisoned forever. An artist such as myself must be free. Surely you agree, Doctor?"

"Try not to touch your mouth with your hands," was Nick's only comment. "You can get an infection that way."

"Haven't you heard a word I've been saying?" Graham shouted, then crumpled back against his seat. "I'm asking too much of you. Only a man of great wisdom would understand. You have an air of smugness about you which I foolishly mistook for the *simpático*. You hear me, but you're not listening. You're too busy categorizing me. Am I a psychopathic personality? Or is it a neurotic personality? You must have some pat term for one who has his own canon of ethics. And I do, I assure you, Doctor. I am a principled man. But I refuse to suffer guilt when I violate a code which is false and not mine! I beat my own different drum and march to it, to go into the matter Thoreauly." Titus raised his eyes to Nick as if offering him his last quip as a present. Not seeing what he sought in Nick's black regard, he wilted momentarily. "And I don't care a fig what you or anyone else might think of my actions," he muttered, like a cranky

child in a pet. He made as if to rise, then sank back. Some
compulsion was riding him, Nick's noncommittal attitude
goading him as no deliberate provocation could have. "License is the prerogative of genius," he suddenly challenged
Nick. "Not mere liberty, license!"

"Mr. Graham, you assert that too forcefully. You protest
too much," Nick said idly. "You don't really think that."

"Ah, don't I? Then let me widen your horizons for you,
Doctor. I think that, and I act upon my belief. There was a
boy I held under the water. . . . It was my ungovernable
temper in that instance. But no breast-beating after, none
whatsoever! He was gone, leaving not the minutest aperture
in the fabric of my life to show where he had been. To this
day no one has ever missed him. So you see, Doctor, when it
comes to carrying out my convictions, I am the soul of
punctiliousness."

"And is that when you wept?" Nick asked. "After you
held a boy under water until he drowned?" He added gently,
"Remorse is the most unbearable mental torture we can
inflict upon ourselves. Isn't that so?"

Titus Graham was trembling; then, rallying, he cried,
"Ah, I did manage to snag your interest, didn't I, Doctor?
And with such a transparent little fabrication. Well, don't
be ashamed, everybody enjoys listening to a confession of
criminal propensities. So lip-smacking. So gratifying."

"I'm not gratified, Mr. Graham," Nick said.

Titus Graham halted his twirling on the stool. "But
you'll never really know, will you? Missing, somewhere on
the face of this earth: one urchin. Maybe. Or mayhap a—
demon—spirited him away. You are a clod, Doctor," he said
dreamily. "I really do fear I ask too much of you."

"A lot," Nick said, "but not too much."

For a brief instant Titus Graham bent on Nick a look
of wild appeal, then to stretch his damaged mouth to its
accustomed mocking smirk. "If you're done treating me, if
you've exhausted your store of medical miracles, I'll be
getting along."

"You'll need a shot," Nick said carefully. "Wound prophylaxis may not be enough for those bites. I'd better give you a TAT shot, just in case."

"TAT? Against lockjaw?"

Nick was unlocking the drug cabinet. If any emotion marred his disinterest in his judging of Titus Graham, it was profound pity. The man had, in all likelihood, been born a psychic carnivore. He could no more be censured for it than a tiger could for not being a housecat. But, unlike the tiger, he was subject to the bleakest grief known to man —remorse. Nick said, to occupy Graham's thoughts, "Since I'm not referring to a Thematic Apperception Test, I must have tetanus antitoxin in mind."

"A perfect example of pedantic drollery." Graham sniggered, his scorn that of one who has been disappointed in another.

Nick fitted a needle to a syringe, then punctured the rubber cap of a drug bottle. He drew in the liquid to the calibration the occasion called for, put the bottle back in the cabinet, label just turned so that Graham could not read it, and then pressed the plunger to expel any trapped air.

"You burly bigot," Titus Graham murmured in afterthought as Nick scrubbed at his arm with alcohol-saturated cotton.

"Make a fist," Nick said politely.

The poet complied, forming the same weapon he had desired to use on Caddy. "This is tetanus anti–what?"

"Tetanus antitoxin," Nick supplied, pushing the plunger home.

"Tet . . . to . . . nuh. . . ." Titus Graham breathed, eyes losing their focus. Momentarily he rallied, fighting the drug, fear-induced adrenalin jetting through his system, coming to his aid. *"Whaaa?"*

"In your own way you asked me for help," Nick told him gravely. "Only I can't cure you; you're fully aware of that. But I can give you the freedom you really long for—

freedom from your compulsion to hurt and kill. I couldn't
loose you on the world again as you are. To you, the world
is peopled solely by victims. Not to borrow your fancy talk,
I am by way of being a horologist right now. I'm going to
fix your clock. Before anyone can stop me."

Titus Graham, with Herculean effort, focused on Nick
for the space of a heartbeat, before his lids eased down and
he sweetly slumbered, slumped against the cool metal arm
of the treatment stool.

Nick counted his pulse, then went to the desk phone.
"Get me Mr. Dick in surgery, this is Doctor Bartholomew."

Mr. Dick came on to acknowledge his important presence on the other end of the line. "This is Doctor—" Nick
began, but fell silent at the sight of Jane Carmody standing
in the doorway taking stock of the comatose Titus Graham.

"What's afoot?" Jane asked briskly. "Who slugged him?
I hope."

"Doctor who?" Mr. Dick was demanding.

"Doctor Bartholomew," Nick said. "Mr. Dick, I want you
to put— Is Sean Maginnis in restraint?"

"Yes, Doctor."

"What?" Jane said, coming to stand over Nick. "Nick,
what did you just—"

"Then put him in the recovery room. I'm counter-
manding Superintendent Keeney's order for his lobotomy.
And after you've done that, get down here to the—" he
had to shake Jane off before he could continue "—down
here to the clinic at once. Take the elevator and bring a
cart with you."

"The clinic, Doctor?" Mr. Dick repeated, his haughty
tone advising Nick that, as usual, he was thinking the world
and all of himself, and of little else.

"Yes, the clinic. But not until you've gotten Maginnis
into the recovery room. He's not to undergo surgery, got
that?"

"Of course, Doctor," Mr. Dick said, offended.

Nick hung up.

Jane sat down suddenly on a treatment stool. She was dazed; she spoke as from some reverie. "You wouldn't have, you couldn't have kept it from me. Unless you really are deranged. I've been around Pawksville long enough to know that half the time the staff are indistinguishable from the patients. But you—you're bizarre, Nick." Her voice took on fire. "Keeney has the scruples of a cockroach, but for you to go in league with him——"

"Now keep watertight, Jane," Nick said. "Don't start leaking a lot of bilge you don't mean. Keeney has the written consent of his parents. And your husband is past all help but psychosurgery—"

"Consenting behind my back," Jane said. "And sending Father Muldroon around to sound me out. And to top it all, your high indignation when I tried to—reach Sean." She stood up. "I'm going up there to make certain that Sean——"

"Oh no, you aren't," Nick said, and pushed her back down as it seemed he had had to restrain one person after another all day. "I'm substituting him." He indicated the slumbering Titus Graham with a nod. "Kox has seven consents lined up, and he's going to get seven patients."

"And if Graham hadn't come along. If you hadn't gotten wind of him and Caddy—— you'd have let Kox *pith* my husband."

"I don't know, Jane."

"There are a world of things you don't know! And yet you storm around Pawksville, plunging into mistake after mistake!"

"I am frequently in error, Jane," Nick said soberly.

". . . jumping to conclusions even God Himself would consider some pretty high hurdles! Are you a sadist? Is that why it's always the 'strenuous convulsion' you like to see, or the exhausting dehydration of insulin, or the degrading stupor of massive sleep, or the Metrazol fractures, and best of all, oh, the very juiciest, watching the Iceman ram that leucotome through an eye socket and squash and mash—"

"Shut up, I hear the elevator coming."

Jane shouted on, "And the next time Kox comes? Who will you substitute for Sean then? That schizophrenic daughter of yours? Oh, don't bother to answer. There's won't be a next time. I'm taking my husband out of here so fast—"

Nick put a hand over her mouth. "You seem slightly out of kilter, Doctor. Since my daughter is not a patient of yours, and your husband is a patient of mine, let's stay on the subject. I did not order your husband's lobotomy. Keeney did, as with all the others. Yet when his order came through to me, don't you think I didn't weigh the matter. You just try being dispassionate sometime, when it comes to meddling or not meddling in the life of someone you love. You try keeping your perspective when your medical judgment tells you one thing, and your emotions another, and your conscience yet a third. . . . All right, all right, I won't go on with that. You order what treatment you want for him and I by-God will administer it. Now get yourself aligned. Mr. Dick will be strutting in here any moment for Graham. Go in the next treatment room and wait for me. I'm going up long enough to make certain this thing goes through without a hitch, and then I'll be back down. I want you here when I come back. You hear me, Jane?" He took his hand from her face. The sounds of the elevator were echoed in the rattling instruments in the cabinet.

Jane looked at him as if she found him contemptible. "I'll never forgive you. I'll work for you and I'll slave for you, but I'll never——"

"Good. That'll be one way of keeping you out of my hair and me out of your bed. Go on, get in the next room."

The elevator made its presence known by a series of door-slammings, gruntings, and cable-whistlings. As Mr. Dick appeared, pushing the cart, a look of dainty disgust on his face at having to perform such a menial task, Jane's white skirt whisked into the next treatment room.

"Here we are, Mr. Dick," Nick said, hoisting the sleeping Titus Graham to an upright position. "Upsy-daisy onto the cart. Is Doctor Kox ready?"

"He *has* been," Mr. Dick said regally, giving not a second glance at Titus Graham. He looked down his nose at Nick struggling with the inert body of Graham, then, unconcerned, bored, Mr. Dick seized the legs and hauled.

The Great Poet was trundled into the elevator. Going up: Main floor, acute psychotics. Second floor, diseases, fractures, and surgical cases. Third floor, Nemesis.

When Nick left surgery, having shaken the cool reptilian hand of the Iceman, the last he heard was Sean Maginnis cutting up in a catatonic abandon in a recovery room. He had ordered Maginnis taken down to the acute ward, where later, he, Nick, would give him a jolt of EST to calm him down. In the other recovery room the patients lay quietly, their eyes neatly bandaged. In less than a week there would be no physical signs of what had befallen them. Mr. Dick was in the act of bestowing his august company on Dr. Kox for the stroll back to the rotunda. Once there Mr. Dick would return Dr. Kox's instrument case to him with the same tomfool ceremoniousness with which he had received it.

The elevator clanked up to discharge the attendants, and Nick rode it down to the clinic. The thunderbolt crash of the doors behind him served notice of Nick's arrival to Jane Carmody, who was pacing the floor, lying in wait for him.

"Now listen," Nick began just before she could launch her diatribe, "He's all right. An attendant is taking him down to acute. And, for your information, he's having himself a real party cutting up and indulging in catatonic capers. I hate to do it, but he's going to go on two ESTs a day for a while, to see if we can calm him down. He's heading for a physical collapse as it is. But you don't think of that, do you, Jane? You prefer to speak of treatment in terms of sadism. Well, I've told you before, and I'll repeat it now: I've had them all. I had EST. I had a Metrazol convulsion that tossed Sonny right across the room. But I'd rather go through that a hundred times over than suffer what your husband is suffering now. But that's the way you want him, that's the way you got him. God help the poor guy, you won't let me."

"You overweening paranoid," Jane said helplessly. "Clapping your big paw over my mouth, and then bawling that you love me, and that you . . ."

"I do."

". . . and that you weighed everything in your mind in the best Clinical Director tradition, and after your mountainous labors came forth with the mouse that—"

"Jane, let's have done with the personal backtalk. Guess what? I'm your superior. D'ja ever think of that? I hired you and I can fire you. Don't think that I don't love you enough to do it, too. That's what I said. Enough. Before I'll stand by and watch you crack up over a man who was hopeless long before you ever set eyes on him."

"All right, today he's hopeless! And tomorrow some drug company sends us a nice tidy sample of a new tranquilizer, or some research lab isolates the chemical factor for what we are pleased to call 'chronic' insanity, and my husband stands to benefit. I'm taking my chances with him this way, thank you. He's not just another hillbilly making a nuisance of himself on the ward, you know. He's a talented—"

"He's a patient like any other patient. You get this straight, Doctor; I'm not going to tell you again. Your husband is not *the* ninety and nine to me. All patients are the ninety and nine to me."

"And especially Titus Graham," Jane sneered on a sob.

"Yes, Titus Graham too. It had never occurred to any of us, had it, that the man was miserable? He walked in here today and taunted me with the fact that he actually murdered a child somewhere. And then he looked at me with such unconscious imploration that I was almost—staggered. So I substituted him for your husband because it was Graham's only chance. He wanted his freedom—from himself."

"And when that gets out, you've lost your job, Nick Bartholomew."

"Yep," Nick said. "It entered my mind when we were riding him up to the Iceman. Are you bucking for Clinical Director, Jane? Do you think you can beat Sonny out?"

Jane flopped into the treatment chair Titus Graham had vacated. Like him, she began turning back and forth. "You know good and well," she said moodily, "that where you go, I go. Taking Sean with me, to be sure. You know why I can't walk out on him. I have to see him restored to what he was, before I can be sure that I've—outgrown him. All that hothouse atmosphere of music and glamor would have proved too rich for my blood, I'm afraid. But I have to know it for a fact. You understand, Nick?"

"I have all along."

"And that's why you would have let Kox go ahead with—"

"No, Jane. I've been going over and over it in my mind. It's for his sake, not yours, that I still think it should be done. Now the decision rests with you. Notify Keeney in writing, and have it entered in the hospital records that you are Mrs. Maginnis, and your consent will be required hereafter. I've dumped it in your lap, Toots, and I don't exactly admire myself for it."

Jane began to weep luxuriously. "Nick, it's hell seeing someone you love, or used to love, or whatever, in the condition Sean is in."

"Well, I haven't been exactly chock-full of chuckles watching you either. If you stay on here at Pawksville you've got to do me a favor. Stop racing down the road of quirkiness, isolation, and disregard for any problems but your own. Try practicing a little medicine, hmmm? I'm not bawling you out, I'm straightening you out. Hell, woman, I need you, Sonny and company are more hindrance than— Oh, godammit, now who's at the door?"

"Me," Caddy said in a bleat when Nick unlocked the door to admit her. "Nick, I've come to make a clean breast of—"

"Caddy. Go . . . practice your vile-in or some damn thing."

Caddy was staring past him to the weeping Dr. Carmody. Such utter abandon of bawling held her both entranced and envious. Sidling in, she remarked dramatically, "Nick, I've got an apology to make to Doctor Carmody. You see," Caddy said, drawing near Jane and addressing her in the loud kind accents of an interfering adult, "I thought you'd ratted on me, Doctor. But after thinking it over, I knew that that couldn't—uh—whatsis—have been the case. In the light of your telephone conversation." Caddy came to a full stop to let the rolling cadences of her phraseology sink in. She turned just in time to bump into the rampageous Dr. Bartholomew, who was treading on her heels. "Oh, it's you," she said in some confusion.

"Caddy, I am tempted to put you under massive sleep. For about a twenty-year stretch. Now, will you please—"

"Don't you want to hear my side of it?" Caddy yammered, wounded. "Everybody got to have their say but me. You even let *him* tell you what happened. I saw him, all right. I saw him come in here. How'm I to know he didn't lie his head off?"

"Caddy," Nick said again in a tone of voice that would have frozen the rotunda fountain in mid-plop, "if you don't—"

"Stop nagging the child!" Dr. Carmody wept. As Nick gaped on, she jumped up to enfold the stunned Caddy in her arms. "If it hadn't been for you, Caddy," Dr. Carmody sobbed, "oh, Caddy, if you hadn't gotten into your silly little scrape with that Titus Graham, my hus—"

"I wish," Caddy mumbled in Dr. Carmody's embrace, "that someone, just anyone, would tell me what this is all about."

"Beat it, brat," Nick said in a tone Caddy did not dare mistake. For an instant longer she dawdled in Dr. Camody's sodden clasp, making what dramatic hay she could of the situation before removing herself from the scene.

"Yes, sir," Caddy said, pulling out of Dr. Carmody's arms. She looked to Nick and saw no sign of his unbending; to the contrary, she read a growing impatience in his black visage. "Well," she said, "farewell, everybody."

"See you around, Caddy," Dr. Carmody managed tremulously.

"Don't bank on that," Nick said, making no sense whatsoever to his reluctantly departing, almost-daring-to-linger, but nonetheless now speedily vanishing daughter.

Slamming the clinic door behind her, Caddy leaned against it, blacking out for a moment under the assault of the direct western sun. Honestly, Caddy thought, the way I've been kicked around these last few days, you'd think I'd committed the Unpardonable Sin or something. And all I've done was strictly mind my own business.

22

The Jumping Off Place

Yesterday I intercepted and chatted briefly with the young man, Marion Pierce, of whom the Holy Dove had spoken so earnestly. He has limited ground privileges, I was given to understand, in that he may go and return unescorted from your little sessions with him, Sonny Boy. He was skittish about lingering for a gabfest; he is as gingerly in his exercise of his privilege as an arriviste from a back ward. His tale of woe I need not record here, Dr. Heall, for it is twice-told, and a third telling has little chance of unstopping your ears. You will be gratified to know, I imagine, that he is of the opinion that cutting and running would be ill advised. The local constabulary hunt down escapees with all the high spirits and sportsmanship of a fox hunt. Mr. Ellis is dead and Pierce could not hide out waiting money wired to him. I am doled out enough to keep me in smokes, and if I wasn't able to give up tobacco for Mitzi, I very much doubt if Pierce's plight can make an appreciable dent in my habit. And yet he must have enough money on him when he makes his break to catch a bus into another state. A few dollars stand between him and permanent rupture of his psyche through your officious psychoanalytic intervention, *chèr Docteur*. We then parted, I calling after him a warning to stay away from the Monkey Tree. He turned to acknowledge my advice, his face as pinched as that melancholy monkey who keeps to himself on the highest limb, contemplating God knows what Darwinian wrong turns in the road. Yes, I could not resist peeping into the grotto to see.

I shall try to slip out a letter to a colleague of mine in California about Pierce. Yes, there is a postman without portfolio on the grounds, though who it is the Holy Dove will not divulge.

The grapevine has brought to my ears a shocking intelligence. I do not pun; EST is but mildly punitive in comparison. The Special Patient, the poet being granted asylum—in the true sense of the word—here was lost for some hours, and finally located in a recovery room off the surgery with his eyes bandaged. His attendant was searching for him everywhere, the Great Poet having gone to the clinic to get attention for some monkey bites. Only Dr. Carmody was in the clinic, vehemently denying all knowledge of his whereabouts. Mr. Hamshot evidently phoned all over Pawksville before he found his man. The story is that Titus Graham was summarily delivered up to the Iceman. Reason? For making inroads on the chastity of the maidenly Caddy Bartholomew—or so the Holy Dove has divined.

Most of the time, then, it pleases Dr. Bartholomew to play the avuncular tyrant; but this time that corruption which accompanies absolute power showed its face. Perhaps he was justified, as Graham was secreted here after severely mauling a child.

On second thought, from what I have seen of Princess Caddy, if ever a child deserved a mauling—say, with her father's belt—that little succubus does.

While on the irritating subject of Caddy, it has been borne in on me increasingly that I seem to encounter her everywhere but on my ward. It all started a day or so ago

when she suddenly burst on my sight from behind a hedge
and shouted something abusive albeit unintelligible at me.
The gravamen of my offense had to do with my sitting on a
bench. Perhaps it is one to which she has claimed squatter's
rights. Then, yesterday, I sighted her behind a shrub, motionless and intent as an Indian, watching the Holy Dove and me.

Cunning little snoop. What a wonderful analysand she
will make for you one day, Sonny-Sigmund. As I look up
from writing this, I espy Caddy's rusty ponytail hanging,
absolutely still, from behind a tree. She seems oddly devoid
of femininity for a girl who is almost a teen-ager. I cannot
imagine her grown, or—I should say—grown womanly. I
bring to mind Mitzi posturing before her mirror, pulling
down her mouth until she resembles a little moose, to
facilitate the application of her mascara. I think of Mitzi
rustling about in full nylon petticoats and taffeta ballerina
skirts. But there, Caddy is destined for medical school, they
say. Quite fitting that the sweet liquefaction of her clothes
will be the clinical crackling of starched whites. She could,
of course, blossom late, and take on the rather wistful *gamine*
quality of Carmody.

Enough of that bratling, Sonny. You must know her
well. And you will, I hope, pardon my resort to pat phrases
and all those desiderata. If you can jargonize of mutism and
autism, then I, in the privacy of my journal, should be permitted the freedom of my own brand of gibberish.

On the whole, the Bartholomews are not an uninteresting family. I have stood to one side, unremarked, while the
husky self-inflated Nick stomps down a ward, fit to be tied,
Sonny, because of some idiocy or other of yours. I prefer not
to meet his gaze; he does not look at one, he reads one with
large black unblinking eyes. His manner is deceptively gentle.
And being read, one fidgets, while he calmly turns a page.
He knows his business; when I made my bow at Staff Meeting, he read me thoroughly, down to the last small-print

footnote of a minor idiosyncracy—searching, searching for a line, a hint, a word, an *ibid.*, if you will, of psychosis.

It is he who gradually has given me to know the true essence of Pawksville. He, with his constant harrying of insanity, his seeking it out and cornering it, and then exorcising it brutally with EST and the dread Metrazol.

Or, to change the figure, because of his concern with the acute patients, he sees them as people driven to the brink, with howling hordes of disappointments and incapacities and traumas and tainted lines of heredity in hot pursuit. And it is Nick Bartholomew, blunt but resourceful, who joins the psychotics at the edge of the abyss to urge them back, to prove to them that savage reality is infinitely preferable to what lies below.

For they are come, and Dr. Bartholomew must convince them of it, to the Jumping Off Place.

23

The Grossly Exaggerated Report of the Death of Dr. Sidney Heall

Caddy had set eyes on something she coveted with all her heart. She set about to plot the manner in which it might fall into her hands. She doubted that requesting Nick to seize it for her would accomplish the *coup*. She was not exactly in favor with him at the moment and, moreover, he'd either tell her to tend to her knitting or get the prize and then keep it for himself. Or, there was the not-miniscule chance that he would belt her one (a quaint Pawksville custom of recent innovation, but taken up enthusiastically by all). I'll have to steal it, Caddy decided in the deeps of a breathless starry night. She rose in the morning to begin her stalking. For three days running she then lurked behind trees and shrubs, beset by gnats and vexed by frustration.

Her prey, a patient downwind from Caddy, either wrote in that which Caddy so desired or sat on it. Several times the Holy Dove came by to rest within a foot of it.

Scratching her bites, one leg thrown over a Dutch wife for coolness—that sheet-covered bolster used in bed by dwellers of a hot clime as something to lean a limb over to absorb sweat—Caddy lay yet another breathless night and

hatched her foul plot. The next day she put it into operation.

The victim and the Holy Dove were taking their ease on
a bench in the shade. Caddy came strolling up, greeting the
Holy Dove and favoring the other with a carnivorous smirk.
Idly glancing past them, Caddy's features froze. "My God!"
Caddy yipped in horror. "Oh—my—Gawd!"

Both patients gawped for an instant at Caddy, then
whipped their heads around. "What?" "*Whaat!*"

"Doctor Heall just jumped off the rotunda," Caddy
screeched. "At least—" she called after them, equivocating,
as they set off at a smart trot in the direction of the rotunda
"—it *looked* like—"

On the bench lay the notebook. Caddy snatched it up
and herself began to run. In the opposite direction.

And that starry night, Caddy lay on her bed licking a
melted Hershey bar from its foil wrapper. Her bedroom door
was open barely enough to admit a cross-current, but not
enough to permit sight of her from the hallway. Though
she could hear Nick and Al murmuring in the soft voices of
those rendered almost torpid by the heavy summer heat,
she was not able to distinguish what they were saying. She
heard clearly only the tinkle of ice in their glasses of gin
and tonic.

"What's she reading now?" Nick demanded of Al. "Shut
up in her room like that."

"Search me," Al said. "Shall I go beard her in her den?"

"Leave her alone. She's quiet, isn't she? Be thankful."

"And for several days," Al mused, "I couldn't get rid
of her. She hung about talking my ears off. Somehow I got
the impression that she was inviting me to extend my visit.
Say for the rest of my natural life. She hinted that only my
presence could avert some family calamity."

Nick was uncomfortable. "Oh, is that so, huh."

"Evidently all is well now." Al shifted her leg on the

footstool. "Or it could be that this is the eye of the hurricane."

Going back a topic, Nick urged, "Why don't you stay on, Al? I'd like you to get to know the twins as well as you do Caddy. At least, stick around until I find out if I'm going to get fired."

"Much as I'd like to get back into harness," Al said, "you tempt me mightily. When d'you think Keeney will blow the whistle on you?"

"He won't. He needs me here for a whipping boy, if and when the Governor finds out about Titus Graham. Then he can claim he was the victim of duplicity and denounce me so roundly that the Governor will focus his ire on me—and not Keeney."

"It ought to be positively ear-splitting," Al said, all anticipation. "But how will Keeney ever get switched over to the subject of the new budget? And that sports car he insists Pawksville needs so desperately. For that matter, how about all the things you had on your begging list?"

"Sonny can ask for them—as new Clinical Director."

"Yes, there could be quite a few hasty revisions of Governor's lists, and in quite a few quarters. I wonder," Al went on blandly, "what's on Jane Carmody's list?"

"A new husband. I hope."

"So that's the way the wind blows?"

"Her present one is all washed up. *Kaput.* Defunct. Always was, as far as that goes."

"That wasn't what I meant, but I'll accept it for an answer. Seems a shame. There are still traces in him of what was once a very personable man. If you like the type."

Nick snorted. "You females. Can't you guess what I had to take out of his case history as soon as I caught on who Jane was?"

For once Al's silence was sterile of any implied retort. "Take out?" Al said finally.

"Expunge. Remove. At least from the retyped copy I left handy in the files for Jane to discover and study. His family thought if they married him off to Jane, he'd stop suffering 'nervous breakdowns' over being separated from another musician he was in love with. Another young man, to be exact. Name of Joel. Hence his destructive excitement in the Morgue House when Jane tried to remind him of the joys of connubial bliss."

"Hence," Al took up, "your willingness to go along with the lobotomy caper. He was already a psychic eunuch, so to speak. Tell me, just how much of this does she suspect?"

"Plenty. And I'm at my wits' end what to do about her."

"Fire her," Al said flatly.

"I wish I had the guts to. But she'd cry and beg. She can't let on to herself she does know; but knowing, she can't go on. Come on, flint-heart, in my place could you do it?"

"Brother," Al said aptly, "I'm not in your place. But if I were filling your shoes as Clinical Director, I could. Tug on the old heartstrings notwithstanding. But then, not being you, I wouldn't have any available means of comforting her."

"Al, you're getting as suspicious as the rest of them around here."

"Oh, I don't think so," Al said cheerfully. "A lot of them are even more suspicious about you two than I am. But I would, if I were you, try to keep Caddy from getting wind of it. I'm afraid she might find your departure from—ah—the exclusivity of fatherhood traumatically Electra-fying. Ummm, Nick?"

"I think," Nick said, "I need some more gin."

"And I think you need your head examined. When are you going to fire that poor woman?"

"I'm not. Since I'll probably be the one shown the door. Then she can stay on."

"A pretty kettle of fish," Al sniffed. "What'll you do with the kids if you're canned?"

"Put them in schools. I'm thinking seriously of sending Caddy to a boarding school, whatever happens."

"You mean, banish her from Pawksville?"

"For a while, yes."

"Well," Al said, "this place could use a little peace and quiet."

24

The Law and the Profits

Rounding the corner of the Hospital, Caddy saw that the author of the purloined journal was strolling directly in her path. Wanting simultaneously to turn tail and to brazen it out, Caddy stood hesitant, foolishly inspecting the rotunda in the distance, though no Dr. Heall crawled precariously along its rim. Then, as if striking a blow for world understanding, she began to walk forward as if to martial music. The adversary toward whom she marched so bravely would not have brought the slightest tremor of fear to the seasoned Pawksvillian. Caddy saw a woman of Dr. Carmody's age, dressed in the usual state-hospital print flour-sack dress. Her hair was a utilitarian tan, cut modishly short, but with a slight variation—two feathery sideburns lay on her cheeks, pointed like a soft sable brush. Her eyes were the color of rain in April, one looked again and again to make sure they were *not* green after all. Taken as a whole, she was a pretty woman without having the least recourse to daintiness. She looked, Caddy suddenly thought, just as she imagined the blond young Pawks Boys to have looked. Downy sideburns, slim but sturdy frame, and wing-waves springing from the temples.

The woman paused, smiled, then moved off the path to

take her place on the very bench where last the seat of her print dress had protected the journal. Challenged and painfully aware of it, Caddy could continue on or join the wronged patient. A dogged Caddy stalked under the shade of the tree. "I'm Caddy Bartholomew, Miss—uh—"

"I'm Leslie Erskine. How are you, Caddy? Come sit down and talk to me."

Caddy sat with the elaborate preparation of one making acquaintance with the electric chair. For a brief space of time she enjoyed a pronounced so-what indifference, but it did not last. Sounding to her own ears exactly like Babs Heall at her most rattled, Caddy hollered, "*I find it very. . . .* I—uh—find it very hot, don't you?"

"Not particularly," Miss Erskine said pleasantly, "but then, I've no cause to."

Caddy absorbed that with lingering pain. Deciding her self-esteem was tattered beyond repair anyway, she abruptly said exactly what she thought. "You know, Miss Erskine, you write exactly like a man."

"That's because in my mind I am a man."

Caddy made a rapid inventory of the rainwater eyes and the lipsticked mouth. "Are you in your mind? I mean, instead of out of your mind?"

"I'm as sane as you are," Miss Erskine said in a tone that declared this alone would have made her certifiable.

With that tone of voice Caddy was in calm accord. "Well, don't brag about it, Miss Erskine. Doctor Heall has me tagged for a garden-variety schizzy. Personally I feel more paranoid. Not a pure paranoid like the Holy Dove," she inserted modestly; "after all, she's the best there is. I couldn't hope to be like her."

"You never know what you're capable of until you try, I always say." Miss Erskine took a pack of cigarettes from her dress pocket and shook one loose. She lit a match and over the flame asked casually, "Tell me—did you like my journal?"

"Oh, very much," Caddy declared.

"Really. Aren't you going to voice any objections to some of the things I said about you?"

"Why, heck no! You caught me perfectly." Caddy was wagging her ponytail, friendly as a puppy. "With me the ugly truth is the only thing that counts."

"Why do people go around qualifying which truth they like? What have you got against 'beautiful' truth?"

Caddy was all unbuttoned admiration. "I never thought of it that way! You certainly do think like a man, you know? You realize, of course, that Nick—Doctor Bartholomew— will give me what-for if he catches me talking to you. I went through just about enough over that crummy poet, and he was completely over on the other side of the street from you, if you catch my meaning. I'm sure you're absolutely harm- less, but when I look back on my life, it seems that every bit of trouble I've had was over some patient or other."

"Indeed?" Miss Erskine said witheringly.

"Well . . . yes," Caddy mumbled, her grandiloquence suddenly having deserted her.

"You know way too much for your age and comprehend much too little," Miss Erskine observed. "And if you were my daughter, Caddy, I'd string you up by the thumbs for some of the fun and games you've been indulging in this summer. You're common gossip on the ward. And while I've the floor, permit me to say that you're way over on the reprehensible side of the dial, aren't you?"

"I reckon," Caddy admitted, moodiness settling on her heavy as the heat.

Miss Erskine relented a mite. "Maybe it's just that I'm not one of your more fanatical champions. The Holy Dove, for one, thinks highly of you."

Caddy did not descend to the obvious by pointing out that the Holy Dove's psychotic notions hardly constituted a high recommendation. "Well, you see, I've known the Holy Dove all my life," Caddy said instead. "So naturally. . . ."

Miss Erskine puffed on her cigarette, her manner easy. "By the bye, when do you think you might be through with my journal? I'd like it back please."

"Back! Fer cryin' out loud!" Caddy shouted defensively. "How was I to know that? I slipped it in on Doctor Heall's desk! After all, you wrote it to him! I thought I was only doing the right thing! When you come right down to it . . ." she ended.

"Stop protesting your innocence so frenziedly, it's a dead giveaway. When did you put it on his desk?"

"This morning." Caddy added for what it was worth, "And he missed lunch completely."

An oddly pleased note entered Miss Erskine's contralto. "You don't say. Do you think then, the good Doctor will greet my efforts with your same critical acclaim?"

Caddy tittered. "It'll take a whole course of Serpasil to get him down off the ceiling."

"Fancy!" Miss Erskine breathed on a stream of smoke. "Sonny missing him's lunch-lunch 'tas him couldn't put my journal down."

Caddy took the opportunity of another careful survey of the feathery sideburns and the bright lipstick. She murmured delicately, "If you don't mind my saying so, you really don't look like one. I'd never have taken you for one on the street."

"You and Doctor Heall certainly share the world's market on tact, don't you?" Miss Erskine rejoined. "What'd you expect me to do? Wear golf knickers and smoke a cigar?"

"Excuse me, I didn't mean to be rude. It's only that Nick has pointed out other lady patients and warned me to stay away from them. They did look the part."

"Think nothing of it. Candor becomes you."

Caddy turned the phrase over in her mind the way the Chinese are said to finger and stroke smooth stones they carry about with them for tactile pleasure. *"Candor Becomes Caduceus,"* she said experimentally. "What a perfect title for

a book. Would you—would you write it for me, Miss
Erskine?"

"I most certainly will not," Miss Erskine said, carefully
stubbing out her cigarette on the bench. "I don't want to be
caught with any such piece of damning evidence. Think I
want your old man delivering me up to the Iceman? In these
parts, it seems you can get your frontal lobe squashed to
a pulp just for passing the time of day with Doctor Bartholomew's darling little tots. Since you've no longer got my
journal, begone, kid."

"I promise it'll be a secret I'll take to my grave with me,
if you'll write the book," Caddy persisted fiercely.

Miss Erskine was unimpressed. "At this moment that
precious pure paranoid, that alliteration-happy Holy Dove
is probably spying on us. On top of that, I suspect she's also
a natural telepath. Hasn't anyone around her tumbled on
to that yet?"

"Oh, tommyrot," Caddy said rudely.

"Oh? Hmmm. Suppose I were to tell you what she said
she foresaw in a vision yesterday? Kiddo, your Old Nick's
going to send you to a boarding school. Yes, ma'am, Princess
Caddy, Father Muldroon is going to drive you to St. Hulda's
School right after the Jubilee ceremony. Maybe the Holy
Dove just eavesdropped under your father's office window
while he and Father Muldoon were making the arrange-
ments. But as you're so avid after ugly truths, how does this
one taste?"

"Vile!" Caddy shrieked. "Nick wouldn't let me leave his
side! Of all the—— The Holy Dove's left the track. She's
off her cotton-picking trolley. I never heard such delusional
eyewash in all my—" She could not continue for some
moments.

Miss Erskine reached for another cigarette. "You think
the Holy Dove is laboring under a mistake of fact? Then
how about her interception of Marion Pierce? Clever spying,

or telepathy, one. She knew about him. As, I'm sure, you do. You do know him, Caddy?"

"I haven't had the pleasure," Caddy said nastily.

Miss Erskine lit her cigarette, taking her time, studying Caddy. "Wasn't it in my journal? He's a representative from *Gadfly*. He came here to get in contact with your partner in crime, the Great Poet." Not missing Caddy's flush of guilt, Miss Erskine resumed in a soft legalistic drawl, "In the meantime, though, the publisher of *Gadfly* has dropped dead. No reflection, I do pray, on the masterpieces a certain unsung prodigy was sending *Gadfly* from Pawksville. Am I on target, Caddy?"

"Bull's-eye," Caddy said faintly.

"Let me review the facts further for your benefit. This Mr. Pierce voluntarily had himself committed in order to determine, if possible, if the great Titus Graham were in truth and in fact insane. The evidence, that is, the unique character of the poetry he purportedly was sending *Gadfly*, pointing strongly to a marked loss of marbles. Now, what do we have?"

"A melluvahess," Caddy gulped, contrite.

"Since it was your doing, have you any idea how this sane young man is going to get sprung from the clutches of Sonny-mund Heall? Surely, you don't think Doctor Heall is going to be galvanized into action on the strength of my journal alone? So what's to be done?"

"God wot," Caddy imparted in a hopeless voice, staring at the ground. "I read that in a poem by—"

"Let's not cloud the issue." Miss Erskine dabbed at the bench with her cigarette. She said briskly, "If God wots, then maybe the Holy Dove does too. I'll get on it right away. I'll expect your full cooperation if need be. But you are not —NOT—to say anything to anyone—your flamboyant father included—unless I give you leave. Have I your word on that?"

"I pledge my—uh—promise," Caddy said, taking fire.

"In the absence of your hand and seal it will have to suffice," Miss Erskine said with a genteel snort. "How much allowance do you get a month, or a week? In other words, how much money do you think you could scare up in the next three days? We'll try for Jubilee day for Pierce's break."

"I've got a buck thirty-seven cents to my name," Caddy groaned. "He can't go far on—— No! Waituh minute! I got three more dollars I should of—you know—converted into stamps. And since I dasn't try to give the money back to the Great Poet, and I don't rightly think I can claim it as profit. Then the money belongs to *Gadfly!* I can throw in four dollars and thirty-seven cents toward—" Caddy's chin lifted, her fist assaulted the air—"towards J-Day!"

Miss Erskine laughed, shaking her head, baffled. "Caddy, if for some reason you find you don't cotton to medicine, give the law a thought, will you? You've got all the makings of a scrupulous shyster. Why, a female scalawag like you could make a fortune!"

"You don't say," Caddy breathed, too full of herself to do more than grin idiotically. Then her face fell. "Naw. I've got to be a dedicated doctor like Nick." Another aspect of the situation presented itself. "Look, Miss Erskine, you are a lawyer. So maybe you have something up your sleeve. The only thing we're going to do on J-Day is help Mr. Pierce escape, right? Then what's your angle?"

Miss Erskine grinned, displaying fine straight teeth with the faintest indentation along the two front ones, bespeaking braces long ago. "No angle. This is purely *pour le sport.* I want to see Doctor Heall's face when he finds out Pierce is gone. And I will if I have to subject myself to his psychic nosy-parkering to do it. I'm entrusting you with all this, Caddy, because I think you're going to keep your promise faithfully, and for the further reason that you may have other uses than merely financing the crash-out. Have we a gentleman's agreement on all points?"

"My hand on it!" Caddy said ringingly and thrust out her mitt.

Shaking hands, Miss Erskine said, "Now beat it. When I need to confer with you, I'll come here and stare over at the rotunda. Just in case—" Miss Erskine explained, as Caddy rose to leave "—Doctor Heall really should take it into his head to jump."

Or me, Caddy thought, if Nick really does want to get shut of me. Oh, but he wouldn't, he couldn't send me off to one of those boarding schools. He knows damn well the first thing they'd do is make a lady out of me!

25

Jubilee

Pawksville had never known such intense heat. The patients
had never been so irritating, nor the attendants (if no doctor
were around) so ready with a blow. Babs Heall lay abed,
ordered to go there and stay there by Dr. Carmody, and
longed aloud for the "baw of cain-dee" Dr. Carmody had
flatly forbidden her. Sonny visited her almost every hour,
the sweat literally steaming up from his limp whites, as he
reported to her how the preparations for the Jubilee were
progressing.

Out on the grounds the ladies of the Baptist church
had vied all morning with those of Father Muldroon's parish
in the decorating of their booths. Both groups would be
selling cakes, though Father's ladies would also be pushing
raffle tickets for a complete set of some encyclopedia no one
had ever heard of. Since the Baptists looked on this as
gambling, there was grumbling among them; it was loudest
when Father Muldroon ambled by, all unhearing, hoping
against hope that he was somehow still in Dr. Carmody's
good graces and that she had a bottle of chilled wine in readiness for him. While promising Dr. Bartholomew to take
Caddy to St. Hulda's after the Jubilee, Father Muldroon had

asked about Sean Maginnis and was pleased, despite his prior convictions and his part in the matter, to learn that the lobotomy had not taken place, and that, furthermore, Sean had mercifully sunk back into his cataleptic state. Father offered up a prayer for Sean, knowing in his heart of hearts that it would be answered in God's infinitely sagacious way.

There were other booths as well as those of the church ladies; there was a hot-dog concession, and a fireworks stand (no items for sale, they were simply on display until the pyrotechnician, hired for the event, would set them off at the conclusion of the Governor's speech), a pop and ice-cream concession, and quite a large booth for the sale of handicraft articles fashioned by the patients in occupational therapy. At this last Caddy had spent the morning helping tack on bunting—that is, when she was not trying to tag after Nick, bending on him an expression woeful beyond description. She had debated everything from staving in her skull with a hammer to swallowing a box of tacks, so that she might require constant medical attention and a prolonged stay at Pawksville under Nick's anxious care. Only her accurate surmise that he would turn her over to Dr. Heall or Dr. Carmody stayed Caddy's hand.

Around two in the afternoon, when the heat was at its height, the busloads of relatives and visitors and the cars of the local citizenry began to arrive. Disgorging their loads at the little bus shelter at the gate, the buses then parked in a meadow across the road. There was an immediate rush for the pop concession, and Father Muldroon set out at once to beguile customers away from the Baptist cake booth to his own. Soon the patients would be led out and seated before the bunting-decorated speaker's stand, erected for the Governor and his party.

At exactly two-ten every single member of the medical staff was standing in the shower, moaning in his or her mind at the very thought of the fresh board-stiff whites laid out for wear. Emerging from his shower, Sonny Heall pranced to his petulant wife's bed, kissed and commiserated with her, and promised to remember and tell her every last thing of interest which might happen during the Jubilee, up to and including any didos the Holy Dove might think to cut if she found herself in conversation with a gentleman of the cloth. "You just relax, Sugar, and concentrate on developing our fetus into a boy," he urged her with medical fatuosity.

Emerging from her shower, Jane Carmody thought only, remorsefully, of the brief glimpses she would get of Sean while keeping herself safely out of his sight. And emerging from his shower, a towel around his waist, Nick Bartholomew encountered—what else—the woeful countenance of his daughter, and, lest he weaken, went by whistling noisily. Not to mention Mr. Dick, who emerged from his shower and marched straight to his pier glass where he admired his full-length reflection for several minutes. Nor should Dr. Diljohn be overlooked; he, not bothering to emerge from the shower, stuck out a dripping arm to take the bottle of Southern Comfort from the window ledge, then stood under the tepid downpour and drank in great fortifying gulps. Dr. Parry, of course, always kept a sharp eye on his condition while in the shower, lest a seizure come on him and he hurt himself badly on the tile. He took his diphenylhydantoin sodium faithfully and had not suffered a seizure in months; still, the fear of one was always with him in the shower—and he had not luxuriated in a tub since he was a boy and had had either his father or one of his brothers to be there and watch after him.

Only Superintendent Keeney and Dr. Ouita were not going to wear whites. The former because he wished to function more as the administrator in his conference with the Governor, the latter because it was her day off and because her new flowery garden-party dress would give her confidence when she murmured to the Governor of having a new little-boy statue erected on the rotunda fountain.

On the wards, the last of the patients were being hustled

into their best clothing. Marion Pierce, for example, was the embodiment of the Ivy Leaguer in the lightweight suit he had arrived in. And Leslie Erskine, with a flair all her own, had borrowed the tapes from a strait jacket and was winding them tightly about her slim waist, to serve as a belt in cinching in her sack-dress. For her part, the Holy Dove—decked out in Billie Noon's best silk print—was going about the ward with a large wet washcloth, wiping the smear from the faces of the busy hebephrenics, preparatory to helping Miss Noon herd them out onto the grounds.

At two-twenty the Governor's entourage, consisting of two Cadillacs, a Plymouth containing reporters, and a motorcycle escort, came wailing through the gate and up to the rotunda portico. Superintendent Keeney, back still damp from his shower, stepped smartly down the broad veranda stair to greet his eminent visitor. Out of the second Cadillac poured the Governor's yes-men, thoughts and actions wired in series like Christmas-tree lights. The reporters tumbled out, the photographers squatting as if in obeisance before the first Cadillac, snapping picture after picture of the Governor's red face as he puffed his way out of the car door and then wrung Superintendent Keeney's hand, booming pleasantries the while, most of which were prefaced with "Yes sir," or "I'm here to tell you." "Yes sir, I'm here to tell you," the Governor said to Superintendent Keeney, "this fine day sure gladdens my heart; yes sir, I'm here to tell . . . ." And so forth. The Governor was not a large man, but he was topped with an enormous head, mostly face, so that he reminded one vaguely of the ancient gods of Easter Island. Then, without further ado, the Governor marched up the steps and into the rotunda, his yes-men and the reporters close at his heels, leaving a somewhat bewildered Superintendent Keeney to bring up the rear. Something was on the Governor's mind, and a chill of premonition coupled with a wild desire to be hundreds of miles away with his family at Virginia Beach filled Superintendent Keeney's being. Speeding up to a trot and skirting the fountain, Superintendent Keeney caught up with the Governor and clung to his side as they exited from the rotunda and out on to the tree-shaded walks for the short journey to the speaker's platform. A line of voluble schizophrenics were shooed along ahead of them suddenly, the Holy Dove marching imperiously at the head of the column, and Billie Noon and her aide clucking and plucking at the stragglers.

"Yes sir," the Governor said, "I'm here to get your solemn assurance, Superintendent Keeney, that things are all hunky-dory at Pawksville. I've got some pre-ty unscrupulous enemies, and they wouldn't hesitate to use any dirt they could—"

"Well, they won't find a speck of it here," Superintendent Keeney vowed.

The party was drawing close to the stand now, clustered around which were Nick, Caddy, Sonny, a frankly curious Leslie Erskine with a hint of a mocking light in her eye, and a number of small boys gulping from pop bottles and inviting one another to enjoy the sight of this or that looney as the patients were led up and seated in orderly rows on the lawn. The Governor set his course straight for Nick, his large head shoved forward as if he would not think twice before using it as a battering ram, if the need arose. Not three feet away from Sean Maginnis, the Governor thrust out his hand to Dr. Bartholomew.

Squatting on the grass cross-legged, or with their feet tucked under them, were the first two rows of patients, the stuporous and mute catatonics, and the quietly depressed manic-depressives and their fellow sufferers, the melancholics; the males on the left, females to the right. After them would come the reasonably tractable schizophrenics and their attendants. The last rows would consist of a gabblement of the merry hebephrenics, the excitable manic-depressives in a manic state, and heterogeneous mixtures, any one of whom might, at any moment, stand up and offer to remove his clothing or deliver a sermon or start a brawl. These patients could be relied upon also to applaud at all the wrong places and howl with laughter when the Governor waxed sentimental about Mother. All in all, an audience to provide excellent training for anyone thinking of entering politics and a quick refresher course for one already there.

Somewhere in a middle row, Marion Pierce sought the eye of Leslie Erskine, as she loitered about, her ground privileges permitting her to sit either with patients or in the visitors' stands, or to avoid the Governor's speech entirely if she so chose. Not making contact with Miss Erskine, Marion found himself instead meeting the grave and—yes —fatherly gaze of Dr. Heall, who smiled slightly to encourage Marion in his mannerly conduct among his fellow acutely disturbed patients. Far, far back, the Holy Dove peered up through the trees and smiled at the sky. Then her bandaged left hand rose into the air, the forefinger crooked, as she unobtrusively blessed Dr. Carmody, who bent to greet the Holy Dove, her eyes roving the front rows for Sean's back.

Though the Governor had patently wished to press straight to the side of Dr. Bartholomew, he was forced to accept the outthrust hand of Dr. Heall, who blocked his way. "Yes sir," the Governor said impatiently. "I'm here to——"

"And this is Miss Erskine, one of my patients," Dr. Heall said with ambassadorial dignity.

Leslie felt strongly obliged to step forward and announce her ward number, years in residence at Pawksville, diagnosis, and prognosis: Ward Seven, sir, one year, paranoid schizophrenic, criminally inclined, and hopeless. "How are you, Governor Jackson?" she asked, magnificently casual.

"There's nothing like," the Governor boomed decisively, "having a lovely lady . . . ," but he had forgotten what nothing was like and wagged his great head at Nick in unmistakable invitation. Nick received the message but, fighting for time, shoved Caddy to the fore. "This is my daughter, Caduceus, Governor Jackson."

Caddy asked sternly, "How do you do, Sir?"

"Lovely child," the Governor pronounced without further thought on the matter.

"I was going to write an Ode for this auspicious occasion," Caddy began, "but owing to circumstances beyond my—"

"Why, that's just lovely," the Governor said. He appealed to Leslie Erskine, "Isn't it, Miss Ruskin?"

"However—" Caddy endeavored to continue, but fell silent when Nick laid a light but menacing hand on her shoulder.

"Much as I would like to just stand around and jaw with you lovely people," the Governor said, "I'm afraid duty calls. Yes," he wagged a rougish forefinger, "I'm going to give a speech. Can't invite a politician around and not expect him to give a speech. Right, Miss Ruskin?"

Deducing that it was she being addressed, Leslie Erskine murmured, "They that govern the most make the least noise, isn't *that* right, Sir?"

Plainly cracked, the Governor's stare proclaimed. "Well, it's been nice meeting all you lovely folks," he said, gathering his wits about him. "But the quicker I can have a little talk with Doctor Bartholomew here, the quicker I can get up on that ole speaker's stand and let fly with a few, and the quicker we can all get to that watermelon feast Superintendent Keeney promised me."

All nodded with great animation. Inwardly Nick warned himself. Well, here goes. If the fat isn't already in the fire, it soon will be. Walking away with the Governor, Nick thought he heard Miss Erskine mutter to Caddy, "All set?"

What piece of preposterousness is she up to now, Nick asked himself anxiously, then recalled with a surge of passionate relief that Caddy would be safely ensconced, or imprisoned—in her case—at St. Hulda's by nightfall or a little after.

Moving through the crowd of visitors, the Governor shook hands absently here and there, asking with noisy intensity, "Well, how are you?" and not bothering to listen to the answer. Father Muldroon called out to Nick, "Take a chance on an encyclopedia, Doctor? Only a few left—why don't you just buy up the last of the book?" Nick handed Father a bill, then hastened after the Governor without receiving his book of raffle tickets. Far behind them, Superintendent Keeney was looking everywhere for the Governor, outdistancing even the yes-men in his dashings hither and yon.

Close by the Morgue House, shielded from the crowd by a hedge, the Governor and Nick sank to a bench, each sighing to himself. The Governor selected a cigar from his person and offered it to Nick. Nick accepting, the Governor found yet another for himself; Nick quite enjoyed having the Governor humbly give him a light.

"Now, Doctor," the Governor began in a sprint, "the news boys aren't going to uncover any dirt around here, are they? Keeney's reassurances aren't worth the air he uses up saying 'em."

"We're not mistreating our patients, if that's what you mean," Nick said cautiously. "Oh, once in a while an attendant does strike a patient, but if I get wind of it, he's fired. Of course, there's no way of hiding the overcrowding and lack of facilities from the reporters. If they ask any patient who isn't mute or acutely disturbed—"

"Oh, don't worry about that," the Governor said largely. "I'm handling that little matter myself. Yessir! I can't say anything for sure yet, have to work it out with the Budget Committee, but there'll be a nice surprise coming your way, Doctor." He looked about him, saw no one lurking near, not even Caddy Bartholomew, but still lowered his voice, "About my wife's cousin. Titus Graham. I don't know how much longer we can keep him here, he prolly wants out, but until after the election. . . . If he does get out, and finds out about—— Well, there could be such a stink, my whole career—— You know what kind of a person he is. Nobody's got any rights but him. But I've *got* to keep him here until—"

"Have you seen Titus Graham this afternoon?" Nick asked, feeling a strange stillness inside him.

"No, no, not as yet. Tell you the truth, Doctor, I can't stomach the fellow. He almost wrecked my career as it was when he—"

"You would hardly recognize him," Nick said in a way that drew the Governor's unblinking gaze. "Physically you would, of course, except that the mustache's gone, but mentally. . . ." Nick decided to have done with it. "I had Doctor Kox, our visiting surgeon, perform a lobotomy on him."

The Governor gasped. "You mean head surgery? My God, if my wife sees him all scarred up—"

"No scars," Nick asserted positively. "The instrument is pushed into the skull through the eye-sockets."

"God!" The Governor shuddered.

"Really, it's quite simple. The patient suffers a little discomfort for a few days, and that's it."

"Are you telling me my wife's cousin is a blithering idiot now?" the Governor demanded, chewing on his cigar in his agitation.

"Not at all. His intelligence, and I guess his talent—he's said to have a great deal by those who profess to—"

The Governor discredited this with a spit of disgust.

". . . at any rate," Nick pressed on, "his intelligence is unimpaired. But his vicious propensities have vanished."

"Tell me that again in plain English," the Governor commanded.

"If you met him for the first time now, all you'd see would be a nice easygoing man. A touch absent-minded at times, but that's all. Incidentally, he wants to stay on at

Pawksville. He has an idea for a new therapy Doctor Heall is anxious to try out. He's going to start a class in creative writing."

"The hell you say!" the Governor commented.

"Yes. I do. Doctor Heall feels that encouraging the patients to write down their thoughts will furnish us with extremely useful diagnostic material."

"Jesus Christ," the Governor mumbled, and wiped his great brow with a ninety-degree sweep. "And he wants to stay on at Pawksville. Only thing, Doctor, about the Special Cottage——"

"It's vacant. Graham liked it on the surgical ward so much that I'm letting him stay there, to help out. He'll have complete ground privileges, naturally. And along with his writing classes he wants to learn to run routine analyses in the lab. Doctor Carmody would teach him."

"Peachy," the Governor said, oddly distracted. "Peachy-keen." He examined his cigar, then suddenly leaned toward Nick, as if presenting the great craters in his huge nose for a dermatologist's inspection. "Doctor, I—uh—have a—uh—friend. You understand. Who just might fit in here in the Special Cottage. Now this is confidential, Doctor."

"I quite understand."

"Well, it's Judge Angst. A wonderful man. Served on the bench for years. A real pillar of the church. The times he's helped me in my career I couldn't begin to name. Only —well, the Judge is in his eighties now. That was prolly his trouble, senility. Anyway, he was in semi-retirement, just a bit of probate practice and that sort of thing. And he was —uh—acting as trustee for several estates. Well, what happened was just one of those things. It seems he must have commingled his own funds with those of his clients. Naturally, nothing has been done about the matter yet, I mean, it hasn't leaked out to the press. Not that," the Governor went on, fixing a forbidding eye on Nick, "he robbed any widows or orphans or anything like that. Nothing like that. Doctor, this is in the strictest confidence, now."

"I understand."

"Yes. So before the thing breaks in the papers, we're all working on some means of restitution of the money he —ah—well, not misappropriated, but—uh—allocated in the wrong direction. The racing stable brought in quite a tidy sum; a constitutent of mine was willing to help out there by buying it up. And then, we simply transferred some stock over to Mrs. Hardesty and her children. You remember, don't you, Doctor, that terrible tragedy when Sam Hardesty was killed in a wreck coming home from my fifty-dollar-a-plate dinner four years ago? Terrible. Terrible." The Governor shifted his cigar around in his mouth in agitation. "The thing of it is, a lot of the money is just gone. Up in smoke," the Governor said, and illustrated by blowing a blue stream in Nick's face. "We've eked out every cent we could, but several of the beneficiaries are just going to have to stand up and take their losses like men. Now, look, Doctor, my wife doesn't know about this. My God, when she finds out that her cousin's dough——" The Governor spread out his hands in appeal. "Graham is wiped out."

"Ah so," Nick heard himself murmuring like some movie depiction of a suave mandarin. "But oddly enough, Governor, I doubt if Graham himself would care. Not so long as he has a roof over his head, and three squares, and is not abused. And can make himself useful." For a moment Nick feared that the Governor was going to burst into sobs of relief. If he does, I'll join him, Nick thought.

"You mean, there's no need to tell him? Since he wants to stay on at Pawksville anyway?" the Governor babbled.

"None whatsoever."

The Governor was beside himself, trying to smoke fiercely and wipe his brow and shake Nick's hand all at the same time. "Then, Doctor, if Judge Angst were to be committed to Pawksville for extensive diagnosis and treatment. . . . Of course, that's your province, Doctor—"

"The Special Cottage can be in readiness any time, Governor."

"I'm here to tell you," the Governor spake, "that that is simply splendid, Doctor!" He stood up, and warmed up on his oratorical boom, "You'll find Judge Angst to be one of the finest specimens of Southern traditions. A wonderful old gentleman. Finest of old families. Just so long as we keep this thing hushed up. And don't think, Doctor," the Governor said with that backwoods straight-from-the-shoulder honesty for which he was renowned, statewide, "that I'm a man to forget past favors, Doctor!" His great face was held aloft as if scanning the skies, his hand outthrust.

Nick arose and shook that hand the many number of times he felt the momentous occasion required. "I would like to remind you," Nick said, himself looking upward, as the Governor had seemed to find something of interest there, ". . . remind you . . ." Nick noted that the day was turning cloudy. *"Remind you,"* Nick said loudly, claiming the Governor's attention, "that what we need first and foremost are more doctors. And we could do with about a dozen registered nurses. Say, eight female, four male. The patients are sleeping with their feet in each other's faces, so if we could have the top floor of the Hospital finished, and then there's the drug budget, what with all these new tranquilizers coming along, though I'm afraid they're a bit expensive—not very, though—but we would like to try the various ones on a statistically significant number of patients so that our results, whether they be negative or positive, though I understand that some near miraculous, naturally a spectacular 'take' can always prove to be just a mere transient reduction, but I'd certainly like to try——"

"Yes indeed, Doctor! I'll certainly keep all that in mind," the Governor said heartily, eye again cast up to the gathering clouds. "Better get to the speaker's stand, Doctor. Can't deprive a hardworking politician of a chance to make a speech!" All joviality, the Governor began his brisk march, in spite of the mugginess of the day, back to the bunting-decorated stand.

Nick followed, musing. What opportunity he had been offered he had seized. Yes, and babbled like an idiot in the doing. But then, Nick brightened, that was not a last-ditch plea. Upon the arrival of the Governor's thieving old jurist, Nick would create some need or other to communicate with the Governor, and in so doing he would set forth the wants of Pawksville in concise detail. Still enjoying the Governor's cigar, he moved through the crowd, stopped again and again by ex-patients, one of whom had named his latest son after Nick, and all of them pathetically anxious to let bygones be bygones, EST, Metrazol, and the nightmares of insulin, notwithstanding.

Also noting the threatening sky, Father Muldroon re-doubled his efforts to guide new customers to his parishioners' booth. There were several cakes left, and a disappointing number of raffle tickets for *The Complete Knowledge of the Entire World* (ten vols.) unsold. He had to contain himself during the playing of the National Anthem—the hospital orchestra, such as it was, sounding like a pack of unbridled traitors, the trumpeter being on a manic toot—and then, eyes morosely bent on the approaching thunderheads, had to stand in rigid respect through three choruses of "Dixie." When the Governor's voice boomed out: "My good friends of Pawks— Is this thing on? Oh, it is. Thank you, I thought the mike was dead. I'm just here to say to all you lovely people—" Father Muldroon went into action. "Last chance to get a raffle ticket for a complete encyclopedia," he said, capturing a newsman hurrying by. "The lady right here in the booth will help you. Look, only one book of tickets left —why not take the whole caboodle? Say a prayer, and I wouldn't be a bit surprised to learn that you'll be the new owner of *The Complete Knowledge of the*— Here you are. That's right, Mrs. Balder, the gentleman wants the entire book. Now. How about a coconut cake?" Extending his hand for the money, Father received in it, instead, a hailstone the size of a marble, pitted as if fashioned for a new cosmos with mountainous upheavals and miniscule craters, a milky moon whose largest crater should rightly have borne the name Mare Muldroon.

At once Pawksville was under the barrage of the new cosmos, tiny ice planets bouncing off the booths and more miniature moons dancing on the grass and walks. A single shaft of sunlight fired the rotunda, the titan of this new universe, its greatest sun. The Jubilee pleasure-seekers began to race for cars and buses, while Father, careless of the hailstone fusillade, worked frantically with his ladies to box up their remaining cakes.

Up on the speaker's stand Superintendent Keeney exchanged a look of anguish with Dr. Bartholomew. Somehow, Superintendent Keeney's eyes said, he had a feeling the Governor was going to hold him personally responsible for the catastrophe. Thunder rolled now, and the Governor, game to the last, wagged a forefinger at heaven, huge face taking a battering from the hailstones, and shouted, "Lord, what've you got against politicians?" As no answer seemed to be forthcoming, the Governor prepared to beat his retreat.

As suddenly as the hailstorm began, it ended. There was a pause, everyone gazing about as aimlessly as the unperturbed catatonics in the first rows. Attendants in the act of herding their charges into line looked to the speaker's stand as if for instructions. Beyond, on the lawns, the fleeing visitors halted in their tracks. The sun was completely obscured, the rotunda a sullen blue dead star surrounded by its melting cosmos. Then a fine pale rain began to fall, seemingly exhibiting a tasteful selectivity. The bunting on the booths and the stand darkened at once, while the flooring of the platform remained dry. Raindrops wept slowly down the Governor's cheeks, but the moisture on his massive forehead was his own sweat of aggravation. The downpour came on at once, raindrops dancing as vigorously as the hailstones had.

Someone surged forward to hold a newspaper over the
Governor's head as he descended from the stand. A bit of
bunting was whipped against one leg, the color bleeding in
streaks on the creamy Palm Beach material.

Taking advantage of the situation, the more frisky of the
patients suddenly began to cause their attendants all kinds
of trouble. Some rushed about trying to get in the wrong
line; the trumpet player abruptly took it into his head to
become disturbed, wrapping his legs about his chair, blast-
ing away on his horn in glorious abandon, breaking off only
to defend himself with his instrument when an attendant
tried to pry him loose. In the midst of the melee, Jane
Carmody strained for a last glimpse of Sean Maginnis as he
was shoved, like an afterthought, onto the tag-end of his line.
Then, out of the corner of her eye Jane beheld the unusual
tableau of Leslie Erskine and Sonny's favorite analysand
conversing ardently in the shelter of Father Muldroon's battered cake booth. The two—Pierce and Erskine—antipodes,
really, now seemed conspirators of sorts; though Jane wondered idly at their hurrying off together to seek the dense
shelter of a tree, she was not alarmed. There was no harm
that she could see they could do one another, and neither
of them, so far, had shown the slightest disrespect for their
valued ground privileges.

The trumpeter was cut off with a final triumphant
blast, so that Billie Noon's "Holy Dee? *"Holy Dee!"* rang out
deafeningly in Jane's ear. "Miss Noon," Jane snapped, "will
you stop that! The Holy Dove has sense enough to come
in out of the rain, I assure you. Now go tend to your other
charges."

Miss Noon did not disobey Jane or ignore her; she
simply hadn't heard her and went off shooing her deterio-
rated gesticulating howling ladies before her, bawling the
while for the Holy Dove.

The Holy Dove, meantime calmly picking her way
from tree to tree on her way back to her ward, stood mo-

mentarily to let a ragged column of men patients pass. Their attendants were yelling at them dispiritedly, not caring in the least who got drenched. The attendants were holding newspapers or their simulated leather cushions over their heads for protection, jog-trotting along at once irritated and bored.

A red-headed patient stumbled and fell at the Holy Dove's feet, his shambling line continuing on without him, his attendant's range of observation narrowed by a newspaper. The Holy Dove bent down and gave him a hand, noting the strength of his fingers as she did so. His eyes under white brows and lashes had the velvety softness of distended pupils, lending him an air of lost bewilderment. For a moment the catatonic and the paranoid exchanged gazes, the one so bereft of self, and the other holding herself in the high regard of an old hand at the game. Thinking what a handsome young man the catatonic must have been even in the recent past, the Holy Dove said maternally, "Why, you're Doctor Carmody's nice husband. Why, yes. I understand you play the piano so pretty. We have a lovely piano in the auditorium, did you know that?" The Holy Dove repeated in a smiling fashion, "Just over there—in the auditorium." Placing her broad chapped hands on his shoulders she turned him to face in the direction she wished. "Over there," she said once again, still smiling. "I'll show you."

The Holy Dove began to lead him from tree to tree, moving her complaisant catatonic along with the unhurried firmness of the long-experienced. At the side door of the auditorium she gave him a maternal little push, and when he moved forward into the gloom, his wet shirt gleaming against his back, his pale head raised toward the looming Steinway C-D, the Holy Dove stood where she was in the doorway but turned to contemplate the steady rain. With a sigh she recalled the days, long ago, when Superintendent Docker's lovely daughter, Moaneen, would play that piano and sing the "Indian Love Call" and all those other classics no one heard any more.

Inside, in the gloom, Sean Maginnis feasted his eyes on the black shape of the Steinway on the platform. A flash of lightning showed him the short stair that led to the platform and, striding triumphantly to the applause of thunder, he mounted to the piano. He opened the lid and contemplated the ivory grin. Then, raising his head he looked across the folded music rack and stared thoughtfully at the closed ebony wing. After a moment he went round and lifted it.

Holding the wing as high as he could reach with his right hand, he laid the fingers of his left along the musical curve of the frame. Then he let the wing drop across his fingers. A glissando of agony shrilled through him. The forefinger of his left hand was nearly struck from the palm. He had to raise the wing with his right hand again because of the shattered flaps of fingers dangling from the left. He made no sound, though his eyes filled with tears. He found he could just support the wing with the heel of his left hand, the forefinger hanging foolishly in the wrong direction. Music and thunder mingled in his head; a Prokofiev cadenza flashed by, yet with each note distinct and given its proper value. He was always able to do it, reel off an entire score in his mind with the rapidity of a single thought. He smiled at his love who was shaking his head in incredulity. It's like Newton's concept of instant velocity, Joe; you comprehend it at once, or you never will. He let the wing drop on his right hand, still smiling through his silent tears. Very neatly done, most of the blood was on the inside.

Now help me raise the lid again, Joe. Pity, there's a great crack in the wood, the thunder must have done it. Sean Maginnis knelt before the noble instrument and applied the heels of both shattered hands to the rim. Slowly rising, like a priest elevating the Host, he got to his feet, wing on high. The applause cracked about him, dashing lightning from the thunder of clapping hands. With a modest nod of gratitude, he slipped his left wrist under the wing support and, lifting it to position, let the wing rest on it. He bowed and laid his neck on the rim of the frame, his gaze fixed firmly on the central E string. His left arm swung out, knocking away the support, and with a joy he had never known he was playing the "Emperor" Concerto in his mind when the wing came down and broke his neck.

Still in the doorway, the Holy Dove had not once turned her head from her contemplation of the rain. She had heard no outcry whatsoever. When the last crashing sound died away with a lingering humming of strings and all was quiet, the Holy Dove thought, "There. There, now. That's better." The Holy Dove began her journey back to her ward.

Sean's sagging knees could not touch the floor, and he hung from the rim as the gloom deepened by the minute. The blood from his dangling hands would be almost dry when they found him.

At the Hospital portico, Caddy stood with her suitcase and tennis racket and vile-in case, unable to look at Nick as she paid him her heartbroken farewell. She received a kiss from her Aunt Al with the listlessness of the despairing. Father Muldroon gunned the motor of his Ford and called up, "Caddy, you coming or not?"

And huddled in the deserted bus shelter, Marion Pierce and Leslie Erskine watched the last of the buses disappear down the highway. The parking lot was empty of all but some attendants' cars. Trembling with the spirit of the chase, Marion asked simply, "Miss Erskine, why did you and Caddy and the Holy Dove really befriend me?"

"Call it a whim on my part. Or maybe I'm striking a blow for the right of all of us to be free of the Sonny Healls of this world. I can't speak for the Holy Dove, of course. Unless she fancies herself as a miracle worker. It is a miracle, come to think of it, how much influence that dotty old dame wields around here. She gets away with murder because her insanity ensures her innocence. As for Caddy—the kid's got a head full of rocks. She's as full of plots as a paranoid. Incidentally, it was she who supplied most of the cash. Something about stamps was all the explanation I could get out of her."

"And who supplied the rest?"

Leslie looked out at the rain. "I suddenly gave up smoking."

"You're—you're womanhood's finest example," Marion assured her.

"Now that's something I was certain no man would ever say to me," Leslie said wryly.

"I mean it! And look, if there's anything I can do for you after I'm safely away. . . . Listen! We've got to figure a way I can get in touch with you, so I can help you—"

"Forget it," Leslie said carelessly, and stood up to wave at Father Muldroon's approaching Ford. "It's either here or the pen for me. And I'm happier here in the raree show. You know, the one thing you ought to ponder at length though, Marion, is the rain. It would have been much harder to pull this off without it."

"Yes, thank God for the rain," Marion intoned as if he were giving response in the litany.

"Or the Holy Dove," Leslie countered. *"She* considers it the same thing . . ." She waved harder, debating stepping into the road as Father's Ford hurtled toward them.

With a shriek of protest from his brakes, Father brought the Ford to a stop. "Oh, that's that nice reporter I was talking to, Father," Caddy said, sticking her head out the window. "He took *such* an interest in me."

"I'll bet he did," Father Muldroon agreed sourly. (Dr. Carmody had not, contrary to his highest hopes, offered him chilled wine—only a chilly smile.) "I suppose," Father went on, "you told him everything you could think of. This reporter fellow. Well, get in, get in!" he yelled out at Marion. "Are you thumbing a ride or not?"

"I missed the last bus," Marion said. "Are you going into town?"

"I am not," Father said with asperity. "I'm going straight on to Arkansas. Are you getting in or not?"

"Why—what a coincidence!" Marion cried, "because I was going to catch a bus in Pawksville that would take me—"

"Hop in," Caddy said to cut all this short, and leaned back to open the back door.

Safely hidden from view in the back of the Ford, Marion stuck his head out in the rain to say farewell to Leslie Erskine.

She waved him back. "Hit the autobahn, boy." Her hand went to her pocket to discover that she had given her cigarette money to Marion. Hiding the acute pain of a habit broken off without sufficient preparation, she grinned bravely. "*Vaya con Dios,* Marion Pierce," she said, and stepped back to avoid the swish of water from Father's spinning wheels.

Skidding out the main gate and onto the highway, Father Muldroon asked, "Doesn't that *vaya* whatever-she-said mean, 'Go with God'?"

Marion's reply could not be heard over Father's tires squealing for purchase on the wet macadam. Then, holding it to a steady sixty-five, Father called out to the back, "This little girl here been telling you a lot of tall stories to print in your paper?"

"Oh, I wasn't sent to cover the conditions at Pawksville," Marion said honestly. "But we've gotten wind of the rumor that the Governor has presidential aspirations. I just wanted to see if he would hint at it in his speech. Then, as luck would have it, my car broke down yesterday, and I had to come in all the way from the city on a bus. Just to get caught in a hailstorm." He laughed a trifle wildly.

"Huh," Father said. "The saints preserve us if he does run for President. Come to think of it, though, why were you talking to that Miss Esquire, then?"

"Who? Oh, the lady patient." Marion coughed modestly. "I've been thinking of writing a book about life in a state hospital. Miss Erskine would make an interesting minor character."

"So would I," Caddy said coyly.

"If you want my advice," Father announced, "you'll write about something you know."

"I guess you're right there," Marion conceded, and could not quite restrain a nervous snicker.

All out of sorts, Father lectured on, "It's you people who don't belong within a hundred miles of Pawksville who cause all the trouble. Snooping around for sensational material, and getting things all stirred up. Insanity is a serious business; why can't you outsiders let them get on with it?"

Marion protested faintly, "But you make it sound almost as if they knew what they were doing."

And Caddy was sorely tempted to observe, "You'd be surprised!" but held her peace. It was coming to her faintly, hazily, nostalgically, that she was an outsider; had been for some time. As Father roared up the ramp to the thruway that would take them straight ahead, bypassing Pawksville, she tried desperately to make herself an insider once again. She babbled, "Did you know, Father, that Mrs. Heall is going to have a baby?"

"I did and I do." In the distance they could faintly hear the sound of sirens. "Must be the Governor's entourage," Father remarked dourly. "All that fanfaroll. Sirens and a police escort—ridiculous!"

That, or the Sheriff's out looking for an escapee, Caddy thought. She yelled gaily, "And the Holy Dove says the baby's going to be a girl and be just like me!"

"God forbid," Father said fervently. He added, "That Holy Dove should be locked up." He pressed down on the accelerator. "I wish," he burst out, "one of my parishioners would have the grace to present the church with a sports car."

If my book sells, Marion Pierce vowed, I'll ship you a car that will knock Pawksville's collective eye out!

"I just happened to think," Father said, "if you're going to be a writer, Mr. Uhh—you should have an encyclopedia for handy reference. How about buying a raffle ticket. . . . Tell you what, I've got just one book of tickets left, and I'm sure the ladies wouldn't mind if I let you have the whole book at a reduced price. Being's as it is the last—" Without warning Father fell silent.

In his mind's eye he suddenly saw that last book of tickets where he had left it in his haste. In the rain, lying next to one lonely, pitted, liquefying cake, under the bleeding bunting, on the booth amid the pop bottles and candy-bar wrappers and dissolving newspapers littering the soaked trampled grounds of Pawksville, was that book of tickets. And it really was the last. This Jubilee, thought Father, the father of all the Jubilees, has been a fruitless, frustrating, hopelessly boring shambles from beginning to end.

They had left the sound of the sirens far behind them.

"Well," Caddy said, "that's that."

"Yes, isn't it," Father agreed.

26

L'Envoi

Superintendent Keeney was entertaining a business guest
in his library. The two gentlemen were taking their ease before the fire, the inlaid game table between them bearing
the cigar humidor, deep ashtrays, the brandy decanter, and
their snifters. Because the guest, a Mr. Schultz, was by way
of being an emissary of the Governor's, Superintendent
Keeney had, after lengthy debate, decided to bring out the
Courvoisier instead of the brandy Mrs. Keeney dumped into
the punch at the annual Christmas party for the staff. Superintendent Keeney had overheard Nick Bartholomew remark
that the second-best brandy had all the bouquet of a dia-
betic's breath, and if he agreed privately, he did not forget it,
either.

Such little unpleasantnesses were far from Superintendent Keeney's mind, however, this rain-heavy afternoon.
Leaning over to his guest, he replenished Mr. Schultz's snifter
generously. That gentleman, a corpulent and affable vulgar-
ian, nodded his thanks and stretched his great feet to the
fire.

"And how is the Governor?" Superintendent Keeney
asked cozily.

"Just great, Doc. He tole me to really fix you folks
up here. Do you a job like I done for the pen." Mr. Schultz
took a swig of Courvoisier as casually as if it were rotgut,
swallowed without comment, and resumed, "Tell you, those
boys up there really get a bang outa their lanes. AMF pin-
setters, the whole shebang. The Gov went up there and
bowled a set with the Warden. I sez, 'Gov, you're getting so
good you'll be shooting in the low three hundreds next.'
Laugh! You know how the Gov can really let 'em yip." As
if in demonstration, Mr. Schultz let a few yip, rolling his bald
head about on his neck as easily as if a greased universal
joint connected the two.

Superintendent Keeney joined in fitfully. When the two
gentlemen had arrived at the stage of intermittent gusts
and tag-end rumbles of merriment, Superintendent Keeney
observed, "I'll have to brush up on my game and invite
the Governor down. After our lanes are in, of course."

"Jig-time, Doc. The way I figure it, those hydro—uh—
hydro, you know, whatsis—"

"The hydrotherapy rooms," Superintendent Keeney
supplied politely.

"Yeah. That. A real waste of good space. Soon's that junk
is ripped out and a coupla walls knocked out, you've got
an area there give you room for five-six lanes easy. 'Course,
I could lay 'em in the basement here, but with all those supporting arches, I don't rightly know just how much of them
are supporting, you unnerstand, anyway, this is a pretty
ole building——"

"No, I agree with you completely, Mr. Schultz. The
bowling alley will be perfect in the Hospital."

Mr. Schultz suddenly beat himself on the knee. "Doc,
you'll never guess what we found down in the basement
here. Way off in some room I don't guess anybody'd been
in for twenty thirty years. A little statue. A little stone boy.
And guess what he was doing!"

"Doing? The statue?" Superintendent Keeney said
blankly.

"Yeah. The kid was peeing!" At the Superintendent's mystified stare, Mr. Schultz explained, "Taking a leak. Get it?"

After a time, Superintendent Keeney confessed, "Yes, I suppose there are all kinds of junk to be found around Pawksville." He was, in truth, something less than enchanted over the discovery of the long-lost Mickey.

"If nobody around here wants it. . . ." Mr. Schultz said tentatively.

"Consider it yours, Mr. Schultz," Superintendent Keeney offered.

Mr. Schultz beamed his thanks and returned to the matter at hand. "Yessir, that Gov's a real sweetheart. Isn't every Gov'nor would bother to fit a bowling alley for the nut farm into the budget."

Superintendent Keeney refrained from looking pained at Mr. Schultz's choice of words. Politically alert, he said instead, "You're right there. We're beginning to be a very up-to-date plant here. Sports therapy, I like to think of it as. Our swimming pool you know, and our Greek reflecting pool—that's very nice in the summer for the patients and their visitors."

"Yuh haven't told the rest of the docs yet about the lanes, have yuh?" Mr. Schultz asked.

"No, as I told you, I'm keeping it as a surprise for them as long as possible."

Mr. Schultz chuckled fondly. "That Gov, what a sweetheart. Bet your staff's going to be tickled pink. Yessir, tickled . . . pink."

The gentlemen found themselves toasting one another with their snifters. They were well met. Both were content that the footprints they left on the sands of time be those of political heels.

In his office, Nick Bartholomew too had a guest. There was no fire, but the Venetian blinds were drawn against the rainy afternoon, and the lamps were on. Across from Nick sat a man in his late twenties, a man of serious mien who could, unexpectedly, reveal a smile of companionable wryness.

"I wish, Doctor," Nick said, "that we could offer more in the way of salary. Of course, there will be maintenance for yourself, and laundry and the like."

"Doctor, I have a wife and a small son. Would there be main—"

"Oh, you have a family?" Nick said, charmed; quite as if he were just in receipt of this fact. "Naturally, maintenance will include them. We have a very nice apartment in the Morgue House that will be coming up vacant soon. As to salary, later on I'm hoping the Governor will see fit to stretch the budget for an increase in that area, among other things. He rather indicated when he was here last month that something in that line would be forthcoming."

"Salary is of secondary importance, Doctor," the guest said earnestly.

Nick threw off his next question in his best offhand manner. "You got through medical school rather late, Doctor?"

"Yes." Only when the guest encountered a word with *s* in it did he reveal his foreign background. "When I first got over here, there were language difficulties, and money— difficulties. . . ." This was accompanied with a wry expressive shrug.

"I had to dig up my own scratch to get through medical school, too," Nick put in sympathetically. "And then, when my wife and I got married smack in the middle of my internship, we were both kicked out. The only place that would have us was Pawksville." Something in his guest's correct smile revealed to Nick his own lack of tact. "I meant to say," Nick stumbled on, "how did you become interested in psychiatry, Doctor?"

The correct smile spread to an easy grin. "I just got in under the quota at the hospital where I was interning.

So . . . I was assigned to the jail ward. And there I saw the psychotic, and the criminal, and the alcoholic, and the addicted, and yesss, even the sane all shut up together. Like a concentration-camp hospital ward."

"Oh," was all Nick could think of to say.

"I took pity," his guest said simply.

A thought so horrendous struck Nick that for a moment he was not able to voice it. The fellow had either a German or a Viennese accent, and those Krauts were notorious for being up to their ears in—— Nick barked, "Doctor, are you interested in psychoanalysis?"

"Why— No. My knowledge of the subject. . . . You see, Doctor Bartholomew, I thought it best I start without any preconceived ideas." The guest concluded diffidently, "I felt I should learn through experience. If that meets with your approval, Doctor."

Beatitudinous, Nick said, "Absolutely. Absolutely, Doctor! How's about my showing you around, now. I want to introduce you to some of the staff. Doctor Heall, and Doctor—" Nick's eyes chanced to fall on Caddy's photograph. What he had thought to be an ulcer, but proved to be only a nervous flutter of the pyloric valve, flared up for an instant. Then, recalling that Caddy was safely many a mile from Pawksville, the flicker of internal fire went out. "My daughter," he said, with a nod at the photograph. "She's away at school. You'll meet my boys at dinner, Doctor. And my sister, who is visiting with me. And Doctor Carmody—" he chattered on "—you'll meet her at dinner too. She'll be showing you the ropes, so I thought it would be nice for us all to——"

The guest was nodding politely. His smile was a touch reserved; he had not, after all, expected anything like so effusive a welcome.

Dr. Carmody's little lab radio was tuned to a classical-music program from Nashville. Two beakers on tripods set over Bunsen burners and containing spiced wine were slowly warming in anticipation of the advent of Father Muldroon. Only in the past day or so had Jane been able to listen to music at all. To re-embrace that which Sean had killed himself for love of—or so she thought—had been her first act of convalescence. Learning of it, Nick Bartholomew had had to avert his gaze lest she read of his profound relief.

Poor Nick, Jane mused, beset on the one side with my self-imposed guilt and withdrawal from him; and Sonny on the other, irritable and smarting from the escape of his Marion Pierce—on whom he, Sonny, had hoped so passionately to rest his psychoanalytical case. Not to mention Caddy's having been instrumental in having Father Muldroon hot-rod Pierce over the state line—— Jane was temporarily so unmindful of her dignity as to giggle suddenly to herself. In her mind's eye she beheld Nick as he had been those first weeks after the Jubilee. Beset on every side by his little brood, with Sonny cranky, and Superintendent Keeney still cross with him, he had stomped around and stormed; until one night he had found himself at the door of the Morgue House, unable to bring his hand to the lock until Jane had gone down and opened the door and said, "Nick, I'm lonesome. Please come in."

The bouquet of the warming wine began to drift in and out of her sensory perceptions like music. Jane turned the burners low. A mild excitement, almost hypomanic, came over her. Everywhere the eye roamed it was met by sparkling glassware or the gleam of polished metal—all the conscientious handiwork of Titus Graham. I'm going to start a bit of research, Jane informed herself. That I am. See if I can isolate a substance, or substances, from the brain tissue of a schizophrenic that might, just might, indicate the chemical imbalance responsible for the disease. Knock Sonny's theories into a cocked hat for him. And as for Helen Daniels—if she isn't lucid, I'll put her on Metrazol and then insulin, in quick order. I'll confuse her psychosis so, it won't know which way to turn. That woman is going to return to her

husband and baby if I have to trephine her and yell for the
devils to come out. If there is one thing insanity is above all
else, it is a waste of human beings, and I refuse to admit that
that young woman is ready for the trash heap yet.

She told herself, You're beginning to think like Nick,
you know that? High time, since I'm going to marry him
one of these days. And high time, as well, I begin practicing
a little medicine. I haven't been within hailing distance
of it for months. I wonder if, after we're married, Nick will
still pin my ears back for me regularly. "He'd better," she
muttered.

"So we've taken to talking to ourselves," a dour dripping
Father Muldroon said from the doorway. "What's that I
smell?"

"The blood of an Englishman, Father."

"In that case," Father said, marching in and taking his
stool, "I'll be having meself some."

Outdoors the grounds and walks were covered with an
inch of water, more in spots, with only the rotunda on its
slight rise not actually awash, like a dismal island in a shallow
sea. Pawksville history was repeating itself; it was again
nothing less than a marsh.

Two patients were trudging, or slopping, along in the
rain. One was Leslie Erskine, bound for her introductory
hour with Dr. Heall. The other was Titus Graham, who
had struggled into an old cracked and yellowed plastic
slicker, common property on the open ward where he was
assigned. At the conjunction of two walks the pair met
briefly.

"Well, it's one for the ducks, isn't it, Miss Erskine?"
Titus said cheerfully.

Miss Erskine merely grimaced, her neon-bright lipstick
dotted with rain. "I can't think of a better day," she said
succinctly, "to start off my little jauntings to the *casa de
tormentos*." With a curt nod she splashed past.

Not dashed in the least, Titus resumed his journey.

But entering the dripping dusk of the grotto, his heart began to ache. Seeking meager shelter in the few leaves which still remained on the Monkey Tree, the small sodden creatures huddled in their wretchedness. The lone monkey, a few feet from his fellows, crouched under a steady drip, his fur black with rain.

"Now, now, here, darlings," Titus called and sat down on the bench, opening his plastic slicker. With cries of welcome the wet stinking little bodies landed on him, their chains whipping his head and shoulders. He clasped them close while they chittered and searched his pockets for the bits of bread he had distributed about his person for them. He murmured to them, calling them by the names he had given them, "Ah, we found a tidbit, did we, little Keats? No, no—Chaucer, mustn't quarrel with T. S. Plenty for all, darlings."

Then, his pets nestled contentedly on his breast, Titus began a steady flow of endearments directed to the lone monkey who sat, anguished and fearful yet filled with unutterable longing just above him. "Come down to Nuncle, little Titus. Nuncle won't hurt poor lost little Titus. Come, darling, you know you want to. . . . Please come down, Titus? Nuncle's got a special bit of cookie just for you . . ."

The monkey who kept himself apart shook his chain woefully. Then, inch by inch, he moved along his branch, his tail curling sorrowfully about him for protection, his thumbtack-round black eyes steady on Titus Graham.

". . . down now, darling?" Titus Graham crooned. "You know you will one day, why not now? Come to Nuncle's arms. . . ."

Just above Graham's head the monkey came to a pause, crying softly in his longing. Gradually Graham's entreaties took on the lyricism of poetry. He wooed his coy trembling namesake with the enchantments of the past. Slowly, slowly, little Titus' prehensile tail eased down to wrap itself gently, sweetly about the poet's neck.

And in this manner they all communed in boundless love, until dusk fell.

To Leslie Erskine's manly rap on Sonny's door there came a manly welcome from Dr. Heall. She entered to find him jumping to his feet, his whites glowing greenish in the light of his forest-green and brass student's lamp. "Come in, come in!" he was crying, so desirous of her presence that she half expected to see him rubbing his hands together. "Good afternoon, Miss Erskine! How are you feeling?"

"Something less than chipper," Leslie muttered glumly.

"Fine! Fine!" Sonny rushed to help her peel off her raincoat, then dragged a chair over to his desk. "Why don't you just sit here, Miss Erskine, and we'll have a little chat."

Leslie sat down lumpishly.

Dancing around to his own desk chair, Sonny said, "Cigarette?"— trying not to sound man-to-man and sounding just that, as he never had before.

"I'd rather not accept a smoke from you," Leslie blurted, "until I state my business. That is to say, I may not be welcome long enough to smoke. Not that I'm not hungry for a cigarette, you can bet your life," she added with a flush of guilt. "But it is good of you to let me have this interview, Doctor."

"Miss Erskine, I am your physician," Sonny said bedsidely. "You're entitled to all the time I can find to give you."

"Yes, I quite understand. But you see, Doctor, I'm here to submit to analysis. If you would care to——?"

"Well-ehl-ehl," Sonny clucked comfortably. "In the first place, I don't want you to feel that you are submitting to anything. And in the second, I wasn't the least surprised to hear you wanted to talk to me. I knew you would come to me when you were ready."

Leslie stared. Was Sonny-Boy really acute enough to suspect she was come to offer herself up in propitiation for Marion Pierce? "Ah?" she murmured vaguely.

"Certainly," Sonny assured her crisply, "your journal, you see, was your way of overcoming the resistance of the id."

Try as she might, Leslie could make no sense out of that hearty reassurance. Then, the subject of the journal opened up, she felt constrained to say, "I'm extremely sorry for some of the . . . I'm afraid, Doctor, there were many instances where you didn't care for the cut of my jibe."

"Jib," Sonny corrected in an absent tone, and pressed a cigarette on her.

Tamping the end of the cigarette on her left thumbnail, Leslie plodded on. "I was abusive, and said things which were unpardon—" She interrupted herself to receive a light. "Thanks." The first drag of smoke was so welcome that even her fingertips tingled. "I can only say in my defense, Doctor, that what I wrote was not meant for your eyes."

"Perhaps not at first," Sonny said with psychiatric forbearance. "It was only an outlet for your aggression in the beginning. But then, when it was no longer therapeutic in that respect, you found that you had overcome your resistance to analysis as well." His smile was a blessing; his tincture-green-soap eyes glowed with silent messages of vast good will.

"But—"

"Otherwise," Sonny said happily, "you would not have gone to the trouble of slipping your journal in on my desk. It was your written cry for help."

Leslie was having difficulties with a lungful of smoke. "Oh, I see," she murmured, tardy in the saying of it. "Yes, I should imagine so," she said, sternly repressing a snigger. What a pompous pill you are, Sonny, she told him in her mind. There was a rather awkward pause, which Leslie sought to end by blurting, "Well, shall I begin?" and which Sonny punctured with an unctuous "You mustn't feel embarrassed, Miss Erskine. Your journal, you know, is a—a— document of great psychoanalytic value."

"You're kiddin'," Leslie said, pleased in spite of herself.

Sonny nodded solemnly.

"I guess," Leslie took up sturdily, "you want me to go lie on the couch."

"No, no!" Sonny said with considerable heat. "Not unless you want to. You see, analysis is an exchange. Yes, an exchange. You're an intelligent woman, Miss Erskine, and I feel I can explain a few of these little—uh—steps to you. No, we'll do much better if we just chat along. Like friends. I don't believe in the analysand doing all the talk— Ex-hem. *Both* of us must contribute, you see?"

Nope, Leslie thought, cheerfully, beginning to enjoy herself. "Well, do I get to suggest the topic of the day?"

"Of course, of course!" Sonny said.

"My trial, then," Leslie said positively. "I don't mind going into that at all. Nor the murder. Would you like to hear how a murderer feels when he's—she's—at her killing? To tell you the truth, so—Doctor—we murderers don't feel much of anything at all. I have no *emotional* recollection at all of having shot down a man in cold—"

"That's natural," Sonny said, and opening his desk drawer took out a ledger. On the spine the name *Erskine* was printed in shaky running letters. "How can you recall an emotion you never felt?"

"Oh, but you see—" Leslie began brightly. "That's what I'm trying to tell you. I didn't——"

"We both know you didn't," Sonny said, not the slightest disputatiously.

"I didn't—"

"Kill anyone," Sonny finished for her soothingly.

Leslie ground out her cigarette. "Doctor, one of us has a screw loose. I not only killed a man, but I did so with malice aforethought. I lay in wait, and with full intent and premeditation I—" Leslie was pounding the desk, shouting into Sonny's grave smile, "I killed him! I blew his head off! My hands are running with blood! I did! Goddam you, I . . ."

"No," said Sonny. He opened the ledger and began pressing the pages flat. To a panting Leslie he said quietly, "Shall we talk a bit about your stay here at Pawksville? How did you feel the first time you were lucid? Do you remember any of that?"

Leslie had once had a dream in which she discovered a string hanging from her mouth. When she yanked the string, all her teeth fell out. She could only stare at Sonny, convinced now that were she to part her lips even slightly, her teeth would clatter onto his desk.

"It was after your course of Metrazol," Sonny prodded gently. "Remember? You looked up and asked me where you were. I told you. And then, you said—'Mitzi.' Remember that?"

Leslie shook her head.

"You mentioned her again during one of your insulin treatments. Does that bring anything back to you? Remember the tea wagon? Or the molasses toast?"

When Leslie remained rigid, silent, Sonny said ever so soothingly, "How about that long refreshing sleep? That nice sleep . . ."

Leslie's head nodded of its own volition. "Mitzi—" she said in a soft wail, and clapped her hand to her mouth to hold her teeth in.

"Yes, shall we talk about Mitzi?" Sonny said, uncapping his pen, and bending on her his unflagging smile of encouragement. "Who was she? Really?"

Leslie shook her head.

"Perhaps," Sonny suggested helpfully, "she doesn't exist. Think about that a moment. Could that be?" He bent his chubby face over the ledger and began to scribble. *"La belle indifférence,"* he murmured to himself, executing the words with a flourish of his pen.

"The beautiful . . . forgetfulness . . ." Leslie heard her voice murmuring hoarsely. "Is that it?"

"Now, now," Sonny said. "Perhaps you'd like to talk about your school days. Do you remember—"

There is no Mitzi, Leslie's mind said in the sure tone of one reading the Scriptures. No Mitzi, and no murder; but madness and to spare. She was filled with repugnance, with dread, for that mind of hers which conceived such sick fancies. How many EST had she had? And Metrazol? She had no recollection of any of them, that invalid of a mind of hers had dismissed them altogether, preferring to occupy itself with fantasies concerning an imaginary little shopworn tart, and a murder trial a freshman in law school would have laughed to scorn. "My God," she proposed to herself softly, "I'm insane."

"Now, now," Sonny said severely. "It's no disgrace, you know, Miss Erskine. You're not to think badly of yourself. Won't help. Here. Have another cigarette." He flipped his lighter for her gallantly.

As if she were the Holy Dove standing outside in the rain-gusty dusk, peeping in on them, Leslie Erskine saw herself and Sonny Heall. Herself, dashing even in her hospital cotton dress, seemingly self-assured as she drew on her cigarette, and sat chatting with a plump man in his early thirties. Contemporaries, two professional people talking together, warm in the aura of courteous respect, as well as warm and dry and cozy in the green lamplight.

When in truth, when in fact, Leslie Erskine was alone in some barren place of wet gray rock and boulders and perpetual nightfall. Alone and standing at the brink of the Jumping Off Place.

"Don't let me go over the edge," she cried out passionately to a startled Sonny Heall. "Help me!"

Recovering his equanimity, he put out a pudgy hand and patted hers as it lay on the desk. "I *am* going to help you, Miss Erskine. And you're going to help yourself. One step at a time, we're going to. . . ."

One step at a time, back down from the edge. Leslie clung to the pudgy hand, steadying herself by meeting his friendly tincture-green-soap gaze. "You're a brick, Doctor Heall," she said thickly.

He coughed in deprecation, pinking a shade. Still, he could not conceal his pleasure. He patted her hand again. "Ready to go on a bit?"

"All right," Leslie said. "Who—who am I?"

Sonny said carefully, "There was no identification on you when you were brought in."

"And you were unable to locate any—"

"I'm afraid not. You did tell us, after a time, that your name was Erskine."

"Which could be only another delusion. Like, like Mitzi."

"I don't know," Sonny admitted. Then added gracefully, "But you do. You do know, Miss Erskine. And in time we'll get the answers. All of them." He cleared his throat and scribbled something down.

When that ledger is filled, Leslie (?) thought, I shall have come a goodly distance down from the Jumping Off Place. She squared her shoulders. "I'll bet you one thing," she said bravely. "I'll bet I was born. Of that I think we can be fairly certain. Now, lemme see. . . ."

Sonny's pen raced.

Dusk had come on, and with it the lights along the walks. The water gleamed blackly, stretching as far as Dr. Ouita's fading eyes could see. She stood at her window looking out, a good day's work—a pair of blue baby booties for one of her innumerable grandnephews—finished and lying in their gift box on her desk. Her old ladies were all snug in their little dining room, gumming their hot sugar-sweetened gruel and cackling happily. Even the bedridden ladies with their multiple fractures were resting easy, and those not under sedation were peacefully dabbing their Copenhagen snuff into their gums and drooling at one another of happenings that were memories before the century had begun.

No one at all was abroad in the black waters of Pawksville. The lights had only each other for company. It was on just such a night, Dr. Ouita recalled—no, no, it hadn't been . . . It had happened in the twenties, and it had happened in spring. The rains had been the worst Pawksville had even seen.

And that spring Dr. Ouita had been overworked, with too many patients under her care. She had her mosquito farm then down in the old lab under the rotunda. There were two wire baskets. One contained mosquitos inoculated with malaria, in readiness to be placed against the hips of those paretics who were scheduled for malarial therapy. And the other wire cage contained Dr. Ouita's sterile stock mosquitos. The uncontaminated mosquitos were fed by Dr. Ouita herself, an alternate arm each day. She was, naturally, at great pains to label and guard her insects well.

But one spring day, when all Pawksville was a marsh, one day, somehow, plashing along the walk with her cage of contaminated mosquitos, Dr. Ouita had dropped it, and the wire screening was ripped, affording a slit through which the malarial mosquitos escaped, in spite of all Dr. Ouita's panicky efforts to contain them, and soon the entire marsh was a mosquito-infested breeding ground, and no matter how much oil was poured on the water, the number of cases of malaria rose to—

But that's another story and Father Muldroon, Pawksville's official antiquarian, tells it best.